DNA NEVER LIES

ALAN D. SCHMITZ

BLACK HAWK PUBLISHING

Black Hawk Publishing
blackhawk340.com

Ordering Information:
Quantity sales. Special discounts are available on quantity purchases by corporations, associations, and others. For details, contact the "Special Sales Department" at the web address above.

DNA Never Lies/ Alan D. Schmitz. —1st ed.
ISBN 978-0-9973573-0-1

Acknowledgements

I want to thank the many, many readers of *Memories Never Die* who encouraged me to bring back Scott Seaver in another adventure. And though *Memories Never Die* was never meant for a sequel, your encouragement helped me create The Senator Series. Truly, without your encouragement, I would not have had the fortitude or will to write *DNA Never Lies* as the first book in that series. So, in a very real sense, you created Steven Westcott.

I want to assure you that I am already working on the next book of The Senator Series. In *The Mexican Solution*, Steven Westcott is recruited by the President of the United States for a very dangerous mission to stem the flow of drugs into the States from Mexico. The plan is bold and creative and will require Steven Westcott to risk his life to make it happen.

****

I hope you enjoy *DNA Never Lies*. The final product is as much a product of my imagination as it is the guidance from my developmental editor, Bronwyn Hemus of Standoutbooks.

Bronwyn always found a way to push me for more suspense, and worked diligently with me to maintain that suspense throughout the book. Her attention to detail helped create an exciting and realistic adventure for you to enjoy.

Developing Steven Westcott as the main character was a fun challenge and with Bronwyn's help, I believe you will discover someone who's adventures you will look forward to time and time again.

Chapter 1

Detective Saltarie ran down the stairs, her breath was hard. The adrenaline surging through her body made it easy to fly down each floor of the atrium. She prayed that the senator would stop running and let her help him. He had been wounded badly by her if not fatally. She had never wanted to hurt him and certainly wouldn't want to be responsible for his death.

Escaping the Hart Senate Office Building was impossible. He was surrounded, and officers were pursuing him inside the building. Saltarie, now on the main floor, ran for the exit door the senator had taken. As she ran, she popped out the nearly spent magazine and replaced it with a new clip loaded with ten more bullets. The steel door of the stairwell felt like paper to her as she yanked it open and raced down the stairs toward the underground parking area.

"Block off the parking garage exits. Nobody leaves, I repeat, nobody leaves." She hollered into her handheld radio. If there had been doubt in her mind that he was in fact the murderer, his actions were now dispelling that thought.

Saltarie carefully opened the steel door of the parking garage and hid behind a concrete post and listened. The wounded man couldn't stay hidden, and he couldn't survive much longer without medical help, of that she was sure.

Back on her radio she called as quietly as she could trying not to give away her position, "I need an ambulance at the Hart Senate Office Building."

She hoped that they would find him in time to save his life. But the safety of the officers in her charge was also important, so haste in capture wasn't part of her plan. She had to be patient. All she had to do was follow the blood trail. He couldn't escape.

Carefully the garage filled with officers, each taking up a protected spot. Chelle signaled some of the policemen to follow her and a few others to stay back. Her team cautiously moved from floor to floor. She could find no blood trail so it was impossible to know which floor the senator had escaped to. After each floor was secured, they moved on.

After they did a sweep of the last floor of the parking garage she realized that a United States Senator had escaped from her. She couldn't believe that, and nobody else including her boss would want to believe it either. Her career as a Washington D.C. police detective didn't seem so bright right now.

Twenty-two years earlier, February 14th, Kuwait:

The soldiers of the 3rd Special Forces Group (Airborne) sat patiently inside the noisy confines of the huge helicopter's fuselage. They had been flying for over an hour now inside the MH-47, commonly referred to as the Chinook. The first part of the trip was through the friendly skies of Saudi Arabia. Now, over into Kuwait, the skies were patrolled by British and US fighters and were mostly safe. However, Iraqi surface-to-air missiles could come at any time. If that happened, the soldiers knew they would be helpless; it would be up to the pilots and the airship's counter measures to protect them.

Sergeant Steven Westcott took out a pack of gum. He unwrapped a piece and slung it into his mouth. Then he slipped another to his partner, Sergeant Denton Jones, who was sitting next to him on a mesh seat. A green mission-ready light went on; it was time to prepare to disembark.

Sergeant Westcott and Sergeant Jones were only two of the twelve special operations troops on board. This mission carried one detachment but they were highly trained and equipped.

This wasn't the first mission for Charlie Company, but it was one of their most dangerous and important for Operation Desert Storm. Sergeant Westcott yelled to his partner over the noise of the twin rotors, "Jojo, time to roll!"

Sergeant Westcott and Jojo Jones held a special part of this important mission and neither would have chosen anyone else to have their back. Both were muscled and hardened by the Green Beret training. And even though Sergeant Westcott's skin was white and Jojo's was black they were closer than brothers.

The two soldiers sat in their respective Ground Military Vehicles. The GMV was basically a heavy duty ATV. The four wheel drive carriage carried a tubular frame and two seats each. On top of the roll cage over the seats was a radio antenna and GPS receiver. Sergeant

Westcott held the brakes while the rest of the team removed the tie-down straps.

"Try not to let it get away on you, Jojo!" Westcott yelled to his bigger and slightly older partner.

"You just try to stay in the saddle, Cowboy!" Jojo yelled back.

By using two GMVs they had a spare. If one broke down they could still use the other for transportation back to the rendezvous area.

The helicopter descended toward the desert. The powerful twin turbo shaft engines of the copter were whipping up the sand of the Udairi Range in southern Kuwait. The two huge rotating blades kept the Chinook's wheels just a few feet off the ground while the rear hydraulic ramp lowered itself to the desert floor. Cowboy and Jojo drove their two GMVs into the swirling, manmade sandstorm. Despite their protective goggles, the sand stinging at their faces temporarily blinded them. Seconds later, they emerged from the sandy void and sped on their way. Their fifty-pound packs were firmly secured to the back of the GMVs. Behind them, their brothers in arms were running off the chopper, carrying their fifty-pound packs and fifty-pounds of body armor.

These men were the best of the best and very highly trained. Green Berets do not go into battle unprepared. February had brought cooler temperatures to the desert, which would hopefully make the body armor more bearable for the next two days.

It was just over a month since Operation Desert Shield had changed to Operation Desert Storm. On that day, a war waged by a UN-authorized coalition force from thirty-four nations, led by the United States and the United Kingdom, began. Their mission was to expel Iraq from the small, independent country of Kuwait, which had recently been invaded.

Now, Cowboy and Jojo found themselves behind enemy lines on a very special mission. It was reported that the Iraqis were using a Kuwaiti experimental farm facility, south of Kuwait city, as a detention and torture center for captured Kuwaiti soldiers and civilians. It was Cowboy and Jojo's job to verify if the report were true, assess the enemy assets, and report back with a recommended plan of attack to stage a rescue.

The rest of their group was to attack a small garrison that satellite reconnaissance had detected. The hope was that the attack on the garrison would draw additional troops away from the detention facility. That would give Cowboy and Jojo a bit more chance of success, and less chance of being captured. Both missions had to be precisely executed and both missions were extremely dangerous. If any team could do it, it would be the soldiers of the 3rd Special Forces Group.

These men had trained as a unit for the last two years. Now, they were a deadly assault force trained in explosives, weapons, and hand-to-hand combat. More importantly, they were highly intelligent and taught not to fail.

As soon as the last of the special forces soldiers were out of the aircraft, the twin rotors pulled the copter away from the earth. In two days, it would return to retrieve the soldiers from their mission.

Even though Sergeant Steven Westcott—or Cowboy, as the squad called him—was in charge of their two-man group, rank didn't mean much between Cowboy and Jojo. Cowboy knew that his best friend of the last two years wouldn't listen to him if he came up with an idea that didn't make sense. This was a team effort and each knew that their life depended on the other. That was what was making this mission so much fun for both of them. Because neither of them would rather be teamed with anyone else, their confidence in each other was absolute.

The two, four-wheeled, all-terrain vehicles, kicked up a small amount of dust as the soldiers drove side by side through the desert. Sergeant Denton Jones pointed to his GMV-mounted GPS unit, then held up the five fingers of his right hand. The signal meant that it was five more clicks to the farm compound. It also meant that it was time to stop and take a careful assessment of the terrain ahead. They stopped just short of a recently developed sand dune. Jojo crawled his way up the dune to scan the distance. The largely flat desert didn't provide much cover, but on the other hand, it wouldn't conceal any Iraqis patrolling the desert either. The last two kilometers would be traveled at night, and they would have to be done very slowly and on foot.

Jojo wasn't necessarily fond of the moniker that his special forces teammates had given him, but he realized very early on that it wasn't up to him. The group seemed to need a nickname for each member. He had become Jojo when, on the first day, he had stuttered his name in front of the entire squad.

Denton Jones had grown up in North Carolina; his dad was an electrician, his mom a teacher. In high school, he was famous for the hard tackles he made on the football field. His grades in high school were another story; if he was famous for them, it wasn't because they were exceptional, that was for sure. But, something clicked after his first three years in the army. It didn't take him long to realize he wanted to be one of the best; he wanted to be a Green Beret. The day he graduated from special forces training at Fort Bragg was one of the proudest days of his life, the other, was when his daughter was born.

Cowboy, on the other hand, was nicknamed because of his sometimes-reckless mannerisms and his last name. Westcott had soon been shortened to West and before he knew it, he was baptized Cowboy, even though he was actually from the East Coast. The difference between Denton Jones and Steven Westcott was that Westcott not only didn't mind being called Cowboy, he relished the title. Cowboy's stubbly white face usually had a persistent wise-guy smirk on it that masked the polished East Coast upbringing underneath.

Cowboy and Jojo had spent the last of the daylight camouflaging the GMVs. Cowboy used the handheld GPS to mark their position. In the endless expanse of desert, it would be impossible to find the GMVs again without the GPS to guide them. The blowing wind had already covered the tracks they had made thus far, which was encouraging.

"We'll belly crawl the last half click or so. Just take your day pack. That should get us through the next forty-eight hours easy." Cowboy said. "You take the radio, I'll bring the camera, extra water, and the portable GPS. If all goes well, we'll slip in and out without firing a shot, but just in case, bring enough munitions so that we can create some holy hell if we have to."

Each attached the AN/PVS-14 night vision system to their M4s. Patience would be their shield.

As they scanned the horizon, the night vision scopes they were using provided a good view of the farm through the darkness, but so far, there was no activity except at the guard stations. After hours of watching the guards, their schedule seemed fairly predictable. If it was indeed a prison compound, it had been very hastily set up. Only certain small areas had been made secured with razor wire.

Cowboy double-checked his watch, looking a bit nervous for the first time. Then chaos broke loose on the farm. A siren wailed in the background as soldiers shouted instructions to each other over its din. Other soldiers started to run out of buildings in various stages of dress. The sound of truck engines added to the pandemonium. It didn't take long for two personnel carriers to be loaded, and soon the trucks were headed down the roadway.

"It looks like our boys have given the garrison a little wake-up call," Jojo whispered.

"Are you ready for a little close-up intel?" Cowboy said.

"Won't be dark much longer, now or never."

Their inside intelligence from a former farm worker had described a cinder block seed house at the edge of the compound; that was their destination. From there, they could monitor the camp for whatever kind of activity was going on. If they discovered that there were no prisoners being held, they would call an airstrike to destroy the camp and the soldiers in it.

Using the moonless night for cover and their night vision glasses, evading the guards wasn't difficult. The seed house was just as expected, and the key they were given worked the old lock on the door. Once inside, the soldiers relocked the door. The rusty lock worked hard, and Jojo pressed it together, trying to not make any noise. They adjusted seed bags to hide behind, just in case someone decided to inspect the small room. There was only the one door and no windows, but there were upper vents in the walls, and by stacking a few strategically placed seed bags, Jojo created a solid platform to stand on.

"This should work," Jojo whispered. "I can see the main building and the steel equipment storage shed. If there are prisoners, my bet is that's where they'll be."

"It's early yet, I doubt that anything will happen until after dawn. Time to get some rest," Cowboy said.

Jojo whispered back, "You sleep, I'll keep watch. I won't be able to rest until we are out of this rat's nest."

"Have it your way." Cowboy made a pillow out of a seed bag and closed his eyes.

Jojo sat down next to his friend, took out a picture from his left breast pocket, and exhaled. "I sure do miss them."

Cowboy tried to ignore him., though he knew it would be unavoidable.

"Yep, my little girl is two years old already. She sure is cute. Do you know why we called her Lorelei?" Jojo started to answer his own question. "It was—"

"Your mother's middle name. Yea, I know. I thought you said I could sleep, dickhead."

"Go ahead sleep; I'm just looking at a picture of my lovely wife and child. If that bothers you I am so sorry," Jojo added sarcastically.

Still whispering, Cowboy frustratingly complained. "Go ahead, look, look all you want, but do you have to do it out loud?"

"You're just jealous," Jojo said.

"Oh, Jesus Christ, just let me sleep."

"You're jealous that I have a beautiful wife and daughter and you have nobody."

"Listen asshole," Cowboy shouted in a whisper. "My M4 is loaded and I have the silencer mounted. If you don't shut up, you will be the first casualty of this mission."

"I knew it, you're pissed."

"Of course I'm pissed, you said I could sleep."

"You're just pissed because you're a lonely fool."

"I wish I was fucking lonely, but unfortunately I have you."

"That's right, that's all you have is me. Me and that hooker you liked back at Spring Lake."

"All right, all right, I give up. Let me look at that picture again." Cowboy knew that sleep was out of the question.

"You're right, your little girl is cute as hell. She really is," he added sincerely. "And Tamara is one foxy piece of ass."

"You goddamn right she is," Jojo whispered back. "I miss her, both of them all to hell. What the fuck am I doing in the middle of fucking Kuwait?"

"Your job, you know, the one you were trained to do." The question was rhetorical but still seemed to require an answer.

"You miss your girl sometimes?" Jojo asked.

"Miss who sometimes? What girl? You know I don't have anybody special."

"You know who I mean."

"You mean the whore? Shatoya? Yea, every time I get an erection, you dumbass. She was a fucking hooker. Hell, half the base is missing her about now. And the other half is fucking her."

"Look man, you had a thing for her, I know you did, you loved that cute little piece of brown sugar. So do you miss her?"

"Didn't anyone ever tell you, never, ever, fall in love with a hooker?" Cowboy said.

"I don't think you took your own advice. I know that you paid her to go on picnics with you."

"Who told you that bullshit? I only paid her when I wanted to get my rocks off."

"She did."

"What?" Cowboy had a hard time keeping his voice quiet.

"She did, just before we shipped out. She also told me that you treated her like a lady, and that was one of the nicest things anybody ever did for her."

"OK, OK. I paid her for a whole day of service a couple of times, like an escort. Big deal. She was in a spot, I had to or her pimp would have beaten the crap out of her for not earning her keep. And then I would have had to kill him. So I thought the money well spent. I can't believe I'm being grilled for not fucking a whore."

"She said she really liked you a lot and she wished things were different. I don't know what she saw in your tight little white-boy ass, but she wanted me to tell you something at the right time. She told me to tell you that she really liked you a lot and that you weren't just another john to her and she's sorry she couldn't take your offer."

"What the fuck makes you think this is the right time?"

"Well, you weren't sleeping or anything, so I thought I might as well tell you. I thought you might think it was important."

"Well it's not; she was a god damn whore and nothing else. I couldn't care less if I ever see the bitch again. What else did she say?"

"She didn't want to tell you how she felt because she knew it would never work between you and her. She was just a black whore and she knew that you were going to be somebody important someday."

Cowboy looked truly hurt, and Jojo wondered if it had been the right time.

"She couldn't know that, it wasn't her decision. I could have changed her life."

"I knew it, you're a marshmallow, a roasted marshmallow."

"What the fuck are you talking about?"

"You are hard on the outside, but all warm and squishy soft on the inside. Listen man, maybe you already did change her life to the better. Did you ever think of that?"

"Damn it Jojo, how am I supposed to sleep now?"

Jojo kept the picture of his wife and daughter in hand well past dawn. Cowboy closed his eyes and tried to sleep but couldn't because he couldn't stop thinking about Shatoya.

"A foreign voice began shouting orders."

Both soldiers instinctively froze in place. Jojo cautiously crawled up the seed bags to take a look out the vent. The morning sun was shining brightly over the courtyard.

"Give me the camera, something is going down. It's civilians all right, two being dragged into the main building from the big shed."

Cowboy had the camera ready and he climbed up the seed bags just as carefully and handed the camera to Jojo as he peeked out the vent which shielded them from view.

An hour later, two soldiers dragged out one of the civilians. He was unconscious or dead, they couldn't tell. Jojo had the camera running, he saw one of the soldiers aim his rifle at the man. A shot was fired and Jojo saw the man's head explode.

"Sometimes I hate this job," Jojo said.

"A scream erupted from the still-open door of the main building."

"They're working someone over real good," Cowboy said.

Time went by as prisoners were moved from the machine shed to the main building. Some came out alive and were returned to the steel building. Others came out dead or half dead and were shot. Some were civilians and some were soldiers.

At noon, a soup line was formed and the guards marched out a long procession of prisoners. The Green Berets recorded the rows of captives on the video camera; it was all the evidence they needed.

With the evidence they needed collected Jojo and Cowboy waited for nightfall so they could sneak back out of the compound the same way they came in. The plan was to leave the farm using the cover of darkness, and walk back to their GMVs. Then they would ride back to the rendezvous point to meet up with the rest of the team. But, sometimes, shit happens. In this case, shit started to happen when a guard checked the lock on the door of the seed house. The door rattled.

Cowboy and Jojo drew their knives and pistols. Silently they went to opposite sides of the shed where they hid behind seed bags they had piled for camouflage.

The door creaked open. The old lock must have jammed when they tried to lock it.

It was just before dusk and still light enough for the two special forces soldiers to see the feet of the Iraqi soldier walking into the small building. They waited silently, controlling their breathing as trained. Cowboy and Jojo couldn't see each other but knew what each was thinking. At the first sign of trouble, one of them would have to make the silent kill with their forces long knife. It would have to be quick, across the throat, so the guard couldn't yell for help.

The Iraqi guard was kicking at the seed bags with his feet. There was no light to turn on, and the setting sun was casting long shadows over the contents inside the cinder block building, making it difficult to see into the back corners. There was a small open area of floor down the middle of the building, and the guard inspected it to the end. As he backed his way out, he continued kicking at the stuffed burlap bags scattered around him. That was when his boot accidentally kicked between two of the bags. The dull thud of his boot kicking seed changed to the sound of something solid. It was Jojo's pack. metal on metal. The guard kicked it again only harder this time it rattled. His curiosity raised he bent down to take a closer look.

In an instant, Cowboy sprang up from behind and expertly twisted the guard's neck back, then used his knife to slit his throat. The guard was dead in an instant, only an instant wasn't fast enough. As Cowboy pulled the Iraqi backward, the guard's finger pressed the trigger of his rifle. Two shots rang out from inside the small hut.

"Fuck!" Jojo said, still whispering, as he stood up.

There was shouting outside.

Cowboy understood some Arabic from training. "He wants to know if his buddy is OK." Cowboy whispered to Jojo.

"Answer him," Jojo coached.

"Fuck!"

"I'm OK, OK, just accident, no problem." Cowboy answered in Arabic of sorts.

The ploy didn't work; soon there was more frantic shouting. That was when all hell broke loose.

Chapter 2

L et's get the fuck out of here!" Cowboy yelled.
Just as he was leading the way out the building, bullets raked the doorway and pounded seed bags, sending up a plume of burned seeds.

Cowboy ducked back behind the block wall.

"Let's go, Cowboy," Jojo insisted. "It ain't going to get any better."

Bullets shredded the wood of the doorway from a few different directions.

"Too late, it just got worse," Cowboy said.

"Shit! We have to take them out or we won't get out of here alive," Jojo said.

Cowboy scrambled up the seed bags and looked out the top vent. "I see two; I can take them out from here. Get ready to hustle."

Cowboy took two shots, both guards dropped to the ground.

"Go! Go!" Cowboy shouted as he flew down from his perch, landing shoulder to shoulder with Jojo. Both shot out the door, one covering the rear and the other the front as trained.

They had only managed to get a few steps from the doorway when the block wall in front of Cowboy exploded. Shrapnel from the concrete peppered his face and hands. Cowboy couldn't see any targets so he plastered his back against the wall and shot his M4 blindly in a level semicircle at over ninety rounds per minute.

Jojo didn't have to see what was happening in back of him, he could hear the sound of bullets hammering the concrete. In front of him he could see what was coming and it wasn't good, An armored jeep was moving toward them fast; on foot they didn't have a chance.

"Back in the building now!" Jojo shouted. More bullets ricocheted off the concrete around them. Cowboy didn't have to be persuaded any more than that. Soon they were back, trapped inside the building, but for now at least, they were still alive.

Cowboy immediately reloaded his gun with a new clip.

Jojo did the same, between deep breaths he said, "There is some sort of fucking armored jeep out there, and it has something that looks like one of our 50 caliber machine guns mounted on it."

"Shit! If it's anything like ours, it'll make Swiss cheese out of this fucking building."

"Yea, and us with it."

"Any suggestions? I'm all ears," Cowboy said as he tried to calm himself.

Things outside had become strangely quiet. "What do you think they're waiting for?" Jojo asked.

"Don't know, give me a mirror," Cowboy said as he positioned himself under a vent.

Jojo reached in his bag and took out a small mirror on a telescoping rod. It was standard equipment for espionage work.

Slowly, Cowboy guided the mirror over his head and aimed it so it reflected the scene outside.

"Some important-looking dude is giving orders; they're moving the wounded. I see only a couple of foot soldiers out there and the big gun aimed right at us."

Jojo had an idea. "Check out the prisoner shed. Is it still guarded?"

Cowboy slowly swiveled the mirror in that direction. "Yea, a couple of guards. Nothing real heavy though."

"I think we took out a few too many of their guys. I bet that they're waiting for reinforcements to come back before taking us on." Cowboy slunk back down, carefully folding the mirror and slipping it back into his fatigues. He pulled out his pack of gum and offered his friend a piece.

Jojo waved it off and took a big gulp of water instead.

"How long do you think it will be before their guys come back?" Jojo asked as his breathing became a bit more controlled.

Chewing on the gum was helping Cowboy control his own breathing and, more importantly, it seemed to help him think. "The plan was for our team to fight the garrison until nightfall and then slowly pull back. After that, it'll take a few hours for them to figure out the fighting is done and then a couple of hours to get back here. My best guess is we have until tomorrow morning."

Steven's jaw worked around his gum. "Pull out the sat-phone, I don't think radio silence is an issue any more, let's call in the cavalry. Maybe they can get some sort of rescue coming before then."

Jojo pulled out his daypack and stuck his finger through a bullet hole in it. The cumbersome satellite phone inside had probably saved his life. He handed what was left of it to his partner. "Houston we have a problem."

"We're screwed," Cowboy agreed as he slunk down a bit farther into a seed bag.

The last remnants of the setting sun were streaming into the small building through the upper vents. The headlights from the armored jeep along with the machine gun mounted on it were aimed directly at them.

****

Time passed slowly for the two soldiers inside, Jojo pulled out the picture of his wife and daughter again. He studied the photos in his hand using the light from the jeep spilling in through the splintered wood of the only door.

"Cowboy, if I don't make it out of here in one piece and you do, you have to promise me that you'll tell them both how much I loved them."

"Don't talk like that, Jojo. We have to get out of here, we have to get the video we took back to base."

"They're waiting for a reason, they want us alive, at least until they can persuade us to tell them as much as we can. You have to promise me."

"Yea sure, man. I promise."

A few shots rang through the upper vents.

"I guess they don't want us to get bored," Cowboy said.

"I'm not going to be taken alive, Cowboy. Just wanted you to know."

Cowboy didn't answer, he was extending the mirror up to the vents again to see what was happening outside. It didn't take long before shots started pounding the building again.

"I guess they don't like it when I take a peek." Cowboy said.

"Too bad there isn't a back door. We could just waltz out of here and out into the desert, nobody the wiser," Jojo said.

Cowboy stared at his friend. "That's it! You're a genius! All we need is a back door, so let's make a fucking back door."

Jojo shook his head. "I was kidding, they're guarding the whole perimeter. They aren't going to just let us walk off into the desert, even if there was a back door. And outrunning that truck isn't in the cards either."

Cowboy had already pulled out his long blade. "If we can take out the mortar between the blocks, maybe we can take out a couple of blocks, enough to sneak out through?"

"I've got some C4, why don't we just blow a hole through it then?"

"Too noisy, they would be showering us with bullets before the dust settled."

Cowboy scraped some of the mortar. "It seems kind of weak."

"What good will that do, you fool? Even if we fight our way out of here, are you just going to call a taxi to get us to the rendezvous point?"

"Yea, something like that."

"What's the plan, Cowboy?" Jojo asked.

"You won't like it anyway. Let's try to make a back door first. If we can't do that it won't matter. Besides, it's the only plan I have."

Jojo didn't really care. Any plan was better than none so for the rest of the night, they took turns carving out the soft mortar. Eventually, they managed to weaken enough of the cinder blocks that, once removed, a man could crawl through.

****

Jojo checked his watch, in another hour the sun would be up. He kicked lightly at the loosened blocks. There was still a bit of mortar holding them in place, but they seemed loose enough to push out with his foot if he had to.

"What's the plan Cowboy, or are you still not going to tell me?"

"This will work,!" Cowboy said.

"What will work? What's the plan Cowboy?" Jojo asked more suspicious than ever.

"Do you want to see your wife and daughter again?"

"Damn it, Cowboy, what's the fucking plan?"

"Remember that taxi you were talking about?"

"Yea, so?" Jojo was afraid of the answer.

"You know that jeep with the gun mounted on it, the jeep that we can't outrun."

"Yea, so?"

"Well, I'm going to steal it."

"What? Are you fucking nuts?"

"See, I told you, you never like my plans. Will you just trust me?"

"Did you hit your head or something? In case you haven't noticed, it's heavily armed and constantly manned."

"That's a problem, I'll admit."

"A problem? A problem?"

"Look, do you want to get out of here or don't you?"

"OK. OK, but if we get caught, you won't have to worry about the Iraqis because I'm going to fucking kill you myself."

"I'm betting you won't have to. At dawn, we, rather, you, create a little holy hell with the C4. Throw them out the vents all around the building. Set all the timers for the same time. The concrete blocks should protect you from the blasts outside."

"Me? Where the hell are you?"

"I'm going to go out the back door, circle around, steal the jeep, stop at the front door, pick you up, and then, we get the hell out of here."

"Oh, well, when you put it that way, it sounds pretty simple. You *are* fucking nuts. You know that?"

****

The sun was coming up as Cowboy and Jojo started their final preparations.

"I'm going to need your M4," Cowboy said.

"You're taking my gun?"

"Yea, I'm going to need it."

"What if I need it? What about your gun?"

"I'll need yours and mine. Besides, you'll have your Glock."

"Sure, no problem, that's all I'll need anyway to kill myself with after this crazy plan of yours doesn't work."

Jojo turned around and started to prepare the C4. As he worked, he muttered to himself about what they were going to try to do loud enough that Cowboy could hear him whine.

Cowboy prepared both M4s and adjusted the straps so that he could shoot from the hip while on the run.

Just as they were ready to start, Cowboy said, "Don't forget to slip the data card of the video in your pocket. This is going to be easier than I thought."

"Oh, and how's that?"

"The other troops haven't come back yet."

"Yea, that's a lucky break," Jojo said.

"Denton." Cowboy looked his friend in the eyes. "I promise, you are going to see Tamara and Lorelei again, real soon."

"Yea, well, if we get out of this, I'll owe you big time."

"Hey, buddy, have I ever lied to you? Trust me, this'll work."

"Yea, you lied to me plenty, but get ready, now or never."

Jojo threw the bundles of C4 out through the broken vents all around the building. He tossed them as far as he could and heard them land with a thump. Then the huge man tossed himself to the ground.

Chapter 3

Jojo looked at his watch and rolled onto his back. With his shoulders pressed against a mound of seed bags he coiled his legs up for a mighty thrust. "Now!" he shouted and kicked as hard as he could with his heavy military boots against the cinder block wall, breaking it open.

The explosives created havoc outside as the building shook from the gunfire plastering its sides. The guards were shooting blindly through the dust and smoke.

Cowboy crawled out the opening Jojo had made. His adrenaline gave him extra strength, and he pushed the blocks out of his way like they were toys. The guards watching the rear of the building were so caught by surprise that they never saw their enemy. But, unfortunately for them, Cowboy did. He quickly aimed his rifle, which was set for single shot. He pulled the trigger and had his sites on the second man before the first fell. He took them both out. The plan had worked so far; nobody was expecting a rear attack. Jojo, who was right behind Cowboy, covering him, got another with his pistol. Then, as soon as he saw Cowboy disappear around the corner, he ducked back into the block building. It was his job to continue the distraction from inside. He had to make sure the guards still thought they were planning an escape out the one and only exit.

A couple more guards went down as Cowboy circled around unseen. All Jojo had inside the building was a pistol and a couple of hand grenades to create the distraction. Cowboy had to work quickly. With both M4s resting on his hips, he shot off the grenade launchers under each rifle. With the ensuing twin firestorms, the Iraqis formed a tight circle. They thought they were being surrounded. Quickly, Cowboy reloaded each grenade launcher and ran out into the courtyard, he switched his gun to full automatic and began raking the area with the twin M4s. He never stopped moving, realizing it would only take one bullet from one unseen soldier to take him down at any moment.

But now he had to cover his attack. He launched two more grenades and they landed on either side of the jeep, far enough away that they wouldn't destroy the vehicle. He couldn't take the chance of damaging their one and only means of escape.

Right on cue, Jojo released several smoke canisters, further confusing the situation. The soldiers in the jeep were at first distracted by the explosions around them but soon realized they were being attacked from the rear. The man on the big machine gun swiveled it around. Now Cowboy had to stop. He had to take the chance; he had time for one shot. If he didn't kill the man on the gun in the next second, Cowboy knew his body would soon be scattered around the courtyard.

Cowboy let one of the M4s drop to his side, dangling from its strap over his shoulder. The contest wasn't for whoever shot first, it was for whoever made contact first. So Steven steadied himself even as the big gun started to fire toward him.

Steven breathed out and a three-shot burst left his gun.

The Iraqi soldier dropped over the gun, dead, but the driver was taking aim at Cowboy with a pistol, crouched behind the steel door of the jeep. Cowboy ran toward the jeep, holding both M4s and shooting at the open door. The driver didn't have time to get off a shot as he ducked for cover. Cowboy ran to the jeep and kicked the door as hard as he could. The steel of the door cracked against the unhelmeted head of the former driver. The pistol flew out of his hand as he fell backward—out cold.

Cowboy slid behind the seat and shot the jeep through the wall of fire and smoke toward the seed building. The door was open when he stopped, but his partner was nowhere in sight. Grabbing both guns off the seat next to him, he used whatever bullets he had left to lay down a cover of hot lead through the curtain of smoke still concealing him.

Inside the small building, he saw Jojo wincing in pain, sitting on a seed bag with blood all around. "My shoulder took a hit. Take the GPS, and get the hell out of here." Jojo reached for the GPS attached to his side belt to hand to Cowboy.

"Not that easy, my friend."

Cowboy reloaded both M4s with new rounds and then said, "Time to go."

Jojo yelled out in pain as Cowboy roughly pulled him to his feet. "You gotta put your bad arm around my shoulder so you can shoot with your good, got it?"

"Oh shit! This hurts."

Cowboy gave Jojo his fully loaded gun and then grabbed his. They rushed out the door, laying down a ribbon of cover fire.

"We have company, and it looks like somebody already explained things to them."

"You said this would work, Cowboy.

"It will. Piece of cake." Cowboy smirked at his buddy.

"You wouldn't lie to me would you?"

"No, never, but I'm afraid you'll have to drive." Cowboy shouted over the sound of gunfire.

Cowboy pushed Jojo into the driver's seat while he jumped up on top of the jeep. Then he threw off the dead Iraqi still slumped over the gun and twirled the mounted machine gun and attached ammunition magazine box around. "Hey Jojo, this looks like a knockoff of our M2 50 cal."

"Thanks for the tour. You ready?"

"Any time you are. And don't stop for anything, got it?"

"Hang on!" Jojo gunned the engine and let out the clutch. The jeep shot toward the oncoming personnel trucks.

The first truck pulled over as the soldiers in it piled out. Cowboy pointed the large caliber machine gun at them and created mayhem in the ranks of the unprotected row of men.

Jojo could hear bullets peppering the jeep from all sides. With his foot to the floor, he had to steer and shift with the same arm, each bounce of the jeep creating sheer agony in his other arm and shoulder. They had just run one gauntlet when another truckload of soldiers established a much more protected stand on the bridge they needed to cross.

Cowboy could hear bullets whizzing past his head. A few times, he felt hard, solid hits against his body armor. He looked back; the soldiers they had left in their dust had formed a line and were bouncing bullets off the steel of the jeep.

"Whatever you do, Jojo, don't you dare stop this jeep for anything or we're toast. Got it?"

"Shut the fuck up and leave the driving to me. How about you start shooting or something."

"One something coming up." Cowboy reloaded his M4 with the last grenade. Carefully, he aimed it ahead of their path as they continued to take gunfire from behind and now from the front. The grenade exploded in the air above the bridge, the shrapnel from it cutting through the bodies on the ground. Cowboy jumped behind the 50 cal. once again. He aimed and shot, first one side of the bridge then the other. The large-caliber bullets created more shrapnel from the concrete as it disintegrated the wall into fragments. Any soldiers taking protection around it wished they hadn't.

Jojo saw at least five soldiers aim their rifles directly at him as they approached the bridge. Cowboy was doing a hell of a job, but there were just too many of them. At the last minute, Jojo dropped his head down behind the steel dash of the jeep as the window above him shattered into a thousand pieces, showering him in glass as he blindly steered the armored truck as best he could toward the bridge.

When Jojo dared to look up again, they were crossing the bridge and racing away. Cowboy twirled the gun around and continued to cover their retreat, trying to keep the soldiers pinned down for as long as possible.

"Jojo," Cowboy said weakly. "Don't stop for nothing. They're getting back into their trucks."

Jojo glanced back at his friend. He didn't look good. But now wasn't the time to stop. Jojo managed to unclip the GPS from his belt and turn it on. He entered the passcode and it pointed the way to the rendezvous point.

The sun was fully up, and he had only one hour to get to the chopper and the rest of the team. Only problem was, according to the GPS, it was at least two hours away. He was crossing the open desert, and the Iraqis were only a half mile or so behind.

A couple of times, Sergeant Jones felt himself almost doze off. The loss of blood was weakening him rapidly. The pain in his arm and shoulder was gone now; in fact, he could feel nothing at all on that side of his body. He looked at his watch. Only fifteen minutes had gone by since his last time-check, and he didn't think he could make another fifteen, much less another hour or two of pursuit.

Jojo looked back at the pursuing trucks. For some reason, he didn't understand, the soldiers were getting closer. He looked at the speedometer and realized that, in his weakened state, he had inadvertently slowed down. He could hear the sound of rifles going off. Some of the soldiers were starting to take low-probability shots at him. Soon, those shots would no longer be low probability.

As he pressed the accelerator to the floor, the jeep sped up. But he soon realized that any faster was too fast for him to control as it bumped along. Jojo was using all his remaining strength just to hang on. He heard a bullet whiz past his head.

Jojo felt dizzy, his vision seemed to be leaving him. Jojo knew that things were quickly going from bad to worse. A sand storm was brewing, and he was heading right into it. If he had his strength, the sand storm would have been welcome; it would have been a chance to lose his enemies. But under these conditions, he could only hope that if he stopped in the middle of it, maybe, just maybe, the other soldiers would drive right past him, blinded by the fine dust.

He was almost into the brown swirling fog. This would be his last stand, his last chance. Consciousness was going to leave him quickly, and he could feel the darkness coming down on him. Jojo drove into the storm and then stopped. He closed his eyes for what he thought would be the last time.

****

When the commanding officer, Lieutenant Tony Wingren, realized that his two special forces soldiers weren't coming, he had instructed the pilot to climb and then circle the area in a search pattern. When the pilot, Captain Bradley, had spotted two moving dust clouds coming toward the staging area, they had cautiously sped forward for a look. Soon, there was no doubt: one of their two missing soldiers was slumped over in back of the jeep. They could only guess that the other was driving it haphazardly through the desert, trying to evade the two personnel carriers chasing them.

The two huge rotating blades created a dust storm over the desert as it descended. Maybe the dust could provide some cover for their men, he hoped.

Captain Bradley swung the right side of the giant fuselage around. Over the headsets, he heard the order from the CO onboard say, "Give them everything we got." Captain Bradley could see and hear the side gunners open up on the soldiers below with their M60D 7.62 mm machine guns.

Then, over the radio, the CO again commanded, "Turk, Justin take out the trucks from the rear ramp." The rear gunners got in on the action as the two trucks came to a halt, and soldiers piled out of them and scattered, finding cover where they could.

"They have SAMs!" came a shout from the side gunner.

Captain Bradley knew that, at this close range, none of his counter measures would be effective. "Don't let them load that thing or we're done for," Captain Bradley called over the open intercom.

Looking out his side window, Captain Bradley saw the jeep with their men in it suddenly shoot out from its desert perch. He clicked his mic open. "Our boys are on the move; keep the bad guys pinned down for another two minutes. And whatever you do, don't let them aim that SAM at us."

The Chinook was taking a beating, the thin sides of the fuselage weren't designed to thwart such a short-range attack. Bullets penetrated the cabin, but so far, nobody had taken a hit, at least nothing that punctured the body armor each soldier was wearing.

"That's it, we're out of here!" Captain Bradley screamed into the headset.

He twisted the helicopter around the carnage below them, making sure the two side gunners on the right side of the craft had open shots to cover their escape. Then he did a side-stepping maneuver as the aircraft danced farther and farther away.

Captain Bradley twisted the cyclic in his hand and pointed the copter toward the fleeing jeep and pressed it forward.

The CO ordered, "Launch a few grenades out the back. Turk, keep the seven mil. going."

"Clear the ramp!" Captain Bradley ordered. "We can't stop to get them, I'm doing a pinnacle. Let's hope he doesn't miss."

****

Jojo heard the sounds of men in anguish and guns firing. He struggled to stay conscious and looked up through the dust storm he was hiding in. The storm surrounding him had moved, he looked up at the angry howl and saw his team attacking the ground targets. He was too close to the enemy for a rescue; he had to help his squad save him and Cowboy. Adrenaline pumped through his body. Jojo dropped his foot on the accelerator and the jeep shot out from its desert perch.

Jojo raced the small jeep ahead over the desert and away from the carnage the helicopter was causing. Somehow, he had to keep himself conscious long enough to put some distance between him and the Iraqis.

He saw the helicopter speed past him, then the strong hydraulic rams lowered the back ramp as far as it could. Suddenly, the twin-bladed Chinook slowed.

"He's fucking nuts," Jojo whispered to himself through his chapped lips when he realized what the pilot wanted him to do.

Jojo looked at his speedometer. He was moving at about twenty miles per hour over a bumpy desert. The helicopter was moving forward at about the same speed, which kept the sand that the huge twin blades were whipping up from blinding him.

Then it stopped about a hundred feet in front of him. The front of the chopper tilted up, and the back of it swung down. Temporarily, the sand was pushed forward away from the oncoming jeep, but that wouldn't last long.

If Jojo guessed right, he would have about two feet on both sides of the jeep to spare if he centered it just right. The sand was starting to whip up around him, his visibility deteriorating by the second. He gunned the motor, and the jeep bounced onto the ramp, and that was when he lost control. The wheels on the left careened off the side of the fuselage, then the jeep bounced to the other side. Jojo held on with all his might with his one good arm, and, on instinct, he hit the brakes.

****

"They're on, they're on," the CO excitedly called over the intercom.

The copilot lifted the switch for the hydraulic ramp and it started to close, pushing the jeep into its belly.

Captain Bradley pushed the Chinook forward, using high-speed terrain avoidance to keep the copter close to the ground until they could get some distance between them and the Iraqis. The SAMs were deadly close.

"Release counter measures," he told the copilot, even though the threat warning system hadn't gone off. "They've got to be breathing down our throat; by the time we find out, it will be too late."

Two high-powered flares shot out of the aircraft, one went high. That was the one the surface-to-air missile decided to track.

There was an explosion in the air above them. The copilot saluted Captain Bradley. His intuition had paid off.

The desert terrain was mostly flat and Captain Bradley wasn't going to give up an inch of it. He hugged the floor of the desert, kicking up a dust storm in their wake as he put more distance between them and the ground forces after them.

An alarm horn started to sound in the cockpit. It was the threat warning system that was shouting at the pilots. It meant another missile was heading their way.

The copilot didn't wait for an invitation; he launched two more counter measures. The pilot twisted the chopper around, turning it into the missile coming right toward them. It was another gamble. The exhaust from the two powerful engines was attracting the deadly missile right toward them. He prayed that by turning the exhaust away from the missile he would confuse the Iraqis.

Captain Bradley knew the missile would be traveling at over four thousand miles per hour. He didn't expect to see the missile until way too late. But he could see the vapor trail it was leaving as it headed toward them.

In another instant, the missile shot past the cockpit and then exploded behind them. He was right, the hot flares once again attracted the missile away.

****

At one hundred and sixty knots per hour in another two minutes, the crew and passengers, and one shot-up jeep, were miles away on their way back to Saudi Arabia. Jojo waved off the medical personnel and pointed to Cowboy. "Take care of my boy first!"

Cowboy was laid out in the back of the jeep, he wasn't breathing. The medics took off the shot-up and bloody body armor to get to the worst of his injuries. Jojo stared at the bloodied body of his friend sure he had been too late. He looked up at the attending medic for an encouraging sign. That was when he saw the chaotic world around him start to spin, then the world went dark.

Chapter 4

Twenty-two years later at Harford County Airport:

A re you sure you want to keep doing this, Cowboy?"
"Yea, I'm sure."

"This could kill you," Jojo said.

"What are you talking about?"

Jojo Jones continued walking toward his car; Senator Steven West-cott had his flight bag slung over his shoulder as he sprinted just a bit to catch up to his friend.

"I assume it was you doing those landings," Jojo said.

"Yea, mostly," Steven said.

"What do you mean, mostly?"

"The instructor had to take over a couple of times," Cowboy admitted.

"Now you know what I'm talking about."

"Hey, it was my first time trying to land the thing by myself."

"Yea, like I said, I could tell."

"Kiss my ass. Is that why you offered to drive me to my flying lesson? Just so you could rip on me?"

Laughing, Jojo responded, "Not the only reason. You're so busy being a senator and all, I hardly ever see you."

Steven slung his pilot's bag into the backseat of Jojo's SUV and jumped into the passenger side.

"Yea, who'd have ever thought twenty years ago that you would end up a policeman and me a US senator?"

"Not me, that's for sure. And soon to be Detective Jones. You hungry?"

"Starving."

It didn't take long before they found a small diner a couple of miles down Churchville Road. Inside, they found a booth.

"Two coffees, black," Jojo ordered as soon as the waitress came over.

Steven busied himself looking over the menu.

"So how's it going at home?" Jojo asked.

"That didn't take you long."

"Didn't want to ask on the way up. I thought it might screw up your landings. Guess I was wrong."

Steven rolled his eyes as the waitress approached with the coffee. "It's going OK, could be better." He turned to the waitress. "I'll have a burger and fries," Steven said.

"Make that two."

Steven took his coffee in both hands and sipped it.

Jojo held his own hot mug of coffee in his big hand and said, "I can't imagine. Losing a child is tough, it's going to take time."

"I don't think there is enough time in the world to make things better again. I can tell you this: I don't know what we would have done without you two this past year. Without your and Tamara's support, I don't think we would have made it." Even as he spoke, Steven's eyes started to swell up with tears. Over the last year, he had learned to deal better with his emotions, but still, just the thought of the loss of his daughter made tears well in his eyes.

"I know it's tough to talk about, but you need to vent to somebody."

"We are seeing counselors. I don't think it's helping much. Maybe, I don't know. I know Lucille is still angry with me. I mean, she doesn't yell at me or anything like that, it's just, well, we've been married a long time and things just aren't the same."

"Is that what she says or what you think?"

"Both, I guess. Pretty much has come out in therapy. She knows it's not rational. But deep down, she feels that I could have or should have somehow saved Rebecca."

"Do you think she could have or should have done more?"

"No, not at all. I mean, it's not rational. Rebecca was an adult, and she was always headstrong. Lucille knows it doesn't make sense to blame me, but, well, I guess she has to blame somebody. It sucks, but at least we identified a problem and are trying to work it out."

The burgers came, and Steven took a big bite, then licked ketchup off his fingers.

"How's Tracy doing?"

"I'm so proud of her. She's a real trooper. We had to spend so much time with Rebecca that we just didn't have much time for Tracy. We are trying to make it up to her now. She's seeing a shrink too, and the doc says she's doing OK."

"Good for her, and as far as you and Lucille go, you know that we are as close as a telephone."

"Of course, but it just won't be the same when you all move to North Carolina. We are really going to miss you guys."

"When you finally get that pilot's license you've been working on, you can just fly down any time you want."

"You didn't tell your wife yet, did you?"

"No, Tamara doesn't have a clue, and it will cost me when I finally do tell her."

"Well good, because Lucille doesn't know a thing about it. She has enough to worry about. I haven't told anybody, and I plan to keep it that way. When I have my license in hand, then I'll tell her and not before. I can't wait; having my pilot's license will make getting home more often a lot easier. And I can't think of anything more important than that."

"Your secret is safe with me."

The waitress came by and poured Jojo another cup of coffee. "Did you see the game on Sunday?" Jojo asked, trying to lighten the subject.

"You bet, I wouldn't have missed it." Jojo and Steven talked sports for a while. By the third cup of coffee, it was getting time to leave.

Then Steven said, "By the way, I'm proud of you, buddy. I mean, making detective and getting the promotion and the new job and all."

"I may not be a United States senator, but it's what I always wanted to do. As a detective in a small town, I think I will be able to make a difference."

"Don't give me too much credit. Being a senator isn't all it's cracked up to be. You sit around for days and days wrapped in details, bored to death, when all of a sudden, all hell breaks loose."

"Pretty much sums up a cop's life too. Most days it's just routine stuff and plenty of paperwork. But one radio call, and it all changes in an instant."

"Kind of reminds you of the service doesn't it? I mean, endless days and days of training. But when that special mission comes through, wow, what a rush."

Steven finished the last of his french-fries and smirked. "Yea, but getting shot at isn't at the top of my list of things I want to do. Considering that, being a boring senator from Massachusetts isn't all that bad."

Washington DC, Barry Farm District:

Destinee Sanford was lying on the torn linoleum floor of the dingy kitchen, rubbing the developing bruise on her left cheek. Her long, dark hair was splayed over her face and spread across the dirty floor. The other girls she'd been talking to when the big, black hand threw her to the floor cowered in a corner.

"Don't give me any of your shit you little, white bitch. Do you really think this is some sort of welfare house, huh? You want crack, you gotta earn it like all the rest. You've given me nothin' but trouble since your mama died. I took pity on you and made sure you didn't hafta sleep in the gutter, didn't I? Well? Answer me, bitch, didn't I?"

"Yea, Clay, you take care of me real good, just look at me, you cocksucker."

Clayton Harris reached down and grabbed the young, white woman off the floor and threw her onto the kitchen table. Destinee's back slapped against the tabletop; her flimsy white blouse tore away in the process. Her hundred pounds was no match against his two-hundred-some pounds of muscle. With his open hand, he slapped her hard across the face. "You gotta smart mouth, bitch. Time you learned some manners." With one hand, he held her cheeks and squeezed hard, then with his other, he unbuckled his belt and slid it out from around his muscular frame. He doubled it up and soon it was whipping down on her.

Destinee curled up into a fetal position to try and protect herself from the beating, her short skirt covering little. "Stop it, Clay, stop. I won't be able to get your money if I'm all beaten up."

The belt came down on Destinee's thigh; the pain gripped deep into her. It hurt so bad, she gasped for air but refused to cry out. The other girls hid in the adjoining room when they heard the commotion. They didn't dare get involved.

"You aren't earning me any money now, you bitch, so what's the difference?" He screamed back as the belt came down on her bare back.

Destinee instinctively arched away and tried to escape as the pain seared her back. The old table she was lying on creaked as she twisted on it. Clayton was squeezing her cheeks so hard, it wasn't easy to talk. Destinee gulped for air, trying to absorb the pain. The heat from the welts that were forming made her feel nauseous.

"Jesus Christ, Clay, stop it, you expect more out of me than any of the other girls."

"You goddamn right. A white girl as pretty as you had better bring in more." Clayton hit her a few more times, the belt welting her back. His strong arms could have gone on all night, but he stopped.

Destinee knew that he had realized she was right. If he bruised her up too bad she wouldn't be able to work and he wouldn't get his money.

Clayton took a towel off the counter and wiped the sweat off his face. It was a hot and humid day in the Anacostia neighborhood of Washington DC, and the old, rundown house wasn't air-conditioned. "You get your ass cleaned up and get back out on the street. Don't you come back without at least five hundred, and if you want a little crack treat, you better bring in more than that." Clayton gave the trembling girl one more whip of the belt across her thigh.

It caught Destinee by surprise, and she lost her breath with the pain. She threw herself to the dirty linoleum floor, hopefully out of Clayton's reach.

"And let that be a little lesson to the rest of you bitches," Clayton said as he withdrew from the room in an angry huff.

After Clayton was gone, three of the other girls in Clayton Harris's stable rushed up to Destinee and helped her back to her feet and then to a chair. For Destinee, there was no escaping her situation, at least not yet. But for now, at least she wouldn't let that SOB see her cry.

Destinee shook like she was shivering from cold, yet the heat from the thrashing burned through her. She cursed silently. Yes, he had taken her in when her mother died, but it was only so that she could take her mother's place in his stable. The years since then had gone by exceedingly slow. She had just barely turned eighteen at the time, now she was twenty-one. If only she had run away back then, but she didn't, and now she was trapped just like her mother had been.

The trouble was that she needed the prick. She was a crack whore and knew that she wouldn't last two days on the street without him and his cocaine. When she felt a bit better, and while defiantly holding back her tears, she got up and thanked the other girls for their pity, which was all they could give. Then she went to her room and began the process of cleaning up.

Her small bedroom was her only haven; she felt oddly at peace in what looked more like a jail cell then a bedroom because of the heavy steel on the windows. Her room was just one of five bedrooms in the rundown, old-frame two-story. It was on the first floor. The bars across the window were meant to keep her locked inside when Clayton was punishing her. But when she heard the frequent sound of gunshots on the streets, the bars on the windows made her feel safe and secure.

The steel-framed double bed and dirty old mattress was comforting to her. The room had been her mother's, and she could still feel her presence in it. Destinee stared at the bed where her mother died, the bed she had slept in with her mother for so many nights.

The beating had her feeling lonesome for her mother. If only she were still alive, they could escape together. She opened a small drawer that contained most everything that her mother had considered important to her.

It was also where Destinee went to feel her mother's presence. There wasn't much in the drawer, but it was all Destinee had. She lifted out the locket with a picture of her mother in it, her most precious item. Her mother was younger and healthier and happy in the picture. Using her shoulder, she brushed away a tear that had formed. She knew that at the rate things were going, she would be dying in that same bed in the near future, it was only a matter of time, years maybe, but not many. She unrolled a bit of toilet paper from off her dresser, blew her nose into it, and wiped away more tears.

The young hooker rubbed her bruises; it had been a small price to pay. She knew that if Clayton ever found the envelope full of cash she was hiding, it would mean a much more terrible beating or possibly death. But she was going to die anyways, she reasoned. Her goal was to get enough money to run away. Then she might have a chance at life. Even if that meant stealing from her pimp.

Heading out the door, Destinee felt safe in the rundown neighborhood despite her near nakedness. She wore a tight, short, black leather skirt that didn't even begin to cover her long and shapely legs. Her silky blue blouse was equally tight; the only buttons fastened were just below her chest, keeping her midriff bare and breasts amply exposed.

She walked down the road past new automobiles parked next to long, worn out, rusting hulks of cars long ago left on the street to rot away. She passed row upon row of public housing. Nobody in his or her right mind would attack her, not here. Clayton would kill anybody messing with one of his whores.

She lived in what some might call a suburb of Washington DC. That would have been generous. Anacostia was a grimy lost city filled with hopelessness and despair. If the greater city could take an eraser and remove this blighted area, it would have been done long ago.

She stopped and looked back at the dilapidated home she had left. But instead of seeing the hellhole it was, she saw something else entirely. She could imagine at one time a well-kept garden and picket fence. Some of the fence was still visible, but it was rotting and pressed down into the weeds. It was one of the few single family homes left in the area. A family had once lived there a long, long time ago. She envisioned a mother, father, maybe a brother and sister playing inside the picket fence next to a flower garden. She fought back some tears, her mother deserved a life like that, and she deserved a life like that. *Someday*, she told herself as she clicked her high heels down the broken concrete walk.

Chapter 5

Senator Westcott pointed the remote at the TV in his small Senate office and turned the volume up just a bit. He was ready to go back to his apartment for the evening, but the culmination of a particular court trial on TV was captivating.

The trial was being shown live, unusual for sure, but so was the trial. The judge was trying to restore order in her courtroom by pounding the gavel on her desk, over and over again. The verdict had just been read. It appeared that the defendant was going to prison for a very long time. He had just been convicted of killing a prostitute he was now known to have associated with.

Senator Steven Westcott shook his head in disgust. *Why would a sports star with everything going for him commit murder?* The senator felt anguish for Deon's family but not for the football player himself. Steven knew better than most that the evidence against the star football player had been insurmountable, despite the man's claim of innocence. There was no doubt in the senator's mind that Deon was guilty. After all, DNA never lies.

The outcome of this particular trial couldn't have come at a better time for Senator "Cowboy" Westcott. It seemed that the case of the "District of Columbia vs. Deon J. Michalski" was made to order. The timing was critical because, recently, in a very contentious decision, the Supreme Court ruled five to four that police could take DNA from people they arrest without getting a warrant.

Justice Anthony Kennedy wrote for the court's five-justice majority: "Taking and analyzing a cheek swab of the arrestee's DNA is like fingerprinting and photographing. It's a legitimate police booking procedure that is reasonable under the Fourth Amendment."

Now that the United States Supreme Court had made the final ruling, he could use this high-profile case to make his point that DNA samples should be taken on anyone convicted of a crime. And this DNA database should be held in a federal registry. The registry would, in turn, help police across the country inexpensively capture more criminals.

After enough DNA was cataloged, it would make finding the perpetrator of a crime much easier. This way, DNA found on crime scenes would be very important evidence in prosecuting and convicting perpetrators. Steven would have to study the details of this case a bit more, but it certainly sounded like he could use this particular conviction as a rallying cry.

His bill, currently numbered S58, would require that all states collect and make available to all the other states across the country the DNA files of all citizens and noncitizens who are convicted of a crime. Working under the assumption that most crimes are by repeat offenders, and on the fact that DNA evidence is left at most crime scenes, DNA collection would become an invaluable crime-fighting tool. Fingerprints would still be good supporting data if available, but DNA was usually easier to find than complete fingerprints. The fact was, DNA markers were the perfect tools for capturing criminals.

And even better, there was a technique that Steven was becoming even more excited about. It was a DNA tracking technique called Familial. Just as repeat offenders commit many crimes, often times, crime seems to run in the family. Criminal scientists had, in a few cases, discovered the perpetrator of a crime because the perpetrator's brother, uncle, or father, who had some of the same markers, had their DNA on file.

Using the Familial technique, the criminologist would run several key markers on a DNA strand against the existing database. If the computer came up with a match on enough of the markers, it would mean that someone in that family was the culprit. Then, it would just be a matter of elimination. When the detectives came up with an exact DNA match, they would have their criminal. There was no doubt in Steven's mind, using and tracking DNA would lead to a revolution in how criminals were caught and tried. The odds of getting away with a crime were going to plummet, making the world a safer place for all, except the criminal, of course.

On his way out of the office, Steven looked in the mirror. He had a bad habit of brushing his hair every which way with his hands when he got lost in thought. As he used his comb to make himself more presentable, he glanced at the torn, bullet-riddled cloth he kept behind a glass frame next to a picture of his old squad. It was there to remind him that in Washington, you had no protection and nobody had your back.

Steven's hands touched the glass covering the swatch of his body armor that had saved his life in Kuwait so many years ago. When he had finally awoken from a two-week coma, the men from his squad had given him the entire jacket as a souvenir, which he kept in his office closet. But they had cut away one small part and framed it inside the glass.

The body armor had done its job, and he had done his. He had been hit numerous times in the back, shoulder, and chest. Each time, the armor had absorbed and flattened the bullets. His body had taken a tremendous beating to be sure, but he had survived. The rest of the tattered body vest was tucked in a closet inside his office; he couldn't remember the last time he had taken it out because the small piece hanging on his office wall was all he needed to remember the mission by.

Steven turned sideways to the mirror, pulled his open-suit jacket back and sucked in his tummy. His face had maintained a mature but still-youthful look. His six-foot frame was solid, but as he let his stomach muscles relax, he had to admit he wasn't as conditioned as he was twenty years ago.

His custom-fit pinstripe suit hid his many battle scars. It had taken Steven two years of intense and painful physical therapy before he could return to active duty. He had worked very hard to get back into physically peak form in the years after his injuries. But looking at his reflection, he realized he was starting to let himself go. The weight was becoming easier and easier to put on. *Once a Green Beret, always a Green Beret*, he reminded himself. It was time to spend more time in the Senate gymnasium and less time in the Senate café.

"Goodnight Shannon," Steven said to the last remaining member of his staff. Shannon Johnston was totally dedicated to him and his office. She was usually the first person in and the last person to leave. Every time Steven tried to remind the young woman to have a life outside of work, another office fire would arise that only Shannon was capable of putting out.

"Goodnight, Senator, and don't forget your meeting tomorrow morning at seven sharp in the Dirksen Building."

Steven hesitated then said, "You worry like a mother hen."

"You already forgot didn't you?"

Steven pulled out his phone and set an alarm for 6 a.m. "Well, you can rest easy tonight, I have my phone set to wake me." Steven held up his phone with a smile.

Shannon smiled back. "Just what would you do without me?"

"Obviously the country and I would instantly be doomed."

Senator Westcott's office was on the fifth floor, and he walked down the open hallway of the Philip A. Hart Senate Office Building on his way toward the elevators. To his right were lines of office doors; to his left was a railing and open air. Steven stopped to reflect on his life and the honor bestowed on him by the people who had elected him. He leaned against the wood-topped railing and looked out and up over the huge nine-story atrium in the middle of the Hart Senate Building. Fifty of the country's one hundred senators had offices here, and he was one of them.

Standing on the fifth floor balcony, Steven was about halfway between the top of the atrium and the ground floor. It always seemed quiet and peaceful out on the open hallway. He could look down or up and see others like him walking from office to office. But from his perch, it all seemed more like a pleasant dance than a hectic office environment.

Steven looked across the bright and airy indoor courtyard in front of the center atrium and the home of an artful rendition of "Mountains and Clouds." It was a huge, black, steel sculpture that represented mountains and rose from the center of the atrium. Floating ninety feet above it, suspended from the ceiling, were four dark clouds made out of aluminum. It was truly massive; first-floor visitors could walk through the giant steel mountain to view it from all sides. Steven didn't particularly appreciate the thing. Art truly was in the eyes of the beholder.

However, he was impressed with the sheer size of the sculpture. Visitors to the Hart Building were always equally impressed; at least they used to be. Starting about a week ago, there was a bit of remodeling going on. Each floor's façade was getting some sort of face-lift.

Workers were just beginning the process of erecting scaffolding and running a huge tarp across the lower floors to protect passersby from any falling debris. So much for the beauty of art, the Hart Senate Building wasn't going to be very pretty to look at for quite a while.

Steven passed his key card over the electronic reader on the Senate elevator. Riding the special elevator took him down to the private parking area. If he wanted, his key card would grant him access to the sub-basement and the private Senate tram system.

Using the private Capitol Subway under the building, he and the other senators would be whisked off to the Capitol Building to conduct their business. Ever since the terrorist attacks of nine-eleven, security had been increased. Now, it was open only to members of the government. It was an efficient and quick mode of transportation for those privileged to use it.

It didn't take him long to find his assigned parking spot. Tonight, he would stay at his small District of Columbia apartment. After his morning meeting, he would return home to his wife and daughter in Peabody, Massachusetts. Summer recess was called, and starting tonight, Steven had five weeks off. It would be a much welcomed respite from the drudgery of Washington DC. Though, just because the Senate was in recess for five weeks didn't mean he didn't have work to do in Washington. In fact, it was just the opposite. However, Steven was going to take advantage of the situation and spend at least two weeks at home.

****

Steven turned the key to his small Washington DC apartment. It had been another long day of meetings, shaking hands, and reading unending paperwork. His apartment reminded him of his college dorm. It was small and simple and sparsely furnished. It was an efficiency apartment with one bedroom. But, unlike some other Senators, at least he didn't have to share it.

Steven set his briefcase on the small, round dining table. With five more steps, he dropped himself wearily onto a sofa in front of his television. He kicked off his shoes, opened his tablet, and used a video-calling app to call home like he did nearly every night.

"Hi Daddy." Steven's fourteen year old daughter, Tracy, answered using her bedroom computer.

"Hi, sweetheart, how are you? What on earth did you do to your hair?"

"Do you like it? Mom helped me streak it."

"It certainly is interesting." Steven didn't particularly like the purple streaking through her blonde hair but knew better than to disprove of a teen's latest experiment. She was growing into a beautiful young lady just like her older sister had, and he understood it was all part of the growing process.

"Did you have a good day at school?"

"It was OK, Nancy said George Meyer got kicked out of school for smoking."

"You mean Nancy from your math class?"

"Yea, she was helping me with homework. George wasn't in school today."

"If he was smoking, he should be held accountable."

Steven tossed his feet up on the couch and forced himself to pay attention to their conversation. To go from dealing with terrorists and voting on missile strikes to keeping track of Tracy's schoolmates, who may or may not have been kicked out of school for a few days, was challenging. Still, Steven knew he was fortunate to have a daughter like Tracy, who would share such details with him.

The nightly video calls didn't and couldn't make up for his not being there, but it helped to keep him involved in her life. When he did get home, he knew almost as much about what was going on as Lucille did.

"Did you just get home from work?"

"Just walked in the door and thought of you."

"I could tell. You still have your tie on."

It seemed that the family was slowly coming to terms with Rebecca's death, but the last year had been a huge emotional strain on all of them.

They talked of home and school and mostly nothing for about a half hour.

"Dad, are you coming home soon?"

"Yes, in a week."

"Can't wait to see you then. Love you Dad. Bye."

"Bye honey."

His home in Massachusetts was nine hours away by car and the commute was grueling. Steven thought about the flying club he had joined. When he finally had his license, he could use the flying club's airplane to be home in about three hours, give or take, depending on wind. The extra precious time at home would be very welcomed.

Across town:

Detective Bruce Harmon saw the bright red hair of the woman he was looking for. She was on a favorite street corner. Harmon guessed that the arrow-straight red hair was her calling card.

The rest of her outfit never varied much either. Despite the weather being cold or hot, she wore skintight, ultra-short white shorts and usually a blue top. The white shorts accented the dark skin of her long thin legs and ample buttocks. The color combination of red, white and blue, was probably supposed to imply she was just your average all-American girl.

"What do you want, Harmon?" Harmon could sense that Tiffany Maddenheart wasn't happy to see him as he stopped his sedan next to her.

Through the open window, Detective Bruce Harmon skipped any pleasantries and said, "Get in!"

Tiffany combed her hand through her deep red hair. She studied the policeman for a moment.

Detective Harmon's pale face looked a bit worn and a bit older than his forty-something age. His long, dark hair was slicked back and looked unwashed.

"Fuck you, Harmon."

"That's the idea. Do you have dust?"

"You're a goddamn cop. Of course I don't."

"Just get in the fucking car or your life suddenly gets more complicated."

Tiffany's lips locked together and her teeth clenched. Though she hesitated for a moment, she opened the door and slid in.

"Meet me at the Washington Arms Hotel at eight."

"Why?" Tiffany asked. "What's wrong with the Saint Claire?"

"What do you care? Just get a room at the Washington Arms. Text me the room number."

Harmon finished his cigarette and tossed it out his open window.

"I'm warning you, Harmon, if you smack me around again, Benny's going to be pissed."

"Just get the fucking room."

Harmon grabbed her hand, pressing her back into the seat and then reached down Tiffany's Camisole top. Between her breasts he found a very small plastic bag with white powder.

"Thanks."

"You know what, Harmon? You're the kind of guy that gives cops a bad name."

Harmon laughed. "Hey, I'll save you some. I am a gentleman after all, and I do want you to have a good time."

Hours later at the Washington Arms:

"Christ, Harmon, look at me." Tiffany examined herself in the mirror, delicately touching the bruise that was swelling up around her eye. Harmon buckled up his pants and secured his holster. "Just stay here for a while and put some ice on it." He took three hundred dollars out of his wallet and threw it onto the disheveled bed. "And don't tell anybody who you were with."

"I told you, Harmon, no more of this shit. I don't want your fucking money. Just stay the fuck out of my life, got it?"

Harmon reached up and grabbed her thin wrist and twisted it. "Shut up, bitch. You know how I like it. You weren't complaining a few minutes ago, in fact, you were enjoying it."

"Fuck you, Harmon. I just wanted you to get off so you would stop hitting me. I'm fucking serious. I don't want to see you again."

"You'll see me whenever I say." Harmon used the leverage of her wrist to throw her to the bed.

"Do you have a new regular?"

"I don't know what you're talking about."

Tiffany watched as Harmon walked over the small garbage can and picked up an empty bottle of Champagne out of it.

"Who were you with before me?"

"Nobody—none of your fucking business."

Harmon pointed to a knife resting on the edge of a cheese platter. "You don't seem to be a cheese plate type of gal. Don't lie to me, it was that doctor guy, wasn't it?"

"So what? It's a free country. How do you know him?"

"Don't, but I saw you and him together before and ran his license plate. Dr. Gregory Merrill."

"Please, Harmon, leave him alone, he's nice to me. He buys me Champagne and cheese and we talk first. And he sure as hell doesn't hit me. And why the fuck do you care anyway? This room doesn't come cheap you know. I have to take it for a whole day. One customer hardly pays."

"Does he supply you with pills?"

"None of your fucking business. Leave him alone, he's a good customer."

"I have to make a call, in private. Take a shower."

"You're such a fucking gentleman, Harmon."

"Here's what's left of your coke." Harmon tossed what was left of her small bag of white powder onto the tabletop.

"Fuck you, Harmon, you know that, just fuck you!" Tiffany grabbed what was left of her cocaine and slammed the bathroom door closed, making a point of locking it loudly.

Detective Harmon looked at the wealth of evidence left behind by the doctor. Finger prints and DNA on the Champagne glasses and bottle. Fingerprints and DNA on the knife used to cut the cheese. DNA was certainly left behind in the used condom he saw in the garbage can, and that was the easy stuff. There was no doubt even more potential evidence of the doctor's visit if he cared to search the room a bit.

Harmon left the room without saying goodbye to Tiffany. He wondered if even a doctor understood the implications of what he so carelessly left behind in the room, just like millions of other travelers the world over did day after day.

****

Ramon Ruben Hayes, the night manager of the Washington Arms Hotel, closed his car door with his white-gloved hand. His parking spot at the Washington Arms was on the far side of the parking garage; he had become adept at gauging how busy the hotel was by the number of cars he walked by. Ramon wore a smart blue blazer emblazoned with the logo of the Washington Arms Hotel. He walked across the concrete, heading toward the main lobby.

As Ramon reached for the door, it swung open toward him.

"Excuse me," Ramon said as he smiled politely and stepped out of the way.

Ramon didn't recognize the person leaving and assumed it was one of the hotel guests.

The man ignored him. Ramon was used to that. He felt his short stature made him invisible to some people. The man was dressed in a wrinkled tan sport coat and was carrying a white plastic garbage bag that, by its bulge, obviously held something.

As the man passed him he noticed through the guest's open sport coat that a badge was clipped to his belt. After brushing past each other, Ramon looked back and saw a bulge in his coat; undoubtedly his gun was hidden there.

Why was a cop wandering around his hotel? And what was he carrying in the white plastic garbage bag?"

At the front desk, Ramon quizzed Jennifer, the manager he was relieving. "Anything I should know about?" Ramon tugged on the white cloth at his fingertips and removed his soiled white gloves.

Jennifer was at least ten years younger and probably six inches taller than Ramon. She chuckled a bit and said, "A hooker came in and wanted an hourly rate. Told her that the Washington Arms was not that kind of hotel. She took a room anyways."

Ramon squeezed out a liberal amount of antibacterial gel on his now bare hands and rubbed them together.

"What room did you give her?"

Jennifer scanned the computer. "Room 435."

"Did you see her customer?"

"I did." Jennifer smirked a bit. "I happened to be checking on the vending machines on the fourth floor and saw him go to the room. Good looking guy, clean enough, probably late thirties or early forties."

"Was he wearing a tan sport jacket?"

"Why yes he was."

Ramon blew his hands dry so he could put on a new pair of white gloves. "Saw him leaving as I came. What time did they check in?"

"About two hours ago."

"Well I guess whether she needs it or not, it looks like she has room 435 until tomorrow morning."

"In the future, keep her off the fourth floor. Give her room 327 if possible. I don't want our other guests disturbed by her type. No sense filthying up all of our rooms with a guest like that."

Chapter 6

Peabody, Massachusetts:

Senator Westcott walked into his red brick two-story home in Peabody, Massachusetts, just like any other returning road warrior. The home was well apportioned but not extravagant by any measure. For a while, he and his wife had considered moving to a more upscale home and neighborhood. But then their daughter, Rebecca, became involved with drugs and everything changed. Moving now would seem like they were trying to distance themselves from their dead daughter, and that was the last thing they wanted.

Twelve hours earlier, he had left DC, and it was a relief to finally be home. He dropped his briefcase like it had been a load of bricks and shouted to the walls, "Hi, honey, I'm home!"

Nobody answered. His wife's car was in the garage and the lights were all on. Then he noticed that something smelled good. Something was cooking with cinnamon in it, of that, he was sure.

Maybe she was upstairs. Steven saw the pile of mail sitting on the foyer table that always greeted him when he came home. He sorted through it, too tired to care about most of it.

"Steven, you're home! I thought I heard something down here," Lucille said as she descended the stairs.

Steven studied his wife. She walked gracefully, with a glass of red wine in her hand. Her long blonde hair was flowing nicely over her left shoulder where it always seemed to naturally gravitate. During the last months, their lives were slowly becoming normal again. As they both tried to change back into the people they had been and the parents Tracy needed. It wasn't always easy.

Lucille gave him a quick hug and kiss. "It's so nice to have you home again. Dinner is ready, probably overdone. I didn't think you would be quite this late."

"Traffic was miserable coming out of Pennsylvania," he said.

"You went to the prison?"

"He's still my brother, it was sort of on my way."

"Sort of on your way? Really? You could have been home hours ago."

Steven tried to sidestep the lecture. "The guards cut us some slack and let us talk for a while. I suppose it doesn't hurt that I'm a US senator. It was good for Ernie to have someone to vent to."

"Tracy and I haven't seen you for weeks either; we need you too, and we didn't commit a felony."

Steven didn't fault his wife for the scolding, she was right. The remaining members of the Westcott family were struggling to put their lives together again and, because of his job, together-time was at a premium low.

When Rebecca was struggling with her addiction, their lives centered on saving her from the self-destructive behavior that wasn't just destroying her but the entire family. With all the energy the couple poured into saving the oldest daughter, Tracy was often ignored just because of the impossible situation. Time and energy were exhausted and suspicion and trust between him and Lucille waned.

Lying to cover up for last minute cancelations or sudden changes of plans became commonplace to protect the family from gossip. Trust was lost, and intimacy was replaced by anger and emotional fatigue.

Finally, the lying and endless nights of worrying if their daughter would survive another day or night ended. Rebecca succumbed to an overdose. The monster that had stolen her from them had won. They had lost.

Steven forced himself back from the past; it hurt to think about those days, but he couldn't help it. And he knew that Lucille couldn't either. Pain and anger were still with them, but with help from Jojo and Tamara, support groups, and therapy, things were improving, albeit slowly.

"Come on, hon, we've been through this before. Yes, he screwed up, screwed up bad. But, he is my only brother. I'm the only person he gets to talk to besides other cons. He needs that."

"He almost killed somebody while robbing a liquor store for a few bucks. He doesn't deserve your time, not one second of it."

"That isn't exactly how it went and you know it. Ernie was an addict. He was high. He didn't know what he was doing. You of all people should understand that."

Steven's comment was instinctual, but he regretted it the instant it came out of his mouth.

Steven stepped gently toward his wife and hugged her. "I'm sorry, I didn't mean to compare Rebecca with Ernie."

"I can't, and I won't. Listen to you, you're defending him."

"Not defending, just explaining it. Ernie isn't a bad person, he just made some very bad decisions in his life that he's paying for every single day."

"Almost killing somebody in a fit of rage *is* the precise definition of a bad person. That's why he is in a federal prison. You need to let him go. Focus on us."

"I do have some good news. Ernie told me that with time off for good behavior, he could be released within the year."

"I wouldn't call that good news. He belongs behind bars. That's what's wrong with the criminal justice system; it's just a rotating door. You tell him that he better not come around here. He is not welcome. I don't want Tracy exposed to him."

Unfortunately, his wife was probably right on all counts. He was risking his career with each visit. This discussion alone was evidence that his brother's mistakes did affect him and his family. And he had to admit; he didn't want Uncle Ernie influencing Tracy either.

"Tracy!" Lucille yelled up the stairs. "Your father is home." Then she gave Steven a stern look and added, "Let's not discuss her Uncle Ernie. Agreed?"

"Agreed," Steven said.

Tracy bounded down the stairs and nearly flew into her father's arms. Steven swung her around just like he used to when she was little. "Daddy, I missed you. I saw you on TV the other day. CSPAN was showing the latest Senate vote. You looked like you were bored."

"I was. It was a procedural vote, meant nothing, but I had to be there. If people knew how much time their senators and congressmen wasted on political BS they would fire us all."

Steven saw Lucille force out a wide smile for their daughter's sake as she announced in the happiest tone she could muster, "Let's eat and get reacquainted."

Sitting at the table in the dining room, Steven set his wine down and took another piece of the fried chicken.

"How about we all go camping this weekend? We could go to Willowdale Forest. You know, where my—"

"Dad used to take you camping and fishing," Tracy finished for him. "I've been there, remember?"

Steven rolled his eyes. "So what do you two say? Campfires, frying up fresh fish, scary stories, smores."

"I'm sorry, dear, I have Benefit League work this week."

"I'll go, daddy, can we go horseback riding?"

"That's a great idea; I'll call the stables. Are you sure, honey? You love to ride."

"Like I said, I have work. You're not the only one who has commitments around here."

"I understand. I didn't mean to imply your work isn't important, because it is."

A little disappointed, Steven was happy for a partial win: time with Tracy.

Lucille poured herself another glass of wine and picked at her food.

"Do you think we can have the horses overnight, you know, ride them deep into the forest?"

"Overnight? How about all weekend, starting Thursday! If you can leave your cellphone home," Steven said.

"Might as well, it doesn't work inside the Willowdale forest anyway, but I do need my music."

"Agreed."

After dinner, Tracy excused herself to visit her friend down the road. Steven was glad to have some private time with Lucille, even if it was just doing the dishes together. Steven carried the plates from the dining room as Lucille rinsed and stacked them in the dishwasher.

When the work was nearly done, Lucille wiped the counter down.

"How's it looking for your bill? Are Senators Williams and Shepard going to sign on?"

"Yes, I think so. In fact, have you been watching the Michalski trial?"

"Who hasn't? I saw that they found his DNA all over the poor girl."

"And that would be the point. The DNA evidence has been critical, and I think that his trial is going to convince some of the holdouts in the Senate that my bill should be passed."

"Anything that makes it easier for the police to catch and convict criminals is worthy of their vote."

Steven put down the dishtowel and took his wife gently in his arms. "Honey, I'm sorry I've been away so much, and I want to thank you for being so patient and understanding. When I ran for senator, we knew how much I would be gone, but what is it costing me? Costing us? I can't help but think that maybe if I hadn't been in Washington and on the road campaigning, Rebecca would still be with us today."

Lucille turned away from Steven to put away some of the dried utensils. Then she turned to look at him. Her face looked tired. The vibrancy was gone from her eyes, her brow was wrinkled with worry and her lips tense with anger.

"You are a good senator. Lord knows the country is short of them and needs more people like you, not less. What happened, happened, and we can't change that. We need to stop the blame game. Rebecca was old enough to know that what she was doing was wrong. She might not have understood the consequences of her actions, but we couldn't be with her twenty-four hours a day to make her decisions for her. You worked hard to be a senator and the country does need you. Tracy and her generation need people like you to protect their interests until they can fight their own battles."

"But that's my point. Tracy is nearly fourteen, growing into a woman," Steven said. "She's going to start high school, and I'm going to be tied to a chair in Washington."

"Yes, that's true. And in four short years, she'll be eighteen, then gone off to college. Then what? Try to get back in as the senator from Massachusetts? Talk about a long shot. Don't feel so guilty. You have to live your life, and I have to live mine, and Tracy will live hers. You are a good father and a good role model."

"As are you." Steven held her shoulders to force her to look him in the eyes. "But what about our lives? What about us as a couple?"

Lucille gently broke the embrace by lifting Steven's hands off her shoulder. Then she walked to the wine cabinet, handed a fresh bottle of Cabernet to Steven, and then reached for two fresh glasses.

Steven popped the cork and poured their glasses half full.

"Sometimes, I forget there is an 'us as a couple,'" Lucille admitted as she led the way into the living room.

Steven took her wine from her hand and set his and hers down on the fireplace mantel. Then he took his wife in his arms and hugged her. "Look, we went through some tough times, but we did do it together. You and I will be fine, I promise. We just need to start living again, start enjoying each other's company again."

Lucille broke the embrace. "I'm sorry Steve, I feel dead inside." Lucille took a few steps toward the fireplace and her wine. "I don't want to feel that way, I just do."

Lucille turned away from Steven. Then, in nearly a whisper, she said, "Maybe we should get a divorce and we can both move on with our lives."

Steven thought his ears had deceived him. Both his hands went to his hair and he brushed them through it in disbelief.

"Divorce! Oh my god, I hope you aren't serious. We can and will get through this, together. I love you, and the last thing I want is a divorce."

"I'm sorry, I shouldn't have said anything. It was just a thought. Let's change the subject." Lucille lifted both glasses of wine from the mantelpiece and handed one to Steven.

Steven wanted desperately to forget what he had heard but couldn't. "Hon, I promise I'll come home more often and things will get better, things are getting better. Time, you, us, we just need some more time. But divorce, that isn't the answer. I swear to you things will get better, we can make them better."

"Sometimes I just don't know anymore. What if we can't?"

We'll be seeing Doc Collins on Wednesday. Let's talk with him about how you feel, but let's do it together."

Lucille gave Steven a smile. "Yes, I guess we should." She took a sip of her wine, then said, "We started planning a party for Tracy's birthday. She is so excited."

"Is her old man invited?"

"Probably not, she's at that age when admitting to her friends that she even has parents is embarrassing. Besides, a gaggle of teenage girls might not be in the same league as the senators and congressmen you hang out with."

"No, I'm sure the teenage girls would be more intelligent conversationalists." Steven chuckled a bit at his own comment. "So, what have you been up to besides planning a party? What ever happened to that issue the Children's Benefit League was having with the IRS?"

"Still working on it."

"Is there something I can do to move things along? I know a few people at the IRS."

"No, not necessary. The Benefit League's attorney is on it and thinks he has it handled."

"Who's the attorney?"

"Sam Kreiser."

"Sam Kreiser? Boy, that name sounds familiar. Do I know him?"

"I don't think so. He started working for us a few months ago; he never mentioned knowing you."

The sun was setting, but, instead of turning on a light, Steven flipped a switch on the fireplace, and soon the fake logs were engulfed in real flames.

The gas-powered flame flickered, casting a pale glow over the room. Steven was happy with the ambience it created. He sat down on the love seat near the fire and was about to pat the empty seat next to him in invitation when Lucille found her favorite chair, turned on an overhead lamp, and started to leaf through a magazine. Steven realized his hand was paused over the seat awkwardly, so he rubbed his pant leg with it instead for a moment.

"He's doing it pro bono for us," Lucille said.

"That's pretty nice of him."

"He was with Cox, Robbins, and Watkins. Maybe that's how you know his name."

Steven took a sip of his wine, searching his memory.

Lucille tossed the already well-read magazine back onto the tabletop. "Sam says he does a certain amount of community investment each year. That's what Sam calls his pro-bono work."

"Who is he working for now?" Steven thought maybe he was a recent contact.

"He went on his own awhile back. He's mainly a Washington lobbyist now."

"Wait a minute. I do remember that name. Cox, Robbins, and Watkins got into some trouble for losing a client's money. Some sort of trust improprieties, I think Sam was directly involved."

Lucille took a sip of her wine. "Sam mentioned it to me. I guess the trust company that they were using got some accounts mixed up and funds were temporarily misplaced. Somebody had to take the fall, and it was Sam."

Steven didn't believe that for a second, but there was no sense in starting an argument. "Well, he should be more than capable of handling the IRS. And he probably has his own contacts in Washington. But, if you need my help, just give a holler."

Steven and Lucille engaged in a bit more small talk, then after an extended awkward silence, Steven suggested, "I'm beat, how about we go to bed and tomorrow night we go to Maccee's for a nice dinner and maybe a movie?"

"I'm not ready for bed yet, but tomorrow night dinner sounds like a good idea. I could call up the Johnston's and see if they could join us."

"Just the two of us would be fine with me."

"Well, I've been meaning to get together with Jean anyway, and this would be the perfect opportunity."

"OK, if you prefer. I was just thinking that it would be good for us to go out on a date, you know, just the two of us."

"I know, but our social life is nonexistent with you gone so much. I think we need to remind people we're still around."

Steven got up, and Lucille accepted his peck on her cheek.

"Good night, love, see you tomorrow."

"Good night."

Steven slowly climbed the stairs up to their bedroom. He was tired from his long day, but still, he was hoping his wife would join him just the same. They needed some catalyst to respark their romance. Just because he was ready to put the past behind didn't mean his wife was. They had both been through a traumatic experience. Time would heal all if he had the patience, he assured himself.

Up in their bedroom, Steven turned on his laptop to check his mail and thought about his suspicions about Sam Kreiser. After a quick search for the name, a picture of the attorney and an article popped up. The article didn't read at all like the story Sam had told Lucille. Apparently, Samuel J. Kreiser's firm had been sued for misappropriating money from a trust. There was some sort of settlement out of court. Sam had been fired but maintained his law license.

Oh well, Steven thought. I can't blame him for spinning the truth in his direction. He made a mistake, was punished, and was now moving on. No foul there. Steven closed his computer and tried to sleep. It had been a long day, and tomorrow he could enjoy his family.

Chapter 7

A few days later in the Willowdale State Forest:

"Hi ho Silver, away!" Steven yelled as he started his horse into a gallop.

Tracy didn't say anything, but the disconcerted face she gave to the stable attendant said it all.

Steven felt relaxed; it wasn't until now that he realized the camping trip was probably more for his benefit than Tracy's. Being in the wide-open outdoors refreshed him and made him feel young again. And to be riding a horse, well, it just plain felt good. The guys in the forces had nicknamed him Cowboy. It had nothing to do with his riding abilities, which they knew nothing about, and everything to do with his name. But still, he liked it, and today he felt like a cowboy.

Steven and his daughter rode side by side in silence for the longest time, content to listen to the sounds of the horses and the forest. It was Tracy who broke the silence.

"Dad, do you think it's wrong for us to be happy, you know, since Rebecca died?"

Steven pulled back on the reins very gently and said, "Whoa."

Tracy stopped her horse too.

Steven looked at the sun, which had seemed to rejuvenate him, and contemplated his daughter's question. Tracy had very simply asked the question that they were all struggling with.

He patted his horse on the side of its neck and looked back to his daughter. He gave the only answer that came to mind. "I think we can be sad that Rebecca is gone, and at the same time, be happy that we had the chance to know her. You had a wonderful big sister. You had a friendship that many other people will never know. Then the monster found her and took her."

"Is that what you call them?"

"Call what?"

"The drugs she took. Do you call them the monster?"

"That's how I choose to look at it. A monster, a terrible monster took her from us. All the mean things she did, all the bad things she did, it wasn't Rebecca at the end; it was the monster inside of her."

Tracy's face found the sun; her hair glistened from its brightness. She patted her own horse on his neck.

"I wish the monster hadn't found her," Tracy said.

"Me too."

"So, Dad, it's OK if we feel happy? Do you feel happy?"

Steven clicked his cheek and got his horse moving again. "Yes, not all the time of course. But yes, riding with you out here makes me very happy. Often, the work I do makes me happy when it helps people. And I'm always happy when I come home to you and mom. How about you?"

Tracy didn't answer for the longest time, and Steven didn't pursue.

"Michael Mitchel makes me laugh when he makes faces in science class. And sometimes, when I go to a party, and I forget about Rebecca for a while, I laugh and have fun. But then I remember, and think I shouldn't be having fun because Rebecca can't either."

"You know when your sister was your age, she was the life of the party. She certainly knew how to have fun, and she made other people laugh." Steven chuckled a bit. "Including me." Steven chuckled a bit more. "Do you remember the time she put on a Halloween mask? I was at home reading the paper. I looked up. I don't know how long she was there. But, all of a sudden I see this face, this bloody and scary face. She scared the dickens out of me."

Tracy laughed. "You got up and chased her right out the house and around the house until you got too tired to run."

Steven laughed out loud. "She was just too fast; I couldn't catch her, that little stinker. She got me good that time."

"That was funny. I can't remember mom ever laughing that hard."

They rode on a bit more until their chuckling died down. Then Steven added, "I can tell you this. If Rebecca were here, she would want you to be happy not just some of the time but all of the time. And I think the best way we can honor her spirit is to be as happy as we can and never ever let the monster get us."

"Do you think mom will be happy again too?"

"I don't know when you got so smart. She will. Together we all will. Mom just needs a bit more time."

Back in Washington DC, a couple of weeks later:

The next Senate session was still weeks away, but Steven felt a need to promote his bill, so he was back in Washington to do just that. He was pacing back and forth in his small uptown apartment. "Thank you for inviting me to your convention. I guess it's true what they say, too many chief's and not enough Indians! God no, no, no. That's awful."

Tomorrow, he was scheduled for an important speech before the National Association of Chiefs of Police and he was practicing his opening lines. Their endorsement for his bill would go a long way. If he could convince them of its value, they, in turn, would unleash their giant lobbying machine and would be able to persuade other senators of its merits much better than he could.

Steven tossed down his notes on the small kitchenette table and tried to come up with a much better opening. Always open with a joke, he was told. What kind of joke would be funny to a group of very serious police chiefs from across the country? *I hate giving speeches.*

The next day in the Convention Center:

"... and so, I want you to think of the possibility, ladies and gentlemen. If my bill, S58 passes, each and every convicted criminal, not just for federal crimes, but state criminals also, will have their DNA markers entered into a national DNA database of known criminals. This testing will easily be paid for by the savings in investigation time, false leads, and screwed up court cases.

"Just think of it, even the great Sherlock Holmes couldn't have imagined such a tool. DNA is much easier to find at a crime scene than a good set of fingerprints. But imagine a bit further: what if we could match fingerprints to families? What if, with a perfect set of fingerprints, we could tell who that person's father and mother were, or brother or sister, or even cousins?

"With familial testing, we can do just that. Just imagine, if one member of a family committed a crime, then, if any other member of that same family committed a crime, we could match their DNA and know precisely who our criminal is. I could go on forever about the merits of this bill, but let me sum up by saying the goal of my bill is to prevent crime, not just catch those that commit it.

"So please, help me put an end to crime. Help me save countless lives and victims of personal injury and theft. I beg you to please show your support for bill number S58."

Steven stopped and held his breath as he looked out over the silent crowd. If he couldn't convince this crowd, he wouldn't convince anyone. The crowd was hushed at first, as if still digesting his statements, and then there was small applause, which started to build, then more and more hands clapped together.

Steven smiled broadly at the audience and waved his hands and nodded in a humble thank you. If this group had anything to say about it, it looked like his bill would become law.

Anacostia district, Washington DC:

Detective Bruce Harmon turned on his blue, magnetically attached flashing light. It only took a couple of blasts from his siren to stop the gold Cadillac in front of him.

Harmon turned off his squad light and walked up to the car he had just stopped.

Clayton Harris didn't get out of his car, but there was no mistaking his strength and size, especially his thick, dark muscular arms. He talked through the lowered window and kept his engine running.

"Harmon, what the fuck you doing in the ghetto? You're making a scene. I don't need to be associated with the police."

Harmon leaned up against the Cadillac and lit up a cigarette. "Just wanted to say hi to my favorite snitching pimp and ask a simple question. I'm looking for a couple of guys, beat up a gas station clerk not too far from here."

"What makes you think I would know them?"

"They needed drug money, you sell drugs. Driving a blue Toyota, black, one big guy, one small. Kids, early twenties, big guy had a tattoo, left arm, naked blonde."

Clayton nodded his head. "I remember, nice tattoo. Dumbasses, might as well tape your ID to your nose when you rob a place with a tattoo. Don't know their real names. Big guy is called Baller, the small guy, Butter."

"Butter?" Harmon asked.

"Yea, smooth like butter."

"Yea, real smooth all right, armed robbery, they pistol whipped the guy for a couple of bucks. He's still in the hospital. Just a kid himself. Should live, but permanent damage. Can't let it go, man, these guys have to do some time."

"Guys in the bing gonna love 'em."

"So how do I find 'em? You know where they live."

"You bet your sweet ass I do. Morris Street, thirteen sixty-seven, apartment two."

Harmon flicked his cigarette down the road and wrote down the address.

"Got any snow?"

"You're gonna get caught, man."

"What the fuck do you care?"

"Next guy might not make the same working relationship. Hell, it could even be that tight-assed chick detective. That would be bad for business."

"You mean Chelle Saltarie?"

"Yea, tried to shake me down a week ago. Hassles my girls."

"Not my problem, what say on the snow?"

"Since my run in with Saltarie, I don't carry. There's a white gal, young, skinny ass, brunette with a blonde streak. Works the corner by the Billy Goat in town. Names Destinee. Tell her I sent you for two bags and it's on the house. For you, no dead presidents."

"Thanks. Remember, if you get pinched by Saltarie, I can't help you, and you don't know me. She plays by the book. Like you said, a real tight ass."

New Jersey Ave., Washington, DC:

The dome of the Capitol was framed down the middle of the wide boulevard as Detective Harmon drove his police sedan down New Jersey Avenue. He pulled his car up to the wide sidewalk next to a ten-story building that seemed to be made of nothing but blue glass. In front, on the walk, was a white girl wearing a short red skirt. She had long legs and long brown hair.

Harmon pressed the button that lowered the passenger side window. "You Destinee?" He called from inside his car.

As Destinee rolled her eyes, she sauntered her hips off to one side looking disgusted. Harmon could tell that she smelled a cop even though his car was unmarked.

"Yea, but I ain't done nothin'!"

Harmon watched her eyes dart across the street. He glanced that way and saw a hotel; its facade was stained concrete and glass. Nothing special to look at, but he was sure it provided steady customers for the girl. She probably didn't like the advertising of his cop car any more than her boss had.

"Get in." Harmon opened the passenger-side door.

Destinee slid inside the car, a bit afraid of being arrested.

"I got a message from Clayton. He said to give me three bags of snow."

"I ain't got no crack on me."

"Want me to search you? You would like that wouldn't you?"

"Clayton will beat me if I come back without the crack."

"Look, it's all right, he sent me and said it was on the house. He said to tell you I don't have to give you any dead presidents."

Destinee reached under her short skirt where she wore a band around her thigh that held the small bags.

Harmon took the coke and then gently held Destinee's face by her chin.

"You're a pretty little thing, young too. Tell you what. I get off of work around five. You get us a room at the Washington Arms, and you and I will have a little party. Text me the room number, nothing else." Harmon handed her a small piece of paper with a number on it.

"I ain't never partied with a cop before."

"First time for everything, sweetheart. Remember, I'm friends with Clayton so you don't want to disappoint me, got it? Now out!"

Detective Harmon drove off feeling smug; today was going to be a good one and tonight even better.

Washington DC, Steven Westcott's Apartment:

Senator Westcott was getting caught up on some paperwork while listening to the local evening news on television. He sat at the small kitchen table with so many papers scattered about, you couldn't see its fake wood surface. Steven was so absorbed in his paperwork that he almost missed the sound bite about a murder in the DC area. It was nothing unique by itself, but the reporter said something about the killer's DNA.

Steven picked up the remote control off the table, reversed his TiVo recording, and played it back. He turned up the sound just a bit. "This is Cynthia Rosen reporting from Baltimore. Three months ago, a body was found in Historic Anacostia near Maple View and High St. It has been confirmed as the body of Jennifer Stoll. The victim apparently died of multiple stab wounds and loss of blood.

"In a strange turn of events, the killer has finally been identified as Father Kelly Millen from Baltimore." The reporter jostled for position among other reporters and bystanders.

"The priest will be charged with a felony: murder while armed."

The television showed a clearly confused priest being placed in a squad car, hands cuffed behind his back.

"The body was brutally mutilated. The autopsy revealed that she died from multiple stab wounds and evidently bled to death in a vacant warehouse. Police have identified Jennifer as a known prostitute, and the suspected motive for the killing is blackmail.

"DNA match showed the priest's hair and body fluids on the victim, and blood and hair samples from the victim were found in Father Millen's car. Father Millen admitted that he knew the victim and that they had met several times at the Hotel Palomar."

The camera panned to an officer in street clothes with a worn, tan sport coat. The cameraman kept filming as Cynthia Rosen unapologetically pressed through a row of people until she cornered the officer.

"Detective Harmon, what happens now?"

"Father Millen will be taken to Washington DC. There, he will be finger-printed, further DNA samples taken, and then he will be formally charged. Bail hearing is set for Monday."

Steven watched and slowly tapped the end of his pencil on the table in front of him. While he hated to see another murder, he did want to know more about this particular case. A murder solved by DNA analysis in a city filled with lawmakers might be another example he could use to promote his bill. Tomorrow, he would have a few of his aids investigate the murder. Maybe the police would be willing to share information with a senator's office.

"This is Cynthia Rosen reporting for channel twelve news."

Washington Arms Hotel:

Detective Harmon was on his back, lying naked across the bed, enjoying another high. Destinee was next to him, already feeling the euphoria wearing away.

Destinee slid off the bed where they had just done everything but sleep.

"Hey baby, where you going?"

"I'm taking a shower." Destinee looked in the mirror for bruises. The cop had slapped her across the face a few times. He wasn't the first or only john that got off on some sort of power trip and got rough. Being high at the time helped her absorb the abuse, but it was never fun.

Though it hurt, her face was miraculously unbruised. Maybe it would be later, she thought. Her arms near her shoulders, however, were bruised where he had held her down.

"You're even better than Tiffany. Do you know Tiffany?" Harmon yelled through the door.

Destinee ignored him and turned on the water. This was a hell of a way to make a living, she reminded the pale-looking girl in the mirror.

Anacostia district, Washington DC:

The next day, Destinee was at home nursing her bruises at the kitchen sink when she saw Clayton. "That fucking friend of yours slapped me around before fucking me. Destinee went to the old refrigerator and popped a handful of ice cubes into an old rag. "I don't ever want to see him again." She gingerly placed the cold pack against her bruised eye.

"Listen, doll, he's my friend. That makes him your friend. He does us favors so we do him favors back."

"I don't care if he's the god damn chief of police, I'm not fucking him again. He hits hard, look!" Destinee removed the ice pack and showed her black and blue eye.

"He's just messing around with you a bit. You're fine."

"Damn it, Clayton! You wouldn't like it if he smacked you around."

"Lucky for me he likes girls."

Destinee stormed away into her small room and slammed the door shut so hard some of the peeling paint dropped to the floor. She threw herself on her bed in frustration and turned on the television to calm herself. The Oprah Winfrey show was on.

Oprah was interviewing a United States senator. The senator was charming and funny but also serious about some new law he wanted to pass.

The camera panned to a close-up of the senator. She didn't follow politics and didn't understand everything he was talking about. But still, there was something about the man that she recognized.

Destinee thought he was handsome; he had full dark hair, a square jaw, and a friendly smile, all packaged in a perfectly fit suit. But more important, he had an amiable character about him. He was charismatic and clever in his fun-natured verbal jousting with the host. Quite the opposite of most of the johns she slept with. Most were drunk or high, filthy, and anything but handsome.

Destinee was getting ready to go off to work. She would have to watch the rest of the show when she got back later that night or tomorrow morning. She double-checked to make sure the recorder was on.

Then she heard Oprah close the segment. "And once again, I want to thank Senator Steven Westcott for being such a wonderful guest."

"Senator Westcott!" Destinee repeated. Her mind wasn't always focused, but her mother had once told her to remember a name. *Westcott, Senator Steven Westcott, tell him ...*

Destinee stopped putting on her make-up and focused on the senator's face. She tried to remember, what was the message? What was it that her mother wanted to tell her about Senator Steven Westcott?

Chapter 8

Two weeks later in DC, 1st street NW:

Detective Bruce Harmon slid into the tattered booth of an all-night diner. It was 7:00 p.m., and Tiffany was enjoying a meal of sausage and eggs.

"Hi, Tiff. Let's go for a ride."

Tiffany Maddenheart finished some sausage and glanced up briefly to look at Harmon, who had slid in the seat across from her.

"I'm not going with you, Harmon. I mean it," Tiffany said forcefully but not loud enough for others to hear her.

Harmon was expecting some resistance as she continued to eat her sausage and eggs doing her best to ignore him. He had found Tiffany at the corner restaurant on 1st street NW. He knew why she worked this area. It wasn't a bad spot, Harmon thought. It had a proper mix of office towers and hotels. Anybody looking for a quickie could leave his office, screw, and then be back before anybody even missed them.

"Look, Tiffany, I'm sorry. That was weeks ago, I had a bad day, and I took it out on you."

Tiffany looked around, making sure she couldn't be overheard. "Fuck you. Besides hitting me, you took all of my coke for yourself."

"Not all of it, baby, I saved you some. Besides, I left you enough cash to buy more."

"Yea, well what about the bruises? You didn't leave me enough for them. No more, Harmon. And I've talked with some of the others; we are all done with you."

"Listen, baby, I want to make it up to you."

The waitress came with the check for Tiffany.

Harmon pulled out a twenty and tossed it on top of the check. It was more than enough to cover the bill.

"What say we go outside and talk?" Harmon said as he got up and lifted Tiffany's arm, suggesting it wasn't a request.

Tiffany's ultra-tight red top, made out of some sort of stretching material, barely held her ample breasts inside of it. Her long red hair seemed to clash against the red of the tight top. As she stood, she tugged on the bottom of her skintight white shorts.

As Harmon followed her out the restaurant, the white shorts didn't leave much to his imagination, and he enjoyed the view from behind.

Once outside in the noisy traffic of the street, Tiffany was a bit more forceful. "Fuck off Harmon. Leave me alone. I know you've been following me. I see your car. What's up with that? Are you some sort of psycho pervert?"

"I care about you, baby, just want to know who you are hanging around with."

"Bullshit! You're scaring my customers away. They can smell your cop ass a mile away."

"Maybe I want you all to myself."

"Let's make something absolutely clear, I want nothing to do with you, nothing. From now on, you can just go fuck yourself."

"Now, that is not being very sociable at all. What if I start arresting your customers? I know who they are. How about I start arresting your girlfriends' customers? You would become real unpopular real quick."

"Yea, well, what if I went to your bosses and told them that you were a whoring crackhead?"

"Come on, Tiff, how about we just let bygones be bygones." Harmon lifted a bag of white powder partly out his pocket. "I just had a bust. I was thinking you and I might have a little party."

Tiffany stared at the bag of coke, then at Harmon, who was smiling widely.

"Come on, baby, let's party. Free coke, and I'll even pay you."

"You know what? Fuck you, just fuck you. You'd better pay me this time or I'm telling Bruno, and I'm not shittin'."

Harmon led her to his car and opened the door for her. Harmon notice a slight hesitation, but she slid into the front seat as he slapped her ass playfully and then closed the door behind her.

Anacostia district, Washington DC, One week later:

Destinee was at home nursing some bruises. It had been nearly a month, but it was still too soon for her when the detective insisted she go with him again. Only this time, he had hit her even harder. When she complained to Clayton, he only told her to suck it up or he would be the one hitting her. The good news was that Clayton had given her some crack to shut up about it.

Alone in her room, she examined her bruised body in the mirror, disgusted with herself for allowing it to happen. The crack called to her, and she found her pipe to heat the crystal treat. She sat on the floor in her room, naked, and decided to play the recording she had made weeks ago.

In the weeks that had passed, Destinee had heard the name of the senator on TV from time to time and had even read an article in a discarded paper with his name in it. She started the recording and inhaled a harsh hit.

Almost instantly, the hit left her lungs and rushed to her brain. She felt at peace as she studied the senator's smile and gestures. Her mind felt sharp, and she desperately tried to remember why her mother had told her he was important. Maybe she just imagined her mother had said the name. Destinee flicked the lighter and heated the small bowl once again. She inhaled deeply and enjoyed the rush. Destinee rocked her shoulders in a small dancing arc. A locket around her neck swung back and forth gently with her. She closed her eyes for a moment to better enjoy the feeling of blissful contentment.

Destinee wondered if Senator Westcott had a girlfriend in Washington DC. She had known girls that had gotten out of hooking by snagging an important boyfriend like a senator. At least they said they did. Maybe she could be one of those girls someday.

When the crack was gone, she fell into a blissful sleep. It was near the middle of the night when she woke in her bed, covered with a single sheet that hadn't been washed since she didn't know when. She flicked on a lamp, the brightness from the bare bulb burned at her eyes. The television was mostly dark though it flickered with white static from time to time. The recording of the Senator's interview had been over for quite a while.

Her mind was sadly clear of the drug-induced euphoria. She stared at the wall, it was dirty and empty, just like her life. To think that somebody like the senator would care about her and take care of her was crazy. For the hundredth time, after a hundred highs, she considered killing herself. But for the hundredth time, she knew she wouldn't or couldn't. Destinee used the pillow to wipe away a tear, then hugged it, trying to will some of her pain into it.

She spotted the crack pipe on the floor and stared at it for a while. Then, with a thought born of desperation, she fell out of bed and crawled frantically toward it. Maybe it wasn't all gone, and she could feel good again even if it was just for ten more precious minutes.

The bowl was empty, so she searched the floor on her hands and knees using the light from the single bulb and the flickering TV to aid her. She prayed that somehow she had not used it all. Madly, she used the palm of her hand to search the floor for any crystals that might be too small to see. Tears washed her cheeks as she realized there was nothing to find.

US Capitol Police Headquarters two weeks later:

Detective Harmon pounded on the steering wheel of his unmarked police cruiser. He was still in the department's parking lot and had just found out that the latest murder in his district was already given to Detective Saltarie. Harmon started his car and then raced out of the lot, squealing the tires.

He knew he was a better homicide detective. Or, at the very least, he was as good as Chelle Saltarie, the department's lead detective. Bruce Harmon wanted the promotion he had been promised. He needed the promotion he had been promised. His lifestyle was important to him, and he had expenses to cover. But how could he stand out if he wasn't given the more prominent cases? Detective Saltarie had been in charge of the high-profile Deon Michalski case, and ever since then, she had been the captain's favorite.

He decided that he needed a little R and R to settle him. His association with Clayton Harris was paying off in more ways than one. As a source of information, Clayton seemed to be in the know. Sure, he was a pimp and drug dealer, but that was a plus too. Harmon headed for the part of town where he might find Clayton.

If he didn't find Clayton, maybe he would find Tiffany. She might even have some of the coke he had given her the week before. Harmon scanned the area for Tiffany. Soon he saw her standing on one of her favorite corners near 1st street.

Three days later, Harford County Airport:

"OK, one more, you can do better, Cowboy."

The small, single-engine plane was bouncing down the runway, mostly under control.

"Sorry, I thought I was going to nail it. I don't know what happened."

"There was a bit of crosswind. It caught you off guard, but it's nothing you can't handle. Let's try it again." The instructor pushed in the throttle, and soon the plane was back airborne.

Steven had asked his instructor to call him Cowboy during his flying lessons. He didn't expect anybody, especially his instructor, to treat him different than anybody else. Calling him Cowboy would hopefully make them forget he was a US senator.

"OK, Cowboy, I don't want to be riding on a bucking bronco again. I want you to keep a nice stabilized approach. You can do this. I know you can."

"Maybe I'm not ready for this. I think the wind is picking up."

"This is real life, the wind changes. And you are ready for this."

The next landing was better, but Steven was still disappointed in himself.

As he drove back to DC, he knew that his mind had not been on his flying.

His bill was in conference; he had to answer what seemed like hundreds of e-mails a day. Yet he couldn't stop his flying lessons or he would regress.

It was an exciting time nonetheless. Ever since he was on the Oprah Winfrey Show, he was being bombarded by requests to be on other television and cable talk shows. He was also being sought out for newspaper and television interviews. His bill was stirring up quite a bit of controversy. More than he had ever expected. Many people and organizations were concerned about the loss of privacy when the encoded essence of each and every being would or could be collected and held by the government. Steven worked hard to dismiss those fears.

At that same time in uptown Washington DC:

Detective Harmon carefully walked around the body of the dead hooker, trying to avoid the puddles of blood. The red-headed woman had been stabbed multiple times. Her hands were badly cut up, which would suggest a bit of a struggle to the medical examiner and a jury if her murder came to trial.

He bent down to examine the purse on the ground next to her. It had blood spatters on it, but he couldn't see any bloody fingerprints. The police photographer was snapping photos from all angles of the body and the blood-washed room.

"After you're done, I want you out and nobody else in here until the forensic guys show up. I don't want anything disturbed in any way," Harmon instructed. With the eraser-end of a pencil, the detective opened the purse and saw Tiffany's ID, then added, "Take a shot of this. You can mark your photos as that of a Tiffany Maddenheart."

The photographer began to write the name down. "You sure?"

"The photo on her ID matches, it's her all right. Shame, pretty girl."

Harmon carefully patrolled the room, looking for evidence. The photographer said he was done but would be waiting outside for the forensic team.

"Thanks. When they show up, tell them to wait for me, there is blood and evidence everywhere, and I don't want them barging in here," Harmon said.

"Got it!"

As soon as the photographer was gone, Harmon went back to the purse on the floor. He carefully examined the contents to make sure he hadn't missed something that might tie him to the hooker. Being the investigator of record on this case was a break that he might as well take advantage of.

Son of a bitch, Harmon thought, looking behind a side pouch in the skinny purse. With gloved hands, he carefully reached in and took out a business card. It said: Detective Bruce Harmon, Washington DC Police Department. He slipped it into his pocket.

The next day, Detective Harmon went to the Saint Claire Hotel. When the manager saw Harmon, he nodded recognition. "I haven't seen you in a while."

"Correction, you never saw me until today. Understand?"

"Yea, sure, Harmon, I get it."

"Tiff was murdered a couple of nights ago."

"Oh no, not Tiffany. I liked her. How are you doing? I mean, she was your girl and all."

"Look, I liked the girl, but she was just a hooker to me, nothing more. But I do want to find her killer. I need to see your security recordings. I need to know who she was with that day."

"Sure, no problem, Harmon, you probably know how to work that equipment back there better than me, so help yourself."

"Thanks Mitch. And remember, if someone asks, you never saw me before today."

Harmon made a point of displaying his hip-holstered weapon.

"Yea, Harmon, I get it. Don't know you."

It didn't take Detective Harmon long to find the recording he was looking for. He had seen the man before in person when he had followed Tiffany's activities.

Harmon called out from the small room, "Mitch, I need you to ID a guy for me."

After a quick look, reluctantly, the manager spoke up. "Yea, I know the guy. And he did like Tiffany. It's Doctor Merrill, Gregory Merrill."

Harmon made a quick note. "Don't erase anything here. I'm going to get a warrant to copy these files. And remember, you never saw me before today."

****

Doctor Gregory Merrill heard the knock at the apartment door. It sounded urgent and angry. He peeked through the small peephole and saw two uniformed police officers and one in a tan suit jacket.

"Greg, who is it?" His wife asked.

"The police, probably nothing."

As he opened the door, it creaked tentatively.

"What is this all about?" The doctor asked.

"Are you Doctor Merrill?"

"Yes."

"I'm Detective Bruce Harmon, and I have a few questions for you."

"About what?"

"Where were you yesterday?"

"Why? What's it to you?"

"There was a girl murdered, and I want to know if you did it."

"Are you freakin' kidding me? Of course I didn't do it."

Just then, Gregory's wife came to the door, realizing it was far from nothing.

"Then where were you, and who where you with?"

"Who died? Who do you think I killed? I want to know."

"Greg, what is he talking about?" His wife said.

"I am about five minutes away from arresting you for the murder of Tiffany Maddenheart unless you can prove where you were yesterday."

"Yea, I knew Tiffany, but I sure as hell didn't kill her."

"I have you on surveillance camera with her the day she died."

"Greg, who's Tiffany? And why were you with her?"

"I'm not saying anything. I want my lawyer."

"Good move. Let me read you your rights before I search your apartment."

Chapter 9

Destinee felt the New Jersey Avenue bus jostle to a stop. She stood and instinctively tugged at the hem of her skirt as if that would somehow make it longer. She knew people stared at her, her clothing was meant to be seductive. But the disapproving looks and whispered jokes about her from the other passengers still hurt.

The bus stopped near the big statue in Columbus Circle. Union Station and the train home were to her left. A number of grassy parks intersected by small avenues were to her right. The day was bright and—due to a kindly older gentleman, who had tipped her generously—she had already earned enough money to satisfy Clayton.

Destinee's high heels clicked across the concrete walk, but the soft green carpet off the sidewalk called to her, so she slipped off her heels and let her feet enjoy the freedom. The grass was cool and she felt it squishing up between her toes, which made her feel a bit giddy. *Is this what happiness is?* She wondered.

A family came by and two children ran up past her toward a small reflecting pool. Their father quickly ran behind them, clearly afraid that at least one of them would over extend themselves into the pool. Destinee laughed just a bit at the father's nervousness.

The young mother, who was pushing a stroller, was also urging caution to the two kids leaned over the pool edge. The little boy in the stroller was holding a small ball, but he was far more interested in what his older brother and sister were doing.

The little boy decided he didn't want his ball anymore and sent it flying across the park ground. A gust of wind found it and sent it even farther. Destinee didn't hesitate. She ran down the grass field after it, kicking it to a stop with her bare feet.

She picked it up and carried it back to the mother, who was now joined by her kids. With a broad smile, Destinee bent down and handed the ball back to the little tyke in the stroller. The mother and father stood by, speechless, shocked by her ultra-short dress and nearly completely exposed breasts.

When Destinee looked up to say hello to the parents, she realized that they were looking at her as if she was some sort of freak. The mother quickly pushed the stroller down the sidewalk. At the same time, she fished the ball away from the child and tucked it in a basket.

The father turned to take the hands of his other two children and offered an embarrassed thank-you while he tried not to stare at her breasts. "Frank hurry or we'll miss the train," the mother said curtly.

As the family rushed off, Destinee sat back down, her smile gone. The girl Destinee saw in herself and the woman others saw in her were hardly the same. Her thoughts went back to a particular day. She was in her early teens when her mother found her as she played with her friends. In a terrible rush, her mother had grabbed her hard by the wrist. In a panic, she said, "We have to go!"

Destinee remembered how she resisted and said she wanted to play longer. That was when she first saw fear. It was in her mother's eyes. "No, we have to go. We have to go now."

When the stunned Destinee asked why, she was told. "They saw me, they know we are here. We have to leave now, no arguing."

Destinee didn't argue. She didn't say goodbye to her friends. The house, the yard, her basketball, and everything else were left behind. Two suitcases packed with clothes became their only belongings.

Destinee stared at the Capitol Building in the distance, framed by the trees of the park. She took out a small handkerchief from her sequenced purse and wiped her tears with it. Her life, her mother's life, had never been the same after that.

Destinee stared at the majestic dome. Senator Steven Westcott worked in that big building. *Why do I care? Who is Senator Westcott?*

That was when an epiphany came to her. She finally remembered what her mother was trying to tell her.

****

Clayton was waiting for her when she got home. She tossed him five hundred bucks.

"Are you holding out on me girl?"

"Honest Clayton, all I could rustle up was a few blow jobs and one date."

"Bitch, if I ever find out you're holding out on me, I'll beat your ass till you break, got it?"

Clayton must not have felt like fighting or arguing because he tossed Destinee a small piece of paper with some crack wrapped in it.

Destinee took the crack without a word.

In her room, she turned on the television like she usually did and then waited another half hour before going to her mother's special hiding place. It had been her mother's secret until one day, years ago, when Destinee found it. Destinee was only sixteen when she spied her mother suspiciously on the floor in her closet. So she watched from behind the door that was slightly ajar and saw her mother slip a box into a hole in the floor and replace a few boards.

Later, her teenage curiosity had gotten the best of her, and she pried open the loose floorboard. That was when she discovered the box of naked photos of her mother with different men.

Her mother had caught Destinee looking at the pictures. She was scolded and told to put them away. Later, her mother had said the photos were important, and that was why she had them. Someday, she would understand, but they weren't for her to look at.

Destinee had nearly forgotten about the pictures and what her mother had told her before she died. It was just a whisper from her mother's dying breath, but today, the whisper had become clear: "If you need money, tell Steven Westcott. Show him the pictures."

Destinee remembered that day clearly now. It was a day she didn't like to remember. It was the day her mother died. She felt tears sting her eyes; she missed her mother so much. She had been her friend and protector. Then she was gone, and Destinee was left all alone.

Destinee dried her tears and stooped down by the closet door. Carefully and quietly, she removed the floorboards as she had done so many years ago. She reached under the floor and found the cavity where the old box was stored.

Lifting it out, her hands shook with anticipation; even the cocaine waiting on the dresser didn't distract her tonight. She opened the box and looked through the photos one by one. There was no doubt what she was looking at.

A much younger and healthier version of her mother was in some of the pictures. She was obviously a whore and some of the men her customers. Though the pictures weren't just of her. The box contained a collection of assorted johns and working girls. By the various stages of undress, she could tell that most, if not all the men, were military of some sort.

Then Destinee saw it: the man from the Oprah show. He was much younger of course, but she was sure it was him. She turned the photo over slowly as if afraid to break it. It said, "Sargent Steven Westcott."

Destinee set it on the floor, away from the other pictures, and continued sorting through the handful of photos until she found each and every one that contained Steven Westcott. She made three piles, one for Steven, one for her mother and one for all the rest.

She lifted a particularly good close-up of her mother's face. If she put her hand over it strategically, she could cover the nakedness and forget for an instant what the photo was. Her mother was much younger than Destinee ever remembered seeing. She was beautiful, and she was smiling.

"Mom, I miss you so much." Tears flowed easily down her cheeks. She wiped her eyes with her blouse and picked up the stack of photos of Steven Westcott.

Destinee concentrated on the young face. Time had treated him well; to her, he was even more handsome now than he had been then. Of course, a young face meant little to her because most, if not all of her johns, were as old or older than he was now.

How her mother had attained the photos was a mystery to her. But that didn't matter. What was important was that her mother had said the pictures were important, and Destinee now knew why. Each photo was marked with the name of the particular soldier in them. There was no doubt the box of pictures was to be used for extortion. Yet her mother had hidden them, and Destinee was sure she had never used them. Her mother had died very poor and very much in the grip of Clayton Harris.

Destinee carefully repacked the photos and slid the box back into its hiding spot. After the floorboards were carefully in place, she went to the dresser and slipped a small piece of crack into the pipe. Now, all she had to do was figure out the best way to use the photos to escape her life. She heated the crystal and inhaled deeply. Peace and confidence overcame her. She had found a way to leave Clayton, but she would only have one chance. Destinee smiled, one chance was all she would need.

Chapter 10

Detective Chelle Saltarie was at her desk collecting her files on Deon Michalski, a.k.a., The Polish Locomotive. Chelle sorted through the stack of manila folders for the last time.

She sipped on her coffee as she shuffled through the paperwork. Her coffee mug had a sleepy picture of Garfield the cat. Chelle read the saying on the mug for the umpteenth time. "Your opinion has been duly noted." Next to it was Garfield shredding a note and dropping it in the trashcan. Chelle set the lukewarm mug down and banded the pile of folders together.

The evidence she collected had all held up in court. With her help, the district attorney didn't have a hard time proving to a jury that the Polish Locomotive had, beyond a reasonable doubt, killed the hooker, his off and on girlfriend.

It was certainly a high profile case, and the prosecutor in charge assured her that if the evidence didn't hold up in court, her ass would be on the line. Chelle had been thrust into the limelight over this case, and she was glad it was over.

Detective Pat Marget walked by and lifted Chelle's Garfield mug. "Looking for a refill? I'm going that way."

"Thanks Pat, a warm up would be nice."

As police officers go, Chelle was a bit small, maybe better suited to have had a career as a dancer. Her curly, dark hair brushed her shoulders gently. She didn't wear makeup on duty, it was a nuisance to her. But her high cheekbones didn't need to have attention drawn to them. And though she looked petite, if you told her so, you might end up on the ground in cuffs before you knew what was happening. Detective Marget was Chelle's sometimes-partner.

At thirty-three, he was a bit younger than Chelle by about four years, and at six foot, he was almost a foot taller. If Chelle looked young for her age, Marget's bulk and the near constant look of needing a shave made him look older. Marget had recently been promoted to detective and Chelle had taken him on as his mentor.

"I'm not sorry to see that case hit the archives," Pat said as he casually looked at a few of the pictures in one of the still-open folders. "Talk about dotting your i's and crossing your t's. You sure didn't leave anything to chance on that one did you?"

"I'd like to think that we would have been just as thorough had it been some no-name assailant."

"I have to admit, I was hoping he didn't do it. I loved watching him play every Sunday."

"Yea," Chelle said as she closed one more folder and added it to the rest, "once I had you convinced, I knew a jury would be easy."

"Hey, I was just playing devil's advocate."

"Devil's advocate?" Chelle grinned. "I thought you were going to steal evidence out of the evidence locker just so your fantasy football team could win."

"Can you blame me? Without him, my season was done. I'll get you a fresh cup and then help you with those files."

"Thanks Pat."

Just as she was about to give her Garfield cup to Pat, Detective Bruce Harmon walked by. She didn't particularly care for the man, but congratulations were in order.

"I heard you solved the case of the red-haired hooker. Congratulations."

"Yea, good work, Detective," Pat agreed as he held his hand out to shake detective Harmon's.

Harmon stopped to accept the compliments but didn't take Pat's hand. Instead, he tossed a piece of gum into his mouth.

Chelle saw the obvious snub and caught Pat's eye to let him know it. "Pretty solid evidence?" Chelle asked, pushing her wheeled chair away from her desk as she leaned back on it.

"The captain thinks so. We have a beer can with his prints and DNA found at the scene. We have the murder weapon; it's being tested for DNA. The girl had hair fibers in her hand, identified as the doctor's. The suspect has no alibi for the time period and, in fact, I have him on video walking into the Saint Claire with the girl that day."

"What about motive?" Chelle asked.

"Who knows? We do know he knocked her around a little before killing her, she was bruised up pretty good. Toxicology thinks she had some bad snow and was pretty much out of it when he slashed her. He might have supplied it. There was no sign of a struggle. If we can match up the coke I found in his apartment to the stuff we found in her purse, we will have more than enough to put him away."

"Well, again, Harmon, good job." Chelle slid her chair back behind her desk to signal that the conversation was over.

"I see you're putting the Deon Michalski case to bed." Harmon took his fingers across a couple of folders, shuffling them about.

"Just making room. Unfortunately, I already have a couple other cases pending."

"Yea, you sure lucked out on that case."

Chelle looked up, her face showing obvious displeasure at the inference.

Harmon deadpanned, "Detective Chelle Saltarie solves the case of the murdered hooker and the Polish Locomotive." Harmon made a gesture with his hands as if displaying a papers headline.

"Lucked out? How?" Chelle said, now as equally upset with Harmon as Pat was.

"High profile, plenty of evidence. You could hardly screw it up. But now the captain sees you as his star player. I, on the other hand, get to arrest a priest, a fucking priest. Can you fucking believe it?"

"Harmon, you're an ass, you know that?" Pat said. "It took plenty of great detective work to nail Michalski. You think it was easy to build a prosecutable case against him? He had millions to fight it. It had to be perfectly documented, and it was."

"Just saying, high profile, and you get it. I wonder what the odds of that are."

"Fuck you, Harmon." Pat's body was tensing, his hands were gripping into fists.

Harmon turned to Chelle, who was unfortunately more used to Harmon's attacks. She was trying hard to ignore him and his words. "If you need help solving any of your cases just let me know. You know where my desk is."

"Thanks, I'll keep it in mind." Chelle purposely turned the coffee mug in her hand around so that Harmon could read Garfield's message.

One month later:

In the weeks that followed her discovery, and for the first time in her adult life, Destinee had hope for her future. Her mother had given her a way to escape the life she had oddly enough inherited from her. Her plan was simple. She needed to seduce Senator Westcott.

She had enticed plenty of men and seduction was something she was good at. Many of her customers were repeats, even steadies if you wanted to call them that. Bottom line was, they liked her. However, for Senator Westcott, she needed to take it a few steps beyond. For that, she reasoned, she needed to know the senator better before she forced their first meeting.

Destinee started a scrapbook filled with pictures and articles about the senator. Ever since she remembered her mother's words, she had watched the newspapers and leafed through any magazines she found lying about for insight into who the senator was. She needed to know his likes and dislikes, his background, even his family.

Screwing a man was one thing, becoming his confidant and friend was much more difficult. As summer turned into fall, Destinee endured her life but also had a reason for living. It made the weeks that passed some of the happiest she had experienced since she was a little girl. For the first time she could remember, she was even trying to cut down on her crack consumption, though so far with little success.

Safely alone in her room, Destinee sat naked on the thin carpeting next to her bed and inhaled a second hit of crack. She picked up the scrapbook and paged through it for the hundredth time.

She had learned that Senator Steven Westcott had a teenage daughter and was married. One of the articles said that his home was in Massachusetts, but he lived in Washington DC when the Senate was in session.

Many of the articles talked about his other daughter, who died from a drug overdose. That tragedy made Destinee feel sorry for him. She set the scrapbook down and closed her eyes to enjoy the high and rocked her body back and forth. The locket hanging around her neck swung gently and made her think of her mother.

She lifted her hand to it and stopped its motion. She held it tightly in her palm. Her mother probably wanted her to use the pictures to blackmail the senator. After all, she had said, "If you need money, tell Steven Westcott. Show him the pictures." True, he was an important man in a powerful position. But after learning so much about him, that was not what she wanted at all.

Besides, threatening a powerful man like Steven Westcott, who also happened to be a war hero, would be very dangerous. No, Destinee reasoned, convincing him through her actions that he wanted her and needed her was much more realistic. All she needed was the proper bait to set the trap. And though she had no intention of blackmailing Senator Westcott, the pictures could be used to advance her plan just the same.

Carefully, she replaced the scrapbook. If Clayton discovered the photos, he would undoubtedly use them himself, and her plan to escape would be ruined. If he found the envelope of cash that was also hidden there, he would probably kill her. It wouldn't take the pimp long to deduce that the cash was really his and had been stolen from her daily take.

She knew the risk she was taking and had already been beaten just because he suspected her of stealing. But if she was ever going to leave Clayton with or without the senator's help, she would need some cash, so it was a risk she had to take.

Peabody, Massachusetts:

Steven walked through the entryway and around the corner toward his home office. He didn't see or hear anybody, so he called out.

"Hon, I'm home!"

Then he dropped his suitcase in the usual spot just inside his office door.

He walked toward the kitchen, and that was when he heard the shower running upstairs in the master bath. It was a bit strange for Lucille to be taking a shower so late in the day. He walked up the stairs. The bed was either still unmade from this morning or Lucille had just gotten up from a late afternoon nap.

With a rap on the bathroom door, he announced again, "Hon, it's me, I'm home."

"Steven! You scared me. I didn't think you would be home until late."

"A committee meeting was canceled, I didn't even go to the apartment first. I just ran to my car and headed home to surprise you."

"Well, you did. I'll be right out."

"I thought we could go out tonight, dinner and a movie. What do you say?"

"That sounds nice, pick a movie and I'll get dressed for Luigi's. How does that sound?"

"Great idea," Steven yelled back through the door, over the hiss of the running water.

Steven smiled. A date with his wife was the most he could have hoped for. Her willingness had been unexpected but immensely welcomed.

Steven bounded down the stairs like he was about to go on his first date. Something had changed with his wife; he could sense it during their nightly telephone chats. He hoped it wasn't his imagination, but it seemed like Lucille had finally found what she had lost in life.

The time past quickly as he got caught up on the stack of mail on the counter. Steven caught himself whistling a tune, something he couldn't remember doing in a long time. He glanced at the kitchen clock for the third time since he had arrived, he was anxious to see his daughter before they left for dinner and a movie. As if on cue, she burst through the door.

"Hi, Daddy, when did you get home?"

"Hi, princess. Not too long ago. How was practice?"

"Jenny Martin twisted her ankle. The coach told her to ice it tonight, we have a meet Saturday, and we could really use her."

"Ouch, that's a shame. I hope you don't mind, but your mother and I are going out on a date tonight. Luigi's and a movie."

"Way to go, Dad!" Tracy held her hand up for a high five.

Steven slapped back.

Tracy leaned in and whispered, "I think mom is becoming happy again. I can tell, little things, and she is smiling more."

"That's great news. See, I told you it would just take a little time."

"How long are you home?"

"Unfortunately, only the weekend."

"Will you be coming to the meet?"

"Why do you think I came home? I wouldn't miss it for the world."

Later that evening at Luigi's:

Steven laughed, "I can't believe she said that to you. But then again, it was Sandy. She says the first thing that comes to mind."

Lucille was still chuckling over the recalled incident from the last week when Steven said, "I am having a wonderful time. In fact, I can't remember the last time I felt so relaxed. And the meal was delicious, good choice."

With a smile, the waitress brought the bill to the table and set down the leather-bound receipt book.

"I've been wanting to see the movie you picked out. It's getting good ratings," Lucille said.

"Can't take the credit, Tracy suggested it."

"I haven't seen a good movie, well, since I don't know when."

"You seem to be in a much better place mentally than you have in a long time."

Lucille didn't respond; instead, she scanned the decor of the restaurant while sipping her wine. Eventually, she broke the awkward silence. "I'm glad we came here to eat. You know that this was one of Rebecca's favorite restaurants. She loved their lasagna."

"I didn't mean to break the mood, I just wanted to say that you seem happier than I have seen you in a long time."

"I know, I am having a good time. Let's just say that I'm starting to adjust to the new reality. It's all right to laugh and think about Rebecca at the same time. I think I finally realized that I was dying a little bit more each and every day."

Lucille glanced around and saw that, as the evening had worn on, the tables around them had emptied. She contemplated for a moment on what she was trying to explain as she took another sip of her red wine.

"I was so focused and stuck on the past, I wasn't living the here and now. Living that way and thinking that way will never bring Rebecca back. I think I have come to terms with the realization that I have to get on with my life as best I can."

Washington DC, three days later:

"Jojo, I'm losing her."

Steven was back in Washington; the weekend at home had gone both better and worse than expected. Alone in his office, he was pacing the floor as he talked on his cell phone.

"She actually said that?"

Steven was fighting back his emotions, trying to talk calmly, but his voice was broken by choked words. His hands were flailing so much it was hard for him to keep the phone up to his ear.

"She says she still loves me, but being with me reminds her so much of Rebecca. Every time she feels herself letting go of some of the pain, when she sees me, it brings it all back. She says it's not my fault and that there is nothing I can do about it. It's all up to her, and she is trying to deal with it in her own way."

"Does she want a divorce?"

"She says she still loves me and that she doesn't want a divorce. But she's afraid it's the only way to move on."

"That's crazy, man. So she doesn't want a divorce but she thinks she has to divorce you in order to make herself feel better? She doesn't really believe that bull does she?"

Steven stopped pacing.

"I'm afraid she does. We had a great time over the weekend. We had a good time at Tracy's gymnastics meet. We had a really fun time going out to a movie and then dinner. We even made love."

"But she wants to divorce you. It just doesn't make sense."

"She says she wants it to work and is going to give it a fighting chance."

"But?"

"Yea, exactly."

"What about a temporary separation of some sort to give it time to work out?"

"That would have to be my plan B. She said that it wouldn't be fair to keep my life in limbo as she deals with her problem."

"Translation: if she decides to move on, you're history, and that is exactly what she wants to get rid of, history, including you."

"I don't have a good feeling about this." Steven sat on the edge of his desk, seemingly calmed down some. His mind was too confused to be agitated at the moment.

"Do you mind if I share with Tamara? She's about due to call Lucille anyway. Maybe they will have a heart to heart, and she can talk some sense into her."

"That would be great."

"I gotta run, but I'll keep you posted if Tamara finds out anything. Call me tomorrow, and we can talk some more OK, buddy?"

"Yea, sure. And thanks."

"Hang in there, guy, this will work out. Trust me."

"You wouldn't lie to me now would you?"

"Of course not, never."

"See ya."

"Bye."

Chapter 11

Washington DC, one week later:

Destinee Sanford felt that she knew as much as she was ever going to know about Senator Steven Westcott. It was time to put her plan into effect. She sorted through the photos one last time. The perfect opportunity had just presented itself in today's newspaper. In a few days, the senator would be a guest speaker for the Greater Washington DC Woman's Shelter.

She wasn't worried about her plan. She had envisioned it so many times in her mind that it was as if it had already happened. She could already hear her friends calling her Senator Steven Westcott's mistress. That didn't mean the risk was any less real, but with confidence, Destinee initiated her scheme.

Two days later:

There was a quiet knock on the private back door into his office.

"Come in Shannon," Steven said to the door.

The private door connected his office with the office of his schedule coordinator, Shannon Johnston.

"Senator, you are gaining a reputation for being late. Do I need to remind you one more time about your appearance today?" Shannon Johnston said.

Senator Steven Westcott grabbed an apple off of a small fruit bowl in his office. "I didn't even have time to eat yet."

"Sorry, Senator, but you insisted on talking to the visiting high schoolers."

"I couldn't say no."

"You also didn't have to spend time showing them your shot-up flack jacket."

"They asked," Steven said.

"Go!" Shannon scolded with a smile.

Steven smirked at his aid and was soon taking the elevator down to the parking garage. He looked at his watch and guessed that if he hit the lights right, and if he found a parking spot right away at the auditorium, he might make it on time.

St. Beatrice Catholic College:

Senator Westcott walked into the crowded private college back stage. A harried-looking short woman, who Steven guessed was in her forties, ran up to him and shook his hand. "I'm Miss Michaels, so nice to meet you in person. Shannon called and said you might be a bit late so we changed the schedule just a little, you will be next. I can't thank you enough for coming."

"Nonsense, I want to help. I respect your organization, and, as you know, this is dear to my heart."

"I want to thank Mrs. Lions for that unique perspective." The MC closed out for the last speaker. "Next, I want to introduce the senator from Massachusetts. I am very honored and proud to have Senator Steven Westcott here with us today."

Stepping out to the podium, Steven worked at hushing the audience who were clapping with encouragement.

"Thank you, thank you. You are all very welcome, and I thank you for letting me speak today. This organization appreciates your attending this conference on the drug epidemic striking our country.

"The college donated this auditorium, and all the speakers are donating their time. That means one hundred percent of your admission price goes to helping people who made some bad choices and now find themselves addicted. The money goes directly to the men and women, young and old, who want to change their lives.

"As many of you know, I lost a daughter to addiction, and I have a brother who is in jail because of an addiction. This is a real epidemic, and the cost to them and to us is something we can't ignore. They need our help and they deserve out help. Each and every person who wants to defeat the monster inside of them has to know there is a way."

Steven then told his story and the story of his family and daughter, hoping it would help others. At the end of his presentation, he added, "For an additional donation, all the speakers will be signing the recorded version of this program. Please open your hearts just a bit more, and I will see you at the back table."

****

Destinee Sanford was clapping louder than anybody. She couldn't have been prouder of the senator. In person, he was everything she fantasized and more.

The line was thinning for meeting the speakers and buying the autographed video. Destinee had waited for just the right moment to stand in that line so that she would be the last person there. The speakers were polite and talked to each contributor and diligently signed the DVD version of the program.

Destinee was the last in line. She politely thanked the other speakers for their time and autographs. After she thanked each one, they left, leaving Senator Westcott as the sole representative at the long table. When she came up to the senator, her heart was pounding so hard she thought everyone could hear it. Steven said goodbye to the second-to-last person in line, looking away for an instant to find his felt-tip pen. Destinee approached. She extended her hand to finally meet the man she had fantasized about for the last two months.

Steven started extending his hand, but when he looked up at the young woman, his arm froze in place for the briefest of moments. The ghost of his daughter was before him. It wasn't that he actually thought for an instant that the girl was his daughter's reincarnation, it was just that, for some reason, the woman in front of him had instantly reminded him of Rebecca. It took him another moment to regain his composure.

"Hi, I am so happy you joined us today." Steven smiled broadly, trying to hide his shock.

Destinee handed Steven the DVD case. "Could you please make it out to Destinee, that's with two e's. Destinee Sanford."

The sound of her voice also haunted him, though he didn't know why.

Steven withdrew his hand, finding it difficult not to stare at the young woman. Steven repeated, "Destinee with two e's, Sanford," as he signed the DVD.

Her makeup was loud and gaudy; that combined with her revealing clothes made her look like a hooker, not a student. It was the same type of clothing Rebecca had taken to wearing.

She was pretty, but looked tired or worn. Too much so for a young woman of maybe nineteen or twenty. That look had also been Rebecca's.

"I loved your talk. I'm a huge fan of yours. Saw you on Oprah," she said, smiling from ear to ear.

The hair on the back of Steven's neck began to tingle. Her voice was so familiar, but he couldn't place it.

He felt his face flush as cold sweat began to form on his forehead. He tried to hide his reaction, but the shock had taken him too much by surprise. His voice cracked a bit as he tried to regain his composure.

"Oh, well, a real fan."

Steven gave a friendly smile as he handed back the signed DVD and caught the dilation of her eyes. It was something he had learned was a tell-tale sign of drug use.

Destinee smiled back excitedly, like a schoolgirl getting asked out on a date with her first high school crush.

"That's perfect," she said. "If you could just sign this too."

Destinee opened her notebook and presented it to him. Steven tore his gaze away from the girl's face and looked at the page.

Steven felt blood drain from his face. It took a moment to digest what he was seeing. It was a picture of Shatoya and a young man. It was himself, but younger. They both were naked and kissing.

He looked up, confused. Destinee pulled the notebook back before anybody else could see it. Then she closed it and held it tight against her chest.

"Senator, I hope we see each other again, real soon. I have this and other pictures to give you; I wouldn't want them to get in the wrong hands. Is there a way to talk to you in private?"

Steven was in shock. He had a thousand questions he couldn't ask. Not here, not now. All he knew was, what he had just seen wasn't possible. Who had taken the photo, and how?

Steven stared at Destinee. He looked into her eyes for an explanation but saw none. Yes, he wanted to talk in private to the young woman—he had to. He wrote down his personal e-mail address on a plain white slip.

Steven handed the paper to Destinee as he stared at her face. There was no doubt in his mind that she was an addict. Unfortunately, he knew personally the outward effects of addiction. And he also knew that addicts only want two things: more drugs, or money to get more drugs. She had damaging photos of him; he could write the rest of the scrip. He knew what his own daughter would have done with a picture like that when she was at her worst.

Destinee took the note and smiled lovingly at the senator. "I don't wanna hurt you. I like you too much, and I don't want your money. I just want to talk, Mr. Senator. I want to give you the pictures, all of them."

Destinee turned away and walked halfway out the hall before turning around and waving goodbye. Her short dress was hiked high on her thighs, barely covering her backside.

Steven didn't wave back.

Chapter 12

It had been a long week since the strange conversation at the Catholic college. Steven hadn't slept well the last seven days, and he looked like hell and felt even worse. He worried constantly about what could happen. Would the pictures show up on the Internet somehow, or be mailed to his wife or the television stations?

There were three reasons that kept him from calling the FBI. First, if he called the FBI, it would become public; it would just be a matter of time, game over. The other was what the young woman had said. She said that she wanted to give him all of the pictures. Nothing was said about a cost of getting them. The third was the way she looked at him. He couldn't explain it, but she seemed trustworthy.

In his office, he tried to distract himself from thinking about the bizarre encounter. The television was turned to a cable news channel. The sound was muted so he could concentrate. Steven glanced at the television to see if the current broadcast was anything he should be concerned about. It showed a gas pump and the current price on it. Not hard to guess the gist of that broadcast.

Steven sliced open some personal mail with a letter opener that had been a gift from the Senate majority leader. It had a thick, curved handle made of brown glass with swirls of teal and tans. The opener was smooth and heavy in his hand, with a brilliant stainless steel blade. But the most important part was the engraving on it. On one side was "Senator Steven Westcott," on the other, it said "Ense Petit Placidam Sub Libertatequietem." Roughly translated, it meant, "By the sword we seek peace, but peace only under liberty." It was the official motto of the US Commonwealth of Massachusetts, and it was hard for Steven to use the special opener without thinking of what the words meant to him as a soldier.

Then, for the tenth time that day, Steven checked his personal e-mail account with his cell phone. Unlike the other nine times, there was a message waiting for him.

It said: "I need to see you. I have the picture you saw and others that are worse. I don't want any money. I just want to give you the pictures so that nobody else gets them. I see you all the time on TV and want to get to know you. I like you a lot. I think you will like me too when you get to know me. We can meet any place you like tomorrow at noon, but I need to know now."

Steven got up and paced his office with the smart phone in his hand. The e-mail had been both what he was waiting for and what he hoped would never happen. It was time for him to decide if he would meet the girl alone, or with the FBI or CIA involved.

Steven felt flush. His hands were becoming sweaty. He read the message again.

The vote on his bill was coming soon. This was bad timing, very, very bad. How did Shatoya take the photos? Shit! He cursed silently. And who was this girl? She was probably a hooker herself, but how did she get a hold of pictures taken over twenty years ago? Blackmail was no doubt the ultimate objective. Or was it? The girl had said she wanted to give him the pictures and didn't want any money.

He wandered his office, lost in thought. Eventually, he found the mirror on the wall and stared at his face, hoping his reflection would give him an answer. Then, out of the blue, it did. The mirror, the bed-room mirror; it had obviously been a two-way mirror.

Steven loosened his tie, breathing was difficult. He slunk down in his chair. It was so long ago, in such a different life. Shit! What was he going to do? Lucille couldn't see that picture. Even if it happened well before they were married, Lucille couldn't handle it, not now, not ever.

The girl had said she had to know now where to meet. Was that an attempt to keep him from coordinating a plan? The girl didn't seem that calculating. Still, maybe she was working with someone.

Steven walked back to the window, trying to think. If he did meet her, where would they meet? Then Steven had a thought. If it was a blackmail attempt, they would try to control the when and where. She had said tomorrow afternoon, but she didn't say where. That was up to him.

Steven looked out the window toward the Capitol. He knew the grounds quite well. The Ulysses S. Grant Memorial wasn't far. It was in the open, but there were a few secluded areas. It was very public, of course, but they would also be able to talk privately.

Steven went to the e-mail and responded.

Tomorrow at twelve thirty in the afternoon at the Ulysses S. Grant Memorial. At the north side, you'll see a big maple tree. Around that tree is a retaining wall you can sit on. It's near what is called the peace circle. I'll meet you there.

He would go alone and meet with the girl and whoever she was with. Maybe she was telling the truth.

The next day:

After another sleepless night, Steven came to the office less certain of his plan than the day before. In the privacy of his office, Steven opened a cabinet and took out a small lock box that contained a pistol. As a US senator and a gun-permit owner, he was allowed to bring a gun into the Senate Building. Being an ex-special forces soldier, he always felt naked without a gun around. It had been locked in a pistol case waiting for his next opportunity at the shooting range. He slipped it into a holster and strapped it to the small of his back. His suit jacket would easily conceal it.

He had picked the Grant Memorial because it was fairly close to his office. He could be there in fifteen minutes or less. It was also not one of the busier attractions, but it was public enough.

"Shannon, I'm going out for a sandwich and a walk."

"You should. You've been a bit tense lately. Where are you going? Just in case I need to find you."

"I'm walking the mall."

"Be back for your meeting at one thirty or I'm calling the Capitol police," Shannon said as Steven stepped out the door.

"You probably would, wouldn't you?"

"Be back on time and you won't have to find out," Shannon teased back.

He walked toward the giant National Mall. It was a little before noon and he bought a hot dog from a not-too-busy street vender. Steven found a place where he could strategically spy on the north side of the Grant Memorial. He waited on the other side of Pennsylvania Avenue. Once in position, he ate his hot dog and kept watch on the small area where he expected the girl, Destinee, to appear.

He hadn't forgotten his training; immediately west of the Grant Memorial was a reflecting pond. Farther west of that was the huge National Mall grass area leading to the Washington Monument. Nobody could approach from the reflecting-pond side of the monument, so it made the entire area a safe zone.

Steven glanced down toward the huge granite and marble pinnacle near the center of the grassy mall; he had effectively taken that entire area out of play. He was north of the big maple tree and was sure he wasn't being watched. Leaning casually against a protected lamppost, he looked past peace circle and concentrated on the area east and south of the meeting spot.

His eye looked for any out-of-the-ordinary tourists, such as singles like him, or people pretending to be reading newspapers, or a wide circle of tourists, who were all in an equal distance of the meeting area. He saw none of that. All the tourists kept moving. Couples walked past holding hands, taking pictures of each other, or asking another tourist to snap theirs. Often, the area was devoid of pedestrian traffic completely. Until one lonely girl in high heels and a short skirt looked around disappointedly, then sat down in the quiet alcove just where he had instructed her to be.

Tree branches on his side of the wide boulevard blocked her view of him, though he could see her quite clearly. She was carrying a grocery-size paper bag under her arm. When she sat on the short stone retaining wall in the shade of the big tree, she slipped the bag down next to her feet. Then she took her small handbag from around her shoulders and set it next to her.

Steven stayed in his position, looking for but not seeing any other pedestrian traffic near her. Steven waited and waited. The girl stood and looked around the corner as if to check if she was in the right place. Then she sat back down and glanced at her phone but never talked on it or texted. He could see the look of eager anticipation on her face. All and all, she appeared quite innocent.

Steven checked his wristwatch; it was past their meeting time. An older couple holding hands walked by the young girl. The elderly gentleman tipped his head toward her as they walked past.

When the older couple was well past the turn and out of sight, he cautiously stepped closer to the boulevard that was separating them. Still convinced there were no other people of interest around, he walked across the boulevard toward the sitting young woman.

"Hello," Steven said, approaching the shaded alcove.

Destinee looked up and saw Steven walking down the sidewalk. She stood and ran toward him.

Steven hadn't expected to be rushed and was slightly unprepared as he slipped his hand under his coat jacket to pull out his gun.

"I thought you weren't coming!" Destinee cried as she reached up to hug Steven.

Steven held his hand on the handle of his gun until he realized his only threat was being hugged to death.

"Please, miss, we don't even know each other." Steven tried to gently break her hug.

"I was so worried. I waited and waited." Then Destinee grabbed his hand and dragged him to the short wall where she had been waiting.

"I brought us lunch, and look." Destinee pulled out a bottle of wine. "This is perfect, we can have a picnic, right here in the shade of this tree. Just you and me."

Destinee pulled out two plastic cups from the paper bag. "I think it's a good wine. And I have sandwiches. I bought a turkey and a ham. I don't care which one you want. You can have them both if you want. I'm not that hungry."

"Destinee, that is your name right?"

"Yes, yes, you remembered."

Destinee sat down, clearly expecting him to do the same. Steven sat next to her. "Destinee, this is all very nice, but I don't have time for a picnic. You wanted to meet because you have some pictures for me."

Destinee already had the sandwiches in her hand and was offering them both to Steven. "This is the ham. Do you like ham better?"

Steven looked around, suddenly worried about the attention the excited woman, and the very short dress she was wearing, might draw.

Steven took the sandwich and set it down.

"We need to talk first."

"Open the wine, I brought an opener, see, I thought of everything."

"OK, OK."

Steven tried not to look at the exceptionally low cut of her blouse as she bent forward, dipping her hand into the bag, looking for the corkscrew opener. Then he noticed the bottle had a twist top. He twisted it off. Destinee's face turned red. "The man said it was a good wine. I'm sorry. I told him I was having a picnic with an important man. You're upset with me now aren't you?"

Steven couldn't believe he actually felt a bit sorry for the girl. She was clearly very flustered. "No, no of course not. Just because it has a twist top doesn't mean it isn't a good wine."

Destinee presented both plastic cups as Steven poured.

Steven checked his watch just as Destinee was forcing one of the plastic cups of wine at him. "I don't have much time. You said to meet you because you would give me the pictures."

"No, silly, I said I wanted to talk to you. I have been waiting for this moment for so long. I saw you on Oprah once."

"I, I know. You told me at the conference. But you said you wanted to give me the pictures, all of them."

"I do, you are naked in most of them. Sometimes you had clothes on, but mostly not."

"Did you bring them?"

"No, I couldn't. They're in a safe place, and I couldn't get them this morning cause Clayton was watching me too close."

"Clayton? Who's Clayton?"

"Kind of like my boss. Don't you want your sandwich? I bought them just for you. I've read all about you, and I like you a lot."

"But I don't know you, and you certainly don't know me."

"No, you're wrong. I do know you. I know all about you."

The mall area was getting a bit more crowded and Steven was beginning to think this was a very bad idea. What if somebody he knew saw them? Or if somebody who knew his face took his picture with the young girl and posted it online?

Steven looked at his watch again and realized his one-thirty meeting was pressing him for time. "Look, Destinee, I think you are a very nice young lady, but you said you wanted to give me the pictures so nobody can use them to hurt me. We need to talk about that. I don't have much time. I have a meeting to go to."

"I know you are a very important man. I like that. I watched you on Oprah over and over again. Remember when you said you like a glass of wine now and then. So I brought you some. Remember the joke you said, I remember—"

Suddenly, out the corner of his eye, Steven recognized a young intern from his office. He had no other choice but to turn his body completely around, shielding his face from the young man's view.

Steven whispered, "Destinee, I am running out of time. If I'm not back to my office in fifteen minutes, people will become worried and send the police out to find me."

Destinee glanced over her shoulder to spy what had caught his attention.

"Let me guess, the person eating an ice cream over there knows you, and you can't be seen by them, and that means you can't leave until they do?"

"Look, no offense, but being seen with such a young girl, alone, in a park. Well, it wouldn't look so good."

"I understand, I look like a hooker."

"Destinee, it's not that, it's ... it's because you're so young."

"I'm twenty-one."

"I'm not."

"Will you meet with me again sometime?"

"Destinee, the pictures are very important to me. If you don't want me hurt, you need to give them to me."

"I want to, I really do, but not today. I want to meet with you again, I want to get to know you better, and I want you to get to know me."

Steven checked his watch again. "I have to get going."

"Don't worry, I can help you."

Destinee looked casually over his shoulder. "The person you're worried about hasn't spotted you yet. His eyes are wandering. Sit tight, I have an idea, and the next time we meet, I'll bring you the pictures. I promise."

Destinee stood up and took the two plastic cups of wine and the wine bottle with her. She sauntered up to the intern.

"Hi," Destinee said with a very practiced smile. Destinee moved directly opposite the park bench and started a conversation with the surprised and innocent intern.

The young man's eyes were immediately locked on the low cut blouse and the pretty girl's smile. Steven knew an opportunity when he saw it. He stood up and walked as fast as he could.

Chapter 13

Washington Arms Hotel:

Destinee stepped into the polished wood interior of the Washington Arms' lobby. The service bell had just been rung at the front desk by another couple. She saw the hotel manager twist his body out the door of his office and quickly emerge to take care of the couple.

"Good evening, Professor Haggerty, sir," The manager announced regally as he stepped up to the counter with a giant smile. "I have room 327 cleaned and ready for you, sir."

"Thank you, Ramon," the bearded guest replied, just as royally. The young girl at his side whispered something into the professor's ear, and then she giggled.

Destinee spied the wedding ring on the professor's finger. Her best guess at the girl's age was twenty to twenty-three, but no more than that. The professor looked to be about fifty-five, though it was hard to tell beneath his perfectly groomed beard and mustache.

The girl wasn't a working girl like her, that, Destinee was sure of. Probably a student, and, according to her body language, her test scores were going to be seeing an improvement.

"If there is anything else we can do for you, please do not hesitate to ask."

The petite blonde stepped up on her toes and whispered into the professor's ear again.

"Could you please have a bottle of Champagne delivered to our room and a fruit and cheese platter?"

"Of course, sir, it would be our pleasure. And might you be needing a taxi later?"

The professor looked at the short-haired girl, who was hanging on his arm as if he were about to float away if she didn't hold him down, and then he quipped, "Not tonight. Tomorrow morning at eight sharp." Then he smiled at the girl and said, "You wouldn't want to be late for class, would you?"

"Oh no," she purred. "Then the teacher would have to punish me." She flashed her impish smile. Professor Haggerty smiled at Ramon as if saying, *Don't you wish you were me?*

Destinee felt slightly embarrassed as the young girl on the professor's arm turned around and gave her an unapproving eye as she checked out Destinee's clothing with an unrepentant stare.

Ramon gave a polite nod and said, "The taxi will be waiting at eight sharp." Then he turned discreetly away.

Professor Haggerty and his girlfriend turned hand in hand toward the elevator. Destinee stepped forward toward the manager.

"I'm sorry, miss, we do not rent our rooms out by the hour."

Destinee understood the immediate insult but was in no position to create a disturbance. "I understand. I would like a room for the night. Is that a problem?"

"No problem at all, miss." Ramon smiled politely.

"I have a very nice room all ready on the third floor, room 331. Do you require help with your bag, miss?" The manager raised his eyebrow as he gazed down at the one small bag.

Destinee was tempted to accept his offer out of spite. "No thank you. I can handle my bag myself."

She turned away from him, feeling dirtied by his comments. Yes, he was right. She was a hooker and, in fact, had several customers lined up for the afternoon and evening. But having been so politely rebuked had hurt her just the same. She didn't like what her life had become. But was she really that different from the college girl? After all, going to college to learn to screw wasn't an option she was offered.

Her small suitcase click-clacked across the tiled floor, as did her high heels as she walked to the elevator. Soon, very soon, she wouldn't have to endure the humiliating stares and verbal and physical abuse. Soon she would be the mistress of a very important man.

Destinee could see herself eating at fine restaurants, wearing expensive jewelry, and having the finest name-brand clothing. But best of all, she would have an apartment of her very own to share with the senator whenever he could enjoy a long visit with her. She knew it happened because the girls talked about it. Destinee's spirits were high because she just knew she would soon be one of those girls.

The other side of town at the same time:

Steven didn't feel he could leave town because of the strange girl. She might demand another get-together at any time. He didn't want to take the chance of missing the opportunity or possibly upsetting the fragile young woman. That was just as well because his bill was now out of committee, and the leader of the Senate was thinking of bringing it to a vote.

Checking his private e-mail for any message from Destinee had become an obsession. It was an obsession that finally paid off when he read her latest message.

If you get a room at the Washington Arms Hotel next Tuesday, I can meet you there. It's a nice hotel. I've been there before. I have to be careful and you should too, nobody will see us there. Text me at the number below with a time and room number and I will meet you there. Please don't call me. I might get in trouble.

Steven had come to a few conclusions he had to act on, at least until he knew differently. Right now, he didn't feel he was being blackmailed. Also, he didn't feel he was in any physical danger. The girl was irrational, but not dangerous. What he still couldn't figure out was her last statement. *Please don't call me. I might get in trouble.* Could that mean she was a minor? How would a telephone call get someone in trouble, and why was a text OK?

Steven had struggled with how to respond all night. The eventual conclusion he came up with was that he had to meet her. Yes it was a risk, but if she really just wanted to give him the photographs, could he afford to pass on such an opportunity? If he had her arrested, or even questioned by the authorities, she, or others, might release the photos out of spite. And either way, the photos would become government property and possibly released through the Freedom of Information Act. If there were any chance of him diffusing this situation, he would have to try. His family deserved it.

One week later:

Steven took a deep breath. He felt like a fool pretending to be someone he wasn't.

"May I help you, sir?"

"Yes, I have a reservation under Fisher, Mark Fisher."

"One moment please ... I believe I have it, yes, here it is." Ramon looked up at Steven.

Steven was sporting a scruffy-looking beard and a new Washington DC visor hat. He was dressed in blue jeans and a T-shirt depicting Arlington Cemetery.

Steven realized the manager was judging him by his clothing, which was good.

"Staying a few days with us, sir?"

"Just tonight," Steven answered, trying not to sound nervous. He had let his facial hair grow out for the last week. That and the baseball hat were the limit of his disguise.

"How many keys, sir?"

"Just one would be fine."

"Would that be cash or charge?"

"Cash." Steven felt uncomfortable uttering the word.

"Room 327 is all ready for you, Mr. Fisher."

Steven felt his face flush as the clerk handed him the key to the room. He reminded himself: he wasn't doing anything illegal or immoral.

"Will there be anything else, Mr. Fisher?"

"No, that will be it." Steven walked to the elevator for the third floor.

Walking away from the check-in desk, Steven realized his heart was beating a bit too quickly, and his hands were sweaty. If he wasn't doing anything wrong, why did he feel so nervous?

Steven tossed his empty suitcase onto the bed. He had brought it to seem less suspicious. The layout of the small room was simple enough. It was on the third floor, but out the window, he could see a rooftop just a floor below. He could jump down to it in a pinch if this was some sort of set up. Steven raised the window to make sure it worked, then he lowered it again, leaving it open just a crack.

He was intentionally early. He left the room and took the short walk to his stakeout position, a small tavern nearby. It was the beginning of fall, the sun was out and the temperature moderate. Steven sat at one of the outside tables at the Billy Goat Tavern. He had a clear view of the Washington Arms Hotel. In two hours, he would meet with the young woman.

He slid his phone out of his pocket and texted the room number to Destinee. Steven nursed a few beers and ordered a plate of cheese nachos as he waited. Then, right on time, he saw her. Destinee was pulling a small suitcase. She had on an ultra-short skirt, a tight top, and high heels. She definitely stood out among the tourists.

Steven waited; he had left the hotel room door propped open with the safety latch. She could let herself in and wait while he watched to see if anyone was following her. There were no loitering individuals or suspicious cars. In fact, the Washington Arms seemed to be having a rather slow afternoon.

Fifteen minutes after he had spotted Destinee, Steven paid his bill and casually walked toward the hotel, keeping a close eye on the surrounding area for suspicious characters. Convinced he wasn't being followed, and absolutely certain nobody had entered the hotel since Destinee arrived, he stepped inside the Washington Arms.

Steven nodded to the manager on duty, the same one who had checked him in. Then he took the stairs instead of the elevator to the third floor.

Steven cautiously opened the stairwell door. The hall was empty. Then he receded back around the corner, contemplating his next move. Luck had been on his side. He could still leave; his suitcase contained nothing and could easily be replaced. But she did have a suitcase of her own. Could be the pictures. He considered.

Steven walked up to his room, prepared to keep on walking if he heard anything suspicious from inside. The door he had left propped open was now closed tight. There was still no activity in the hallway. Whoever she was, she was alone. No bodyguards, no photographers, or journalists. He took a deep breath. Whatever happened in the next few minutes could mean the difference between quenching the fire of disaster or inflaming it.

He double-checked the loaded pistol that was tucked under his shirt into the small of his back. With his gun still hidden, he slid the electronic key through the lock and entered the room. She wasn't there; the room was empty. He looked toward the bathroom. The door was closed, but only partially, and the shower was running.

He made sure the door locked behind him, then moved the safety latch into position. Steven walked past the bathroom door and shouted loud enough to be heard over the splashing water.

"Hello!"

"Be out in a minute."

Steven thought it bizarre. Why would a stranger walk into another stranger's room and start taking a shower? And even more to the point, why would a woman walk into a strange man's room, get naked, and take a shower? Unless ... *oh boy! I'm not going to let that happen.*

He felt uncomfortable just standing around waiting and decided a drink might be a good distraction. The room had a minibar, and he noticed the ice bucket was full of fresh ice. He mixed himself a drink, then sat down on the bed and heard the shower turn off. He shifted uncomfortably and felt like an idiot.

He took a couple long sips as he stared at a poster on the wall of fireworks going off over the Capitol Building. The reproduction wasn't inside a frame. Instead, the material of the print was wrapped around the outside of the frame. When he heard the squeak of the bathroom door open he instinctively turned toward it. That was when the glass fell from his hands.

Chapter 14

Destinee giggled, "Haven't you ever seen a naked woman before?" Steven couldn't help but look at the completely naked form in front of him. He had expected many things, but this wasn't one of them, and it paralyzed him.

"Don't you think I'm pretty?"

"Ah, yea, ah ... sure you are, I mean of course. But ..." Steven stopped himself. He didn't want to upset her in any way. All he wanted was the pictures. Obviously, the young woman wanted more than to hand over a few photos to him. More than he was prepared to give her, but he couldn't tell her that just yet. He had to know more.

"But what?" she asked coyly. "I love your beard. Did you grow it for me?"

"What? Oh, ah, thank you. No, no I just thought ... never mind."

"I can't believe we are finally alone." That was when she closed the small distance between them in a rush. She reached out to Steven and flung herself down on him like they were long lost lovers finally united. Her naked form crashed into Steven and they both fell back onto the bed. Destinee started to kiss him all over.

"No. Stop it." Steven tried to object but was rewarded with a kiss on his lips. He twisted his head away and more forcefully cried out. "I mean it, please stop." He grabbed her by her thin wrist and forced her off of him. The smell of cheap perfume engulfed him as he stood, pressing Destinee away firmly by her wrist.

Destinee stood in front of the senator, completely unabashed. "Don't you like me?"

"Like you? I don't even know you."

"You don't have to pay me or anything if that's what you are worried about. Don't you think I'm pretty? Most men think I'm pretty."

Steven didn't know how to respond to that. Something was wrong, way wrong. He remembered the message in the letter. *I like you a lot. I think you will like me too when you get to know me.*

"Yes, yes of course you are pretty. I'm just a bit confused. I thought you were going to give me some pictures. You said you didn't want anyone else to get them."

"Oh no, nobody else should see those pictures. You are an important man; it would be bad for you. It will be a secret just between us."

Steven stood, afraid of being tackled again. Destinee stepped closer to Steven and took his hand. Tenderly, she looked into his eyes and spoke softly. "I was sure that when you saw me you would want me. Men pay a lot of money to have me. They all tell me I'm beautiful."

"Yes you are. You are very pretty. But, I don't know you yet, after all, we didn't have much time to talk." Clearly, the girl wasn't completely rational. Her thin, light brown hair and pale complexion reminded him of his daughter. The more addicted she became, the more irrational and very easily irritated she became. Steven proceeded with caution.

"I am married you know," Steven said.

"Yes, I know. Your wife is very pretty, so is your daughter."

"You know my family?" Steven asked, becoming more and more uncomfortable as the young girl touched his face. Steven backed away, but the girl followed.

He grabbed her hands a bit forcefully.

"I can't do this with you. Like I said, I don't even know you. You said you are twenty-one, how do I know that?"

"Don't worry, I'm legal. I can prove it if you want."

"Yes, please. It's important to me," Steven said.

Steven felt a hint of an opportunity to stop what was happening. He hadn't been this close to a naked woman other than his wife for twenty years. And he had no intention of breaking his vows to her over a twenty-one-year-old's fantasies.

She went back into the bathroom and found her ID in the suitcase she had carried in.

Still naked, she handed it to him. "See, I'm twenty-one."

Steven looked at the ID. He was, in fact, very interested in her age. Being with a young girl was bad; being with an underage girl was jail, even if unintentional.

The picture and age checked out. He read her name, and it meant nothing to him except that she was exactly who she had said she was. Steven stood up, he wanted to offer her a blanket or towel to cover her with, but he was afraid she would take it as an insult. He walked over to the minibar and offered her a drink.

"Why don't you join me for a drink and we can get to know each other?" Steven said.

"Sure, why not. How about a rum and coke?"

Steven scavenged around in the minibar, thankful for the excuse to divert his eyes, and found the right ingredients. He kept his back to her as he prepared her drink.

Steven stalled a bit by making himself another drink as well. Good idea or not, it was all he could think to do. When he looked back at the naked girl, he couldn't help but insist, "Please could you cover yourself up?" He offered her the top blanket off the bed.

"Don't you want to look at me?" Destinee said.

"Yes of course, but I also want you to be comfortable."

"I am comfortable. I think you aren't. It's OK if you are a bit shy; we have plenty of time to get to know each other. We can have the rest of our lives together."

Destinee wrapped herself up in the blanket loosely and bounced down on the bed. Then asked, with a slight pout, "What do you want to talk about?" As she propped her back up against some pillows and the backboard.

Steven was near panic. Things were going exceptionally wrong.

He handed the drink to Destinee and then retreated to the foot of the bed. He wanted to pace the floor, but there wasn't enough room, so he stood awkwardly by a small desk. "The pictures—you said you had more pictures."

"I do, but I didn't bring them all here."

"Why not?"

"I don't know, didn't feel like it I guess."

"How did you get them? How many are there?"

"Let's fuck, I don't want to talk about the pictures anymore."

Steven choked on his drink. Destinee giggled.

"Tell me about yourself," Steven said once he stopped coughing.

The blanket slipped down off her left breast, Destinee didn't notice, or she didn't care, either way, she left it that way. Then, with a disgusted huff, she complied.

"My mom raised me, I didn't know my father. Mostly Mama and I lived in Vegas. She worked in a casino; I forget which one. Then we had to move. That was when Mama became a hooker. We had a house and everything, but then something happened. Mama never told me why, but we moved to DC and Mama met Clayton Harris. He gave us a place to stay. Mama was real pretty like me, and he made her work for him. We wanted to leave, but whenever Mama said we were going to, he would treat her real nice. Eventually, Mama got hooked on his drugs so she couldn't leave.

"Clayton Harris, he's the guy you said is sort of your boss."

"Yea, sort of."

"And your mother knows you are hooking for him too?"

Destinee looked down at the blanket covering her lap. "Mama died a couple of years ago, and he said I had to work for him to pay off what Mama owed. Clayton gave me Mama's room. Now I'm one of Clayton's bitches. That's what he calls me."

Steven was beginning to understand certain things, valuable things. Things he might need to know if he was to gain the girl's confidence. He sat down on the chair next to the small bureau.

"I saw bruises on your shoulder. Are they from Clayton?"

Destinee's cheeks flushed. Steven watched her eyes as she looked at the purple bruise on her left shoulder. She pulled the blanket up to cover it, realizing it was impossible to miss the dark mark against her pale white skin.

"Mostly. Sometimes johns think they can hit me cause they pay me. But mostly from Clayton. He gets angry sometimes, and then beats me. I really don't mind that much. Sometimes I have it coming."

"Destinee, it is not OK for anyone to hit you, ever."

"He's too big, I can't stop him. And, mostly, if I do what he says, he doesn't hurt me too bad."

"Nobody should ever hurt you."

"You would never hurt me," Destinee said confidently.

"Of course not. I mean, look, Miss Sanford, I'm not sure what you expected to happen here, and I'm sorry if things didn't work out like you planned. But I was under the impression that you were going to give me more pictures."

"I am having a wonderful time so far. You are nicer than I imagined. I knew from the first time I saw you that you were different. That's why I want to be with you. Do you know that I know everything about you? You were in the army, and you are a hero. I read all about it. You almost died. You got married and had two daughters, but one died. She was pretty. I saw a picture of her with you. Your other daughter is very pretty too. You built a business of some sort, made a lot of money, and you have a brother in jail somewhere. Now you are one of the most important men in the country."

"Wow. You certainly do know a lot about me, but that doesn't mean you know me."

"But I do know you, and I want to get to know you better, much better. And then when you know me better, we can be happy together. We can have an apartment together, and I won't have to work for Clayton anymore, and he won't hit me anymore. I will love you, I promise. I will make you very happy. I know I can."

Steven realized that there was much more going on inside the young woman's mind than giving him compromising pictures. For some reason, she had chosen him as her fantasy savior from her miserable life. Rational thoughts had nothing to do with the situation. He knew all too well how the drugs over time numbed the mind and often reverted it to childlike insecurities. Maybe if he handled this right, he could help her out of her dilemma and him out of his. He had an idea.

Steven sat down on the bed—at the far end—then suggested, "If you give me all the pictures that you have, maybe I can help you get away from Clayton."

Destinee looked up at Steven. There was both hope and suspicion on her face. "If I give you the pictures, how do I know you will help me?"

Though she was a grown woman, he saw her like a child in need. Steven started to reach out his hand, tempted to just reassure her with a gentle touch. Then thought about the bizarre situation he was in and pulled his arms back.

"Trust me, I will help you if you let me. Remember where we first met, at the addiction conference? Those are good people. I can call them for you; they will give you a place to stay. You will be safe; nobody will hurt you."

Destinee moved her long legs over the edge of the bed and sat up near the foot, closer to Steven.

"I listened to you talk about your daughter at that conference. You said you always loved her even though she did mean things to you."

"Of course. My wife and I and her sister all loved her."

"You said she died from an overdose."

"Yes."

"But you are rich, she grew up in a nice house with a family."

"We were comfortable, and Rebecca did have a nice home and family." Steven seemed oddly relaxed talking about Rebecca with Destinee. He assumed she used and abused illegal narcotics as well, maybe that was why. At least she wouldn't be judging Rebecca as others might. He continued talking about his daughter while staring off at the picture of the Capitol lit by the surrounding firework, but he wasn't studying it, his mind was in the past.

"Drug addiction doesn't know any boundaries. Young or old, man or woman, rich or poor, it doesn't matter. My Rebecca was a wonderful person, smart, kind, honest, full of life. But once she became addicted, that all changed. It was like the girl, the daughter I knew, had been stolen and replaced by a stranger."

Destinee reached over, touched Steven's arm, and squeezed it.

He looked at her and gave a small smile of gratitude.

"What kind of girl was she? I mean, before she became addicted?"

Steven chuckled sadly.

"What?" Destinee said. "Please tell me."

Steven smiled. "I remember it like it was yesterday. She was about fourteen. We were riding away from a local stable on the horses we had just borrowed.

Rebecca was a fairly accomplished rider at this time and we rode those same horses often enough. I still don't know why it happened, it just did." Steven chuckled again.

"What happened?" Destinee tugged on Steven's arm playfully. "Tell me more."

"She fell, I mean, she just somehow lost her balance and slipped off the saddle. She didn't get hurt, but she did land in the most awful mess of horse manure you ever saw.

She looked up at me and the look on her face was priceless. I couldn't help it, I started to laugh so hard."

"Oh no!" Destinee laughed.

"But did my Rebecca get mad? Nope. In fact, as she stood up and wiped the manure from her hands and jeans, she looked at me and smiled. I still can't believe she did it!" Steven laughed again.

"What, what did she do?"

"She slowly walked up to my horse with a wide grin on her face. I was laughing so hard I could hardly stay on the saddle. Suddenly, she reached up and tugged me hard. Before I knew it, I was lying in the same manure pile. She then took a fresh pile of horse poop and worked it into my shirt."

"Oh my god!" Destinee put her hand up to her mouth in disbelief. "What did you do?"

"I took a big handful of horse crap and ground it into her jeans. All the while, we were laughing so hard we couldn't stop. The stable hands thought we were crazy."

"You were!"

Steven laughed again. "Yea, I guess we were. Eventually we cleaned ourselves off as best we could and had a very smelly ride home."

"Tell me another, please, this is so fun."

"OK, just one more. That reminds me of the time ..."

Steven shared the story, and then another as Destinee coaxed more out of him.

Steven never forgot about the reason he was in the room alone with the naked girl. But the conversation with her was harmless enough, and he hoped that the more she considered him a friend the more likely he would be to retrieve the photos.

"That's enough about me, what about you?"

Destinee shared stores of her time with her mother and the dangers of hooking and some of the funnier stories of particular customers. Destinee's laugh was contagious, and there was something else about it. It seemed strangely familiar, yet Steven couldn't place it.

"You make me feel almost as good as when I smoke crack. You make me laugh."

"You make me laugh too, Destinee. But can you tell me how you got those pictures?"

"Mama had them. They aren't just of you, most are of different soldiers and different hookers. When I saw you on Oprah, I remembered your face. I went to the box of pictures and found yours. Before she died, Mama told me the pictures were important and to use them to get money. I think Mama stole them from somebody because she told me not to ever tell anybody about them or she could get into trouble. I think that might be why we had to leave Las Vegas so fast. Mama said somebody saw her, and we had to leave."

Abruptly, Destinee changed subjects again, which Steven was starting to get used to. "Do you think I'm an addict? I don't think I'm an addict at least not like all the way. I smoke some crack sometimes, I think I could stop using if I wanted to, but I like it too much. It makes me feel good, so I don't even try. My mama didn't die from an overdose, she just got sick, real, real sick and died."

"I'm sorry about your mother, Destinee. But if you don't stop abusing drugs, you will get very sick too, or die someday from an overdose like my daughter. What happened to my daughter and your mother doesn't have to happen to you. I can call my friends. They would welcome you and help you."

"Would you take me? I mean, would you be with me?"

"Yes, I could call them right now. But I do need those pictures so nobody can hurt me. You don't want anybody to hurt me do you?"

"Oh no, I want to help you. I want to be your friend. You can trust me."

"First we need to build that trust. Give me the pictures, all of them, and I will find a place for you to go so that Clayton can't hurt you anymore."

"Will they give me crack?" she asked sheepishly. "Cause I get really sick if I don't get my crack."

"They will help you, I'm sure of it."

Destinee's phone rang, but she didn't answer it. She looked at the name it displayed and froze. "It's Clayton, I got to go. I didn't think he would miss me so soon." She stood and rushed back into the bathroom in a panic. "If he thinks I'm stealing from him, he is going to hurt me real bad this time," she said as she changed back into her clothes. "Can you really help me?"

"I know I can, but not if you go back to Clayton."

"I don't have any other place to go. I need my crack, and he is the only one who will give it to me. I have to go back. But I brought some pictures; I have even more at home. I promise I don't have copies." Destinee tossed a few pictures at him as she clipped on her short dress over nothing at all.

Steven looked at the three new photos. All were of him and Shatoya. One was fairly innocent looking, the other was the same photo she had already shown him, the third, well the third made the second photo look modest. "What was your mama's name?"

"Jasmine. She could have used 'em for money, but she didn't. Mama was a good person even if she was a hooker."

The name Jasmine Sanford didn't ring a bell. "And what's going to happen to you if you go back?"

"It all depends on Clayton's mood. I was supposed to be out hooking. But I wanted to be with you instead. I had to go across the city from where I live. I thought I would have time tonight to make some money. If I don't have any money, Clayton thinks I'm stealing it. Then he is going to beat me up real bad. I might not be able to see you again for a while."

"Wait!" Steven didn't know if he was thinking selfishly or selflessly. But he couldn't let the girl be beat up and possibly killed by her pimp. He needed the rest of the pictures. Steven thought about the money in his wallet. He had brought extra. He wasn't going to be blackmailed, but he realized that he might have to do a little business if he wanted the pictures back. "I have some money, how much to keep him from hitting you?"

"I don't want your money, I don't need it. He's right; I have been stealing from him. I'll give him all I have, and he'll think I made it today."

There was something special about this particular young woman that appealed to Steven's sense of chivalry. Maybe because Destinee reminded him of his daughter. If only a stranger would have helped her at the right time, maybe she wouldn't have died. He looked at the photos in his hand and at the young black woman in them. Destinee also reminded him of Shatoya. It was certainly a different time and place, but very much the same problem. Both trapped by a situation not entirely of their making.

"How much?" Steven demanded. "I said I wanted to help you, how much?"

Destinee didn't respond immediately. Instead, Steven could see that she was studying him, judging what she saw in his eyes.

"I told you that you would like me once you saw me."

"I don't want you to get beat up, that's all. How much?" he said again.

"Three hundred will make it not so bad. Five hundred and he'll be happy."

"Here, take the five hundred." Steven hastily counted out five from the ten hundreds he had in his wallet. "Save your money, you might need it someday."

Destinee gave Steven a quick kiss on the lips and rushed toward the door, cash in hand.

"Wait, when will I see you again?" Steven said.

"I'll send another e-mail, or text you. But don't call or text me. Sometimes Clayton takes my phone. If he finds out I'm meeting with someone and not getting paid for it, he'll get angry."

As the door closed behind her, Steven stood, dazed, wondering what had just happened.

He locked the door and picked up his drink. The ice had all melted, but he downed everything that was left as he collapsed on the bed, three pictures richer and five hundred dollars poorer.

Chapter 15

Destinee recounted the money as she rushed out of the hotel. She stuffed the cash into her small sequined purse. Before leaving the hotel, she double-checked her hair in a lobby mirror. It was a bit upheaved from the shower she had taken. In her rush to leave, she had forgotten to comb it. She pulled out a brush from her purse and touched up her long, light brown hair. In the mirror, she saw the night manager watching her with some interest.

"Bye Ramon!" Destinee said cheerfully as she finished and walked out the door. Destinee took one glance back in time to catch the mouse-faced little man with the thinning hair watching her backside.

Washington Arms, Room 327:

Steven finished another drink and, for one of the few times in his life, he realized that he didn't know what to do. He smelled of cheap perfume, and a look in the mirror confirmed that he had lipstick smeared all over his face and some on his clothes. He could do little about his clothes, but he could shower and wash the scent off his skin. Steven felt dirty. He had been in a hotel room with a naked woman, not his wife, for the last two hours. Yes, he didn't want it; yes, it had been out of his control; but still, he felt like he was the initiator, not the victim.

Steven double and triple checked the door to make sure it was locked. Then, before stepping into the shower, he looked at his aged face in the mirror. He was old enough to be the young woman's father. He took a wet Kleenex and wiped his face until his cheeks were red from the abuse. Now he really felt dirty. The young woman had kissed him. Had he let her? For even just a few seconds, did he like it?

He stood under the hot water as it softly sprayed over him. His wet hair dripped water over his face, and he let himself become immersed in the relief from the soaking sheets. He completely lost track of time as he went over the strange encounter over and over again.

Steven didn't feel like seeing anyone that night, so he elected to stay in the hotel for the evening. The next morning, he showered again and was happy the hotel had supplied him with a complimentary toothbrush, toothpaste, a comb, and a plastic shaver.

Steven needed to shave off the week's worth of stubble; he had a television appearance scheduled, and he needed to look his best. If he left the hotel through its side door, he was sure he could avoid anyone who might recognize him.

Steven started to shave off the thick growth and realized his hands were shaking. He couldn't stop thinking about the previous night and the photos Destinee had given him. And she said there were more too. Which was bad news. The new pictures she had given him were already worse than he imagined. What else had he been caught doing?

"Shit!" He winced as he nicked himself with the shaver. His neck started to bleed. Eventually, with enough tissue, he managed to slow the bleeding down, then he stopped it completely with a small bit of tissue held in place with dried blood.

Steven drove back to his small apartment to change clothes. He rushed from the underground garage to his unit. The first thing he did when he entered his apartment was to feed the pictures through the paper shredder next to his small desk. That was when he noticed that on the back of each photo was his name. It clearly said, "Senator Steven Westcott." It was a small consolation when they were in a million pieces, but he couldn't breathe easy until he had all the photos. Knowing his name was attached to them made them even more important.

After changing clothes, it was back down to his car and then to his drycleaners to drop off the clothes from the night before. Then it was on to his office where he would need to work at pretending today was just like any other day.

Weeks later:

"I don't care what Senator Rupert wants. His amendment to my bill would take all the teeth out of it. I'm sorry, Mike. Either the senator wants to cosign the bill as is, or he can watch from the sidelines. ... Of course I want the senator's support, but I can't agree to this type of change. Please tell Senator Rupert that I appreciate all his help."

Shannon Johnston burst into his office just as he hung up. "Not now Shannon!" Steven rubbed his brow. "Sorry, Shannon, what is it?"

"Don't worry about Rupert," she said. "Senators Lindel and Fischer are on board and they say they know others who will vote for passage."

Steven didn't know who actually ran his Senate seat, Shannon or him. But right now, it didn't matter. "I hope you're right, because I think I just pissed off Rupert."

"You did, but don't worry about it."

Steven wondered how Shannon knew so much, but thought it better that he didn't question her talent.

"I got a call from both senators' offices; they are in full support. No changes, just like it is. Your bill can finally come out of committee. It's going to a vote, and it's going to pass," Shannon said with conviction.

Steven knew if Shannon said it was so, it was. She was seldom, if ever, wrong. With the two positive committee votes, it would be a done deal. But, hearing it out loud made it all the more real.

In the first weeks following the meeting at the hotel, the strange encounter with Destinee had consumed him. But now, there were times when he didn't even think about it anymore. Steven stepped away from his desk and looked out the window. He stared at the horizon, coming to terms with the fact that his horizon would never be the same again; not as long as the pictures were still out there somewhere.

"Senator," Shannon said. "I know it's not my place, but you don't look happy. You have been on edge, you're coming in late, and you always look tired. Is there something you would like to talk about?"

"Believe it or not, there is a lot you don't know. And no, there is nothing I want to share with you. That will be all. I am very busy."

Steven turned away from the window and looked back at Shannon, who was fighting back tears. Steven lowered his head. "I'm sorry, Shannon. I'm just a bit overwhelmed. I've been working at this a long time. It's hard to believe it will finally happen."

"It's a good bill, Senator, and it's going to help a lot of people. It's going to put a lot of criminals behind bars where they belong."

"I hope so, Shannon. I hope so."

"Are you still meeting with my dad?"

Steven glanced at his watch. "In about an hour at the Capital Grille."

"Try to relax a bit, Senator. Have dad tell you some of his corny stories."

"Thanks Shannon, good advice. Relaxing I mean, not your dad's stories. I believe I've heard them all at least three times."

"Count yourself lucky, I've heard them all a lot more than that."

Washington DC, Capital Grille:

Later that evening, inside the Capital Grille, on Sixth and Pennsylvania, Steven was sitting with his old friend in one of the semiprivate dining areas. "Listen Steve, don't budge an inch on the way your DNA bill is written, not an inch." Teddy Johnston lifted up his glass of scotch on the rocks and knocked down a bit more.

Steven looked at his drink and swirled the ice around in a circle for a moment before responding. "Senator Rupert is pissed. I don't want him working against me, not now when we are so close to getting it passed."

The Capital Grille was so crowded that anyone, except maybe the president himself, could just blend into the noisy throng. It was more like a country club than a grill; a few dead animals with massive antlers graced the dark mahogany walls. The senators were a protected group, and though the restaurant and bar were open to the public, certain areas were unofficially off limits to them, reserved for the regulars. In a comfortable back corner, Steven and Teddy sat on suitably plush leather dining chairs, disturbed by no one.

"Yea, he's pissed, he wanted to hijack your bill." Teddy spoke plain enough and didn't care who heard him.

Steven looked over Teddy's shoulders. It was obvious the closest table had heard Teddy's rant.

"Keep it down, Senator Rupert has ears all over."

"Let him hear. He knows that it's going to happen, and he wants to take credit for writing it. That was why he wanted to change it to meet his personal criteria. Hell, you would be lucky to get second billing by the time he's done with it."

Steven looked thoughtfully into his glass of swirling ice cubes as if the cubes themselves would give him sage advice. Much more calmly, he replied, "Ronald Reagan used to say that you could get a lot done if you didn't mind who gets the credit. Senator Rupert could get this thing passed in an instant."

"Yea, well Teddy Johnston used to say, 'Fuck him!' You don't need him, Steve. Besides, his version would water the thing down so far that it wouldn't mean anything anymore. I threw his version of the bill past some of the supporting police chiefs. They told me that you might as well not even pass the damn thing."

"You what?"

"I got a copy of his additions and changes. I know a few people in the association, so I asked them."

"You got his changes and went to the Police Chief's Association?"

"Yea, sure, why not? I went through their lobbyist."

Steven wasn't upset, just surprised at his friend's initiative.

"They hated it. Fuck him." Teddy finished off his drink with one last swallow. An attentive server saw him hold his empty glass in the air. She came over to the table and Teddy ordered another. "Shannon tells me that it's in the bag. She also tells me that you have been unusually upset lately. And what's up with the beard and mustache? I don't like it."

Anticipating another meeting with the young hooker, Steven had let his beard grow out again. Steven chuckled, picturing Shannon's reaction to the beard. Shannon was more like her old man than either of them knew. Direct, abrupt, fiercely loyal to him, and usually right.

"What's so funny?" Teddy asked.

"Neither does Shannon, and she isn't shy about it either. Did she tell you that I chewed her out?"

"She didn't mention that."

"Well I did, and it wasn't her fault."

"So she is right! She thinks you need a vacation not a beard."

"There's a lot going on, a lot of pressure I didn't expect. I just wanted to change my look a little."

"Whatever. But remember this, if Shannon says your bill is solid, it's solid. Stop worrying so much."

"Your daughter has a talent, and I am lucky to have her."

"Then don't screw it up. Relax a bit, everything is going to be OK."

Teddy Johnston had no idea how badly Steven wanted to believe he was right.

Steven's cell phone vibrated in his pocket with a short burst. A text had come in, probably from Lucille. She usually texted before calling. Steven slid it out of his pocket and with a tap, his phone lit up. The text message on it read, *I'm better now, I got beat up some and I didn't want you to see me that way. I have more pictures to give you. I can meet you this week same place and time.*

"What's wrong?" Teddy asked.

"What? Ah ... nothing. Why?"

"Cause you turned white as a sheet in about two seconds."

Steven was a poor liar, and he knew it, but he made up something just the same. "A friend of mine is sick, very sick."

"Anybody I know?"

"No, no. Somebody I've met recently," Steven said as he stood up. He didn't want to be questioned anymore, so he excused himself.

"Sorry, Teddy, I have to leave. I promised Lucille that I would call her tonight."

"Sure. Maybe you, Lucille, Shannon, and I could get together for dinner soon, Tracy too?"

"That's a great idea. Maybe we can all meet the next time I get home, if that ever happens again in my lifetime."

"We'll make it happen, and soon too. By the way, I'm sorry to hear about your friend."

"My what? Oh, yes right, let's hope he gets better soon."

Steven slung down the last of his drink and then patted his friend on the back, "See you soon, buddy."

Steven walked out, trying to politely maneuver past the group nearest them. "Excuse me," Steven said.

"Certainly, Senator, no problem," one of the men said.

Steven smiled a thank you at him. The man's face looked familiar and Steven was trying to place it when his phone vibrated again, reminding him of the waiting text message. A path opened up in front of him, and he hustled to the door, stepping into the cool night air and some privacy.

"Steven looked up at a streetlight and saw that it was raining. The beginning of October was bringing in the dampness of winter. The evening had started out overcast, but now, water dropped cold and wet on his face.The entrance to The Capital Grille had no canopy so there was no protection. The double concrete lions guarding the door just feet from Pennsylvania Avenue seemed to be scowling as the water darkened their features. Steven pulled out his handkerchief and sneezed into it. Perfect weather for a cold. The strange thing was, he felt as if he deserved to feel miserable.

Steven thought about the message from Destinee. He tried to distance himself emotionally from the young woman. But he had just eaten in the lap of luxury while she was forced to sell herself, and for what? The chance to get smacked around again? The chance to get high again? She didn't have a life, and nobody deserved that.

The doorman signaled to a waiting taxi for him. The rain picked up and the wipers on the cab flip flopped back and forth, literally throwing water at him. He looked up at the sky again, the streetlights reflecting off the falling rain. Steven didn't mind the rain. He felt gloomy and welcomed the soaking.

Steven decided that he would meet with the young woman again. He was certain he could find time on his calendar. Nothing bad had come from the last meeting. In fact, for five hundred dollars, he had gained three photos, any one of which could ruin his career and marriage. It had been well worth it.

While they bumped down the road, Steven deleted the text messages and e-mails from Destinee. He made a note to close down that particular e-mail account. If needed, he could always start another just to communicate with her. Senators had enemies and enemies had a way of finding things if you were sloppy.

Hopefully, with the next meeting, he would get all the pictures. He felt more prepared for her quirky behavior. Had she conned him or had their interaction been real? Steven didn't feel conned; she just didn't strike him as devious. Still, she admitted to stealing from her pimp. But was it stealing when you earned the money in the first place, no matter how it had been earned?

If it was true that the girl had gotten beat up by her pimp, then that made him angry. He didn't have any rights to do that to anybody much less the small girl. Steven wanted to help her but he was enough of a realist to know that if an addict didn't want help, nobody could help them, not even their parents. That was something Lucille and he had to learn the hard way.

Chapter 16

Steven parked his car a block away from the Washington Arms Hotel. He was taking the same precautions as he had before. Three long days had passed since he received Destinee's text inside the Capital Grille.

"Reservation for Mark Fisher."

The hotel manager looked up at him. Steven had hoped that there would be somebody else on duty. No such luck. He was sure the manager remembered him.

Today, Steven wore his blue jeans and the same visor cap. Steven could feel his loaded gun in the small of his back, concealed by an oversized sweatshirt.

"Certainly, sir. I have your key right here. Room 327 is all ready for your stay. How many keys would you like, sir?"

"One key is fine." Steven took the key, realizing that it was the exact same room as his last visit. Was that the manager's way of telling him that he remembered him? And did he know he had met with a hooker?

Check in time was two o'clock. It was now two-fifteen. He had told Destinee to meet him at three-thirty. Avoiding the elevator, Steven carried his small suitcase up the stairs. Once in his room, he placed the cash he had brought inside the room safe.

He cautiously left his room making sure he wasn't being followed. Then he left the hotel out a side door and walked the block to the Billy Goat Tavern so that he could watch the hotel from a safe distance.

"A cup of coffee and some cheese fries," Steven ordered, sitting at a table near the window. The waitress served his coffee, and as soon as she was gone again, he texted Destinee with the room number. Steven's cold had become worse over the last few days, and he didn't feel up to any sort of meeting, but he had no choice. However, he did consider that a good, old-fashioned cold could be an excellent excuse to avoid any intimate contact.

Steven watched the hotel uneventfully for a while.

"More coffee?" the waitress said.

"Please."

"Not very hungry?" The waitress stared at the mostly uneaten fries.

"No, I think my cold has gotten the best of me. But the coffee is just what the doctored ordered."

"I'll be right back. Don't want to mess with doctor's orders."

As three-thirty approached, he saw no sign of her. Then, right on time, Destinee Sanford sauntered into the hotel, pulling her small suitcase again. He slowly sipped on his coffee, then left.

He had planned this meeting differently. His suitcase wasn't an empty prop this time. This time, he brought spare clothes in case Destinee marked the ones he was wearing in some way or tore them or made them reek of perfume.

He had brought extra money too. Though he promised himself that he wouldn't use it to pay off a blackmail. There was a very thin line between a simple business transaction and paying off a blackmail. But he was confident he would know it when he saw it.

The number of things that could go wrong kept growing the longer he thought about the situation. He had to consider that perhaps the first visit had been a test of some sort, a blind test to see if he would show and if he would be alone. After all, he was a US senator; the stakes were fairly high. The holster in the small of his back and the Beretta M9 in it was of some comfort to him.

This time, as he walked up the first flight of stairs, he stopped on the second floor and peered over the railing to the lobby below to see if he had been followed. Not seeing anything suspicious, he went up to his room, prepared—he hoped—for whatever happened.

He took a deep breath as he entered the room. His right hand was behind his back holding on to the grip of his gun. Steven braced himself for anything; not exactly sure what he might see this time.

It didn't take long to find Destinee. She was posed seductively on the bed, her arm propped up on a pillow, her head nested into it. She was on her side, smiling sensuously at him. Her firm breasts were exposed, and the wispy, white cover sheet just barely concealed her thighs, though not her shaved genitalia.

"I've been waiting," she purred.

Steven quickly scanned the room and bathroom. They were alone, and Destinee had already made them both a drink. Hers appeared to be half gone.

"You're bruised again," Steven managed to say just before he rushed to grab a Kleenex off a night stand and sneeze into it.

"This is nothing, you should have seen me two weeks ago. A cop beat me up. He kind of likes his sex rough, but he brings me coke."

"A cop?"

"Yea, I've seen his badge and gun. He's a cop all right."

Steven was furious. "Who, what's his name? I'll have his badge, I promise."

"It's OK. He pays me good and gives me coke."

Steven was about to scold Destinee for her cavalier attitude when he sneezed again.

"You don't sound too good."

"Just a cold. It's nothing." He threw the used tissue into the small wastebasket under the table. "But what about your arm? It looks swollen."

"Oh, the cop didn't do that, Clayton did, I think he broke it. It's starting to feel a lot better now though."

"Didn't you go to the doctor and have it x-rayed?"

"Clayton ain't paying for no doctor. Besides, Clayton wouldn't trust me not to squeal on him, he knows that they would ask me a lot of questions."

Feeling very protective of the young girl, Steven sat on the edge of the bed and slowly and gently covered her up with the remaining blanket. "I talked to the people I told you about. They will take you in and protect you. You don't have to get beat up anymore; you don't have to hook anymore."

"Mr. Senator, you are so nice, I want to love you. Let's not talk anymore, let's fuck. I can fuck real good!"

"Destinee, look at me, do I look like somebody who wants to fuck?" Steven wouldn't normally have called it fucking, but, when in Rome. "I'm feeling terrible."

"I brought something that might make you feel better."

"Can't wait, but please forgive me, I need a moment in the bathroom to clear my nose."

While Steven stepped away into the bathroom, Destinee slipped out of bed, went to her suitcase to get something, Steven hoped it was the rest of the pictures.

Steven saw her go back to the bed through the reflection in the mirror. But what she had in her hand looked more like a notebook than the pictures. He blew his nose once again and took a few extra tissues with him as he walked toward Destinee, who was examining the booklet she had retrieved.

Steven sat down at the edge of the bed as Destinee started to explain. "I made this. I found all of these things in papers and magazines. People leave papers lying around all the time. I would go through them looking for your name."

She sat down next to Steven, still completely naked. Spending literally hours with the naked young girl last time had taken away the novelty.

"See, these are all about you. You are a very important person."

Steven saw the pride and the tenderness in her hands as she turned the pages of the old tattered spiral notebook. It was filled with pictures and articles about him.

"I read all of these. That's why I know so much about you."

"This is very impressive, Destinee." Steven was truly flattered. After examining the pages, he handed the book back to Destinee. Her hand lingered on his, and he let it. Then Steven stood and walked the short distance to the table where his drink was waiting.

The girl had been stalking him in a manner of speaking. In her mind, his life and hers were now intertwined. She wanted something from him, but it wasn't money, at least not directly. Steven was afraid he knew what she wanted, and it was something he couldn't give her. He was playing with explosives of the worst kind: human.

"What happened? How come Clayton beat you up? I gave you money."

Destinee closed the book, ashamed. "I had to use some of it for crack. I'm sorry, but I just had to."

"We have to get your arm looked at. If you brought the pictures, you don't have to go back. I can call someone right now, and they will come and get you, or I can take you there."

"What about my crack? Will they give me crack?"

"Better, they will help you so that you don't need it any more. You won't have to do things just to get high."

"Is that why you don't love me? Because you think I'm a drug addict? I'm not, I know I can quit if I really wanted to."

"I didn't say you were an addict. But quitting can be hard and they can help you."

"I brought more pictures, they're in my bag." Destinee turned her eyes toward the roller bag on the floor. Then looked at the floor seeming to be debating their discussion silently.

Steven walked over to it, tossed it on the bed and opened it. Four pictures were in the case. He sorted through them, disgusted and still not used to seeing himself in such compromising and candid photos.

Destinee looked up and caught Steven's eyes with hers. Steven though she must have read his mind because she said, "I think you're sexy in them."

Steven felt embarrassed thinking about the young woman fantasizing over the photos. He looked up at her and remembered that, in her mind, she was paying him a huge compliment.

"Is your mother in any of these prints?" he asked.

"Nope."

Steven pointed to a shot of him with Shatoya. "Do you know her? Was she a friend of your mother's?"

Destinee didn't even glance at the photo. "Yea, I think so, but I never knew her."

Destinee finished the rest of her drink with a gulp.

Steven examined the four photos a bit closer. They seemed to be like the other pictures: old, not computer printed. That gave him some hope that they were not only the originals, but also the only copies. Steven slid them into his suitcase.

Destinee who was sucking on an ice cube asked, "Are we going to screw? I'm so fucking horny I could scream."

"I told you, I am not feeling well." For once, Steven was happy to have a cold. Then he blew his nose again, not afraid of making a spectacle of it.

"You're stalling, Mr. Senator big shot. Are you afraid of me?" Destinee purposely uncovered herself and formed a seductive pose.

"I'm a bit older than you in case you haven't noticed. I need a little time to ... adjust," he said.

"Come over here, and I'll help you. I know just what to do. I'm quite good at getting men to ... adjust." She mimicked his exact inflection.

"I'm sure you are, but what I need right now is a drink." And boy did he.

He opened two small bottles, one of scotch the other rum and made them both another drink. When he finished pouring his scotch into a cup with some fresh ice, he asked, "So how did your mother come across these pictures?"

"I don't know. She just had them."

Destinee sat up in the bed and propped her back up against two pillows She reminded Steven of a pouting toddler as she folded her arms and pressed a pillow against her breast in a bit of a huff. She realized her immediate desires were to be postponed once again. Her tone clearly indicated she wasn't in the mood for more talk but Steven pressed her just the same.

"She must have got them from somebody?"

With a disgusted sigh, Destinee answered, "I think she got them from another hooker, who stole them."

"Stole them from who?"

"I was just a little girl. I don't know."

Steven handed her the drink, convinced that Destinee knew more than she was sharing.

"So a friend of your mother's stole these pictures?"

"It was a whole box of pictures. My mama said that they were all soldier boys. There were two-way mirrors in the house. When you soldier boys fucked whores, somebody else was taking pictures to blackmail you. I sort of figured it out."

Destinee lifted the rum and coke to her lips and downed most of it.

"Mama said that one of the girls stole the pictures and then left. I think it was the woman you pointed to."

Steven showed Destinee the picture again and pointed to Shatoya. "You mean her?"

Destinee glanced at the photo. "I think that's her. I don't want to talk about this anymore. Can't we just fuck?"

"This is important to me Destinee. Please tell me what happened when you were little."

"My mama became friends with that hooker in Vegas, and she gave them to Mama for safekeeping. I don't know what happened to the other hooker. Mama said she just sort of disappeared one day. Mama kept them because she thought they might be important, but she never did anything with them; she just kept them hid in her closet till she died."

"And how exactly did your mother die?"

"Just got sick and died. Hookers don't seem to live real long you know."

Destinee sat her now-empty drink down on the night table, then tossed off the blankets and moved closer to Steven. "I don't want to talk anymore. Let me show you what I can do for you. I can make you real, real happy."

"Destinee, I'm sure you can, but ..." Steven covered up the girl once again but this time, held her hand gently in his. Steven was not feeling the least bit sexually aroused, and he knew it wasn't because of his cold. He wanted to help her like a father. "You know I'm married. I took an oath that I would be true to my wife. You understand that?"

"I've been with lots of married guys."

"Not this one, I'm sorry. It's not that I don't think you're pretty, because you are. And I think you're very sweet. But I can't get into bed with you. "

But still, the girl's nakedness had served a purpose; Steven had seen that her body was terribly bruised, worse than he had thought. "Destinee, you are hurt and bruised, you can't go back to Clayton."

"She said you were her favorite. Now I know why."

"Excuse me? Who said I was her favorite?"

Destinee hesitated, looking away from Steven's eyes. "My mama's friend."

"What happened to your mama's friend? What was her name?" Steven was becoming suspicious of the girl's story.

"I don't know what her friend's name was, Mama didn't say. Mama was pretty sick the last year and didn't always make sense. But I do know that you only liked her 'cause you aren't with any of the other girls in any of the pictures."

Steven knew that statement was true. He had met Shatoya quite by accident, literally. He had nearly hit her with his motorcycle as she crossed the street near the base. Shatoya had been distracted and hadn't looked for traffic. Steven had been equally distracted looking at the beautiful woman he didn't expect to step into the path of his bike.

He narrowly avoided the startled woman, but felt compelled to stop his motorcycle and check on her just the same. He eventually learned of her profession, but by that time he was already in love and often the only way he could see her was by paying to visit her at 'The House' as they called it.

Destinee still wasn't looking at Steven; she was a good liar, but for some reason, she felt bad to be lying to him. Steven could tell that she was holding back some information.

Destinee sat up and let the pillow against her fall as she tilted her head down and brushed her hair back from her eyes. Steven caught the glistening of tears when she lifted her head back toward him.

"You miss your mother, don't you?"

"Mama was all I had. We were a family, just her and me." Then, with a tender smile and pleading eyes, she added, "But now we can be a family, just you and me. We can be happy together."

"I'm so sorry, Destinee."

Steven handed her the box of tissue paper. She pulled out a few squares to dry her tears with. Steven knew he was becoming emotionally attached to the girl. Maybe he saw too much of his daughter in her. He actually wanted to give her a hug but knew that would give the wrong message.

"You can be happy, and you will be happy when you get off the drugs. Then you will find a man, a good man, a man more your age, who will care about you. You don't want to be with a doddering old man like me. You are young and pretty and smart."

"You think I'm smart?"

"Absolutely, very smart, you just need a bit more school."

Destinee sat back and hugged the pillow against her again as she thought for a moment.

"I don't want somebody more my age, I want you, and I won't let you leave me," she blurted out. "I have more pictures, lots more. You can't leave me or I will show the pictures to the newspapers."

Chapter 17

Steven showed the opposite reaction that Destinee expected. He calmly insisted, "I don't want that to happen. It will hurt a lot of people besides me. But I can't make love with you. Not now, not ever."

Destinee stood in a fit of anger. The fact that she was naked meant little to her. She knew what she wanted and wasn't going to let it slip away. "You are going to leave me just like everyone else. You are no different than any of the johns I fuck. You just want the pictures, and then I'll never see you again. So long whore, here's your money, now shut up, and get out of my life."

"Destinee, you're wrong. I want to help you."

Destinee suddenly felt embarrassed being naked in front of Steven. It hurt her to feel rejected by somebody so important to her. As she hastily got dressed, she ranted. "You think you're too good for me. You think I couldn't possibly be someone you could love. Maybe we should see how much your wife loves you after she sees the pictures of you with a whore?"

"Destinee, I want to be your friend. I want to be a good friend, but I can never be your lover, I'm sorry. I have a wife and a daughter not much younger than you. You know that. I know you do. Please, listen to me. As your friend, I want you to go with me now. I want to take you to a place where Clayton won't be able to hurt you anymore. The people I know will take good care of you. Nobody but me will have to know where you are."

"I don't want a fucking friend. Nobody helps me. Nobody cares about me. And that's the fucking truth isn't it? I thought I could trust you. I wanted to love you. You know what? Screw you!"

Once she was dressed, Destinee stomped about the room still angry and voicing it through her tears. "I don't need you, you'll see. I don't need anybody. I'll leave Clayton, I have some money. I don't need you or your pity."

Destinee saw Steven slowly approach her with arms out. He was offering her some tissue despite her anger.

"Please do it for me. You need a friend, a friend who can help you get out of this kind of life. Let me be that friend."

Destinee let Steven dry her eyes with the tissue. She didn't really want to leave; she believed she did love him. The truth was she did need a friend; a good friend was something she hadn't had since her mother had died.

Steven took her in his big, gentle arms. It felt so good to be held in Steven's strong, loving arms that Destinee cried and cried, but they were tears of relief. She felt something that she hadn't felt for a long time, if ever. She felt safe and loved. She wondered if this was what if felt like to have a father.

Destinee finally managed to stop her tears but found it harder to let go of Steven's embrace.

"Rebecca, you have to do it now," Steven said. "You can't wait."

Destinee pushed herself away slowly and stared up at Steven. He apparently didn't realize his mistake. She looked into his eyes; they were glossy from his own tears. Destinee knew then that she did have a friend, a friend who could never be her lover anymore than his own daughter could be.

"I'm too afraid."

"Afraid of Clayton? He won't find you, I promise."

"No, I'm more afraid of needing my crack; you said they won't give me any."

Destinee was still drying her tears when Steven reached out and grabbed her shoulders. He made her look into his pleading eyes. They were filled with tears and hope.

"They will help you so that you don't need it anymore. They will give you medicine, and a doctor will x-ray your arm and make it feel better too."

Destinee looked down at her sore arm and thought about the of-fer. "There are more pictures of you in my room, hid real good. But someday soon, Clayton says they will tear down the house. Somebody will find them. I have to go back and get them, all of them. Your name is on them."

"No, Destinee, don't go back, it's not worth it. You have to leave it all behind, and you have to do it now."

"I have to think about this some more. I really need my crack. Clayton says I might die without it. And I get real sick when he won't give me any. I don't want to get that sick. It hurts all over."

"My friends can help with that. Let me call them. We'll worry about the pictures later."

"Can I stay with you, at your apartment?" she asked hopefully.

"No, Destinee," Steven said softly.

Destinee wasn't surprised but was disappointed just the same.

"You can't stay with me, that's out of the question. But I can drive you someplace where you'll be safe."

"I can't. I have to go back. The locket my mother gave me is there, and my money, and the rest of the pictures."

Still holding her shoulders, Steven added dryly, "And your drugs. "Don't you see? The more you take the drugs, the more you need them. You can quit, but you have to do it right now."

"I can't, I have to get back to work." Destinee felt ashamed when Steven's arms dropped from her shoulders and his head fell just slightly. She needed to explain. "It's just the way it is. I just want a little more crack first, and then I'll be ready to quit. I'll call you in a week or so."

Destinee saw the disappointment in his eyes. What she didn't see was that Steven was saying a prayer that she would be spared, unlike his daughter.

"Where do you live?" Steven said.

"I live on the other side of town. It's over at the Barry Farm District, on Talbert Street."

"Would you like a ride home?"

"I don't think you should go there; it wouldn't be safe for you. But nobody messes with me because they know I'm one of Clayton's girls. I'll be fine. Besides, it would be bad for me if somebody saw you drop me off."

"I can drop you off at a corner somewhere."

"I can't go home yet. I have to get back to work. I need to bring some cash back or Clayton will beat me again."

"Look, Destinee, I don't want you working tonight. I want you to stay here and rest. It's a warm bed and a clean room. How much do you need so that you don't have to leave until tomorrow morning?"

"It would take a thousand for an all-nighter. But I'll stay with you for free and just use my hidden monies. It won't cost you a cent, honest." Destinee shot a hopeful smile. "We don't even have to do anything. I mean, I won't make you fuck me or anything if you don't want. We can just talk. We can talk all night long; it'll be fun."

"I can't. You know that. But I would like it if you stayed here, alone. At least I would know you were safe for the night. Think of it as a small gift to me. I have a thousand dollars I can give you."

"I don't want your money. That's not why I came here to see you. I don't want to be your whore, I never wanted that. I love you," Destinee said.

"Destinee, I'm sorry. I didn't mean it that way. Look, I care about you too. Please stay here tonight and take the money so that you don't have to worry about Clayton, at least for tonight and tomorrow. It would mean so much to me to know you're safe tonight." Steven stood and cleared his nose one more time.

Destinee looked over the room; it would be nice to have a comfortable place and clean sheets for a night. "I would like that," she finally admitted. "We both know that you don't have to do this. You have been kinder to me than anyone except Mama."

"I'm flattered."

Steven checked his watch; hours had gone by very quickly. He opened up the room safe and counted out a thousand dollars. "Take this, but I want you to promise me something. If at any time you feel in danger, I want you to leave and hide. Then call me. I'll find a way to get you. And don't use this to buy more drugs or Clayton will hurt you more.

"And how do I contact you if I need to?" Steven held his phone out to take down her number.

"Please don't. Clayton watches me real close. Only johns he knows can call me. He checks my phone for messages and e-mails all the time. She lifted herself up on her tiptoes and gave Steven a quick peck on his cheek. "Don't worry, I can take care of myself."

"Please think about my offer before it's too late. OK?"

"I will."

"And one more thing. Could I have a picture of you?"

"You want my picture?" Destinee asked a bit surprised and flattered.

"Yes, I want to remember you just like this."

Steven used his phone to take a close-up photo of her face. Steven smiled. "Perfect, very pretty." And it was. It also looked familiar to him, like he had seen it before but couldn't remember where. The picture was for a hunch. It was a long shot, but he had to play it out.

Steven left the Washington Arms feeling strangely at peace and reassured. The next time they met, he had high hopes he would be able to make a difference in the girl's life. He admitted to himself that she was only one of hundreds of thousands, but it was a start.

At his apartment that night, Steven printed up the picture of Destinee that he'd taken. Then he took the portrait of his daughter down from the wall. He set the two photos next to each other.

All alone in his thoughts, he swirled a couple of ice cubes around in the scotch he had just poured. It certainly could be his imagination running wild, but he saw an uncanny resemblance to his now-dead daughter.

Was it just coincidence? He couldn't take his eyes off of the pictures. The photo of Rebecca was just as he always remembered her. Her face was energetic and happy with a mischievous gleam in her eyes and with skin that needed little makeup. Unfortunately, as the drugs took their toll, her looks had changed too.

Maybe he was only seeing what he wanted to see. He wanted to hug his daughter again, and Destinee was the aberration that would permit it.

Steven recalled another picture he had of Rebecca. It was from just before she died. He pulled up the photo on his phone and expanded it until only Rebecca's face was visible. It was the same face, yet so much had changed.

Rebecca looked pretty, posing with her younger sister; it would be their last photo together. Steven remembered the night well. Rebecca had helped Tracy get ready for her first big dance. The daughters collaborated on clothing and Rebecca even did Tracy's makeup for her.

In the photo, Rebecca was proudly showing off how beautiful her little sister had become under her direction. But on closer, unbiased examination, Steven could also see Rebecca's sunken cheeks and sick-looking sad eyes, her pupils dilated. She was forcing a smile, but the vibrancy was gone. In fact, she didn't even look like the Rebecca he remembered so vividly. She looked like Destinee, eerily so.

The hair was certainly different, but the resemblance was unmistakable. Steven rushed to crop the photo and print it. By the time he had all three photos side by side, the ice in his scotch had completely melted.

He picked up his watered-down drink and absently sipped it. Then he moved away the healthy version of Rebecca and stared at the photos of the two drug-addicted girls. He was sure it wasn't his imagination. They looked like sisters. Had God given him his daughter back? Was God giving him a second chance to save her?

Steven poured himself another drink and walked away from the photos so he could think. How could it be possible? Steven thought of an old quote from Arthur Conan Doyle Sr., the creator of Sherlock

Holmes. "Once you eliminate the impossible, whatever remains, no matter how improbable, must be the truth."

Steven held up a small, clear plastic bag. Inside, were strands of Destinee's hair. When he had excused himself to go to the bathroom he had taken them off Destinee's hairbrush. There was only one other woman in the world he could have fathered a child with.

If Destinee was Shatoya's daughter, there didn't seem to be much resemblance. Certainly skin color hadn't been passed on or the luscious full lips. If Destinee was his daughter through Shatoya, it would indeed be a long shot, but ... the laugh, he had finally remembered why Destinee's laugh sounded so familiar. He hadn't heard that laugh for over twenty years, but there was no mistake; it was Shatoya's laugh too.

The photos tugged at him like a powerful magnet, he walked back to the table and stared at the pictures of the two young women side by side. It certainly looked like a possibility to him. Even Destinee's age and birthdate would be about right. The last name didn't match, but if Shatoya Anderson was running and hiding, she could have changed her name to Jasmine Sanford. His mind could be playing tricks on him, but at this point, he had to know for sure.

In another bag, he put in samples of his hair. He labeled them A and B. Tomorrow, he would mail them to his friend Paul. Paul Willer owned and ran Genepool Medical; his help had been invaluable in writing the law Steven hoped would pass. Steven was sure that Paul would keep things confidential.

At that same time at the Washington Arms:

There was a light knock on the door of room 327. Destinee went to the small peephole and saw her expected guest and opened the door.

Detective Bruce Harmon walked in. "So you missed me, baby?"

"Did you bring some dust?" Destinee was as disgusted with herself as with the man she invited in.

Harmon smiled as he held up a bag of white powder.

Steven had been right. If the drugs didn't kill her, the things she did to get them would. Still, she forced a smile back while swearing to herself that tonight would be her last night with Harmon and drugs. This way she wouldn't have to use the money Steven gave her to buy drugs, and she could keep her promise to him.

"I don't care if you want to screw me, but my arm is hurt real bad so you better not beat me. If you hurt me, I'll have to go to a hospital, and they'll ask what happened."

"Take your clothes off, gorgeous, and let's get the party going."

Chapter 18

During the fall break, Steven left most of his cares behind in Washington to go home to his wife and daughter. When Steven pulled into his driveway, he noticed that the Halloween decorations were up. For some reason he would never understand, Halloween had become a major holiday at their household. He chuckled at the latest addition to the usual array of ghosts and skeletons. There was a huge black spider web made out of ropes, and on that oversized web was a huge spider. It was undoubtedly a collaboration between his wife and his daughter. The special haunted evening was still weeks away, but clearly the family was already getting into the spirit of things.

"Hi, honey," Steven announced as he walked into the house.

Lucille was on the phone when he entered. She hung up then gave him a quick kiss hello. "Wow, you taste good," Steven whispered into her ear.

"Thank you. Tracy should be home soon."

Lucille went to the small bar and poured Steven a glass of wine. "Welcome home. I heard a little celebration is called for."

"Oh ... and what would that be for?"

"I've heard through the grape vine that soon Westcott's law will rule the land."

Steven took the glass of wine with a smile.

"Really? And what grape vine is that?"

"Secret sources. If I told you, I would have to kill you."

"Well I hope your grape vine is right. Things are looking fairly positive right now."

"That's good, very good. You should be proud. You worked hard at it."

"Thank you, hon. I appreciate that, I really do. It has been a struggle, a very time-consuming struggle."

"I was thinking we could either go out for pizza or order delivery from Tommaso's."

"Works for me. Let's go out."

"Do you know who else is very proud of you?" Lucille asked as she picked up a picture of Rebecca and Tracy off the fireplace mantle.

"Do you mean Tracy?"

Lucille studied the picture in her hand. It was from a camping trip. The two sisters were lit up by the glow from the campfire. Each had a wide smile and held a roasted marshmallow up as a trophy.

"Yes, she is very proud of her father. She even talks about you to her friend. Most teens don't even want to acknowledge they have parents. And if Rebecca were here, she would be proud of you too."

Steven's mind went to the scrapbook Destinee had made. That made at least two fans of his. "Tracy is a gem in our lives, I'm proud of her too."

Steven saw a small plate of Halloween candy laying out and unwrapped a piece to nibble on, then asked, "I saw the new decoration out front, whose idea was that?"

"Hers of course." Lucille smiled at the picture still in her hand. "I helped; it was fun. She is growing up so fast. In many ways, she is so much like her sister."

Steven could see the tears welling up in his wife's eyes as she headed for the always-handy tissue box.

"It's hard not to miss her." Steven knew what his wife was thinking.

"Did I tell you about the Halloween party we're planning?" Lucille said, bringing a tissue to her eyes.

"When?"

"In two weeks."

"Ouch. Too bad, I'll be back in Washington. I mean who wouldn't want to be around all those high-pitched, shrieking teenage voices squealing all night long."

Lucille gave a quick smile and repeated, tongue-in-cheek. "Yea, too bad!" Her tears were starting to dry.

Steven gave a slight smirk and shrugged his shoulders.

"You know, the truth is, it does sound fun. I could even give them a scare or two."

Steven rounded his face, lifted his eyebrows, and raised his hands into claws.

Lucille laughed.

"Next year, I promise I'll be around more."

"Don't make promises you can't keep."

Steven wanted to tell Lucille about the flying lessons he was taking and how things would change but thought better of it. Now was not the time.

"What is that all about?" Lucille pointed to a Band-Aid on Steven's neck.

Steven touched his neck where she had pointed. "Oh, that, I keep nicking myself with my razor. It bleeds like a son of a gun. I have a small tag there. I'll have to go to the doctor sometime and have it removed before I shave it right off and bleed to death."

Steven remembered that Destinee had asked him about the Band-Aid on his neck too. It seemed lately that everything reminded him of the young girl. He tried desperately to push the thoughts of Destinee out of his mind. The rational part of him knew that the odds of Destinee actually being his daughter had to be slim to none. He had to admit that it would be a relief to know that she was little more than a stranger whose path had crossed with his. The complications of having a long-lost daughter reintroduced into his life would be immeasurable. He tried to sell himself on the notion that he wasn't responsible for her situation, good or bad. But he was doing a poor job of it.

Still, if she was his daughter, she was his responsibility. And strangely enough, he would welcome that, though he couldn't be so sure about Tracy or Lucille.

"What's the matter?" Lucille asked.

"Oh ... ah ... what, what do you mean?"

"Your face. Suddenly, you were gone, someplace else. I could see it in your eyes."

"Just trying to imagine what it would be like to quit Washington."

"If you did, I would think you're doing it for me. I appreciate the thought, but neither of us would be happy with that. You, Mr. Senator, belong in Washington. The country needs people like you."

"Thanks, honey. Just thinking."

"Stop thinking. You are here for a little R and R so let's have some fun with Tracy while we can."

His wife was right, his family needed his attention and he was devoted to giving them 100 percent of it as soon as he put the new bill to bed.

Just then, Tracy came through the door, dropped her book bag and rushed up to Steven for a quick hug.

"Daddy, Mom said you couldn't be home long."

"Only about a week I'm afraid. So let's not waste a minute of it. How about we go out for pizza?"

At Tommaso's:

As they ate pizza, Tracy seemed excited to have the attention of two parents.

"Did Mom tell you about the party?"

"She sure did. Sounds like a lot of work and a lot of fun."

"Michele Morgan said she would help. I don't want Molly to; she's too bossy. She thinks she knows everything."

"I don't know if I'll be able to be home that weekend."

Tracy took another slice of pizza. Whatever Lucille's thoughts had been, she seemed to have shelved them for her daughter's sake.

"Mom said she didn't think so either," Tracy said with a mouthful of pizza. "That's OK. Mom is buying decorations and everything. Tom Peters said he was coming."

"Boys too?" Dad asked, looking at Lucille.

"She's not ten years old."

"How many people are you expecting? How many people make up a gaggle of teens?"

"Daddy, I can't invite Molly if Becky doesn't come and Becky will only come if Todd comes. Becky thinks Todd likes her, but he's too shy to talk to her. Butt Todd won't come unless Tom does."

"OK, OK, I get it," Steven surrendered. Clearly he didn't know the finer points of teen etiquette.

Lucille chuckled.

"I just hope you two know what you're doing." He laughed, then looked directly at his daughter.

"How about we all go to a movie this weekend? Maybe we can find a scary Halloween movie."

"Daddy, I can't, the school dance is Saturday, and we have to make decorations this Friday. Teresa and Michele are expecting me to help them, and we are all invited over to Molly's for pizza on Friday. Then after the dance, Molly is having a sleep over. Her mother said it was OK; mom already asked."

"I thought you didn't like Molly."

"Daddy, she's like my best friend."

Steven had his mouth open to say something, then decided he was better off just putting some more pizza in it, so he did.

Later that week:

Steven found himself helping out with the school decorations, or at least trying to. It seemed the other adults thought that decorating a high school gym was beneath a senator. Everybody was constantly taking things out of his hands, leaving him standing with nothing to do.

Before he knew it, he had volunteered his wife and him to chaperone the dance. So, come Saturday night, the Westcotts found themselves at a high school dance. Watching their daughter enjoying herself brought back wonderful memories for Steven. They even joined the younger crowd in a dance. Not because they had to, but because they wanted to. He also managed to make his wife laugh a few times.

Back home that evening, Steven took the initiative and handed Lucille a glass of wine. "I had a wonderful time tonight. I can't believe how grown up our little girl is. I swear it was only a month ago she had sworn off boys completely."

"I had a wonderful time too. Tracy is growing up and moving on with her life. Maybe it's time for us to move on with our lives too."

Steven leaned forward and gave Lucille a kiss. She kissed back. Then Lucille suggested. "We have the whole house to ourselves tonight, how about you bring that bottle of wine upstairs with you, and we pretend we are twenty years younger?"

Steven took Lucille's wine from her and set it down, then started to unbutton her blouse and gave her a kiss. "Like you said, we have the whole house to ourselves, let's not waste it."

On the way to Washington:

Back in his car, on the way to DC, the pressures of the world started to fall back onto his shoulders. For a while, he was mostly able to forget the rigors of Washington and the feeling of responsibility for Destinee. Now, his mind raced back to his dual life.

Steven was only a mile out of town when he pulled over. He lifted the phone he used for private calls to check his personal e-mail. There still wasn't one from Destinee, and he was worried.

He was also haunted by his suspicions about Destinee, so he placed a call.

"Genepool Medical," the receptionist answered.

"Paul, please."

"May I say who is calling?"

"Senator Westcott."

There was a pause then a couple of rings. "Hello, Senator."

"Hi Paul, any news yet?"

"Sorry, buddy, not yet. You told me you want me to run this myself."

"Yea, I know, just ... just—"

"Just anxious, I don't blame you. I've started it, shouldn't be long. Do you want me to call you?"

"That would be great, call me on this number. And, Paul?"

"Yea?

"I'm sorry, I mean, well, I don't believe that Tracy isn't my daughter. I just need to know for sure."

"Steven, I get it. This is what we do here all the time. Just a confirmation, and it will be strictly confidential. I promise."

"And, Paul, if I don't answer, don't leave a message. I'll get back to you."

"Understood. I'm sure whatever you think happened didn't. So relax a bit, OK?"

"I know, I'm sure you're right. It's just something I have to know."

"That's what we're here for. I'll be in touch."

On his way, Steven made time to visit his brother at the Pennsylvania Correctional Institute in Schuylkill. Steven walked through the metal detectors then was hand searched. The guards knew who he was but couldn't make an exception.

The visit was face to face. His last visit was limited to a telephone and a glass partition between them. They weren't supposed to touch, but they did share a coke as they talked.

"I just got final word," Ernie announced anxiously. "The parole board meets in a week, and they have agreed to see me. That's a good sign, a very good sign."

"Ernie, that's great. I wish I could grease the skids for you a bit, but it actually could backfire on you. People, especially parole boards, don't take kindly to friendly persuasion."

"I get it," Ernie said. "Good behavior, that's what the warden told me. He wrote a report. I think that did help. There are no guarantees, so I'm trying not to get my hopes up too far. But, if they recommend release, it could mean weeks, not months, and I would be a free man."

Ernie looked over his shoulder at the wandering guard as he passed behind them, close enough to hear their conversation.

"I suppose when you get out, you'll have some sort of supervision."

"I'm sure of that, probably restrictions. No alcohol, drug testing, attending AA meetings, getting a job, that sort of thing. As far as getting a job, I'm willing to work doing anything; I know I can't be too picky."

"Maybe I can help you out there. I do know some people who are always looking for good employees."

The guard did another loop and wasn't bashful about letting the Westcott brothers know he was watching.

"I appreciate that, I do. But I want to do this on my own if I can. I need to prove to myself and others, like Lucille, that I can make it on my own."

"I know you can. You made some bad decisions, that's all. Now it's time to put it all behind you. You're a smart guy. If anyone can do this, you can. But if you need some help, don't be afraid to ask."

"I saw the news, you're making the big time, bro. You're going to get a law passed. You're not very popular with some of the gang guys though. They know they're going back to dealing or whatever when they get released. So they're afraid of your law making it easier to send them back. But most of the guys in here don't care, they think whatever they did was a one-time deal."

"So what do you think?"

"I'm going straight. They can have all the DNA they want.

At the end of the allotted time, Steven gave his younger brother a big hug, which apparently was allowed. "I'm proud of you for getting through this, Ernie."

"You don't have to be proud of me yet. But I promise, I will make you proud someday."

"Just stay clean and out of trouble. If you do that, everything else will work out, trust me."

From the prison parking lot, Steven looked back at the melancholic building. He wondered if he would be man enough to spend years in such a place and still come out the same man, or a better man for that matter.

He didn't have a jacket on, and the autumn weather urged him into his car. October in Washington was a transition month from pleasant fall temperatures to the chill of winter. It could bring anything from sunny and pleasant to an early season snowstorm. On the drive back, Steven enjoyed the best the season had to offer. The last of the fall colors were clinging to the trees.

The time spent visiting with his brother, who was otherwise alone and locked in a dingy cell day after day, made him appreciate his life all the more. Despite Lucille's wishes, he knew he couldn't and wouldn't abandon his brother—not yet. He deserved another chance to get it right. Maybe he was a sucker; a pushover for people willing to take advantage of him and his success. He had made the right decisions. They hadn't. People like Destinee, she didn't have to become a hooker, did she? She didn't have to become an addict; she had choices, didn't she? He wasn't responsible for her decisions any more than she, or Ernie for that matter, was responsible for his successes.

The short visit home had caused Steven to reevaluate his life. He realized how fortunate he was that he hadn't died in Kuwait so many years ago. He had been gifted many years of sunsets and fall colors. Many other soldiers had not been as fortunate, and he thanked those that had fallen and God for his life. Why had he been blessed with a loving wife and daughter? Other men as good as or better than he had died in combat, some right in front of him, one of them in his arms. Was there a reason, was there a plan, or was it just plain old luck? Some win. Some don't.

Steven didn't have the answer and realized he didn't need one. Whether it was a divine plan, or dumb luck, Senator Westcott didn't plan to waste his life. He was here to help others in one way or another. It was something he always knew somewhere inside of him, but just the same, he reaffirmed it to himself as he drove down the freeway.

Chapter 19

The next day:

N ice landing," the instructor said.
"Winds are light and right down runway ten, that made it easy."
Steven didn't take compliments easily.

"Taxi over to the fuel station."

"Lesson over already Gary?" Steven looked at his watch as he pressed on the brakes.

"Not quite yet." With that, Gary Wilson, his flight instructor, opened the door on the small Cessna. "Time for you to solo." He shouted as he closed the door again and walked carefully away from the still-spinning propeller.

Senator Westcott, in his apprehension, pressed his feet into the two brakes harder than necessary. Gary gave a thumbs up.

Reluctantly, Steven gave a return thumbs up. He had heard stories about how your first solo often happened when you were least expecting. This was it. If Gary thought he was ready, then, Steven reasoned, he must be.

Steven taxied back for a takeoff on the same runway he had just landed. He had picked this particular airport for two reasons. First, he had been told that the instructor was first rate; second, the airport was small and far away from the restricted airspace around Washington. To get arrested or fined for breaking one of the new rules about flying around the sensitive area wasn't a headline his enemies needed to see. The airport had three runways and two were grass strips. It was an uncontrolled airport, meaning there was no tower to contact for takeoff or landing. As a student, that made it less intimidating.

Over the local radio frequency in his headset, he heard Gary's voice. "OK, Cowboy, just like we practiced. Go over the pre-takeoff checklist.

Remember the plane is going to accelerate faster without me in it. Just watch the airspeed, the airplane will do the rest."

"Rodger," Steven answered nervously.

I shouldn't have to worry about a crosswind landing, he reminded himself.

"You can do this. Just take it around once in the pattern and land. Piece of cake," Steven heard through the head set.

Steven uneasily looked at the empty seat next to him. If he took off, there would be no instructor to bail him out if he panicked. He could taxi back now and insist he wasn't ready. But, damn it, as sudden as it was, he was ready. If not today, when?

He pressed the throttle full forward while holding the brakes. Steven listened closely to the sound of the engine as it roared to full power. Then he released the brakes and the Cessna 182 quickly accelerated. The broken painted lines of the center of the runway sped by. In fact, it was much quicker than he had anticipated. The airspeed indicator came alive, and before he knew it, the plane felt like it leaped off the runway and into the air. The bouncing and shaking of the small plane stopped as it left the bumpy asphalt and was carried away from the earth. He watched the airspeed indicator, making sure it didn't slow to a critical speed and cause a stall. He knew that if he climbed too fast and the airplane stalled, it would fall out of the sky. There would be a warning—a stall horn was installed—and if it went off, he'd have to tip the nose down and, if possible, add power. It was simple really; keep the airspeed needle in the green area and the airplane would fly just fine.

"Yahoo!" Steven yelled once he was five hundred feet above the ground.

His training kicked in, and he proceeded to climb the aircraft to pattern altitude. At a thousand feet above the field altitude, he proceeded on the downwind leg. There was no turning back now; he had to land it.

Looking out the left window, the airport seemed small and the runway even smaller.

Steven clicked on the carburetor heat. At slower engine speeds during the landing phase, and with the right temperature, the carburetor could ice up and cause the engine to quit. An engine-out landing wasn't on the lesson plan today, he hoped.

He looked out at runway ten. It was parallel to his path. The two other grass runways were clearly visible, but the winds were right down the lone asphalt runway so that was his target. Two thousand feet of asphalt forty feet wide—piece of cake.

"Cessna 182 Mike Delta on downwind for runway 10 Churchville," he announced proudly. "Time to suck it up, Senator," Steven said out loud as he pulled the throttle halfway back.

Airspeed was just as critical during the decent as it was during the climb. Without full engine power, it would be easy to lose airspeed by instinctively raising the nose of the aircraft upward. To keep his airspeed up, he needed to point the nose to the ground.

"Cessna 182 Mike Delta turning left base," he called out again to let any other aircraft in the area know his position.

"Altitude looks good. Watch your airspeed and turn for final," Gary confirmed.

"Cessna 182 Mike Delta on one mile final for runway ten," he announced.

The plane was responding differently than it did with an additional two hundred pounds of instructor next to him. Steven pulled back the power a bit more, afraid he would overshoot the target. "Airspeed check," he said to himself. "Fuel check, mixture check, carb heat check." If he remembered everything, the plane should be ready to land.

The big number ten on the runway was quickly growing bigger in the windscreen. But Steven was too busy concentrating to be nervous. "Airspeed check," he said to himself again. Just as the plane crossed the end of the runway, he pulled the power lever back full. The wings flared nicely over the runway, then a bit of ground effect lifted the plane again. The ground effect had been greater on the lighter aircraft than he had been used to. But he held the yoke back and let the plane settle slowly as it lost lift. Just at the end of his landing flare, he heard the stall-warning buzzer go off, but the wheels settled to the asphalt at the same time. It was a perfect landing. His hands were shaking as he taxied to his instructor's position.

As soon as Steven got out of the now-quiet airplane, Gary came up from behind him with a pair of scissors and promptly cut off the tail end of his shirt. A very small group of his hanger buddies clapped and congratulated him. It seemed even a US senator wasn't immune to tradition. The piece of his shirt was proudly handed to him to be displayed.

At the small airport, it was also tradition for the newly minted solo pilot to host a small party. Because Steven hadn't known he was soloing that day, the small crew took it on themselves to order in sandwiches and soft drinks. Steven proposed a toast to his flight instructor and all present lifted their plastic cups up in a salute as they enjoyed their sandwiches in the cramped flight room.

Leaving the airport in the very best of spirits, Steven peered into the sky and squinted at the morning sun. He smiled as he contemplated how, with a bit more hard work, he would soon earn his pilot's license and be able to make the long commute to and from Peabody, Massachusetts much quicker.

The next day, Steven took a long walk through the National Mall before the start of the Congress session. Known as America's "front yard," the mall was a two-mile stretch of grass and trees surrounded by monuments, memorials and museums. From the steps of the Capitol to the Lincoln Memorial on the Potomac, the mall offered a usually peaceful respite in the middle of Washington.

The high from soloing the aircraft the day before was still with him. Unfortunately, he couldn't share his accomplishment with his family. At least not yet; not until he had his full license.

Temperatures were only in the fifties, but the sun was out and the wind calm. Walking through the National Mall was a spiritual experience for him. A great cross axis, marked by the obelisk of the Washington Monument, descended from the White House to the picturesque Tidal Basin, famous for its blossoming cherry trees.

The walk past the various monuments, and war memorials grounded Steven. It reminded him of who he was and why he was in Washington. He was humbled by the fact that great people had come before him and built what he was merely a custodian of.

His mind drifted to Destinee. He had managed to push her out of his thoughts for most of last week, but now he couldn't stop thinking about her. Strange, he thought, she held his future in her hands as long as she had the pictures, but he knew that, like it or not, he also held hers in his. He was the girl's best chance at a real life.

Steven also knew that the time might come when he had to walk away from her and from the situation. Steven was nothing if not a realist. He didn't believe in miracles, but he didn't believe in coincidence either. Bringing a drug addict and hooker back from the brink wasn't an easy task, and the odds were against him. But that doesn't mean you don't try, he thought. All around him were monuments to people who never stopped trying. With their encouragement, he would persevere.

Steven picked up his pace; the walk through the mall awakened his spirit. He felt ready to do battle, to fight those in Congress that might fight against him. His bill was just; it was right. He would win for the safety of the people he represented, and that was every man, woman, and child of the United States of America.

Back at his small apartment that evening, he kicked off his shoes and checked for new messages. There was nothing from Paul, and the suspense was killing him. So he decided to call Paul. Steven put the phone on speaker as he poured himself a drink.

"Senator, I was just going to give you a call."

"Did you learn anything?"

"Yes, very good news. Tracy is positively your daughter. I was very thorough, one hundred percent guaranteed."

There was a long silence on both sides of the phone.

"Steven, are you there? Did you hear what I said?"

Steven had set his glass down and was filtering both of his hands through his hair. It was impossible. He had been sure his imagination was wrong.

"Yea, sure did, I, I'm ... just relieved. So, no chance of a mistake?"

"Positive. I mean, if it was your DNA and hers, then she is definitely your daughter. All the paternal markers matched perfectly."

The hair on the back of Steven's neck was tingling. He slunk down onto the chair by his phone.

"Listen, Paul, please keep this quiet. I didn't mean to question Lucille's fidelity."

"Say no more, buddy. It never happened. I did it off the books."

"If I have more questions, can I call?"

"Certainly, any time. But trust me on this one. She is your daughter."

"Paul, thanks. You don't know what that means to me."

"Rest easy my friend. Go home and give Lucille and Tracy a great big hug and everything will be fine."

"Good advice. Thanks again."

Steven sat, dumbfounded, rubbing his hands through his hair over and over. He picked up his phone to call Destinee; she had to know. But even as he searched for her number, he realized he couldn't just call her and say he was the father she never knew.

Then he thought of Lucille. How and when would he tell her? And Tracy, Tracy had a sister, a big sister. Was this good news or bad? He didn't know. Good news of course, he corrected himself. It had to be; he had another daughter.

Steven couldn't decide what he should do next. He wanted to call Lucille, but no, he needed to tell her in person. It wasn't the type of thing you casually dropped into a phone conversation. He stood up with his phone in hand to call somebody, but who? He had to tell somebody, anybody. Should the first person he tell be his lawyer or maybe Ernie? He could trust Ernie to help him sort through this, but you can't just call a prison and ask to talk to an inmate.

Steven sat back down at the table, his nervous energy had turned into contemplation. Then Steven thought of Jojo. He could trust Jojo, and Jojo had known Shatoya. The story might actually make some sense to Jojo. He could trust Jojo's advice and make his decisions from there.

"Hi, Tamara." Steven tried to make his voice sound calm.

"Cowboy, I mean, Senator, how are you?"

"I will always be Cowboy to you, Tamara. Is Jojo around?"

"Not tonight. He's working. Anything I can help you with?"

"No, just wanted to shoot the crap. Just tell him I called, and I'll be in touch."

Steven slowly put his phone down on the table and replaced it with his drink. Sadly, he walked into the small living room and stared out at the city lights. He was alone with the information, at least for now.

Chapter 20

Sleep didn't come easy for Steven. After an evening of constantly thinking about his new daughter, he realized how little he knew about her. He only had a vague idea of where she lived: in an old run-down home somewhere on Talbert Street. And even if he did somehow find the right house and her, barging in and trying to take her away could get them both killed.

Though it hurt him not to drive up and down Talbert Street and every other street in the Barry Farm District, he didn't want to put his daughter in further jeopardy. And what if she wouldn't go with him? What if she denied even knowing him? Would her pimp kill him? Even if she did want to leave, her pimp would never let her.

Somehow, he had to meet with her again in the privacy of the hotel room. Convincing her that he was her father might not be that easy. After all, why would she believe him? If it had been a shock to him and hard to believe, how on earth could he expect Destinee to accept it?

Without anyplace else to go, Steven went to his office early. He prayed for an e-mail from her. She had said she would contact him to meet again and warned him not to contact her. Steven had to trust her instincts.

Shannon rapped on his office door lightly.

"Come on in." Shannon stepped inside.

"Good Morning, Shannon."

"Good morning, Senator. I saw your light on, would you like a coffee?"

"Yea, sure. Thank you, Shannon."

Bringing in the coffee, Shannon said, "Remember the university lecture today, it's still scheduled for noon."

Steven was looking at his personal phone, waiting for his e-mail to load.

"Noon, got it. I should probably leave at around eleven. Could you see to it that I'm not disturbed until then?"

"Yes, of course, Senator. But if you do need me, I'll be right outside."

Steven looked up and smiled. "Thanks. I'll be fine."

Steven was itching to talk to Jojo, but if he had worked the night shift, then he would be sleeping now, and he didn't want to wake him. They could talk this afternoon after his speaking engagement.

On his way to Georgetown University Law center for the noon program, Steven drove down New Jersey Ave. He wasn't far from the Washington Arms Hotel. He peeked at his phone again. Nothing from Destinee. That was when the thought struck him. She had said in her letter, "It's a nice hotel, I've been there before." This particular area of town was a sort of an upscale hotel row. It was the perfect spot for a hooker, Steven thought.

Steven glanced at his watch. He was a bit early and had some time, so he turned his car down New Jersey Ave. He knew it was a long shot, but he didn't mind wasting a few minutes driving around. Traffic was light, and his suspicions were right. On a few of the intersections, women were standing in pairs. Funny how he had never noticed them before. A couple of the girls whistled at him and motioned for him to come over and talk. Steven smiled awkwardly at them as he continued past.

Then he saw her, alone, walking—more like sauntering—away with exaggerated hip swings, begging for attention. At least he was fairly certain that it was her. The hair, height, and shape were right. Steven decided to pull over next to the Billy Goat Tavern and wait for the girl to pass so he could know for sure.

Steven glanced over his shoulder at the approaching woman, his heart raced with excitement. It was her. He had found his daughter.

Steven lowered the passenger side window. He was about to shout out, but Destinee came to the open window of his car out of habit. She was used to being approached in this way.

"Senator!" she said. "You shouldn't be here." Just the same, she rushed into his car. "They could arrest you for picking up a prostitute."

Steven hadn't thought of that, so he accelerated the car away from the curb, nervously glancing in his rearview mirror. "I was worried about you. You didn't text or call."

"Clayton, the son of a bitch, trashed my phone. He's watching me real close. I think he knows I'm stealing from him. He beat me up real bad again, but I didn't tell him nothin'."

"That's it," Steven said, "I'm taking you away from him. I have a place all lined up. You'll be safe.

Steven put on his signal to turn the corner then said, "I'm going to pull over, I have something very important to tell you."

"No don't." Destinee twisted her head just enough so she could use the side mirror to look backward. "Clayton is following. Don't stop."

"Destinee, that's what I am trying to tell you. You don't have to worry about Clayton anymore."

"I still do, just for a little while. I have a plan, but I need your help."

"Destinee, you don't understand."

"You don't understand. Clayton can be very dangerous. Now do as I say. I don't have much time. You have to drive around the block and kick me out of the car at the same place you found me. You have to push me out, got it? Like you're pissed at me for something."

"Destinee, I have something very important to tell you."

In deep breaths, she said, "I have something to tell you too, a favor to ask."

Confused, Steven turned another corner then nodded that he was listening.

Destinee's breathing was rapid. "I've been waiting and waiting to somehow see you again. Take this key, you're the only person I can trust; it's for a safe deposit box at Bank First National, Central DC. I've been carrying it with me just in case I found you. I'm so scared. I'm afraid that Clayton is going to find out I have a bank account. I think he saw me go into the bank. Some cash and the rest of the pictures are in the lock box. Go to the bank and take everything. If he gets those pictures first, you'll be in big trouble. I have another key hidden; if Clayton makes me take him to the bank, I'll be able to show him an empty deposit box. I'll contact you somehow as soon as I can."

Steven's head was spinning as he took the key in his hand reluctantly. "Destinee, you don't understand. You don't have to go back. I'll drive you away right now. I'll take you to a place you'll be safe."

"I can't. I can't just yet. I have to go back one more time."

"Why? Why Destinee? You don't have to go back, not now, not ever."

Steven's nervous glances picked up a car that seemed to be following them. "Does Clayton drive a gold Cadillac?"

"That's him," She said sadly.

"You can come with me right now. We'll get away. He won't catch us, I promise."

Steven glanced at Destinee; her eyes were swelling. He could tell tears would be next.

"I can't, not yet. There are some of my mama's things I have to get."

"No Destinee, I'll buy you whatever you need. You don't have to go back," Steven said.

"I can't leave them behind, it's all I have of her; I can't leave them there with Clayton, not her special things."

Destinee looked at Steven, her eyes red and puffy. "Get the pictures and the money. I trust you. You are the only person in the whole world that I trust. I love you so much for caring about me. Nobody else but Mama ever cared about me."

"What does Clayton want?"

"He's making sure I get paid for sucking you off."

"What? Destinee no, I'll go with you; you don't have to go alone."

"You don't know Clayton. He'll kill you and ask questions later. I'll be all right, I promise. Just do as I say."

"But how will I find you again?"

"I'll find you. I will. I know where you work. When you push me out, yell at me, call me a bitch, and swear a lot."

Steven pulled the car over to the curb.

"Now reach over and start pushing me out the car."

Steven pushed Destinee away by the shoulder. He wanted Clayton to see.

Destinee flailed her hands and pushed back. "You son of a bitch. Get your hands off me!" Destinee yelled as she pretended to fight off the attack. Then she opened the car door and cussed on her way out. "You're a goddamn asshole!"

Steven was so taken aback by the sudden name calling, he almost forgot his cue. "Yea, well, you're an asshole too!"

Destinee shot him a disgusted look, slammed the door, then motioned with her eyes for him to drive away.

Steven pulled away from the curb, tossing her the bird as he drove off. He saw the gold Cadillac stop at the curb right after he left, but he also thought he saw a smirk on Destinee's face. She must know what she was doing. Her acting was pretty convincing.

Steven looked down at his hand that was still holding the key Destinee had just given him. He saw a small, bleeding cut. Apparently, Destinee's long nails had scratched him a bit during their mock fight. His hand was shaking, and he couldn't stop it. Everything had happened so fast.

Chapter 21

That evening, in the privacy of his small apartment, Steven dared to take a closer look at the items he had removed from the safe deposit box. He had them locked safely inside his government-issued briefcase. It was more than it appeared from the outside. It was a special government-issued case that had a secure lock and a steel and Kevlar skeleton wrapped in leather. Anything could eventually be broken into, but the case was designed to ward off the casual thief and buy precious time from all others.

Steven turned the dial to the right code and then pressed his thumb against the security reader. With a click, it signaled it was open. He took a deep breath and opened the case. He stared at the three items from a distance, as if by touching them he would somehow contaminate both him and the items.

Tentatively, he picked up the largest envelope. It was a standard eight by ten. In his Senate supply room, he had stacks of the exact same thing. Nothing special at all, yet it scared him to open it. He held it gingerly as if it might blow up in his hands.

Steven had handled explosives with calm steady hands, never afraid of the damage it could do. Today, his hands shook as he reached into the envelope and slid out its contents. Destinee hadn't lied, the photos were every bit as revealing and potentially life-damaging as the previous. The fistfuls of photos were of many different men and mostly the same set of women, including Shatoya. Steven cursed his naivety; certainly the hookers knew that they were the bait for an ugly trap. They had to know that behind the mirror was someone taking photos for the express reason of blackmailing their customers.

It was so many years ago, but the pain he felt was new and real. Staring at the photos, it was difficult seeing Shatoya with other men. Shatoya Anderson. He reflected on her full name to try and distance himself from her. He knew what she was, who she was so many years ago. But seeing pictures of her having sex with other men made him feel sick and ashamed.

Then a thought struck him. In a way, she had betrayed him—not just once, but over and over again. She had to have known that pictures were being taken to blackmail him, yet she never warned him. But she had been trapped just like her daughter was. No, Steven corrected himself, just like *their* daughter was. Steven stared at the face he knew so well. The smooth dark skin, quick smile, luscious lips, and eyes that always seemed to say, "I love you."

But had she betrayed him? Apparently she had stolen the pictures and ran away with them. She had changed her name and, despite hardships, never used the pictures to try and get money from him. Possibly, even probably, Shatoya had gone through great lengths to protect him.

He had more questions for Destinee, but it looked like, unwittingly, her daughter—his daughter—had adopted the quest from her mother. She had protected him too.

Steven quickly glanced through the stack, one at a time. He recognized some of the men from his past. Why he had to look at them, he didn't know. But he had to just the same. Every now and then he would recognize his own features and thank God that he had the photos in hand. Toward the bottom of the stack, the photos changed. One was a small photo of Shatoya and him in a park. Steven remembered that day, that park, even what they had eaten during their picnic. In another picture, they were at the beach. Her body looked gorgeous in the bikini he had bought her at her urging. He smiled as he remembered their innocence. Though in reality, they weren't so innocent.

Another was of them standing in front of the local movie theater. He remembered the day quite well. It was a wonderful evening, with a warm breeze he could still feel. It was just before he had to ship out for Kuwait. That was the evening he asked Shatoya to marry him. She had laughed and asked him if he asked all the hookers he slept with to get married.

Steven thought back to that moment, the picture tipping in his hand. "No!" he had said. "You are the only person I sleep with. And you don't have to be a hooker anymore. We can get married before I ship out." Steven caught himself whispering the words he had spoken over twenty years ago.

Steven remembered Shatoya's response as well. It had haunted him for years. Steven looked at her photo and imagined her lips moving as she said to him, "You are dreaming, Sergeant. Can you even imagine? Sergeant Steven Westcott, a prim and proper East Coast Blue Blood bringing home a southern black hooker. What the fuck do they do to your brain inside those walls? Do you really think that could work in a million fucking years? Just how many promotions do you think you'll get when the brass find out you married a whore?"

Steven remembered his shock at those words. He had expected her to swoon into his arms, not to scoff at his proposal. "We could live anywhere we want. We don't need anybody's approval. And don't call yourself that. You can't help it. You have to live and eat."

Steven clenched the picture in his hand and closed his eyes. The movie that had been his life so many years ago came alive. He heard Shatoya's response.

"Listen, sugar, trust me, it won't work. I know you don't like hearing it, but I am a whore. I do what I do because I want to. Don't ruin the time we have left with silly talk and false dreams. I know my place, and being Sergeant Steven Westcott's pretty uneducated hooker wife is not what I want."

She had put a dagger in his heart. That was the end of the evening and the end of Shatoya for him. The hurt lasted well after deployment. That was the last time he saw her. And though his mind had accepted her refusal, his heart never did.

Steven sent every single one of the pictures through the shredder next to the kitchen garbage can. One by one, he fed them through the whirling sharp teeth. He set them in upside down so that he wouldn't have to look at them again, until he came to the last picture. It was the one in front of the movie marquee and was the hardest to destroy. He took a long last look at his beautiful Shatoya. Then he sent the photo through. The shredder whirred, then fell silent as it shut itself off.

The evidence of the past was now destroyed but not the memories. Steven remembered the most painful part. Shatoya never came to visit him in the hospital, not once, even though he was there for months. Jojo told him that he had called her to let her know where he was, and that he was hurt real bad and needed her. She told Jojo she knew, but that she was leaving town in the morning and never coming back.

Steven stared out at the lights of Washington DC. Suddenly, he understood the hurt Shatoya had caused him. *Shatoya never came to visit because she was pregnant with Destinee? She didn't want him to know she was pregnant because she was afraid he would find out the child was his. Shatoya knew he would insist on doing the right thing. Only that wouldn't have been the right thing for her.*

"I will make it up to both of you," Steven said.

Steven went back to his briefcase and the remaining items. His life had come full circle. Another hooker was in his life. A young woman desperately needed his help, and he wasn't going to let her down. He lifted out a thick letter-size envelope. It was filled with twenties and fifties and hundreds. Steven counted the stack of wrinkled bills. Destinee had managed to steal just over three thousand dollars.

He stared at the crumpled stack. She had risked her life over and over to gain that advantage. Steven thought about how easily he could spend double that amount on a vacation or household furnishing or landscaping and never miss it. He was now making trillion dollar decisions in the Senate. He saw millions of dollars of government money wasted every single day and was powerless to stop it. And here, with a mere three thousand dollars, a hooker was betting with her life that she could change hers.

Another item from her bank was the tattered spiral scrapbook she had made; it was so important to Destinee, she was so proud of the pictures and articles she had found of him. He remembered the day Destinee had showed it to him and how carefully she had turned the pages. It made Steven wonder if she had made the connection between him and her somehow? Did she already know he was her father? Had Shatoya told her? No, Steven reasoned, that didn't make sense; she had wanted to have sex with him and was upset with him when those attempts failed.

Steven lifted the final item. It was a locket; he opened it. Inside were two photos. The first was a photo of a young girl, obviously Destinee. He could see the resemblance to Tracy. The photo was small and creased.

On the other side of the locket was a photo of Shatoya. Steven held it gingerly in the palm of his hand. If he had needed further proof, he had it now. Maybe Destinee didn't know her by that name, but Shatoya was undoubtedly Destinee's mother. Steven could only imagine how precious the locket and any other remembrances of her mother were to Destinee.

Two days later:

Steven couldn't stop the tears. At last he was alone in his apartment, free to cry like a child. His stomach hurt, and his chest felt as if it would explode. Just an hour earlier, he was at his office going about his normal routine. As usual, Shannon had the news on. Steven was just walking through, not even paying attention, when his ears caught the words, "A known hooker was found murdered in the Barry Farm District."

The odds of it being Destinee were nearly infinitesimal. Just the same, he glued his eyes to the television with trepidation. The photo of the victim soon appeared with the announcement that her throat had been savagely slashed. Steven rushed to the bathroom, making it just in time. He threw up into the toilet as his stomach twisted and turned. His pulse had quickened to the point where he thought he was going to have a heart attack.

"Are you OK, Senator?"

Steven looked up from the floor, his head leaning against the cool water tank.

"I'm OK, Shannon," he croaked.

"You don't sound OK, Mr. Westcott, do you want me to get help?"

Steven felt his stomach turn, and he heaved once again into the toilet.

A minute later, the door creaked open. It was Shannon. "Here, Mr. Westcott, use this." Shannon handed him a bundle of soaked paper towels and some dry tissue

"Thanks," was all Steven muttered as he wiped his face.

Chapter 22

Steven sat in his apartment, squeezing the locket. He waited for any further information on the murdered hooker. Reports were long in between; another murder in Washington wasn't headline news.

When the news of the murdered hooker finally came back on, the knot in his stomach came painfully back. The television displayed a close-up of the girl's face. There was no doubt; the ashen white face of the dead woman was Destinee.

"I'll kill the bastard," Steven swore under his breath, meaning every word of it. He was certain that her pimp, Clayton, had been the murderer.

Steven knew death, and had seen it often; he had lost many brothers in arms and had seen the atrocities of war. He had killed his share, sometimes up close and personal with his long blade. Killing Clayton wouldn't be a problem. But losing two daughters in such a short period was something no parent should ever have to experience. Rebecca's death had hit him hard, yet it didn't steel him against another. He had known Destinee for only a short time, but that made it all the worse. Now he would never know her.

Destinee's death was different from Rebecca's. Maybe it was because of the unexpected nature of seeing her dead body on TV. All alone, so very alone even in death.

He rolled his arms into his aching stomach and cried. "I'm so sorry, honey. I wasn't there for you, and I should have been."

Without even knowing he was her father, she had reached out to him and said she trusted him and only him. He was her father, and he had failed her. A United States senator trained in self-defense by the best instructors in the world, a man with money, power, and prestige. Yet, she was dead just the same.

"I never got to tell you that I'm your father, and that I do love you."

Finally, the television news devoted another thirty seconds to the dead hooker. Steven wiped the tears from his face with his sleeve as he stared at the screen. The newsperson announced: "I am with Detective Chelle Saltarie of the DC police. Detective, what can you tell us at this early time?"

"The police have no suspects at this time. However, it is of course very early in the investigation. The police believe the young woman was murdered two days ago and then dumped here in this alley."

Steven quickly realized that his daughter had died the day she gave him the key to her safe deposit box. That day she had said that if her pimp found out what was in it, he would kill her. Steven picked up his phone. He would tell the police about how the girl had been beaten up by her pimp and how she was afraid he was going to kill her someday.

Just as he was about to press the call button, he thought of the consequences. Questions would be immediately raised. *How did he know the hooker? How did he know that her pimp had done it? What about their meetings at the hotel? Why did he meet a young hooker in a hotel? What pictures? Where are the pictures? Did they have sex?*

Steven dropped his head into his hands. If he was tied to the young woman in any way, his career was sunk. Steven knew that nobody would believe the truth; he sure wouldn't. The story was way too crazy. Then he thought of Lucille. Could he expect her to believe him? Just as things were starting to get better between them. This would probably be an ending event. He didn't want to find out. And maybe now Tracy wouldn't have to deal with the fact that her father wasn't the man she thought he was.

There was absolutely nothing to tie him to the young girl besides his own admission. Steven desperately went through his phone, making sure any reference to her was gone. Clayton had destroyed her phone, so they couldn't trace his number back to her. Steven abandoned the e-mail accounts they had used and erased anything connecting him to Destinee. Luckily, he never made the call to Jojo or anybody else. Nobody on the planet knew he'd been with the girl.

Doing nothing about the murder was against every bone in his body, yet it seemed like the only logical course of action. When Clayton Harris was caught and punished, his life would go on as if none of this nightmare had happened. It would be a cross he alone would have to bear for the rest of his life.

Steven made a decision he didn't particularly like and set the phone down on the table. Any competent detective would know the girl had a pimp and would question him. There wasn't much more he could do other than wait for the system to do its thing and hope justice would be served.

Steven walked to his liquor cabinet. He was going to ease his pain the only way he knew how. After pouring a full glass of scotch and then drinking half of it in one gulp, he had a dark thought. If the police or the courts failed to properly convict and punish Clayton Harris, then he was going to take matters into his own hands. One way or another, Clayton Harris was going down.

Talbert Street, Barry Farm District, Washington DC:

Days had passed by the time Detective Saltarie tracked down the murdered woman's home. Precious evidence could have been removed by this time. But she had a knack for finding evidence that a casual criminal might not even know existed.

She was inside an old house that was the centerpiece of a run-down neighborhood. It was two-story, and the outside of it badly needed a paint job it would never see. The windows had bars on them to prevent intruders, which was probably smart because the home was in one of the rougher areas of the Washington DC general area.

Inside, the home didn't look any better than the outside would suggest. She was wandering around the bedroom of the murdered prostitute Destinee Sanford. The bed wasn't made, and the bed sheets were dirty and scattered haphazardly. The room was sparsely decorated. Beside the steel frame bed there was an old wood dresser with a cracked mirror above it.

Clayton Harris, the owner of the home, stood by the doorway as Detective Saltarie inspected the room.

Saltarie asked, "Who is this picture of?"

Clayton Harris looked at the framed picture that had been propped up on the dresser. The big man's hands were behind his back, secured with handcuffs. He was being watched closely by a uniformed officer and Chelle's partner, Detective Pat Marget.

"Why the cuffs? Are you arresting me or not?"

"I'll let you know when and if I get around to it."

Chelle could arrest the man any time she wanted even if it wasn't for murder. There were probably drugs somewhere on the premises if she wanted to spend the time to find them. He was obviously a pimp; she could arrest him for operating a house of prostitution.

But of course, the charges wouldn't mean anything. She would end up with hours of paperwork and time in court. He might get some time in jail, but in the end, she wouldn't accomplish anything, and she knew it. It was just the way the system worked.

Chelle focused on her job of catching a killer. She asked again, "The picture, who is it?"

"Destinee's mother," Clayton said.

"I don't see the resemblance," Chelle deadpanned.

"Yea, well, me either, but they both showed up here together, and I didn't ask questions. I assumed she sort of adopted the little tramp."

"Where is she now?"

"Right now she's six feet under."

Chelle thought she might have a connection. "When? How?"

A couple of years ago. Aids, I think. You can check it out."

"Trust me, I will. Mind if I keep this?" the detective asked.

"Be my guest, I sure as hell don't want it."

Then Chelle looked at the pimp with cold, steely eyes and asked, "Where were you four days ago?"

"I was at forty-thousand feet on my way to Vegas."

"Really? And you want me to believe that?"

"Yea, I want you to believe that, cause I was, and I can prove it."

"Good, because if you can't prove it, your ass is mine."

"I can, and you can still have my ass, sweet thing."

"OK, so prove it?"

"I have a plane ticket, and it has my fucking name on it. My boarding pass is still in my bag over by the wall."

Shit, she thought. If he isn't lying—and why would he?—a legitimate boarding pass would give him a plausible alibi. With the heightened security, if TSA said he was on a plane to and from Vegas, then he was. Even if they screwed up, he would have a legal alibi. Clayton didn't know that the coroner had given her a pretty exact time of death. If Clayton was gone during that time, he would be in the clear.

She walked out the small room to where the bag was lying, then motioned to her partner to search it. It didn't take long for him to find two boarding passes. There was one to Vegas and one back to Dulles International. Chelle's eyes went to the flight time information. He was right. According to the ticket, he would have been midroute at the time of death. Even if the coroner was wrong about the exact time, Clayton had hours of time before the death accounted for.

She handed the passes back to Pat. "Check them out."

The alibi seemed too convenient. What were the odds of her first and best suspect being away during the murder and having a perfect defense?

Chelle walked back to Destinee's room. She signaled the officers to escort Clayton into the room too. Once inside, she began opening up drawers with her gloved hand and turning things over with her pen.

"What's this?"

"I don't know, I respect my guest's privacy."

"Yea right, you rape these women whenever you want."

"That's harsh, sweet thing. I love my girls, and they love me."

"I know better, but I also know they're too scared to testify against you."

Clayton gave a smug smile that said it all.

Chelle did her best to ignore the big man's audacity.

Inside a drawer were small photos. One looked like a trip to the zoo, another looked like some sort of school function. Next to them was a small collection of cheap jewelry. "Are these Destinee's things?"

Clayton stepped over and took a serious look at the drawer of trinkets and old photos.

"Most of the shit looks like it was her mothers. I recognize some of it."

Chelle studied the pictures, hoping for some insight. She lifted some of the jewelry gingerly.

"What was the mother's name?"

"She called herself Jasmine."

"And her last name?"

"Sanford, just like the daughter."

"Do you have the mother's wallet, purse, or ID? Anything?"

"The ambulance guys took it when they came for the body."

"What was the name of the ambulance company?"

"I called the police and they called somebody. I don't know. They came and took the body away, and that was it. They asked for her ID, and I gave it to them."

"What happened after that? Where did they take her, what morgue?"

"Hell if I know. They just left with her and that was that. Maybe they told her daughter, but I don't know."

The detective looked at the scum in front of her with contempt. The poor woman had died and nobody even cared enough to worry about her remains, not even her pimp.

"Hey, you don't have no right to judge me. I let the bitch's daughter have her room. What more was I supposed to do?"

"Just so she could take her place. You are such an asshole."

"Yea, well, it was that or making her live on the street. It's easy for you to talk."

Chelle studied the photo she had in her hand. Mother and daughter were at what appeared to be a school function. The young girl was grinning widely; several teeth were missing, which wouldn't have been unusual for a little girl that age. She was holding an award up for the camera. Chelle swore to herself that the daughter's death would be avenged for both women's sake. She walked away from the big black man and continued to look though the small room without much success.

"I'm going to take these things too, if you don't mind."

"I told you, I don't want the stuff, so go right ahead."

"Can you think of anyone else who might have wanted to hurt or kill her?"

"As far as I know, she just did her work and came home. I never saw her with anybody, like, on a regular basis."

"I'll need to talk to all of the girls that live here."

Pat came back into the room and whispered into Chelle's ear. "It all checks, he flew to Vegas on that date and flew back three days later."

She looked at the uniformed police and said, "Uncuff him." She hoped the big black man would do something stupid like run, so she could actually arrest him. Saltarie was sure he did it; she just couldn't prove it yet. But the boarding pass would be a problem if she couldn't punch a hole in it somehow.

"Let me see your ID," she demanded.

Clayton looked confused; probably because she had already checked his identification just before the officers handcuffed him. "Sure, sweet thing, can't get enough of me in person?"

She compared it with Clayton's face. It matched, but with a hat, maybe glasses, somebody could pass as him, maybe a brother.

"Do you have a brother, Mister Harris?"

Clayton's face suddenly wasn't so cocky looking. "Yea, but he lives in Philly."

"Let me guess, he looks a lot like you."

"Fuck you bitch. I didn't do it. I told you."

"I'm thinking he had better have an airtight alibi, or I will be charging both of you. You with murder and your brother as an accessory to a murder." It was still a long shot, but she had made cases before with less to go on. "Cuff him again, and bring him down to the station for more questioning. Pat, find his brother, I don't care if he lives in fucking LA."

Chapter 23

It had taken a week to fully investigate Clayton Harris's alibi and to find his brother. Detective Saltarie hated coming back to the slum dwelling and hated what she was there to say. Clayton Harris answered the door himself.

"What you want, bitch?"

"I've checked out your story," she said as she stared at a tattoo on Clayton Harris's forearm. It was a blue dragon holding a sword in its talons and breathing a red and yellow flame. "In fact, Caesar's was good enough to provide me with a video of you gambling in Las Vegas on the night in question. It was you. I saw your tattoo. Your brother also checks out and so does the plane ticket."

"Then why the long face, sweet thing? Everything is right with the world. Maybe now you and me, we can get it on. I mean as long as I'm innocent and all."

"Fuck you," Chelle sneered. Her blue-suited backup was ready with his gun in case she or Clayton erupted.

"As you said, sweet thing, my alibi is solid. I didn't kill the bitch, not that she didn't have it coming."

"May I come in?"

Clayton stepped out the doorway onto the outside porch.

"No. You said I had a solid alibi."

"You are in the clear. So would you mind telling me why she had it coming?"

"Look, the truth is, I didn't do it, and I don't know who did. Maybe she was stealing from somebody else too."

"What do you mean? Who was she stealing from?"

"The bitch was stealing from me."

Clayton lit up a cigarette. He exhaled a puff of smoke toward Chelle. Chelle backed up, tempted to slap the cigarette out of his hand.

"So you did have motive?"

"Yea, I had fucking motive. But, I didn't do it, and you know it. Like I said, maybe she stole from somebody else too. The bitch was a thief and somebody didn't like it much."

"Mr. Harris, do you mind if I take one more look around the girl's room?"

"If I let you in the house one last time, will you take the police lock off it and let me give the room to another girl."

"Let me inside, and we'll see. If you don't, I can guarantee that if you or anybody else goes in that room, you will be arrested."

Clayton let Chelle in, and she crossed through the kitchen where a scantily clad woman was smoking a cigarette and drinking a coffee. She had a Hollywood rumor-mill magazine in front of her but was eyeing the detective.

Chelle's best hunch had evaporated, her next best guess was that Destinee was killed by a trick gone bad. The truth was, at this point, she had very little to go on. Precious time and capital had been spent tracking down Clayton's brother in Philadelphia and Clayton's time in Vegas. Clayton's brother had a perfect alibi: he had been in jail the whole time. So if it wasn't the pimp, who did it? And why?

Her gut had brought her back to the girl's room. Walking through it again, she saw that Clayton had obeyed police orders and kept it unoccupied. Chelle checked the drawers again and under the drawers. She moved furniture, sure that something had been missed. But again she found nothing helpful. She stepped into the closet and felt all the empty shelves for something besides dust. She checked each and every pocket of the dead girl's clothing—no receipts, no money. On the floor in the closet was a crumpled up sequined pair of jeans. She searched all the pockets even though she was sure they had been carefully searched before. Then she found a pack of matches in a small pocket inside a bigger one. The matchbook read, "Billy Goat Tavern," with an address on New Jersey Ave. It was a start, not much more.

Chelle started to step out of the closet, but the edge of her shoe caught on the side of a raised board. The weight of her foot had pressed a section of old wood flooring down a half inch and raised the opposite end.

She pressed carefully around the area with the sole of her foot, putting on pressure and releasing. Getting down on her hands and knees, Chelle lifted the few loose boards. To her disappointment, nothing was under them. If it had been a secret hideaway, it wasn't anymore. Saltarie reached into the dark crevices, searching for anything hidden within reaching distance. She felt something smooth, metallic. It was very small. Using her fingernails, she was able to lift it and bring it out into the light. It was a key, a small, flat key.

Back at the station:

"Hey, Chelle, heard your case has gone cold. What's up, ace?"

Chelle rolled her eyes as she turned around. She had tried to be chivalrous, but it had become extremely difficult. Detective Harmon had been basking in his own glory the last few weeks.

"Good morning, Detective. I guess that's what I get for assuming the obvious."

"Yea, so the easy solution didn't present itself. I heard the girl's pimp had a perfect alibi. Lucky for him I guess. Looks like you've burned through not just a lot of time and money, but a lot of good will with the Chief too. Oh well, easy come, easy go."

Harmon was right, unfortunately. The murder of the young hooker wasn't her only case, and the sad truth was that her death wasn't the only homicide still not solved. It seemed that Harmon was taking her place as the Chief's go-to person. His case-solved record had improved steadily the last year.

The reality was that the city had only so much money and so much time to spend on each case. Sometimes, priorities had to be set and a hooker that had died because of a drug deal or, like Clayton had suggested, a theft gone bad, wasn't very high on the list.

But that didn't mean she had to stop trying. She had one more lead. It was a long shot, but it deserved some attention.

"It's not over yet, Harmon."

"Well, it better be over pretty soon, for your own sake. Captain promised me the next homicide, which is fine with me; my plate isn't that full right now. Don't know if you heard, but I just wrapped up another one. Guy killed his girlfriend. Said he didn't do it of course, but I proved otherwise."

"Was she stabbed to death?"

"Yea, and we have the murder weapon."

"How many is that now? My hooker was killed with a knife too. Her throat was slit."

"If you're suggesting a serial killer, don't even go there. Just because that seems to be the latest method of killing *du jour* doesn't mean you can turn your case into a serial killer publicity stunt."

"You don't think it's a little too coincidental?"

"Do you want me to go over the evidence list with you? DNA, fingerprints, even the coke we found in his apartment matched.

"Motive?"

"Probably she was threatening to out him to his wife if he didn't keep supplying her with drugs. The guy says he didn't do it, didn't have any reason to kill her. The evidence says otherwise. So you can scratch her off your serial killer theory. The hooker the priest killed too. He also had motive and there was plenty of evidence to convict him.

"Keep thinking like that if you like going down dead ends. Is Polish Locomotive part of your theory too? She was stabbed multiple times. Oh the captain will love that. Why don't you tell him you want to go back and prove he didn't kill the girl? I want to be there for that."

"You know you had better start picking it up a bit, I've been solving two cases to your one. Go ahead, check. Oh and, Detective, there is one other small thing you are missing in your serial murderer theory. It's called unsolved cases all possibly committed by the same person. We don't have any. Correction, I don't have any."

"Fuck you, Harmon. Next time you stop to chat, don't."

Chelle took off out the station, fuming. By the time she got to the Billy Goat Tavern, she had settled down some. She parked her unmarked city vehicle on the street next to the fence guarding the outdoor sitting area. She stepped out of her car and onto the sidewalk. This area of town was close to Georgetown University and was modernized with wide walks and trees surrounded by steel cages to protect them.

But what was just down the street was even more of a coincidence. The Washington Arms. Foot traffic was steady. The location might not be a bad place to set up shop, that was of course, if you were a hooker.

It was late afternoon by the time Chelle went into the tavern and flashed her badge. She showed a picture of the hooker to the man tending the bar. The spritely black man wore the outfit of an old-time barkeep, with a white shirt and a ruffled red stretch band around his right bicep.

"Have you ever seen this woman before?"

"Sure, haven't seen her for a while, but she would stop in for a drink every now and then. She would hang out at the edge of the outside fence. She was a working girl, if you know what I mean."

"You mean a prostitute?"

"I thought she was fairly obvious. I guess you need to be too, in that line of business."

The bartender wiped down the wood counter separating him from Chelle.

"Did you know her name?"

"Yea, sure, checked her ID enough, she looked pretty young, but I can assure you, she was of age."

"No problem there; what was her name?"

"It was just a little strange; I'll have it in a minute." The bartender leaned against the bar and stared just over Chelle's head.

"Like I said, I haven't seen her in a while and after the first few times, I didn't need to see it again. Began with a D, I think, Dusty, no, no not Dusty. Destinee, yea that's it, Destinee. Only, it was spelled differently."

"That's her, and the reason you haven't seen her much lately is because she's dead, murdered."

He went back to wiping the bar top and shook his head, "Sorry to hear that. She never gave me any grief."

"Did you ever recognize any of her customers?"

"Nope, we had an arrangement early on."

"What was that arrangement?" Saltarie asked suspiciously.

"Simple, she could have a drink, but I told her I didn't allow any hooking around my establishment. She respected that. That's why we never had any problems. Lots of hookers in this area, good area, I guess. Most don't give me any problems. The streets are their office if you know what I mean. Everybody knows who they are."

Chelle thanked the bartender. She realized that she could go up and down the street and stop at all the hotels and bars, and they would all say they remember the girl. But that would prove nothing and solve nothing. Yet it wouldn't be the first time that she pulled on a small thread that eventually lead her to a big breakthrough.

Chelle's next stop was the Washington Arms. It was in easy walking distance, so Chelle left her car in the Billy Goat Tavern's parking lot.

Chelle stepped up to the check-in counter and pressed the service bell.

The bell made a small ding. Soon after, a short, portly, and balding man in a logoed sport coat came out from a small office to the side of the front counter.

"May I assist you?" the night manager said.

"I'm Detective Chelle Saltarie." Chelle flashed her badge.

Ramon held out his gloved hand. "Welcome to the Washington Arms, Detective."

Chelle's gaze settle on his white gloves. Ramon held up his hands. "I touch money and suit cases all day long, not to mention shaking hands with visitors. It is all quite filthy, and one can't be too careful these days in preventing the collecting of bacteria and germs."

"I quite understand ... Mr. Hayes." Chelle read his nametag hanging loosely on his dark blue sport coat. "I'm afraid that I'm here on official business, and I was hoping for your help."

She pulled out the photo of the woman again. "Do you recognize her?"

"Ramon slid his glasses down his nose a bit and then answered. "Yes, of course. She was friends with some of our guests."

"She was a hooker." Chelle was becoming frustrated at all the code words.

"Yes, well ... I would have no firsthand knowledge of that, Detective." Ramon sounded insulted.

"Mr. Hayes, I just was wondering if you could help me. She was murdered. Do you remember the last time you saw her?" Chelle smiled at Ramon, realizing that a little honey might be the best way to get information from the manager.

"Please call me Ramon."

"May I see that picture again?"

Ramon reached out his white-gloved hand and held the photo up.

Maybe it was her imagination, but the night manager seemed eager to stand close to her. The manager gave a wide smile. His catlike face and short squat body made her think of the Cheshire Cat from Alice in Wonderland. The white cotton gloves reminded her of white paws.

"I don't remember the last time I saw her. It may have been quite some time ago. She usually never checks in. She just goes to a guest's room and generally leaves alone. Might not even use the front lobby door, so I wouldn't see her at all."

Chelle looked around the lobby and up at the ceiling and didn't see any security cameras.

"No cameras?"

"Our guests don't seem to mind."

"I would imagine some of them actually prefer it that way. Mr. Hayes, if you do remember anything, would you give me a call?" Chelle handed Ramon her card, not expecting a call.

"I will most certainly give you a call if I think of anything at all that might help you." Ramon tugged off the white glove of his right hand and offered it to Chelle.

Chelle didn't know how she could refuse, so she reached out and took his hand in hers. She forced a smile despite the unnatural feel of his scaly skin.

Ramon walked with Chelle to the wide doorway and held the door for her. "Please feel free to visit any time."

Chelle just smiled back and hoped she would never have to return. She walked across the street toward her car and the Billy Goat Tavern. Then an idea struck her. The hotel didn't have cameras, but—Chelle looked up at the steel pergola over the outside seating area of the tavern—the Billy Goat Tavern did.

Senator Westcott's office:

Weeks had passed since Destinee's death, and Steven was becoming obsessed with the guilt of her disappearance. Sleep had become a rare commodity. He had changed, and the most visible changes were seen at work. He had become a recluse. He shut himself in his office and instructed Shannon not to bother him unless he paged her.

It guilted him to no end that he hadn't claimed the body of his daughter. He didn't even know where she was interred, or if her remains were just cremated and disposed of. He had abandoned her and he couldn't forgive himself.

Steven purchased every local newspaper he could find. Maybe somebody would report on the case of the murdered hooker. He couldn't afford to not know what was happening. While he skimmed the papers for any small lead, he also flipped through the local television channels.

Why hadn't the police arrested Clayton yet? Steven was contemplating how he could help the police. How could he lead the detective in the right direction without placing himself in the middle of the investigation? Or was he already? Maybe the police had already found out that he and the girl were seeing each other. Maybe they had made her connection to the Washington Arms. "I've been there before," she had e-mailed him. Maybe the hotel manager had recognized him and the girl and reported it to the police. Maybe he should just call up the detective and tell her everything. Maybe, maybe, maybe. All the maybes were killing him.

The police station:

Chelle tapped her pencil on her desk nervously. It had taken the DNA analysis awhile to get back to her. Now that it did, she was scanning the report on her computer.

There had been no reason to run an expensive familial DNA test on the murdered girl's DNA. Knowing if any of her relatives were in the DNA database wouldn't help to solve the case. But what was important was any DNA that wasn't hers.

The opening notes said that there was a familial match on DNA they had found inside the girl's vagina. Chelle scanned the report past the technical jargon to find out just who her suspect was or at least who they were related to.

Detective Chelle Saltarie's face turned ashen. The DNA markers matched a convicted felon. It didn't take long to track the individual's records. It turned out the convict was in prison during the day of the murder. So that meant the suspect had to be a close relative. The federal prisoner the DNA markers matched had only one sibling, a brother. Chelle's stomach began to churn. If arresting a sports star had been difficult and unpopular, how could she possibly face up to the fact that she had to arrest Senator Steven Westcott for murder?

Chapter 24

Later that afternoon, armed with a search warrant, she hoped to find the final bit of evidence. Chelle tried to imagine a delicate way of handling the task. This wasn't going to be pleasant.

Harmon, Pat, and a uniformed officer were her backups. Chelle knocked on the apartment door. She knew the senator was home because Harmon had been watching the entrance to the parking garage and saw him return for the evening.

Steven opened the door slowly. Saltarie struggled to maintain her best professional voice and a stoic manner. She displayed her badge and announced, "I have a search warrant for your apartment, Senator."

"There must be some mistake, Detective. Why? For what?"

"It's on the warrant, you are the suspect in the murder of a young woman named Destinee Sanford."

"I must object. I have sensitive government information here. There must be a misunderstanding."

Saltarie handed the document to him and the two other detectives entered the apartment not waiting to be invited. Chelle carefully studied the senator. She made sure the uniformed officer guarded the doorway. Nobody was allowed in or out until they were done.

Steven scanned the document. "This is a restricted warrant. You are not authorized to search my office and office effects and that includes my home office."

"I understand, and we won't. Where is your office?"

"Right here, all around you. Where do you think it is in this tiny apartment? Usually I sit at the kitchen table," Steven said as he slammed his briefcase closed, "and maybe I can help you. But you can't see state secrets," he insisted as he pointed to his now-closed case.

"I don't want to know state secrets, just yours."

"Detective, please tell me what this is all about. Why do you think I killed a hooker?"

"I never told you she was a hooker."

Steven realized he had made a mistake, but he tried to recover. "It was on television. You were on television and said she was a hooker."

Steven saw it in Chelle's eyes. In that instant, he knew his credibility had been compromised.

That was when Detective Pat Marget walked out of Steven's bedroom with a flat key in his hand. He handed it to Chelle.

"Where did you get this?" Chelle said. It looked very familiar, very much like the one she had found in Destinee's closet under the floorboard. On closer examination, it had the same stamped number on it. But she needed the other key to compare them side by side to be 100 percent sure.

"It's a safe deposit box key." Steven sounded insulted.

"What bank? Would you mind showing me its contents?"

"I want my lawyer," Steven said.

"I haven't arrested you yet, Senator. Are you sure you don't want to talk to me first? It could save us both a lot of problems, and you a lot of bad publicity."

"Whatever you are fishing for, I want my lawyer present."

"This is a very touchy situation, Senator. If this key matches the one at my office, you will need your lawyer because I will be back for you. I would arrest you on suspicion right now, but you are a United States senator, and fortunately for you, I have to be extra ... well let's say, politically correct. Besides, do you really think you can run from this? You are a public figure and would be recognized wherever you go. And I wouldn't plan on taking your car anywhere; it is being impounded as we speak. Are you sure you wouldn't like to get something off your chest?"

"My lawyer will be in contact with you, your boss and their boss."

The two other detectives were searching every drawer and box and cupboard in the apartment as Chelle stared down the senator. Pat continued his search of the senator's bedroom and private bath while Harmon searched the television room. Photos were taken of the apartment and the only object left alone was the closed briefcase. Chelle stared at it and threatened, "I hope you are not withholding evidence, Senator. I can get you extra time for that."

Chelle looked at the two phones sitting on the table next to the closed and locked briefcase.

"And I will be taking your cell phones, laptop, and electronic tablet."

"Oh no you won't! My phone and laptop are official government property. Off limits, restricted warrant. Remember?"

"The computer had better be or you will be obstructing justice. As for the phones, do you want me to figure out which one is your private phone, or will you surrender it?"

Steven grabbed one of the phones off the table and tossed it to her. "Be my guest."

"We will be in touch, Senator. Oh, and we'll be watching you, so I wouldn't try anything stupid."

****

Steven closed the door after them, then slumped his back against it, suddenly exhausted. As his weight pressed against the door, he whispered a simple word to sum up the situation. "Fuck!"

Steven paced the small apartment. He went to the faucet and poured himself a glass of water, then set it down without tasting it. *Now what?* he asked himself. He had promised the detective that he would get a lawyer. He saw no way around it. His Senate phone was sitting on the table, so he picked it up to make one very unofficial personal phone call.

"Come on, Teddy, pick up. I need you, buddy." Steven was just about to hang up when Teddy Johnston answered.

"Teddy, that you?"

"Hello, Steven, great to hear from you. What's the good word?"

Steven paced the floor between the kitchen and the living room and back again.

"Shit, Teddy, I'm in deep crap here!" Steven's heart was pounding harder than ever.

"Whoa, settle down there, can't be that bad."

"Wanna bet? I'm a suspect in a murder."

"Are you serious?"

"Damn right I'm serious; I've never been more serious in my life."

"Have you been arrested?"

"Not yet, but I think it's only a matter of time. They took my car, my phone, and stuff out my apartment."

"Don't say another fucking word. Steven, as your lawyer, I'm telling you not to say another fucking word over the phone. Just shut up and don't talk to anybody until I get there. I'll drive all night if I have to. Just don't say anything to anybody. Do you hear me?"

"Yea, I hear you. But Teddy, I don't know why they think I killed her."

"Steven, shut up!" Then the phone went dead.

Chapter 25

Pouring his third cup of coffee, Teddy asked again, "How did you meet her?"

"The first time was at a conference on drug addiction."

It was early the next morning. Teddy had gotten little sleep, and Steven had gotten even less. They were having their meeting in the privacy of his Senate office.

"That's when you gave her your e-mail address."

Steven got up from the small conference table and poured himself another cup of coffee as well.

"Yes, a private account for nongovernment and noncritical type of stuff."

"So she sent you an e-mail?"

"Yes."

"But you don't have it anymore?"

Steven sat down at the table again as Teddy did the same. Teddy's yellow notepad was full of notes. He was still trying to understand what had happened and was listening intently, going through Steven's story over and over again to see if he missed something important.

"No, I couldn't take the chance of anybody seeing it. When I heard she was murdered, I made sure I canceled that account, and I never printed her letter out. The account is gone, so I don't know what happens to the e-mails. Erased I suppose. I panicked and made sure I erased, deleted, and destroyed anything that could tie me to her. All texts and e-mails gone."

"So you met the girl several times."

"Yes, to get the pictures back."

"But she wasn't blackmailing you?"

"No, never."

"But you paid her?"

"Shit, Teddy, I didn't pay her. I gave her money so she wouldn't get beat up by her pimp."

"Which means you knew she was a hooker, who you paid money to, but you never had sex, even though you met in a hotel room twice and picked her up off a street corner one day."

"Aww fuck! If you don't believe me, how will anyone else?"

"Good point, and I'm trying here, but you have to understand how this sounds. You got the pictures back, but you shred them, so no evidence there either."

Steven stood up as he pounded the tabletop.

"Of course I shredded the goddamn things. They were burned in the building's incinerator weeks ago. That was the whole point. They were nothing to be proud of."

"Steven, please settle down. I'm not asking anything they aren't going to ask. You have to keep your calm. The detectives found a key. Tell me again about it, and don't leave out anything."

"She was trying to run away from her pimp, and I said I would help her. She gave me a key to a safe deposit box with the pictures in it and some money she had saved."

"So you took the money and pictures out of her safe deposit box?"

"Yes, but that was the last I heard from her, I swear. The next thing I knew, she was dead."

"But you never told the police that you knew her?"

"No, I didn't want them to find out about the pictures."

"You mean the pictures that don't exist."

"Yes! But look, I have the money." Steven pointed to his open briefcase.

Teddy looked at the cash without touching it, and then he gave Steven a look that easily said, *That proves nothing.*

"You have to understand, she was already dead. I couldn't help her, and I was sure that her pimp killed her and that they would arrest him, not me."

Steven pounded on the counter top, rattling the coffee pot.

"Dammit! He did it. I know he did it. Destinee said he would kill her if he found out she was stealing money from him. He broke her arm, he beat her. I saw the bruises."

"You only know what she told you."

"Oh fuck, Teddy. I'm screwed. How did they tie it to me? I saw her only briefly the day she died. She sat in my car. We didn't do anything, honest."

"I'm going to place a call to find out what I can. They have to tell me why you are a suspect."

Teddy called the police department. He had to go through a few people but finally, he was talking to somebody who was willing to share some information with him.

Steven just buried his head in his hands, thinking. He lifted it just in time to see his long-time friend's face turn white.

"What? What?" Steven said.

"That can't possibly be," Teddy said firmly. "I don't believe it."

Steven wanted desperately to hear what was being said but waited in silence.

"My client maintains he is innocent."

Teddy ended the call and spent a few seconds collecting himself and motioned for Steven to sit.

"Sit? Are you kidding me?" Steven paced to the window, rubbing the back of his neck. He walked back to the conference table.

"Sit down, Steven," Teddy instructed calmly.

"I don't feel like sitting down."

"Please sit down, Steve. They have DNA evidence. I am going to ask you a very important question. Please answer me honestly. Remember, I am your lawyer. You can tell me anything and you have to tell me everything. Steven ... did you have sex with the girl?"

"No, never ... Teddy, she was just a little girl."

"Fuck, Steven, she was twenty-one, she was of legal age. Hell, if you didn't pay her, you could legally screw her all you wanted. So let me ask you again. Did you fuck her?"

"No, I didn't fuck her! She was my daughter!"

Teddy Johnston fell back against the bookcase. "What? What are you talking about?"

"I didn't want anyone to know, not even you. You have to promise me you won't tell anyone. Do you hear me? Nobody. Lucille doesn't know, and it's something I have to tell her myself. I ... I ... just haven't been able to. When I heard the girl was dead, I didn't think I had to anymore. Everything is just so messed up, Teddy. I just don't know what to do."

Teddy, who was normally unflappable, walked to the nearest chair and fell back into it, temporarily stunned.

"How ... when? Who?"

Steven sat back down, brushed his hands through his hair before looking up.

"I never knew about her, my daughter I mean. I dated her mother back at Fort Bragg. After Destinee and I met a few times, I got suspicious, I thought she looked an awful lot like Rebecca so I took a gamble and sent her hair sample along with mine to be tested. It turned out to be positive. Destinee is ... was my daughter. And I can get the paperwork to prove it."

It took more than a moment for Teddy to digest the new information. Then he said as calmly as he possibly could. "That was the detective on the phone, and she didn't have anything nice to say about you. They found your DNA on the dead girl and now they have a key that matches one found in the dead girl's room. Let's go over that car ride again."

"Like I said, the last time I saw her was when I found her on a street corner and picked her up. Then she gave me a key. It was about a day or two before they found her body I think."

"Very possibly the day she died. Then what happened? And don't leave anything out. Not anything."

"We just drove around the block in my car. I had just found out I was her father, and I wanted to tell her. That's why I searched her out. But I didn't have time because she was scared and insisted on giving me a key and telling me to get the things she had in her safe deposit box. She was frantic and said if her pimp found the money in it, he would kill her. Then we had the make-believe fight."

"So you touched."

Steven thought about it. "Yea, but just barely. She was afraid of her pimp. She wanted it to look like we were having a fight so she wouldn't have to explain why we didn't have sex, I guess. She swore at me, I swore at her, and then I pushed her out the car. Hell, I even gave her the finger, but it was all an act for her pimp, I swear." Then Steven looked down at his forearm. The scratch had healed, but he remembered it.

"And that was when she scratched me." Steven rubbed his fingers over the general area. "Her fingernail scratched me. It wasn't bad, but it did bleed a little bit. It was an accident. We were pretending."

"Pretending or not, that could very well be where they got your DNA from. Two plus two equals prime suspect."

"Teddy, what am I going to do?"

"There has to be a way to prove what you are telling me, but we just don't know what that is yet. Here is what I do know. Your story does match theirs. They have you on security camera, picking up the girl on the day of her murder in your car. And they have you fighting with her and pushing her out of your car and then driving away the day of her murder. Unfortunately, you must have been fairly convincing because they don't think it was an act. They think you were fucking a whore who was going to go public."

"Teddy, I know how it all sounds and looks, but it's just not true. Her pimp did it. I know it."

"Steven, you have been under a terrible amount of pressure lately. You and Lucille haven't been getting along; you live here, your family hundreds of miles away. You have the pressure of getting reelected and trying to sponsor and pass a bill into law. I'll ask one more time, and you must tell me the truth. Were you seeing a hooker for a little emotional and physical relief? I'm not judging. You're an adult; she was an adult. Even if it's true that you somehow found out she was your daughter, you didn't know it to begin with."

Steven shook his head and looked his old friend in the eyes, tears starting to swell.

"Teddy, I just wanted those pictures back so my family wouldn't be hurt, so I wouldn't be hurt. And she was giving them to me; I didn't have to threaten her or anything. She just used them to make me spend time with her, hoping I would like her and make her my mistress. She wanted out of her miserable life, and I don't blame her. We talked, and the more I got to know her the more I started to like her, but we never had sex. She reminded me so much of Rebecca, I couldn't have slept with her even if I wanted. I tried talking her into going to a clinic. I swear Teddy, even before I knew she was my daughter, I pleaded with her to leave Clayton. But she was afraid. Not because of Clayton, she was afraid of not being able to get drugs. I don't know how anybody could think I would be capable of killing her. My god, Teddy, her throat was slit. That bastard Clayton slit her throat and is going to get away with it. We can't let that happen. We have to prove he did it; that's my only way out."

Teddy looked back at Steven and paced the office in a dead silence. Steven slunk into a chair, a beaten man.

"Steven, I'm not going to lie to you. This doesn't look good. If this girl is your daughter, and I say *if* because I haven't seen any evidence to prove it yet. But if she turns out to be your love child, it's even more incriminating. It's not hard to connect the dots here. Senator doesn't want to be exposed with a drug addict, hooker, and daughter who he went to bed with. And as far as the court or a jury believing you are capable of slitting somebody's throat. Well … we all know that you were trained by the army to do just that."

"What about you, Teddy? What do you believe?"

"I want to believe you, I really do. I guess, as your attorney, I have to believe you."

"Do you believe I killed her?"

Teddy paced the office floor some more, and then he sat on the edge of Steven's desk and looked Steven in the eye.

"No. I believe you didn't and couldn't. But we had better come up with something damn good real soon or nobody else in the world will."

"Why? Why do you believe I didn't do it?"

"I believe that you think she is your daughter."

"She is. Paul at Genepool Medical can confirm the test he did."

"I believe you, Steven, because if you were planning on killing the girl, you wouldn't have wanted to know if she was your daughter first. And if you didn't kill her, the rest of your story seems plausible to me. But that's just me. I know you. To anybody else, it might mean the exact opposite. I have to leave; I have to think. I'm going out to get some air and sort through how to handle this. And one more thing. I don't want Shannon in your office any longer. This is going to get messy, and I don't want her hurt. Besides, with her father as your attorney, it could put her in a compromising position. I'll call if I get any more news.

"If you think of anything, and I mean anything, you call me and tell me. Do not talk to the police or anybody else for that matter. I'm going to reach out to some of the finest criminal defense lawyers I can find. In the meantime, think, and think hard."

Teddy stopped at the door before opening it, he turned around slowly, then said, "You know what's ironic? If you are convicted, this crime will cement your bill into law. The DNA off the girl was searched using the familial technique. Your brother's DNA turned up, except he was in jail. Yours would be the only other match. Congratulations, Senator, your law works."

****

Steven paced his office. DNA didn't lie, yet he was the only person in the world who knew that, in this case, it was lying. Strike that. There was another person. The real killer also knew the truth.

Steven searched his mind for evidence, an alibi, or whatever he needed to prove to the detective that he didn't do it. He couldn't think of anything that would help his case. Then another awful thought crept into his mind. His wife. He had better tell her soon, because this wasn't going to be a secret very long.

Steven knew that, until this was settled, he would be a hostage to the situation. He opened his briefcase and looked at the pile of cash in it. They probably knew by now that the matching keys were for a safe deposit box that belonged to Destinee. There was undoubtedly security video of him entering the bank's depository vault.

Then he noticed Destinee's precious locket next to the pile of cash. Instinctively, he picked it up and opened it and talked to the small photo of Destinee. "My life became instantly different since you entered it, and it will never be the same again. I want you to know that I don't blame you." Then he slipped the locket into his inside suit jacket pocket.

Teddy was right; he needed to know everything, and by that, Steven meant everything. He had nothing else he could do, so he took a yellow legal pad out of his briefcase and started to write down everything he could possibly remember, starting with the letter he received. Steven tried to write the letter exactly as it was written to him. No detail was too small.

The one thing he couldn't put in writing was that Destinee was his daughter. He had sworn to himself that the next person he told would be his wife. And until he did, he just couldn't bring himself to put it in writing, even if it was just for Teddy's eyes.

Steven knew that he had to be the person to tell his wife. He wasn't looking forward to it, but it was his responsibility.

That was when he remembered a small overlooked detail: Destinee's scrapbook. The one she had made of a collection of pictures and articles about him. It would prove that the girl had an ongoing fascination with him. The old and torn spiral notebook was still hidden in his briefcase. If nothing else, it would further corroborate his story to Teddy.

Steven lifted it carefully, as if it might crumble in his hands. He went over the pages. There wasn't any particular order, at least not that he could discern. Early history of his life was mixed with new. What he was really disappointed about was that there was no writing. There was nothing to demonstrate the young woman had made the book. Which meant the notebook could have been made any time by anyone, including him.

The next morning:

As the sun washed light over his eyes, he forced himself upright on the sleeper sofa in his office that he used for late night legislative sessions.

Steven rubbed his sore eyes and scratched at his now two-day's worth of beard. He glanced at the coffee maker and remembered it was out of water. That was just as well because it was also out of coffee.

Lifting his body off the bed took immense effort. What he wanted to do was sleep, to sleep and dream of better days. His feet took him to his desk, and he picked up a photo of his family. It was all of them, Rebecca too, smiling in front of a giant flowerbed that showed the face of Mickey Mouse. Steven smiled at the memory, then set it down as his smile disappeared.

Then he picked up the worn, yellow legal pad that was filled with pages and pages of dates and details. The edges of the yellow pages were turned up from his thumbing them through the night. Unfortunately, besides the incredible story that nobody could possibly make up, he had run across nothing that would exonerate him.

Writing down the timeline and the details of his time with Destinee had been good therapy. Somewhere inside the notes was the clue or clues he would need to eventually prove himself innocent. The problem was, he hadn't discovered them yet. Maybe Teddy would. Steven walked over to his open briefcase and dropped the yellow pad into it like it weighed a thousand pounds.

He showered and washed up in the basement gym. He changed back into the same blue suit he had worn the day before. Steven felt the stubble on his face. There was an electric shaver back in his office, and he made a mental note to use it. Walking back up to his office, he felt as if he was walking up to his own gallows, and, in many ways, he was. Not knowing what the day would bring was emotionally killing him. Any minute now, the staff would be coming in for work. He rushed through the double door of his office, not ready to face his staff yet.

Steven sat at his big, polished desk and placed his hand on the office phone to call his wife, but he couldn't lift it. The weight of guilt over what his family would have to endure as he tried to prove his innocence was overpowering. All he could hope for was that she knew him better than anybody in the world and would know that her husband was telling the truth. He could only hope that she would believe him, but the truth was, he wasn't even sure that he would believe himself under the circumstances.

He stood up again and walked to the window, looking out at the bustle of Washington in the morning, hoping for inspiration. How would he even begin the conversation? "Honey, there's been a bit of a problem in the office I think you need to know about. I'm being charged with murder, and I can't prove I didn't do it. They have evidence I killed a hooker I was meeting with. Oh, guess what? Funny thing was, she turned out to be my daughter from another woman."

Steven decided to present himself to his office staff. They would all be in by now, except Shannon Johnston of course. That would mean questions and gossip. Shannon Johnston never missed work. Maybe talking to them first would help his dilemma. He walked slowly to the doors; never had they looked so big and so ominous.

Steven opened one of the doors and stepped into the front office. The faces he saw were unaware of how their lives were about to be changed. If, or rather when, he was arrested, his Senate seat would for all practical reasons be shut down.

He walked to the water cooler and filled a paper cup, then turned around and spoke to his team. "If I could have all of your attention, I have a small announcement."

This was unusual for the Senator, and the office quickly became hushed.

"Shannon will not be in for the foreseeable future, but I hope it's temporary. Her father is representing me in a sensitive matter, and she didn't want to be exposed to a conflict of interest. I can tell you that there is some damaging false accusations against me. For legal reasons, I can't discuss it, but I would imagine the press will get wind of it real soon. This will probably go to court, and it is there that the truth will come out."

Steven could see the questions in their eyes, but he had told them all that he could at this time, even if it wasn't much. Not wanting to get into a question and answer session, he turned and quietly disappeared behind the fancy mahogany six-panel doors of his office.

He was cleaning up his office from the night before when Teddy came barging through the same mahogany door and broke the quiet. "They're coming for you! The Capitol police are on their way. A guy I posted at the station to watch for unusual activity tipped me off. This is a big deal to the cops, and I'll bet it's already been leaked to the press."

"What?" Steven froze in shock.

"I'm afraid, old buddy, that you are in real deep shit."

Steven slunk down in one of the guest chairs.

"They're going to arrest me? Take me out of my own office in hand cuffs?" Steven looked up at his attorney, his eyes pleading, trying to understand the impossible situation he was in.

"There must be something you can do? Some sort of an injunction. I know some judges, maybe they could help us?"

"They're coming, and we can't do anything about that right now. Look, Steven, I'm going to talk to them first. I'll guarantee you won't resist. You're a US senator with no place to run to. Everyone in the world knows your face. Maybe I can keep them from cuffing you.

"At the very least, we can drape a coat around your hands to hide the cuffs, and it won't look so bad on television. You know the television and cable bastards will play it again and again. Straighten your tie; we want you looking as professional as possible.

Steven stood and did as told. Looking at himself in the mirror, he wished that he had shaved. The man in the mirror looked a lot older than he remembered. He looked tired, and his face was creased with worry lines.

"Remember, let me do the talking. When they come in, I want you to hold your hands in front of you like this and don't move a muscle."

"I want to thank you Teddy. I wrote down everything I could remember, I mean everything. I want to give it to—"

Teddy's phone rang. "Yea, OK got it. They're out in front of the building, about ten officers and Detective Saltarie. I told you they were going to make a big deal of it. As far as they're concerned, you did it. They have all the evidence they need. I'm going into the hall to wait, just stay calm and wait here. Don't say anything to anyone, got it? Nothing. Anything you say can and will be used against you, so just zip it. Let me do the talking. Anything I say, wrong or not, cannot be used as evidence."

Steven felt a cold sweat come over him, and his heart was racing. Out of need, he slunk down onto the nearest chair. He felt light headed like he might faint. Teddy gave him a gentle pat on the back and walked out the office and closed the door.

Steven leaned forward and crossed his arms in front of his stomach. It hurt. He realized that he might never hold his wife again, or hug his daughter, or see her grow up. He could be going to jail for the rest of his life, starting within the next couple of minutes. If anyone in the country understood the conclusive evidence that DNA provided, it was him. Nobody was going to be looking for the real killer because Detective Saltarie already had her man. In short, he was screwed for life.

Chapter 26

If he went to jail now, he didn't believe that he would ever be able to prove his innocence. It certainly didn't look like the police would believe that he didn't do it and spend more time and money looking for the real killer.

Sitting in jail, hoping others would tirelessly seek out the truth wasn't in his nature. It was a sad fact that he wouldn't be the first innocent man that went to jail. Steven abruptly came to the conclusion that he had to discover the truth himself, and he couldn't do that from jail.

"Please forgive me, Lucille," he said out loud.

If he were going to run, he would need cash. He stared at the envelope in his briefcase. He had no choice, so he grabbed it and tossed it into his suit jacket pocket, then he slammed the briefcase closed, locking it.

There were very few things he could do to tip the odds more in his favor, and his military training had taught him never to leave a percentage behind. So in the few remaining minutes, he did what he could. His office was on the fifth floor; Steven contemplated exiting via the small balcony behind his desk. With a rope and proper gear, repelling down would have been a snap. Unfortunately, repelling gear and rope wasn't standard senator issue. Each balcony was two stories apart, so climbing down would be exceedingly difficult, and the last two stories would have to be jumped—climbing them was impossible. The small back office door was the only other way out of his private office besides the huge mahogany doors. The back door was a direct entrance to Shannon's private office.

Steven took the two blankets off the fold-out bed. Then he ran to the balcony and opened the glass door. The air was cold and windy as he quickly tied the end of one of the sheets to the railing. If he didn't slip, he could use the blanket like a rope to get to the third floor balcony directly below him. Tying the other blanket to the next set of rails would possibly get him to the ground, even if he had to jump the last five feet. It seemed doable. Steven tied the second blanket and tossed it down two floors. The wind grabbed it, but that didn't stop it from landing on the balcony below. The wind continued to twirl it and soon it was twisted around the railing.

Steven heard loud voices from outside his office; it didn't sound like negotiations were going very well. He could hear Teddy's voice. "I insist you let me bring you Senator Westcott, I will handcuff him myself."

"Out of our way, or you will be arrested for obstructing an officer!" Steven heard Detective Saltarie shout back.

Steven hoped his escape or at least attempted escape didn't get his friend into too much trouble, but it couldn't be helped. There was no more time for debating right or wrong. He pulled the curtain closed to shield his exit. Then he grabbed his briefcase. It was mostly empty, but his precious notes were in the case, and they could be vital in finding the real killer.

He never heard the rest of the argument.

****

When they found the room empty, Detective Saltarie turned and yelled at the attorney. "You are now the accessory to an escape. Where is he?"

"He was here, he was here waiting for you." Teddy searched the room for his client.

Chelle saw the curtain twisting and turning from the wind of the slightly open glass door. "Check the balcony!" She shouted at the officers closest to the doorway. "Be careful. He is very dangerous and could be armed."

Cautiously, they walked up to the doorway. Chelle drew her gun, covering the two men in blue. Once the curtain was pulled back, they all could see the balcony was clear. Chelle raced past the two officers and out onto it. She lifted the sheet going down to the balcony below. Beneath that was another sheet blowing in the wind, caught on the lower balcony's rail. "Shit!" she screamed.

Chelle had stationed her men at the inside of any exterior doors; they were now in the wrong place. Instantly, she was on the radio. "The suspect has escaped. I repeat, the suspect has escaped. He climbed down the northeast side of the building." Chelle turned to the attorney. "What was he wearing?"

"A suit."

"What color?"

"Blue. Blue," he repeated, "with a white shirt and blue tie."

"He's wearing a blue suit, white shirt, and blue tie." Which Chelle knew would mean half of Washington DC. She turned and looked back at Teddy with fire in her eyes. "You purposely detained us. Arrest him, and don't forget to read the fucking lawyer his fucking rights," she shouted.

****

Senator Westcott looked around the corner of the small back office area. Shannon's office had been empty, so sneaking into it had been easy. Once the commotion started in the main entranceway, everybody had moved to the front office to watch the spectacle of his or her boss being arrested. The private stairs to the lower level wasn't being watched right now.

He still held his briefcase in his hand. Nobody bothered to check the rest of the office, it seemed like his plan worked. His heart was pounding. He was live game now. The stakes couldn't be higher.

Each senator's two-story duplex suite was designed with movable partitions and a small stairs so the senator's entire staff could work in close proximity. Steven had carefully gone down the stairs to the unused portion. His staff had never grown to the point where he needed both floors.

Steven heard sirens wailing outside. He carefully peeked out the back window. He could see policemen on foot, policemen in cars, and policemen on horseback all looking for him. If he thought getting out of his office might be difficult, getting away from the Hart Building might prove impossible. Still, first things first, he was already committed.

Steven slowly opened the lower office hallway door. He peeked to the left and to the right. The inside balcony around the huge atrium was busy with onlookers. Good, he thought, most wouldn't yet know who the police were looking for. The more people moving in the hallways the better camouflage for him.

Steven took a deep breath, then moved out into the hall as if he owned the place. He nervously buttoned his suit jacket. The next big decision was whether he would take the stairs down or the elevator. In a stairwell, he wouldn't know who might be around the next corner. With the elevator, he could at least be sure that no police were on it when he entered. But what happened on each floor would be the risk.

He decided to walk slightly past the stairs in order to better see the elevators. In fact, by leaning over the atrium rail just a bit, he could see down another floor. The elevators one floor down looked clear. Steven glanced back at the door to the stairwell. The decision had to be made.

Just then, the door opened and Detective Saltarie stepped out. Their eyes locked. She quickly raised her gun. "Stop, Senator! You have nowhere to run. The building is surrounded!"

"I didn't do it, Detective, I have to prove it because I know you won't or can't. I know who did it. It was her pimp. I'm sure of it."

"Not possible, checked him out. He literally has an airtight alibi. He was on an airplane heading to Vegas at that exact time."

"That can't be. He's fooling you; he's fooling everybody. I'm telling you. He did it, not me."

"Lay down on the ground, now!" she shouted. "Then we can talk."

"You don't believe me. Nobody believes me. Ask Miss Michaels at the women's center. I was trying to help the girl."

"Fine, that's good. But I still have to arrest you, so don't do anything stupid. I will shoot."

The gun was pointing at his midsection, the largest target.

The odds were now way against him, and he knew it.

Steven lifted his briefcase up in front of his chest and started to back away toward the rail.

"Don't do it!" Chelle said. "Freeze right now. I'm not kidding. That case will not protect you."

"I have to prove I'm innocent or die trying. Tell my wife I love her, and I promise her that I didn't do it." Steven rushed toward the officer. He only wanted to knock her down so he could escape down the stairs. The detective instinctively shot twice with her Beretta 9 mm. Her shots both hit on target.

The sound of the Beretta echoed loudly through the open atrium. The briefcase slammed into Steven's body, but it did its job and deflected the bullets with a shower of sparks.

Saltarie took two more shots. The briefcase absorbed the bullets again. Steven felt the force of the shots pounding into his body. He staggered backward but was still on his feet.

"Senator, I have another six rounds and then another full clip. You can't protect your whole body with that thing. You are not leaving this building, Senator. Please, please set the case down on the ground and then lie down with your hands behind your head or you will soon be a dead man."

Steven backed up against the edge of the railing to the atrium. He looked over the railing at the floor four stories down, then at the detective. Officers were racing into the atrium and up the stairs on both sides. He tossed his briefcase at Chelle and jumped over the railing.

****

Chelle instinctively ducked, which gave him just enough time to disappear. She ran to the railing and saw Westcott clinging onto the canvas tarp that the workers had placed to catch any falling debris. He had slid most of the way down the concave section of tarp. His weight had stretched the canvas down two floors, and then a four-foot section he was on started ripping. The canvas ripped apart as Steven held on for dear life, still two stories up. He fell a bit more as the cloth pulled apart from itself. That was when the canvas caught on a seam and suddenly held fast. The police were now running up each stairwell, convinced he was trapped between them.

The detective called for backup and positioned herself to take another shot. She had to take him down.

She saw Steven trying to swing to some scaffolding. She took two shots. The first one missed, but the second one didn't. Chelle saw it hit her target squarely in his chest as it pierced his shirt. However, Steven's momentum kept him swinging until he fell onto the scaffolding.

Unbelievably, Steven stood up, looking for a way out. Chelle took another shot, and it splintered wood near his face. Steven dropped himself over the edge of the iron scaffold and tried to push it over.

Chelle ran along the upper fourth story balcony of the atrium, looking for another open shot. It was time to put him down for good. Chelle took careful aim, then fired. As the steel structure tipped over its center of gravity. She saw the senator's body flinch and a hole explode into his shirt as the bullet hit his midsection. It was a stomach strike—painful, but probably not fatal.

With a screeching sound of steel against steel and sparks flying, the scaffold slowed its fall and finally stopped on a diagonal with the floor. He was only a few feet off the first floor when he let go and ran for his life.

Chelle stared in disbelief. Nobody could take hits like that and run away. Still, the hits were solid, of that she was sure. He would be losing a lot of blood and would soon be down.

Chapter 27

Chelle ran down the stairs. Her breath was hard. The adrenaline surging through her body made it easy to fly down each floor. She prayed that the senator would stop running and let her help him. He was wounded badly if not fatally. She had never wanted to hurt him and certainly wouldn't want to be responsible for his death.

Escaping was impossible. He was surrounded, and officers were pursuing him inside the building. Now on the main floor, Chelle ran for the exit door the senator had taken. As she ran, she popped out the nearly spent magazine and replaced it with a new clip loaded with ten more bullets. The steel door of the stairwell felt like paper to her as she yanked it open and raced down the stairs toward the underground parking area.

"Block off the parking garage exits. Nobody leaves. I repeat, nobody leaves," she hollered into her radio.

Chelle hid behind a concrete post and listened for the senator. The underground parking structure had multiple floors to hide in. But the senator couldn't stay hidden forever and he couldn't survive much longer without medical help, of that she was sure.

Chelle was breathing hard into her radio. "Suspect was hit. I need an ambulance to the Hart Building." She truly hoped that they would find him in time to save his life. But she also had to keep her officers safe, so rushing the capture wasn't part of her plan. She had to be patient. All she had to do was follow the blood trail. He couldn't escape.

Chelle walked back up the stairs to look over the path Senator West-cott had taken. She looked around the main floor of the Hart building. All exits were guarded; the senator was trapped. She motioned her officers to hold in place as she looked for the path of blood. Slowly, methodically she retraced the senator's steps. She walked all the way back to the tipped scaffold, to where he landed on the floor. There was no blood, not a drop. That was impossible.

Chelle picked five officers to follow her. They ran down the stairs where the fugitive had last been seen. From there, her team cautiously moved from floor to floor, checking between and under each and every car. With no blood trail, it was impossible to know which floor of the parking structure the senator had escaped to. After each floor was secured, they moved on.

On the last floor, Chelle discovered her error when she saw the sign pointing to the Capitol. The bottom-most floor contained the senator's private shuttle train security entrance.

Chelle ran up to the security guard manning the little sign-in booth. He was on his radio. Chelle heard it warning him against the senator's escape.

"Did you see Senator Westcott?" Chelle asked with her heart thumping and her chest heaving in and out from exertion and the adrenaline rush.

The guard looked up at Chelle and pointed down the track.

"Turn it off, shut it down!" Chelle ordered.

The guard raced for the control system. "Center, this is Jack in the basement of the Hart Building. Shut down the shuttles."

Over her own radio, Chelle warned, "The suspect is probably not injured as suspected. No blood was found on scene. The suspect is somewhere between the Hart Building and ..." Chelle looked at the guard for any insight.

The guard looked at his watch. "He could be as far as the Capitol by now, or he could have gotten off at the Dirksen Building."

Chelle had a sinking feeling in her gut. She radioed out, "The suspect could be at the Dirksen Senate Building or the Capitol, consider him armed and dangerous, lethal force is authorized if necessary."

The guard thought for another moment then admitted. "He could really be anywhere by now. The buildings all interconnect."

****

Only minutes before, Steven was counting on the fact that his security card still worked. Steven walked this building every day; this was his turf, and he still had a few tricks up his sleeve. If security had already disabled it, he would be trapped in a dead end, but he had to take the risk.

Three stories down, he stopped running and walked calmly down a concrete ramp. Steven held his jacket together to cover the torn shirt underneath as he approached a security gate. Jack, the guard on duty, hardly paid attention as the light turned green and the gate opened, then said, "Hello, Senator Westcott, how is your day going?"

As calmly as he could muster, Steven replied, "Thank you Jack, just a bit challenging, nothing I can't handle I hope."

"The Capitol subway shuttle is ready to go. Be safe and have a nice day."

Steven boarded the private automatic shuttle express three stories under the Hart Building. Ever since nine-eleven, only senators and their staff could use it. The first stop would be the Dirksen Senate Office Building, and then it would go on to the Capitol. Steven didn't know yet where he would get off. The Capitol police might determine that for him. Another light beeped green and soon a tramcar was ready for him.

Senator Westcott decided to bypass the first stop at the Dirksen Senate Office Building. He hoped his luck held out for a few more minutes. The tram's top speed was fourteen miles per hour. In just over two minutes, it had gone the half mile to the Capitol. His plan was to hide in plain sight by merging with the throngs of tourists.

Steven took in a huge breath and realized it hurt. His chest was badly bruised but the tattered special forces vest that had been just a conversation piece kept in a closet all these years had saved him. It was the exact same vest that had saved him in Kuwait; once again, the Kevlar had done its job. He would be badly bruised by the two shots he had taken, but that was all.

Steven's white shirt that covered the Kevlar vest was shot through and torn, but miraculously, his suit jacket suffered nothing worse than a torn-off button. It was dirty from the scaffolding but otherwise unscathed.

Steven exited the open-air tramcar and thanked the guard. The Capitol Building over the decades had turned into a sort of Grand Central Station. From it, somebody with proper credentials could fan out to the Russell Senate Office Building, the Dirksen Senate Office Building, the Rayburn House Office Building, or the Hart Senate Office Building.

Time was now on his side. Steven tried to estimate just how much time he might have. Certainly there were security cameras documenting his travels. The United States Capitol police were in charge of protecting the Capitol grounds and, incidentally, the congressmen and senators on those grounds. So it would take a few minutes for the USCP to be notified and then receive confirmation that they had the authority to track and arrest a US senator. Searching the cameras would take a few more minutes. That should buy him at least ten minutes, maybe fifteen at the most. Steven pushed his coat sleeve up and checked his watch.

What he needed was a place to hide. And what better place than inside the bowels of the huge five-hundred-and-eighty-thousand-square-foot underground visitor center built on the east side of the Capitol Building?

Because there were auditoriums and offices for senators and congressman inside the visitor center, a tunnel connected it to the Capitol Building. It was built that way so the business of running the country could continue without interference from or to the visitors to the Capitol.

So, instead of walking up and out of the Capitol Building, he walked down a few nondescript hallways until he was at yet another tunnel. This tunnel led to the relatively newly built Capitol Visitor Center, and what he hoped would be throngs of visitors to the Capitol.

Steven walked hurriedly, like he was late for a meeting. He made sure the one button left on his coat was keeping it closed, which covered the bullet-ridden white shirt and body armor.

Steven cautiously exited the tunnel and followed the signs to the main lobby of the visitor center. A few other Capitol employees had passed him in the hallway; he kept his head down while pretending to talk on his phone, hoping none of them recognized him.

Emerging from the tunnel, Steven bypassed the elevator and decided to use the stairs. He checked his watch; five minutes remained of the ten he had given himself. He could start to hear the throng of tourists on the main level as he rounded the last corner toward the first floor.

He dashed around the corner and was both happy and apprehensive at what he saw. There were tons of people, which would help hide him, but he was well known and the little bit of hairy stubble on his face from twenty-four hours of not shaving would hardly conceal his identity. If somebody recognized him and pointed him out, he could be hopelessly encircled and trapped by well-meaning guests.

Luckily, most of the guests were being mesmerized by the view of the Capitol dome through the center's strategically placed skylights. Cameras were flashing and clicking and all heads were staring up as Steven proceeded directly for the north gift shop. He slipped into it and used his credit card to buy an extra-large sweatshirt with a picture of the Lincoln Memorial on it and a hat with an embroidered picture of the Capitol Building.

He carried his bag of souvenirs along with him as he merged into a group of tourists. As the group moved past, the guide walked them to the edge of Emancipation Hall. She pointed to the far west center and down to the original plaster model of the bronze Statue of Freedom.

As the group eyed the allegorical figure from above, Steven checked his watch one more time. The ten minutes were up. He headed for the first bathroom he saw. Once inside, he peeled off his suit coat and tie. Then he slipped on the sweatshirt over his shot-up white shirt. The large sweatshirt nicely hid the bulk of the body armor he was wearing under it. He folded up his blue suit coat and carefully placed it in the paper shopping bag. He took the baseball type cap with the picture of the Capitol Building on it and tucked as much hair into it as possible. He pulled it low on his forehead.

With his disguise in place, he felt a bit more confident to step out into the crowds once again. As he did, he saw Capitol police and DC police chatting and pointing in various directions. The tourists were far too busy listening to guides, reading signs, and examining statues to notice.

Steven ducked back into the gift shop and kept his face hidden among the souvenirs and racks of assorted T-shirts and various other clothing. That was when his phone rang. The caller was Detective Chelle Saltarie.

Steven stared at the phone. The number was blocked, but he knew who it was.

His phone was a detail he had forgotten about. He knew that phones could be traced, but it had only been fifteen minutes since his escape began. He doubted that the detective, or anyone else for that matter, had the time to get authorization to track him yet. Steven shut his phone off.

He saw two police walking past the store. They stopped and scanned the store, looking at all the faces. Steven hid behind the display of men's jackets. Soon enough, they moved on. They didn't know exactly where he was, but they had a good idea. Eventually, the area would be swarming with police.

As the officers walked away, Steven was about to leave the small store when he saw a sign by the register next to him that advertised, "Buy your hop-on/hop-off tour bus tickets here."

"Could you please give me a tour bus ticket?" he asked the clerk.

"One day or two day?"

"The one-day." He used cash to purchase the ticket for the double-decked sightseeing bus. With the pass, he could get on and off a hopefully crowded bus from any of the many stops it made throughout the city. Getting out of the visitor center without detection would have to be his next priority if he wanted to use that ticket.

He was at the south gift shop. The southeast exit was to his right. The exit was also next to a tunnel to yet another building. This tunnel would take the visitors directly to the Library of Congress Building. There wasn't much choice. Those were his only two potential exits, and he had to take his chances with one of them. The tunnel would undoubtedly lead to more security on the other side. But if the main exits were blocked with additional security, he would have no choice but to take it.

He walked down the hall; two police came toward him, so he latched on to a group of tourists, pretending to listen to the guide repeat a bit of something or another that had some sort of historical value.

Steven reached up to tug on his hat, his hand helping to conceal his face. With the hat pulled tight over his hair, the stubble on his face from the night before, and a frumpy looking sweatshirt covering his white dress shirt, his disguise was as good as it was going to get for now. The shopping bag he carried completed his look as he casually stayed as close as he could to other tourists. He stopped when they stopped and looked at the same monuments and sights as they made their way across wide expanse, staring up at the skylight and Capitol Dome whenever possible.

The police all seemed to be moving in his direction. Steven followed the group down the hall to a statue of Julius Sterling Morton of Nebraska, an early Legislature. He heard something about Arbor Day but wasn't really paying attention. He was much more interested in seeing what was happening to visitors leaving the building. But he couldn't see around the corner, so he didn't know if every exiting tourist was being screened or not.

The fifteen minutes he had given himself were over. Now was the time to make his move. So he left the relative protection of the tour group and headed toward the two different exit points. He was going to make a last-second decision, possible a fatal one.

In front of him, a bit of a bottleneck was forming, which wasn't a good sign. Most people were taking the southeast exit, while only a few were taking the tunnel under First Street to the Library of Congress.

In front of him was a young mother pushing a crying baby in a stroller. At the same time, the mother was trying to negotiate with an older child. Steven guessed by the older child's looks that she was about four years old. The little girl was making quite a commotion about not being able to ride like her brother. The young mother looked completely frazzled.

Holding the stroller and rocking it back and forth with one hand to try and pacify the baby, she tried as best she could to hold on to the hand of the protesting tike. The woman strained to look over Steven's shoulder. She was clearly looking for someone else who was apparently somewhere behind him.

An elderly couple holding hands and walking slowly were the first in line for the exit. They disappeared around a corner. Another family of five left with the dad insisting he had left his phone on the car seat.

Steven needed to make his decision soon. Would it be the main exit or the tunnel?

That was when all hell broke out in front of him. The four-year-old had decided to take the bottle away from the baby in the stroller. Mom scolded the child as the baby started to cry. Then the four-year-old tossed the bottle down the small exit hall in defiance. Mom raced down the hall toward the rolling bottle, grabbing the arm of the uncooperative four-year-old.

Steven saw a chance and rushed up to the unattended stroller and pushed it through the exit hall up to the mother just as she caught the bottle.

"I hope you don't mind. I couldn't help but notice you were a bit short handed."

"Oh thank you so much, you don't know the half of it. My husband is here somewhere, but I don't know where. He said go out the east exit and he would meet us while he bought some juice downstairs for the little one. This was such a bad idea."

Steven laughed. "It wasn't that long ago my wife and I were you. There are two east exits, a north and south; he probably went to the other one and is looking for you outside. I can help until your husband shows."

"Oh would you? You are so kind."

"No worries. I'm sure your husband is outside; you'll find him. I'll just help you get out of here, and then I'll be on my way."

The four-year-old had stopped screaming for the moment, probably trying to understand the situation.

The mother picked up the still-crying baby then said, "Janice, climb into the stroller. You wanted to ride in it, so no more arguing, and no more fussing."

The four-year-old looked up at the strange man but decided she had got what she wanted, so she climbed into the now-vacant buggy.

Steven pushed the stroller while the mom rocked the baby gently in her arms, trying to get him to calm down. The Senator pretended he was busy with the stroller and kept his face down. He tucked in gear and shifted things around as he pushed it past the guard.

The guard had of course heard the commotion the four-year-old had been making and was happy to wave the distressed couple through.

Outside, Steven helped the mother find a bench to sit on and parked the stroller. True to his suggestion, in the distance, a man called out and ran toward the woman and children.

"I told you. Have a good day." Steven nodded with his hand on his hat in a near salute.

"Thank you so much," she said as he walked away without turning around.

Steven waved over his head and merged into the relative security of yet another group of tourists. He walked toward the street with them. As he approached the street, he turned his phone back on and flagged down a taxi. As soon as it pulled over, he opened the back door and then apologized, saying that he had forgotten something back at his hotel. The taxi driver left in a bit of a huff with Steven's cell phone going along for the ride.

Walking in the opposite direction, he stopped at the marked tourist stop area. The sightseeing bus came along on schedule and he jumped on it, making his way to the top of the open-deck vehicle. It was a bit cold out so he was left mostly alone. The bus pulled out onto the street and continued down the boulevard.

Chapter 28

Steven walked a few blocks away from where the bus had let him off. The area he was in was mostly industrial. He saw a few old houses, all were unkempt and were interspersed between factories, which were equally uncared for. Steven watched his footing, being careful not to trip over the cracked and upheaved sidewalks.

Washington was a big city, and he wanted to become lost in it until he could come up with a plan. The farthest the series of buses went was to the corner of Martin Luther King Jr. Avenue and V Street. That was where the tourists would be treated to see the Big Chair, which was once billed as the biggest chair in the world—so big that, as a publicity stunt, someone actually lived on top of it for a month.

Steven looked down at his shiny, black Allen Edmonds shoes and his pressed, and creased, dress pants. Even his new clean sweatshirt made him look out of place as he walked past grassy areas that were more trash-strewn field than yard. He was in the Anacostia area. As he remembered from the history of Washington DC, this area of town had started out poor back in the eighteen hundreds and had never given up that unfortunate distinction.

He passed a tattoo parlor and noticed a hand-written sign: "Room for rent." Steven knew he had to get off the streets. It wouldn't take long for the police to guess at how he escaped the Capitol area, and all stops and busses would be searched.

He walked into the store and saw a counter with signs advertising an assortment of body jewelry. Inside a glass case, were smaller signs distinguishing nose rings, navel rings, tongue rings, eyebrow rings, and other displayed items that Steven couldn't even guess what they were for.

"How much for the room?" He asked a fully tattooed young woman, who was guarding the counter. She had three piercings in her lower lip.

When she talked, a metal bar of some sort that was pierced through her tongue clicked on her teeth. "How long you want it?"

"A month?"

"It has a bed and blankets, a hot plate, and a table and two chairs. The bathroom is down the hall and is shared along with a shower. You need your own towel though, and we don't do no laundry. This ain't no hotel. I can show it to you."

"Please." He was less than anxious to see it, but wanted to know what he was getting into.

The room was everything he had expected and much less. But there was a window and a fire escape. He could wash the sheets and fumigate the mattress. The bathroom down the hall was even worse, but his time in the army had often offered him less.

"How much?"

Steven realized the girl was eyeing him up and down, guessing at what he might be able to afford. "Eight-hundred bucks, cash up front."

Steven's face turned red. He came from a credit card world and didn't carry much cash, didn't need to. He did have some cash in his wallet, but it was maybe two hundred tops. But even if she accepted cards, he couldn't use one. It would definitely be traced.

"Thank you, I'll think about it."

Stepping back outside into the sunshine, he thought of the portentous situation he was in. His home was certainly being monitored, so contacting his wife was not an option. And even if he could call someone, who would he call? Teddy was definitely being watched. And even as his lawyer, there were limits to what he could or even would do for him. Steven's thoughts turned to Jojo, *Detective Jojo, he reminded himself. No, that would be bad for both of them.*

Walking in no particular direction, he played over the events of the last hour. In a mere sixty minutes, he had gone from respected senator to a murder suspect on the run.

For the first time in his life, he was all alone. Up to now, even during some of the worst times, he had family or friends to help him. Even in the special forces, Jojo Jones always had his back. Today, suddenly, he had nobody.

Nobody had his back. In fact, not only did nobody have his back, now, all he had were the clothes on his back and enough cash to buy him a few meals. He had to find Destinee's murderer, but that would take time and money. He had neither.

Steven was concentrating more on his situation than his surroundings. When he heard some voices mocking him he picked up his pace and tried to appear as if he knew exactly where he was going. There was a small group of young men watching him from across the street. If he were mugged, he could lose what precious little he did have, if not his life.

Steven walked around the block until he found himself walking toward the Big Chair. It was the safest place he could think of, but it was also a tourist stop, which meant it may be under surveillance. He couldn't continue to wander the street, but he couldn't just check into the nearest Marriott Hotel either. The dingy old room was his only option, but how could he come up with the money? Even if he found an ATM machine within walking distance and without getting mugged, would he dare to use his card? And that was assuming the police hadn't somehow cancelled it.

An old brick building guided his path down the street; its facade came out nearly to the sidewalk. Steven slumped against it as he dropped the shopping bag carrying his suit jacket.

Steven's mind raced through the surreal dream of the last hour. Everything had happened so fast. His escape was a minute-to-minute challenge that he had met. It was hard for him to believe that he had just done what he had done.

That sanctuary of the small apartment was across the street. *Destinee, he thought. What have you gotten me into? I know you didn't mean to, but now you are gone, and I am being framed for your murder. I wish you had left me more clues. I have nothing but a guy named Clayton who lives, who lives ... Steven repeated the thought to himself, who lives not far from here. That's right. You said he lived in this area. You lived in this area, not too far from here.*

He considered a plan. Instead of waiting around to get killed roaming the streets of Anacostia, he had to take the fight to the pimp. He would have the element of surprise if nothing else. If he didn't have time, he would have to take bold actions. With a bit of luck, he would find the pimp and beat the truth out of him. If that were the only chance he had, no matter the odds, he would have to take it.

Steven picked up the shopping bag and headed for some industrial dumpsters against a beat-up brick wall. Just as he was about to toss it, he thought of Destinee. In that instant, hope flashed across his face. He remembered Destinee did help him. He looked around and didn't see anybody. He reached into the bag and pulled out the jacket. Inside the inner pocket was the money from his briefcase. As he searched the pockets for the cash, he came across Destinee's locket. He opened it to look at the picture of the girl that had caused him so much trouble. He tucked it away into his pants pocket for safekeeping. Then he counted out eight hundred dollars and put that in one pocket and stuffed the rest in another. He decided to take the coat with him. If the area were searched, no sense leaving a clue as to his whereabouts.

Walking back to the tattoo store, he asked the clerk again how much for the room. This time he tried not to look so desperate.

"Eight hundred a month, like I said."

Steven pulled out five one hundred dollar bills. "Five-hundred for that rat trap."

"It's eight," she insisted.

Steven needed every dollar he had; he wouldn't give up that easily. "Five or I find somewhere else."

"OK, asshole, five hundred." She took the cash and tossed Steven a key. "One month and you're out, especially if I find someone to pay me more."

Steven caught the key and didn't act grateful. Walking up the stairs to the grungy room, he felt a bit lighter on his feet. Where there was a will, there was a way. His only little problem was that he hadn't thought of the way yet, but now, with the cash, he had time. Time would have to be his ally, his only ally.

Chapter 29

Detective Chelle Saltarie sat alone on a park bench, feeling very dejected. She couldn't believe it. A United States senator was on the run for murder, and she was the detective that let him get away. Of all the bum luck in the world, she had to be on duty for this case, she had to be the one to arrest a US senator.

And why couldn't this senator be some fat seventy-year-old SOB that could hardly walk, much less run and take bullets bouncing off him. Not only would her bosses be all over her, but also the talking heads across the country would be questioning her abilities on TV, radio, and newsprint. *Shit*, she thought. She was toast.

Of course, now she realized that the blanket tied to the outside balcony was a ruse to distract them. The briefcase he used to defend himself happened to be especially made to deflect bullets. It was now in her possession as evidence, though it was still locked. But the biggest surprise of all was that the senator had a flak jacket as a war souvenir in his office. The fact that he had the wherewithal to slip it on under his shirt and jacket proved intent to escape. *No shit, Dick Tracy.*

The phone call she had made to his phone had led them to the Capitol Mall. Even though the senator had never answered it, the phone records had shown where it was when it rang. The phone itself was eventually found inside the cab of a stunned cab driver.

It had been confirmed that a man matching the senator's description had bought a sweatshirt and bus ticket. Nearly every step he had taken since escaping his office had been traced. The only thing they didn't know is exactly what stop and what bus he had finally disembarked on. Any leads had evaporated along with the day's tourists. And so a US senator had disappeared right in front of her nose, and she looked like a fool. *He would have to pay for that*, she swore. But, sooner or later, he would have to reappear again, and then she would pursue him without underestimating him. That is, if her superiors kept her on the case.

One month later:

Sitting at her desk at the Metropolitan Police Department of the District of Columbia, Chelle tapped the eraser end of a pencil onto a blank yellow notepad. Her nerves were frazzled; the last four weeks had been grueling. She lived each and every day anticipating that at any second, night or day, somebody or anybody from the president on down could be calling her expecting more information on the missing senator. Only she didn't have any—zip, zero, nothing—and neither did anybody else. That or they weren't sharing.

Chelle desperately wanted to know what was in the briefcase that the senator had used as a shield. Only she couldn't because as far as she was concerned, it was stolen from her. Stolen from right out under her nose. Some men in black suits had flashed a badge and a letter to the captain, then walked out with it.

Chelle wasn't in the station at the time, which was probably a good thing. The captain couldn't tell her who had it, just that it was procedure for government property.

The suitcase was gone, just like the senator. And as famous as he was, he was even more famous now. His face had been on the television, magazines, and newspapers around the country over and over again. The missing senator was now one of the greatest crime mysteries in the United States.

Chelle had no idea there were so many investigative agencies. And each felt as if the missing senator fell into their jurisdiction. The CIA, FBI, Department of Homeland Security, Secret Service, National Security Agency, Office of National Counter Intelligence, State Department, and others had interviewed her. There were also several very serious-looking gentlemen who she had been instructed to unquestionably cooperate with. They didn't bother to mention what agency they were from, nor did she ask. It seems the United States takes a missing senator very seriously.

The only good news over the last weeks was that she was still on the case. Her boss was pissed as hell at her for letting the senator get away, but, with so many agencies to coordinate with, he didn't think it wise to switch contact persons. Nobody else at the department would be able to get up to speed fast enough. Besides, the fact was that Chelle was as good as or better than anybody else he had. Detective Harmon was a close second, but the captain still had his reservation about him. She would just have to clean up her own mess.

Chelle popped a few more Tums into her mouth; they had been a staple of her diet lately. She looked up at the big clock on the wall. It was almost noon. So far, today had been the first day in a long time when she had actually had time to work on the case instead of answering e-mails and telephone calls and personal visits by the mounting number of contacts all claiming they were critical to solving the case of the missing senator.

Soon it would be one o'clock and time for her daily news brief. Even the reporters were becoming bored with seeing her as she reported the same thing day in and day out. Most had moved on to create another news cycle to keep the public's attention. The fact was, the senator had disappeared, and she didn't know how he did it.

The State Department was worried that he had been kidnapped by a foreign power. The Secret Service worried that he was being tortured to obtain sensitive information. Homeland Security and the FBI were sure a terrorist plot was underway with the senator being used as a hostage.

But Chelle was sure it was none of the above. She had seen him last and his actions told her he was nothing more than a murderer running from the law. Sooner or later, he would make a mistake, and she would catch him. She could sense that he was still in the DC area. He was hiding in plain sight and was good at it.

Chelle stared at the few leads she had written down on a yellow legal pad. The first point she noted was, "Telling the truth" next to the name Miss Tannen Michaels. The poor girl was now scared out of her wits. Chelle had been the first to visit the young woman, but after that, every agency even remotely connected to the case had contacted Miss Michaels at the woman's shelter and asked the exact same questions over and over again. Eventually, the tabloids had connected her to a romantic fling with the senator, which was a complete lie, but it did sell papers.

Miss Michaels readily admitted that she had talked to the senator about helping a hooker and drug addict that he knew. She had never asked the senator how he knew the girl, that wasn't important to her, especially back then. She explained that Steven Westcott had been especially kind to the woman's shelter and had assisted with fundraising for the shelter and helping her navigate governmental red tape. Tannen explained to the detective that Mr. Westcott had never been anything except a perfect gentleman with her and the other staff.

Chelle wrote down, "Perfect Gentleman" next to the shelter's name, and then added, "Benefactor." So far, that information didn't imply a cold-blooded woman-killer. But then there was the security video from the bank. It clearly showed the senator entering the safe deposit vault. He definitely took something out of Destinee Sanford's safe deposit box, which was now empty. The fact that the senator had the key and wanted something from inside the box was problematic for him. It could be the reason he killed the woman. Chelle wrote down, "Safe deposit box," and then added, "Intent?"

Then there was the DNA evidence. The DNA link was undeniable and incriminating to say the least. Next to the letters, "DNA," Chelle wrote, "Close personal association."

The senator's lawyer seemed as upset with his client as she was. After she had cooled down and thoroughly interviewed the lawyer, she believed Mr. Johnston that he knew nothing about the escape plans. But she also sensed he did know something, which was protected behind the lawyer/client privileges. In fact, even if the lawyer wanted to tell the detective something, he legally couldn't, and if she somehow made him, it couldn't be used in court. She wrote, "Lawyer—knows secret."

To catch the senator, she needed to think like him, and to think like him she needed to understand him. Most of what she knew wasn't very helpful to that end. She had researched his past, his military career and family life. He seemed like the perfect soldier, the perfect husband, the perfect businessman, and the perfect senator. In fact, the only blemish she found was that his daughter had been a drug addict and died from an overdose. And then there was his brother, who had been safely tucked away in prison at the time of the murder.

A camera on the bridge over the Anacostia River had shown the senator on the top of a tour bus leaving the city. If she were leaving the city, that would be how she would have done it. Find another bus outside the DC area and go to a big city such as Richmond Virginia. He could have pulled it off while they were still busy looking for him in DC.

Saltarie wrote down, "In DC or GONE?" She thought long and hard. "Still here," she wrote. It didn't make sense, but it was something the senator had said to her. "I didn't do it, Detective, I have to prove it because I know you won't or can't."

It wasn't just what he said; it was also how he said it. Very few criminals, or murderers for that matter, ever acknowledge that they are guilty. But the conviction in the senator's voice seemed to her that he actually believed it. Some murderers in their grief at killing someone they loved can't accept that they committed the atrocity themselves. Though he had certainly killed during the war, as far as Saltarie could tell from her research, he had never raised a finger against anyone since. She accepted as fact that he wanted to help the girl, so it would stand to reason that he did like her or even love her. For whatever reason, the young woman was more than a casual hooker to him. The senator could very well be in denial. Truly believing that the real killer is at large could be part of a psychosis, and the delusional part of him now had to find the true killer.

Chelle stood up and stretched. She hadn't brought a bag lunch and didn't want to waste the time going out. She eyed the sandwich machine across the room. Between that and the coffee machine, she could scrounge together a meal.

She took her wallet out of her purse, hoping for enough singles to buy a sandwich and another coffee. Chicken salad or egg salad or ham and cheese? All plausibly edible. Didn't really matter, and she did a kind of eeny, meeny, miny, mo over the buttons, and then pressed one of them. An egg salad sandwich dropped into the lower bin.

With a coffee in one hand and a plastic-wrapped sandwich in the other, she walked back toward her desk to eat.

She thought about her theory. It was possible, but not probable. Though, if the senator was deluding himself that someone else had committed the murder, the longer he believed and told himself the same story, the more real it would become to him.

She sat down and looked at her pad and wrote "Invisible."

Of the hundreds of investigative talent looking for the senator, all had come up empty. No expense had been spared. She was sure that technology she didn't even know existed was being used to find the man. A tail had been put on the attorney Ted Johnston, so she knew that no physical contact had been made. She couldn't be sure about telephone or mail. Monitoring a call or any type of communication between an attorney and their client would be illegal. That didn't mean it wasn't being done. It just meant she wasn't in that particular loop, which was all right by her. However, there was no such presumed privilege between the senator and his wife. Per his wife's permission, his house and phone were being monitored twenty-four hours a day, seven days a week.

The first week, law enforcement wouldn't even had to have been on station. With the number of news vans and reporters surrounding the place, nobody could get in or out. The urgency of the story had eventually evaporated. Last she had checked, most of the onsite cameras and reporters had moved on to greener pastures. The FBI and Secret Service had a bit more patience; Mrs. Westcott and her daughter were still being followed closely any time they left the house.

After she broke through two layers of packaging, she started munching on small bites of the sandwich. Small pieces of egg and mayo clung to the side of her mouth as she chewed and read another brief in front of her, suggesting he might try to contact his wife.

Chelle thought back to her very unpleasant meeting with the senator's wife. Chelle had met with Mrs. Westcott late the same day Steven had eluded her. She had convinced Mrs. Westcott that if she wanted to help her husband, the best thing she could do would be to convince him to give himself up if he contacted her in any way. At first, his wife had given her the cold shoulder, but a brutally honest discussion eventually changed her mind.

"I don't care what you say," Lucille had said. "Steven didn't do it. You are wrong. You don't know my husband; he couldn't do something like that."

"I would like you to identify the car and the person in this video."

Lucille's face turned white, eventually she admitted. "Yes, it looks like our car, and it certainly looks like Steven, but I couldn't swear it's him."

"The license number confirms it's your car. Here are copies of the DNA analysis of the blood, the hair fibers, and semen found in her. They all match Steven's."

"Semen?"

"I'm afraid so. It's definitive."

"God no ... god no." Lucille took the document, stood, and walked away from the detective. The name Steven Westcott was all over it. One column said "original sample," another said "crime scene." The "match" column showed percentages. All were 100 percent.

Lucille slunk down in a chair in the living room and began to sob uncontrollably.

Chelle couldn't help but feel the woman's pain, so after giving Lucille time to cry, she approached her, woman to woman. "I'm sorry I had to show you those things. But you needed to know the truth."

"We haven't been close lately, ever since our daughter died. It's not all Steven's fault; I could have been a better wife. But ..."

Chelle handed Lucille some Kleenexes.

"But things were getting better."

Chelle put her arm around Lucille. Maybe it wasn't professional, but if she he been in the wife's position, it would be what she might want.

Lucille tried to dry her tears. "I mean, I thought things were getting better. But, a whore? He was seeing a whore, and he would come home and make love to me? Sorry, I'm not feeling well." Lucille got up and left the room.

When Lucille came out of where Chelle guessed was the master bedroom, her tears were dried and her makeup was cleaned away where it had been a smeared mess before.

"My daughter, how will I tell my daughter?"

"I don't know, but she will find out soon on her own if she hasn't already. She needs to hear it from you."

Lucille looked up at Chelle, searching for an answer. "How, how can I tell her that her father is wanted for murder? That he's wanted for the murder of a hooker he was known to sleep with."

"Mrs. Westcott, I can't possibly explain why Mr. Westcott did what he did, but by running, he has put himself in a lot of danger. And inadvertently or not, I'm afraid he may be putting you and your daughter in danger also. Catching him for his own good and for yours and your daughter's is the best thing we can do right now. In that end, we need to watch your home closely and monitor your phones. We believe he will try to contact you or your daughter."

"Yes, of course, anything to help."

Chelle reached for the other half of her sandwich before realizing that she had been so deep in thought that she had unconsciously already eaten it.

Chelle wrote on her paper, "Hasn't contacted family."

Detective Harmon walked by and caught Chelle staring off into the wall. "Detective?" Harmon waved his hand in front of Chelle's eyes.

"Just thinking. Haven't had that luxury for a while."

"Thinking about your escaped senator, I presume?"

"He's still here. I know it."

"Hey, I just had a thought. Maybe he didn't do it; maybe it was your serial killer. Didn't he tell you he didn't do it? I mean, what more do you need?"

"You are a first class asshole, Harmon, you know that?"

"Stop worrying. If you believe he is still in the DC area, all you have to do is search about a hundred square miles and you're home free. Maybe you'll be able to do the impossible just like the president."

Harmon walked off, Chelle could tell by his smirk that he was sufficiently satisfied that he had rattled her cage enough for now.

A subject on everyone's mind, especially in the DC, area, was that the president of the United States had somehow managed to get the Israelis and the Palestinians together for peace talks at Camp David. It was still months away, but security planning had already started.

"I'll find the son of a bitch," Chelle whispered to herself. She circled the words, "Still here," and added an exclamation point.

"I know who did it," the senator had said. "It was her pimp, I'm sure of it." When she told him it wasn't possible, he had insisted. "That can't be. He's fooling you; he's fooling everybody. I'm telling you. He did it, not me."

Chelle wrote another note, "Visit Clayton Harris again."

Chapter 30

Ramon Ruben Hayes had found a new hobby, as had millions of Americans. And that hobby was watching the television for news on an escaped murder suspect. With the TV in his back office barely audible, he stood against the office door, hoping for an update. The last he had heard was that the senator was still missing. Many of the news pundits believed that war trauma had caused the senator to go rogue, and that was what made him so dangerous.

Ramon listened to Detective Chelle Saltarie on the television as he fantasized about her touch and the smell of her hair. She assured the viewers that it was just a matter of time. But Ramon and most of the public understood that the trail leading to him was getting colder each and every day.

Ramon debated his wisdom in withholding the information that another detective named Bruce Harmon had liaisons with the now-dead hooker too. He wondered if that information might have helped Detective Saltarie in some way. Ramon also knew that Harmon knew another murdered hooker. A redhead named Tiffany.

Protecting Detective Harmon wasn't his goal. What he didn't want was to be connected in any way with Harmon or the hookers. Ramon didn't see how he could have one without the other.

Ramon didn't feel his added information would help Detective Saltarie. He had confidence that she would eventually catch the senator regardless; the detective seemed more than capable. Ramon's personal opinion was that the law never rested. Sooner or later, the senator would make a mistake and would be caught. Just as, sooner or later, without his help, the detective who abused his authority would be caught. Ramon reminded himself to be patient because God worked in mysterious ways and on his own timetable.

Across town:

Clayton Harris looked out his window; he had heard a car door close. It didn't take long before he heard the knock on his door.

"What do you want?" He hollered through the door.

"It's Detective Saltarie. I would like to talk."

"I thought we were done talking, sweet thing."

"May I come in? It's cold out here?" The December winds cut through her thin layers. Chelle hated to admit it, but winter had come to Washington and she needed to start dressing for it.

"I thought I was in the clear. That senator guy did it, everybody knows that. Even you said I didn't do it."

"That was a month ago, and I said I couldn't prove you did it, and now I believe you."

"So why are you here?"

"I think you might still be in danger."

Clayton laughed. "You think I might be in danger? Yea, so do I, from you."

"Let me in, let's talk." Chelle was tempted by the cold to give up and not let Clayton in on her suspicions.

"I don't trust you, sweet thing. You still need somebody to pin the murder on and a big black pimp would suit you just fine."

"Clayton, you need to listen to me."

"Why should I? You just want to trick me into saying something incriminating. You're a white bitch and can't be trusted, that simple."

"We found his blood on the girl and her blood in his car along with hair fibers. The DNA all matches. May I come in?"

"Fuck you, Detective. I know my rights. Take off."

"We found his semen inside the girl. I know you didn't do it. I'm not here to trick you."

Clayton unbolted the door and let the detective inside.

"Why are you telling me this?"

"Because nobody will believe you if you repeat it, and I want you to listen to me. I still think you are in danger from this guy, the senator."

Chelle stepped inside the small hallway. At least it was warm, she thought.

"I think Senator Westcott is in the area and is going to come after you."

"Why would he do that?"

"Because he's blaming you for her death."

"That doesn't make any fucking sense. If he did it, why would he blame me?"

"I don't know why, but even as he ran from me, he was blaming you specifically, by name. He also said that you were just fooling us and you wouldn't be able to fool him."

"Big deal. If I was him, I'd blame it on somebody else too. But that doesn't mean he's going to fuck with me. Shit, he knows he did it. What would be the point? Does he think I'm going to admit to something I didn't do so he can go free?"

"I don't know. Maybe he's delusional or in denial. I don't know why he believes you killed the girl, but he does. I'm convinced of that. Hell, maybe he thinks that if he supplies the police with the body of a big black pimp who could have done it, his troubles will go away. He told me that if I didn't or couldn't find the killer, he would.

"I can take care of myself. I'm not going to worry about a fucking senator."

"It's my duty to warn you. I don't really care otherwise. But if something strange starts happening, call me."

"Strange? Like what?"

"Like if you think you are being followed. He's ex-military; he will probably follow you, learn your habits, that sort of thing."

"You're just trying to fuck with me, make me paranoid."

"I'm trying to save your worthless life."

Clayton opened the door. "Don't let the door kick you in the ass. And don't wait for no fucking call."

Clayton watched until Chelle was back in her car. He glanced around, making sure nobody was spying on him. The only other person he saw was a bearded homeless man, who was pushing his shopping cart on the broken-up sidewalk. The old bum didn't seem to mind or notice the police cruiser. He stooped down to pick up a few stray aluminum beer cans rolling about between patches of dirty snow. Then he moved on again, hunched over, barely able to walk. The wind was blowing in a gust. The old bum's winter coat blew open with one of the sharper blasts; apparently the old coat didn't have a working zipper.

Clayton closed the door and went straight for his gun. Maybe the cute little detective was right. He would keep the loaded gun close until the senator guy was caught.

At the police station:

Chelle went to work on another case. Maybe if she cleared her mind of the escaped senator, she would be rewarded with a sudden inspiration. Chelle took the elevator down to the basement. It was the securest place in the building and housed the evidence lock-up. It was more like a giant safe, and Officer Mitch O'Connell's job saw to guard the contents of that safe.

When she stepped out the elevator, she was greeted by an unfortunate surprise. Detective Harmon had also apparently checked on some evidence and couldn't resist the chance to harass her again.

"Afternoon, Detective. Hey, we got another girl stabbed to death. Maybe you want to add it to your serial killer list. Just because a professor dude's fingerprints were all over the knife shouldn't imply he had anything to do with it. Or the fact that his DNA was found all over the murder scene or that she was his student that he was fucking. Why should any of that matter when Chelle Saltarie has a theory about a rogue serial killer?"

"Harmon, you're a real piece of work, you know that?"

Chelle walked past Harmon, intentionally brushing her shoulder hard into his side. She walked up to the sign-in desk as the elevator door opened for Harmon. Chelle heard the ding of the elevator and was thankful that, at least for the time being, Harmon was out of her hair.

Officer Mitch O'Connell was sitting behind his desk and munching on some M&M's. Chelle thought that a year walking a beat would be healthy for him. Mitch was quite overweight but he was amicable as the log officer, and Chelle had never had issue with him.

"Hi Mitch."

"Hi, Detective. What can I do for you?"

"I need to take a look at some evidence, case number S5348."

He twirled around a sign-in and sign-out book. "Sign in, find what you need, and then I'll sign you and the evidence out. You know the drill. You can go to the examining room with it but you can't leave this area with the evidence."

"Sure, it won't take long."

Chelle signed in and noticed Detective Harmon's name above hers. But he had not signed anything out. A little unusual, but maybe it was just a quick look at something to refresh his memory. Chelle scanned the rest of the sheet. "It seems that Detective Harmon often comes down to the evidence lock-up, but he almost never takes anything to the examining room."

Mitch didn't think much of it. "Naw. He usually is just confirming what's in storage. He has caught some discrepancies. Somebody is effing up when cataloging evidence. I wouldn't want to be them when Harmon finds out who they are."

"What kind of discrepancies?"

"You know, evidence in the locker but not on the report. That could really screw up a case if an attorney finds out there was evidence they weren't told about."

"I can imagine, though I have never had that problem."

"Well, Harmon certainly has. And important stuff too. You know, DNA samples, like hair or things. He just recently found some hair samples not listed for a professor guy who killed a young girl. Unlucky for the professor that he caught the error. It was critical to his arrest. He also found out that a bag of cocaine had been missed. He even showed me the bag in the evidence locker. He had originally found it the perpetrator's home. Never listed, can you imagine? It became a direct link to a murder, just not listed as evidence. Between you and me, Harman can be an ass, but he's a good detective, very thorough."

"Mitch, if that ever happened to me, what would I do?"

"Simple really, you just show me the evidence missed. I verify it is there, and I add it to the case file. No big deal. I do it all the time for Harmon."

"Thanks Mitch. I'll get what I need and be back in a second."

Chelle didn't believe in coincidences. A bit more investigating was due.

Then, just as she stepped out of the elevator, Detective Pat Marget rushed up to her. "Captain is looking for you. The briefcase the senator used to block your shots is back in play."

Chelle's eyes sprang open. "You're kidding? Where was it? Who had it?"

"Past my pay grade, Chelle, but you're welcome to ask the captain."

Chelle shot right to the captain's office. She almost didn't knock first and then thought better of it. She rapped on the frosted glass door with Captain Walker's name stenciled on it.

"Come in."

"Captain, I heard we got the briefcase back."

"Hold on, Chelle, not exactly." Captain Walker stood and put a file away in one of the twenty or so steel file drawers lining the wall of his office.

"What do you mean, who has it?"

"I don't know who had it, and I don't know if it's been tampered with. All I know was that we got a letter that says to see what is in it, we have to go to a special magistrate. And then we can only see what they want us to see."

"What kind of bullshit is that?"

"I don't know, but I do know we can't argue with it." Captain Walker sat back down. The chair squeaked loudly as he wheeled it tight behind his desk again.

"The letter said that it's only because it was used as a weapon and shield that we can claim the briefcase itself as evidence. If there is anything of value to the investigation inside of it, I was assured we would see it."

"I'm sorry, but a magistrate wouldn't know police evidence or clues if they bit him on the ass."

"We'd better hope this one does."

Chapter 31

The private office of the chief magistrate for Washington DC:

"My bailiff will act as witness as I remove the items one by one from the senator's briefcase," Chief Magistrate Celia LaRosa said. "I alone will examine the contents and make a determination as to the sensitivity of each piece."

Chelle held her breath and her tongue. It was possible the magistrate would decide that nothing in the case was to be shared with the police. Chelle cursed the situation. The way the senator closed the case in front of her when they first searched his apartment meant it certainly did contain something she wanted to see.

Chelle wasn't standing alone. Her boss, Captain Walker, and Pat were not quite as emotionally involved as she was, but they were on hand as additional witnesses to whatever they were given.

Magistrate LaRosa decided to go through the briefcase in a methodical order. First, she examined the top lid and its partitions, starting from the back, working toward the front. Last, she removed the loose items in the base of the case.

With her hands gloved in latex, paper after paper left the briefcase, and paper after paper was examined and then handed by the magistrate to the bailiff, who was also wearing latex gloves. Then, each item was carefully placed inside an evidence container.

Chelle was doing everything in her power not to jump over the magistrate's desk and rip the documents out of her hand. The tediously slow process was killing her. The upper case had been emptied, and not one piece of paper was allowed into their hands. Then the magistrate lifted out the contents in the base of the case.

After very carefully examining several of the papers, she looked up at the officers in front of her and then took the stack of papers and flipped them upside down on her desk.

"It seems we have a situation that I need to resolve before giving these particular documents to you."

Chelle crossed her arms and then uncrossed them and then crossed them again all in a matter of seconds. She saw her captain give her a signal to contain herself. Then Captain Walker asked much more calmly than Chelle ever could have managed, "What seems to be the problem?"

"These papers are not sensitive to the government and are indeed pertinent to your investigation."

"Then please let us see them. Every minute is important," Walker insisted.

Chelle seriously considered grabbing them and running. But her partner grabbed her forearm to keep her contained.

"I have a dilemma. The letter is written to his attorney, specifically. Even though it was unmailed, it is still privileged information."

"No! That's not right," Chelle interjected. "It was not mailed. It is in our possession. Everything in that case is theoretically evidence, everything!" she said. "We are obliging the court and the Senate with your prior inspection, but the case and everything in it is our evidence, and we are entitled to see it."

"Well then," the magistrate settled back into her chair comfortably. "You can see my dilemma. I don't see it that way at all. Communication between an attorney and his client is strictly confidential. That is the basis of our law. This letter is very clearly written to his attorney. It isn't some random rambling, or something like a suicide note written to nobody in particular."

"Oh my god!" Saltarie was losing it.

Captain Walker scowled at Chelle. The magistrate was nobody to be trifled with, and his headstrong detective should know that.

"Detective Marget, please take detective Saltarie out to the hall and wait for me there," Captain Walker insisted with a voice that conveyed his displeasure.

Chelle and Pat left the room. Chelle realized she was fighting her partner's gentle guidance as they left.

The magistrate continued to go through the briefcase. Then, under the protection of the briefcase cover, she browsed through the scrapbook. It was an unexpected revelation and was clearly not government business, but it also could clearly be insight into Senator's Westcott's frame of mind. She handed it over to Captain Walker along with a ballpoint pen and some paperclips and a pocket calculator. The rest of the contents stayed inside the evidence container, which the bailiff padlocked in front of the captain.

The only item not either given to the captain or the bailiff was the letter to Senator Westcott's attorney. Magistrate Celia LaRosa carefully placed it into a one-time use envelope and sealed it.

"I will have to research case laws to see if there have been any specific rulings on the basis of evidence. You wouldn't want Senator Westcott to go free simply because you choose to ignore the law," the magistrate said.

"Madam, we have enough evidence to convict Senator Westcott already. We and the nation simply want to find him. If you have information that would help us find him, I strongly suggest that you give it to us."

"Unfortunately, it is not that simple for me. If you are legally entitled to this information, you will get it. If you are not, then it shall be delivered to his attorney as intended."

"We don't know that," Walker argued. "It wasn't mailed, maybe he wasn't going to give it to him. That was why he still had it."

"I certainly can't assume that, even if it is a possibility."

Magistrate LaRosa stood up and handed the now-empty case to the captain. "The case itself is yours to keep as evidence. I would assume the bullet marks on it are quite important. If you are entitled to the documents, I will return them to you."

"When? Time is of the essence."

"As soon as I can. I have nothing further to add."

The magistrate excused herself. Then she and the bailiff walked out a side door, leaving the captain holding on to an empty, shot-up briefcase. He looked at the closed hall door and dreaded to go back to Detective Chelle Saltarie with nothing but a strange scrapbook that the senator made, which was some sort of sick narcissistic tribute to himself. This wasn't going to be pleasant.

****

Chelle and Pat were in the basement evidence examining room. Chelle had signed out the spiral notebook that they believed Senator Westcott had made. Officer O'Connell had even got up and opened the glass door of the glass-enclosed viewing room for them.

They sat down at one of the long metal tables. Pat's chair screeched across the concrete floor as he pulled it up as close as he could to Chelle's chair and the table.

Chelle and Pat wore gloves as they carefully paged through the spiral notebook.

"He certainly is full of himself," Pat said and then added. "And of all things to carry around in your briefcase. It has certainly been looked at enough based on the rough edges. It's like he needed a narcissistic high from time to time."

Chelle sat back in her chair, thinking as Pat continued to flip through the pages.

"Doesn't seem to be in any order, which is strange. I would think it would be chronological, oldest to newest," Pat surmised, then added, "I don't know how it helps us much. It's all about him, nothing about Destinee or hookers in general. We have his early life, getting married, and articles about his daughter who died of an overdose. There are some about his election. Just random stuff. I don't see any pattern at all."

"I'd give anything to know what else was in that briefcase," Chelle voiced the same wish she had said a hundred times already.

Outside the glass window of the evidence room they were in, Chelle saw Detective Harmon walk by.

"Pat, how would you like to help me stick our noses where they don't belong?"

Pat saw Chelle watching Harmon. "If it has anything to do with sticking it to Harmon, I'm in."

****

Later that same day, back at Chelle's desk, she and Pat were examining an open file.

"How about that, Pat?"

"I see it. The Washington Arms was their favorite place to have their little tryst."

It was after hours, and Chelle had convinced Pat to stay a little later. They were looking into the stabbing death of a college student. It was a recent case that Detective Harmon had already solved.

"Not exactly the same as Destinee and Senator Westcott, but close enough."

"Don't believe in coincidences do you, Chelle?"

"Let's just say I've become a bit more suspicious about them."

"Don't you think it a bit strange that Harmon never went to the hotel to confirm their visits?"

"Didn't have to I guess. The girl had the professor's DNA all over her. And the murder weapon had his prints and DNA on it. And if you look at the evidence list, the professor's personalized lighter was found at the scene."

"Remember that other case Harmon bragged about, a redheaded prostitute?"

"Sure do, a doctor is sitting in jail right now for killing her."

"What was her name?"

"Tiffany something."

Chelle sat up at the computer and searched until she found the right file.

"Tiffany Maddenheart."

Pat stood up and read the computer from over Chelle's shoulder as she scrolled through the file.

"Doctor Merrill is in jail awaiting trial, bail denied," Chelle read. "He admitted to giving her prescription meds but denies killing her. She also had some bad cocaine in her system, the same that was found in the doctor's home. They usually met at the Saint Claire Hotel. She was also killed with a knife, which had the doctor's prints on it."

"How about the priest and the hooker?" Pat asked.

Chelle did the search. "DNA evidence—killed with a knife that had the priest's fingerprints on it."

"What hotel?"

"The Hotel Aster."

"Wasn't that the hotel Deon Michalski stayed at?" Pat said.

"You mean my case? That was over a year ago."

"We have two out of four right now that stayed at the Washington Arms—just a hunch."

"Well, your hunch is wrong. They used the Continental. But," Chelle continued, "she was killed with a knife too. His fingerprints and DNA all over it."

"Are you thinking what I'm thinking?" Pat asked.

"Serial killer. Somebody is killing prostitutes with a knife and getting other's blamed. The knife is always on the scene or nearby with the perpetrator's DNA and fingerprints on it."

"What does Detective Harmon have to do with this? Maybe he got a bit lucky with some of his cases lately, but that's the way it goes."

"You know me, Pat, I don't believe in coincidences. His arrest and conviction rate has skyrocketed lately. And ..."

Chelle filled Pat in on what the she had found out from the officer in charge of the evidence lock-up.

"So you think he's framing these people by searching their private residences, collecting evidence, and then retroactively saying he found it at the crime scene?"

"I ... I don't know what I'm thinking right now. Keep this between us. We have to be careful we don't go on a witch hunt just because we don't like the witch."

"But that would make Harmon a serial killer. He's killing people just so that he can make an arrest. I can't believe that."

"Maybe, or he is just planting evidence to make it easier to secure and arrest and convict. He would have motivation in the form of prestige and advancement, and he has the means to plant the incriminating evidence. Everybody has a knife in a drawer somewhere with their fingerprints and DNA on it."

"But how did he plant the evidence when it wasn't his case?"

"I didn't say he did, just that he has the motive and the means, particularly on his cases."

Chapter 32

Another day had gone by. The wind was raw and cold as the old bum eventually made his way back to his small flat above a tattoo parlor. The tattooed and pierced clerk glanced at him when he moved past her counter and slowly crept up the stairs with his garbage bag of aluminum cans.

Steven placed the garbage bag down next to another that was as full as it could get it. Tomorrow, he would look for some more cans and then sell the lot to a recycle center. He had some of Destinee's money left, but he dared not use it for anything but rent. Steven took off his dirty coat and immediately smelled his own odor. He hadn't showered in two weeks; the smell it produced was good cover. To the police, an unwashed bum was somebody to leave unmolested, and if at all possible, they usually kept their distance. In the special forces, it was called going local, and so far, his disguise had worked perfectly.

He was sure the pierced young girl behind the counter had forgotten completely what he had looked like when he first walked into her life over a month ago. Besides, she wasn't the paper-reading or television-news type. He doubted she even knew there was a US senator at large.

During the first two weeks, he hadn't left the apartment. The only exception was to buy enough food and books to last him while in isolation. He had let his hair and mustache and beard grow. After the first two weeks, when he looked and smelled the part, he visited a nearby resale shop. That was where he found the rest of his costume. It included a worn old pair of sport shoes and a torn jacket. They became his trademarks.

As the weeks of seclusion went by, his loneliness became a bigger and bigger burden. It was now the Christmas season, and every Christmas song he heard during the quiet of the night made his stomach ache. Nobody had even once wished the old bum a merry Christmas.

He had often spent Christmas thousands of miles away from home on a mission, but never was he alone. Never was he so lonely for his family that he felt sick to his stomach. Steven thought of his family over and over again. Certainly the season was being ruined by the bizarre turn of events for them too. It was hard to imagine his daughter pretending to enjoy the season with her friends knowing her father was a fugitive from the law and possibly not even alive. Did she even have friends anymore?

Christmas Eve eventually came. A Christmas snow was falling, and Steven spent his time integrating himself with the neighborhood, learning the area inch by inch. The last five weeks, he had become a fixture, walking up and down the same streets day after day and picking his way through the same garbage cans. He was sure that, by now, most of the residents were of the opinion that he had always been around, just unnoticed.

His military training had taught him the value of patience. It had also taught him the value of good reconnaissance. First he had to find Clayton Harris, it wasn't too difficult. His disguise had allowed him to walk the neighborhood undisturbed as he scoured through the garbage for aluminum cans. Eventually, he had seen the same gold Cadillac that had followed him the day Destinee was murdered. In the garbage can outside Clayton's house, there was plenty of unopened junk mail addressed to a Mr. Clayton Harris.

There was only one thing going for the senator, and that was time. He couldn't hide forever in plain sight, but rushing to his objective wouldn't serve him either. Steven was budgeting himself carefully; he thought he would have enough money to get him through another couple of months, maybe longer if he collected enough cans.

He would wait for another month to make sure Clayton's home wasn't under surveillance. In the meantime, he hoped the police wouldn't become interested in an old bum collecting cans and taking them to the local junkyard.

Washington DC police station:

The station house was its typical hectic self. The only differences were a few Christmas decorations that hung on some of the walls still left over from the Christmas Holidays. Everybody mostly ignored them. They were the same decorations used for the last ten years. It was already a week into the new year and Chelle thought if somebody else didn't take them down soon, she was going to. She was getting tired of looking at them.

Captain Walker walked up to Chelle's desk with an envelope that had been sent certified mail from the chief magistrate's office.

He showed it to her. Chelle looked at her captain with quizzical eyes.

"She came to a conclusion," Captain Walker explained.

"What type of conclusion?" Chelle asked suspiciously.

"It seems that the magistrate ruled that the letter inside the briefcase was now the property of Senator Steven Westcott's attorney."

"That's bullshit, sir!" Chelle said.

"But she also made another decision."

"Can't be bad news, because it couldn't get any worse."

"No it's not, she also decided that because of legal discovery laws, and the special nature of the case, the attorney would have to share it with us."

"You're kidding!" Chelle said.

"Nope, right here." Walker handed the letter to Chelle. "Some good stuff I think. I don't know if he was being perfectly straight with his attorney, but it's pretty detailed for being all lies."

Chelle wasn't even listening to her captain anymore; she was already absorbed by the contents of the letter. It explained a lot, but not why the girl had been murdered. In fact, the one consistency was that even to his attorney, the senator denied killing her.

New pieces to the puzzle were added, none explained.

The senator knew the girl quite well, though not intimately, he claimed. That was expected, nothing new there, but there were pictures, many pictures, intimate pictures, that *was* new information. The senator had attained the pictures and destroyed them. It sounded like a blackmail scheme, which would be motive enough. He also confirmed the visits he had with the girl at the Washington Arms Hotel.

The scrapbook that hadn't made sense up to now was explained. That was, if she were to believe the senator's explanation. It wasn't a self-appreciating collection. According to the written notes, it came from the safe deposit box. It belonged to the hooker. She was stalking him, and that was how they originally met.

Chelle needed to see the scrapbook again, so she stood up, stretching her legs a bit, and walked down two floors to the evidence holding area.

Chelle signed out the scrapbook, took it to the side examining room, and opened it with new eyes.

Yes, it was possible the deceased hooker made the book, and using touch DNA sampling, it would be easy enough to verify. The tape used to hold the collection in place would also hold the DNA of the maker. Chelle studied the book from cover to cover. There was no writing, no connotations, nothing besides roughly cutout newspaper articles haphazardly taped in place. The more Chelle thought about it, the more she couldn't imagine that someone like the senator would produce a tribute to himself in such a haphazard way.

Chelle made sure Mitch registered the scrapbook as returned evidence when she placed it back into storage. That made her think back to the discussion she had with Mitch when he explained how Bruce Harmon had corrected nonlisted evidence.

Chelle took her brush out of her purse and looked at it. It certainly had her hair samples on it. If she was to put those hair samples in an evidence bag and tell Mitch that it should have been cataloged months ago as evidence for the Destinee Sanford case, would she then become a suspect if it were traced back to her? And if, as the detective in charge of that case, she also reported the collection of that evidence, would it ever be questioned?

It had never before been considered by her as a way to change the facts in a case. For a detective to do that, it would be unconscionable. But, the point was: was it possible?

Chelle signed herself out of the evidence room with Mitch witnessing her signature. This time, she waited for the elevator to take her back upstairs. Once upstairs, she rinsed out her Garfield mug and filled it with fresh coffee. Back at her desk, Chelle looked at her copy of the senator's reproduction of the e-mail from the hooker. Chelle sat back with her hot Garfield mug in both hands as she sipped on it, deep in thought. The e-mail was even more interesting and also more perplexing than the scrapbook. It was rewritten in quotations marks. Undoubtedly, it was supposed to be an exact duplication.

Chelle stared at the blank, gray walls of her cubical. If the entire story was a fabrication, it was a dandy. And in it, he had covered many of the unexplained evidences, but nothing that would exonerate him—quite the opposite. Chelle felt more exasperated than ever. She certainly had more information, but none of the facts had changed. The letter still didn't explain the DNA or Steven's blood and fingerprints at the murder scene.

In fact, if she was to believe the letter, it would mean the senator never had sex with the girl, so there couldn't be any semen left behind to incriminate him. But that obviously was not the case, so did that mean the whole explanation was also false? Chelle took out her note-pad and wrote down next to all her other notes, "Doesn't make sense."

It was certainly an elaborate story. If it was all lies, it was exceptionally written. But the senator was an exceptional man. However, if she were to write a believable alibi, she wouldn't include numerous references to conditions that would imply motive over and over again. The senator was much too smart for that. The writing of the letter was in itself enigmatic. Why even bring up blackmail pictures if you later admit that you weren't being blackmailed and that you got the pictures and destroyed them. What would be the point, especially if the reason for going through all the trouble of attaining them was to keep them secret in the first place?

Chelle hoped that maybe she could use her marked-up copy of the letter as a blueprint of sorts to provide clues to his current where-abouts. She needed to go back to the Washington Arms again and confirm the exact days of the two visits and see if it concurred with the letter. Strange, she thought, the hotel had become quite the frequent stop for her lately.

Meanwhile on the other side of town:

Steven was cold, hungry, and miserable as he walked down the sidewalk, pushing the recently emptied shopping cart. A half hour ago, he had cashed in his precious bags of aluminum cans. With the thirty dollars in his pocket, he felt darn near rich. He caught a whiff of his own scent, which disgusted him. Passing a coffee shop window, he saw his reflection and didn't recognize the man looking back at him.

He had lost his identity, his inner self. He used to know exactly who he was and what he wanted to accomplish in life. Today, like many days before it, the man in the window didn't even know if he cared to live another day. Day after day, the torture of not being able to share even the small fact that he was still alive with his wife and daughter wore on him.

Without my family, what's the point? What was left of the man that used to be Steven Westcott had to constantly fight off the temptation to contact his wife and daughter and calm their fears. He missed them desperately and the void in his heart ate at his soul. He stared at the man in the window. The old homeless man didn't have a family and wouldn't until he proved his innocence.

Steven couldn't imagine what his family thought of him, and the knowledge that his daughter might believe that her father was a murderer ripped at his insides. The letter explaining everything he knew about the hooker and why he knew her and why he had done the things he did was evidently still secured away from the media. Even if the written ranting of a lunatic weren't believable, it would have been perfect fodder for days' worth of sound bites. Yet the newspapers hadn't mentioned it.

The letter and Destinee's scrapbook had been in the briefcase that he threw at the detective in desperation. She had it, of that he was certain. Maybe Detective Saltarie was checking out those leads, maybe she would discover he was telling the truth. *Maybe, maybe. He looked away from his own reflection. Maybe I'm just dreaming.*

Steven wondered if the detective had shared the letter with his attorney, and was Teddy Johnston trying to use the information in it to help him? Had Lucille read the letter? Did she believe it or did she believe he was a killer too? The uncertainty was killing him. He needed to hear her voice. He needed her assurance that everything would be OK. He needed to hear from her that she believed him and trusted him completely.

But Steven knew better. He assumed that his wife was being watched night and day. Her phone was most certainly tapped, their house probably bugged. He was a big fish and the government wanted him back. National security could produce a big veil to commit many constitutional sins. He was afraid that the government was pursuing the philosophy that if they weren't caught, they didn't break any rules. And in their efforts to find a rogue Senator, he was sure that many rules were being broken in the name of protecting the homeland.

Disappearing in today's world was not an easy task. Sacrifices had to be made. A letter to his lawyer might get through unnoticed, but he couldn't be sure. E-mail would eventually lead them back to the very computer he had sent it from. And a telephone call would also be traced to his location. He had apparently successfully disappeared and he had to keep it that way.

Steven had gone over his options a thousand times and, unfortunately, always came up with the same near-hopeless conclusion. Without proof of who had killed the girl and why, a call would accomplish very little besides letting his wife know he was still alive. While that was important, it would not only reveal to everyone else that he was still at large, it would show them where to start looking for him. Unfortunately, it just wasn't worth the risk. He said out loud for the thousandth time, "Honey, I'm so, so sorry for all of this."

Steven hunched his back over and started to walk away. He glanced up one more time at his reflection. Then, on the television inside the coffee shop, another face caught his eye. It was his wife, and she was stepping up to a microphone outside a courthouse.

Next to her was a man he didn't recognize. He was dressed in a heavy dress coat over his suit and was acting protective of Lucille. The cold January winds made the bottom of his coat flap.

Steven had to hear her voice and see her up close, so he walked into the coffee shop, oblivious to everything but the image of his wife. She was as gorgeous as ever, and Steven almost reached out to touch the TV screen. His wife looked sharp in a winter hat he didn't recognize and a white long coat that, though thick against the cold, hugged her shape nonetheless. He sat down at the first empty table he saw and listened. Lucille's voice was music to Steven's ears.

"As my attorney said, the last months have been extremely difficult on my daughter and me. At this time, I have come to a difficult conclusion. Some decisions have to be made so that my daughter and I can move on with our lives as well as possible under the circumstances. I want you to all know that I stand by my husband and believe that he should not be judged by anyone but a jury. And to that end, I would like to remind everyone that he is innocent of the charge of murder until proven to be guilty."

Lucille paused as if unsure of her next words. "However, I have to accept the fact that my husband, by his own choice, has disappeared from our lives. He ran from the police for reasons that I can only speculate. But the important thing is, he didn't stand up for himself in a court of law. I do not know where my husband is, but I can see no circumstances in which mine or my daughter's lives will ever be the same. Our family has been destroyed by the attention and constant distractions. For my daughter's sake, we need to distance ourselves from the ongoing ordeal. I have had no contact with my husband, and I will not have any contact with him. I have just filed divorce documents with the court. We need to move on with our lives and for the sake of my daughter, I beg of you, the public and the media, to please leave us to some much needed privacy.

"To my husband, if you are listening. Please give yourself up before you or someone else is hurt or worse. If you still love us, please do not contact your daughter or me. Understand that your actions have robbed her of her youth and have done irreparable harm to her already."

The man in the suit came back to the microphone and promised to answer any questions he could as the former Mrs. Westcott was led away by another man in a custom-fitted suit. This particular man he did recognize. It was Sam Kreiser. In an instant, it all made sense to him. Lucille didn't know many attorneys, and she had said that she was working with Sam through the foundation. Sam must have set her up with a big-shot divorce attorney and had apparently become her personal adviser.

A big guy in a white T-shirt and dirty white apron came up to Steven's table as he stared at the television in shock. "I'm sorry, buddy, but you have to go. Some of the other tables are complaining about the smell, and they ain't wrong. Time to move on."

Steven didn't move; in fact, he was barely paying attention. Then he felt a strong hand grab his arm. With a start, Steven twisted his arm in a reflex move, stood up, and soon had the cook facedown on the table. A shocked waitress ran to the phone, probably to call the police.

Steven realized what he had so automatically done and immediately released the man. Then he ran out the restaurant, leaving his shopping cart behind.

Chapter 33

Steven ran down an alley between two abandoned factories. The tired, discolored, red brick facades sheltered him from the wind. He slumped down next to a rusty dumpster with a wheel missing. Then he held his head and wept like a child. His wife had abandoned him. She was divorcing him, and he was absolutely helpless to stop her or even explain to her what had happened. He needed her. He needed some hope for the future. He needed more reasons to live.

Tears ran down his face. He thought about the embarrassment his daughter must be feeling. The shame she must have to face every day. He hit the broken pavement beside him with both fists and thought about how much she must hate him right now. It hurt him so bad to know that not only could he not comfort and console his daughter, but he was the cause of her despair.

Up until now, Steven had chosen to pretend that everything was going to be all right, that Lucille and Tracy would both greet him with open arms when he returned home victorious against the wrongs committed against him. Now he realized that not only might he never see them again, the two women he loved more than anything else in the world would despise him for the rest of his life.

The world looked bleak and unwelcoming. What was he doing? Did he really think he had a chance to find a murderer? Who was he? He wasn't a powerful senator anymore. He looked at his tattered and smelly clothes. He was a bum, a poor, stinking bum. He didn't have any money; he didn't even have a phone. For over two months, he had filled his head with delusions. He had pretended he was a man with a plan, a man who was on a great and righteous quest.

The fact was, he was a bum who needed to go through other people's trash to eat. A plain old bum that could be picked up by the police at any time and spend the rest of his days alone behind bars. *My god! He was his brother, only worse. And he knew how much Lucille despised his brother. What was it that she had said? "You tell him that he better not come around here. He is not welcome. I don't want Tracy exposed to him."* That statement now applied equally to him, only more so.

Eventually, Steven lifted his cold body off the ground. He didn't care if the police captured him, and he didn't care if he was mugged. In fact, he wished someone would try. God, it would feel good to beat the crap out of somebody.

About halfway back to his small room, he passed a liquor store. His money had been so little and so precious that alcohol had been off his diet for months. *Fuck it,* he thought as he walked in and bought a bottle of whisky. Outside, he uncorked it and began to drink.

By the time he got to his room, he stumbled in and the room spun round and round. He fell to the bed and passed out.

When he woke, he didn't know what time it was or what day. He didn't care. Thank God, the bottle still had some whisky left in it. Steven saw himself in the mirror; he saluted the dirty, hairy bum and toasted him by raising the bottle and guzzling a bit more. "To you, you old, rotten bum. We are what we are." Steven looked at the almost-empty bottle and then at the old bum in the mirror again. "You've been a good friend my good man, too good," he said.

"I'm starting to like you too much, especially when you're drunk. Like now." Steven belched. "Sorry, excuse me. But it's time for us to leave each other," he slurred. "But not before another toast. To us!" Steven took another swig. "To Destinee!" After another swig, he stared at the mirror as seriously as he could. "And to beating the fuck out of Mr. Clayton Harris." The last of the bottle disappeared down his throat.

That same night at the Washington Arms Hotel:

As she entered the Washington Arms, Detective Saltarie reluctantly asked for the night manager by name. "I would like to speak to Mr. Ramon Hayes."

Chelle flashed her badge and the young woman behind the counter didn't ask any questions. Soon, the night manager stepped to the front of the check-in desk. He was dressed in a stiff white shirt and blue tie that matched the blue sport coat he was wearing, which was tastefully embroidered with "Washington Arms Hotel."

"Ah, Detective Saltarie, how pleasant to see you again." The manager's short stature and round face combined with his wide smile immediately made her think of the Cheshire cat once again.

Apparently, the Cheshire cat felt self-conscious about wearing the white gloves around her because he nervously began to remove them. Only after he had his gloves off did he offer her his hand in welcome.

Chelle took the rough, red, scaly hand in hers and gently shook it.

"Mr. Hayes, I have a small favor to ask. I have a few specific dates in which Senator Westcott claims to have stayed here. Would you mind verifying these dates for me? I don't think it will take us very long if we work together on it."

Ramon's pulse was quickening a bit. Working together with the detective would be a dream come true. "I ... I guess you are right. I, or, I mean, the Washington Arms, would be doing a service to the community in this case."

"Not just the community, Ramon. The nation. This is a national priority."

The Cheshire Cat puffed out his chest and gave an even wider smile. "Why don't you step around, we can look at the computer together."

"I really appreciate your help, Ramon," Chelle said as she moved into the position suggested by the manager.

"Under the circumstances, it would be very unlikely that the senator used his real name on registration." Ramon stared at the set of filthy computer keys, then at his bare hands.

When Ramon's hands hovered over the keys without touching them, she asked, "Something wrong?"

"I ... I usually type with my gloves on. I can't ... I mean I have to put my gloves on first."

Chelle was beginning to understand; the manager had a phobia. It would explain his red, raw hands.

"I can do it if you don't mind. I'm pretty good with computers."

"It's just that I just washed my hands. I ... I just don't want to get them dirty again."

"I understand, Ramon. Cleanliness is next to godliness."

"I ... I don't like to get dirty."

"No need to explain." Chelle meant it too; she had seen various phobias in her lifetime. In some, it became a severe handicap to daily living.

Chelle stepped past Ramon to the computer.

****

Ramon knew it wasn't his imagination; the pretty detective had purposely rubbed her breast against him. He was sure of it. Ramon inhaled the lovely scent coming from her hair. It was hard for him to concentrate. Still, he suggested, "If you press the history tab we can just scroll through the list to whatever date you want."

"According to my information, he would have checked in later in the afternoon."

Ramon dared to reach out toward Chelle's hand as he pointed to the page-down button. "Just press that a few times."

"How would I know if somebody paid in cash?"

Ramon felt sweat building under his sport jacket. His arm couldn't help but rub slightly against the detective's left breast as he pointed to a particular column.

"This notation means that whoever it was paid in cash."

He could have sworn that the detective moved even closer.

"There," Chelle said. "Mark Fisher. Does that sound familiar?"

"Yes, I can't be one hundred percent sure, but I think it was the senator. He had a beard. But when I saw the senator's picture in the paper, I thought he looked a bit like Mr. Fisher."

Ramon found it hard to concentrate. The smell of Chelle's hair made him feel aroused. He pointed to the screen and stepped even closer to her.

Their hands touched as they both pointed to the computer screen at the same time. Ramon's hand lingered. He thought the Detective's hand had too.

"There should be another date after that," Chelle said. "Let's see if we can find the same name again."

Chelle worked the keyboard some more quickly proceeding to a particular date. Though several times Ramon noticed she seemed to be interested in other names as well. Then when she reached a date weeks later than the first she scanned the list much slower until she found the name Mark Fisher again.

"You might be right about him. Mr. Fisher paid in cash again," Ramon said though now he knew that she knew exactly what name to look for.

Chelle turned toward Ramon. "Thank you so much."

Slowly, she slid her hand over his. He was sure she left it linger a bit longer than necessary.

"Ramon, you can't believe how helpful you have been."

Ramon held the big lobby door open for Chelle as she thanked him one last time.

****

Outside, the night air was cold, and she walked briskly back toward her car. Chelle chuckled out loud to herself as she walked in a light snow. The night manager certainly seemed to be smitten with her. His nervous flirtations and embarrassment over his germ phobia were quite obvious.

The important thing was that she had gotten what she had come for and more. Chalk one up for the senator, Chelle thought. The name and time was exactly as he had told his attorney in the letter.

The senator's letter had been particularly detailed. He mentioned that he always paid in cash and that he had let his hair grow out to hide his identity. That also checked with the manager's memory.

But what surprised her even more was that she found another name that was familiar. Apparently, Tiffany Maddenheart used the Washington Arms as well as the Saint Claire. Chelle wondered if Detective Harmon knew that as well.

Her day had been long, and it was time for a break. The truthfulness of the letter struck her as very odd; she needed some time to think, and the Billy Goat Tavern looked warm and inviting. Chelle sat by a high table next to the window, watching a light snow fall against the streetlight. It looked so peaceful; she spotted the camera that had captured the senator in the act of picking up and discarding the angry, and now-deceased, hooker.

In his letter, he had said it was all just an act to fool her pimp, Clayton Harris. It was a good act, because the video footage was very incriminating. But if the senator were telling the truth about that too, could it be that someone else was the murderer as he claimed? But that didn't make sense. Chelle's head began to spin. If it wasn't Clayton Harris, who? Harmon? Was that possible?

"It is a pretty snow isn't it?" A tall, good-looking man stopped by her table, looking at the snow falling passed the window.

Chelle had been deep in thought, she was surprised as the comment drew her out of her trance. She looked up at the man's face, assessing that he posed no threat. She looked back outside. "Yes it is."

"Mind if I have a seat? It's a beautiful view. The snow is pretty too."

Chelle rolled her eyes. She was in no mood for small talk or a date. "Yes, absolutely, help yourself. I was just leaving."

Chelle stood up, slipped on her jacket, left a tip, and went out the door. She walked into the night and the gently falling snow. Chelle cinched the belt of her black leather winter coat, and glanced up at the video camera once again. Something wasn't right, but she couldn't quite put her trigger finger on it. Then it came to her. The same camera may have captured another customer of Destinee's.

When they had originally searched the camera recordings, they stopped when they found the senator's car. It proved a motive. So, along with the other overwhelming evidence, they never felt the need to go any further. Her job was to collect enough evidence to make a conviction stick, not to poke holes in her own case. But what if someone else did kill the girl? Possibly somebody who also picked up the hooker the day she died.

Chelle wrestled with her conscience. The senator was the murderer, plain and simple. In this particular case, she had found and supplied ample motive and evidence for any idiot of a prosecuting attorney to make a conviction stick. Now it was time to let the district attorney's office do their job. Her only duty now was to capture Steven Westcott so the DA could bring him to trial. At that point, it would be a slam dunk. Spending the taxpayers' money and spending her time to prove otherwise would be a waste of precious resources.

But the nagging feeling persisted. Why would a man who knew so much about DNA evidence be so sure that he could prove somebody else was the murderer? He must know about the semen inside the girl and the blood in his car and the knife with his prints on it. Those things would be all but impossible to dispute.

Chelle thought back to the notes he had written for his attorney. If they were accurate, his semen shouldn't have been inside the girl. There certainly wasn't a knife, and the only blood was from one small scratch.

If the senator were telling the truth, he wouldn't know about the evidence collected against him because, as far as he was concerned, it didn't exist.

Chelle stared up at the camera as gentle snowflakes drifted around it. She lifted her leather collar around her neck and slowly turned away.

Anacostia, Washington DC, three days later:

"Harmon, where you been?"

"After your white bitch was killed, you became contaminated."

"Tell me about it. I was under surveillance. What I want to know is when is that bitch detective going to leave me alone? She says she knows I didn't do it."

"Not you they're after. They thought the senator was going to come after you. You were the bait. But it's over. Ran out of time and money. It was all Chelle's idea, and nobody buys it anymore."

"We still got the same deal going? I haven't felt the love lately, bro."

"I told you, you were too hot for me to go near. But it's over. So you give me some snow, and I'll give you some information that will make it worth your time."

"I got a girl, black, tall but built. Wears her hair in braids and goes by the name Tanya. Tell her she should give you two quarters and you don't owe no dead presidents. I'll call her and tell her to expect you. Same corner Destinee used to work. And Harmon, when are you guys going to catch the senator dude? I've been jumpy ever since the bitch told me he was going to kill me."

"Don't worry about it. It was all a figment of her imagination. And you won't have to worry about Chelle much longer either. She is wearing out her welcome real quick. After this thing dies down a bit, the department is going to have to fire her for losing a US senator. Then I'm going to be the top cop."

"It's not just me, my girls are spooked too. They think there is a killer out there who likes to kill prostitutes with a knife."

"Tell them to notch down. No such thing going on. They have nothing to worry about with Detective Bruce Harmon watching out for them."

"I'm telling you, they're spooked."

"I'm telling you that I would know about it if there was something going on. There isn't. For every bitch that was murdered, we caught the killer."

Anacostia, Washington DC:

Steven's stomach still wasn't feeling too well as he cleaned up the room. Bottles and garbage and junk food wrappers were lying all about. It looked like the aftermath of quite a party. He had hidden for long enough; if anybody had even an inkling of where or who he was, he would have been caught by now.

He had studied Clayton's home and habits. There had been constant surveillance, but that had stopped as far as he could tell. He had waited them out and had won. Like an omen, Steven noticed a crumpled up newspaper on the floor that he'd used to protect his cherished bottle of whisky. The headline said, "In several weeks, the leaders of Israel and Palestine will meet at Camp David."

Steven picked up the paper to read the article. He was very aware of Camp David. It was in Maryland, not far from Washington DC. It was a military base that was used to give the president of the United States a safe place to unwind and experience some privacy. The paper went on to say, "It is where peace was brokered between Israel and Egypt back in 1978."

Steven lifted the paper and set it on the table, unfolding it as if he were just handed the Holy Grail. This was not only good news for the world, but it could be good for his current situation as well. *Divide and conquer.*

Steven started to formulate a plan. He took off the dirty, old coat and stripped down to his underwear. It was time for Steven Westcott to take back what had been taken from him or die trying. He looked into the mirror and promised to himself, in two weeks, Clayton would pay for what he had taken from him.

Before the last week of self-pity, he had a fairly steady exercise routine. If nothing else, it eased the boredom. That meant he wasn't totally out of shape, but that didn't mean he was ready for a fight. Steven needed to become a soldier again.

With a newfound sense of vengeance, Steven started an exercise regime. He installed a pull up bar and other simple equipment that he had found in trashcans over the last months to get back into shape. Steven also practiced his own form of Tai chi. In slow-motion, he performed self-defense moves. They were done slowly for pace and balance and correct breathing. But with the mental exercises he incorporated, he could see the move happening ten times faster and with deadly force.

Recusing to the small room for days at a time, he spent four weeks nearly constantly exercising. Besides Tai chi, he practiced defensive skills that he had become more than rusty on—there was little need for a senator to disarm an armed assailant. But with practice, it was all starting to come back to him. Steven felt strong and confident and impatient. Soon, very, very soon, his ordeal would take a change for the better or ... or he would die trying.

Four weeks later:

Steven flexed his muscles a bit vainly in the mirror. He had kept the pact he made with himself. He was as ready as he would ever be. Steven set down the scissors in his hand and brushed his neatly cropped beard and newly trimmed mustache, and he ran his fingers through his cut and cleaned hair. The old bum was gone, nowhere to be seen. But he had to admit that he hardly looked like the man who had run from the police months ago either.

He had somehow survived the worst of winter; the small calendar he had in his room reminded him that March was about to begin as he crossed out the last day of February. There was a lot of winter left, but the coldest and worst should be over. With only four hundred dollars left to his name, it was time to move on.

He tossed on the old, tattered coat for one last mission. The coat's oversized pockets were convenient for a few special tools. Steven looked back over the room, it had served its purpose, and he would miss its security. He closed the door behind him and locked it for what he assumed would be the last time.

Chapter 34

The old bum, hunched over and pushing a grocery cart full of aluminum cans, made his way toward Clayton Harris's house. Steven moved slowly, searching through garbage cans along the way as usual. It was late afternoon as he pushed his cart toward the garbage cans outside Clayton's home. As he suspected, Clayton's gold Cadillac wasn't in its parking spot.

Steven strategically placed the shopping cart between him and the street. He pretended to search through the garbage as he listened for any sounds from inside the home. Through previous surveillance, he had detected a certain pattern in the homes activities. Usually, Clayton and the girls arose late morning. After some hollering and screaming at each other, they would eventually leave in the afternoon. The girls first, and then Clayton would drive off hours later. Usually, Clayton was the first person back home, where he waited for the girls and collected their earnings from the evening.

That had been a pretty consistent pattern, and Steven was counting on it for tonight. It was very possible that tonight would be Clayton Harris's last night alive. Clayton had taken Steven's family and life away from him; the least he could do was repay the favor.

Steven was counting on the Camp David peace negotiations. The dangers to the high-profile participants were very real. That meant the FBI, CIA, DHS, Secret Service, and the local police would all be stretched pretty thin right now. And that meant this was the time for him to make his move.

Steven slipped on the black balaclava over his head. When it was pulled down tight it covered his hair and face, even his beard. His eyes were all that were visible. Steven dared to peek through the windows, looking for activity. So far, it didn't seem as if anyone were home. He checked the back door, hoping to jimmy it open, but it was securely locked with a padlock on the outside.

Then he checked the windows. They had steel grates over them, but they were mounted also from the outside. It seemed that Clayton was more worried about keeping someone in. That was even better than Steven had hoped. The mounting brackets were accessible from the outside. With the multi-tool he had picked up from the resale shop, he went to work removing the mounting brackets.

Under the cover of darkness, Steven lifted off one of the steel grates. He could feel the coldness of the metal pushing through his black leather gloves. At that point, it was fairly easy to pry up the old window. Warm air greeted him as he stepped inside the home of Clayton Harris.

Steven waited in the unlit room. He kept his gloves and balaclava on. His eyes had ample time to adjust to the dark. He closed the drapes to keep the streetlights from casting shadows. The dark would be his ally tonight. Steven felt an unusual calm as the lights from Clayton's Cadillac brushed through the curtains and gently washed over the wall on the far side of the room.

Steven's plan really wasn't much of a plan. The idea was to beat Mr. Clayton Harris to within an inch of his life. As a special forces operative, killing was a trained instinct. The hard part would be keeping him alive enough to give useful information. If he died, so would the answers that he desperately needed.

Steven calmly stood up and positioned himself next to the door. He reached into his coat pocket and pulled out a length of wash line he had found lying about. It was thin but strong. As the door creaked open, Steven waited in the shadows. The trap was set. He calmed his breathing. Every muscle in his body was ready.

Steven saw Clayton reach for the light switch, but nothing happened. Steven had taken out the bulbs.

"Fuck," Clayton cursed the darkness and then closed the door.

With one lunge, Steven was on the big pimp with the wash line around his neck.

Clayton tried turning toward Steven unsuccessfully with his hands thrashing wildly.

Steven pressed his knee deep into Clayton's back.

The line tightened on Clayton's throat, choking him. Desperately, the pimp tried to get his hands under it as he gasped for breath. Steven held on as tight as he could, knowing the struggle would soon be over.

The much bigger and younger Clayton arched his body forward, lifting Steven off the ground. Steven kicked a lamp to the floor as his feet struggled for a foothold. It crashed into pieces.

Clayton pushed back with his entire weight as hard and fast as he could. Soon both men were heading backward.

A two-hundred-and-seventy-pound sledgehammer slammed Steven into the corner of the doorframe. Clayton pressed forward and then back again even harder.

"Oomph!" Steven's lungs seemed to collapse as the air tore out of them.

Now it was a race to see who would stay conscious the longest. In a last, desperate move, the pimp did the completely unexpected. He rolled his head and body forward into the death grip of the line. Steven's legs thrashed wildly as they came off the ground. At the same time, Clayton dropped to his knees.

With nothing to stop Steven's forward momentum, he flew over Clayton's back.

Clayton grabbed at Steven's neck, but all he got was a handful of balaclava.

With a hard thump, Steven's body pounded flat on the floor in front of Clayton.

Steven was learning a few hard lessons. First, he wasn't the man he was twenty years ago. Second, a few weeks of exercising didn't compensate for years of complacency.

Clayton reached for his throat, clearing the line away from it as he gasped for air.

Steven's plan had failed, he had just lost the advantage. Now he was in a fight for his life. He rolled out of harm's way. With his face exposed, he stood up, only feet away from Clayton, who was staring him down as he gasped for air.

Clayton pulled out a gun from the small of his back. Steven didn't waste a second. He bull-rushed the big man, hoping he could attack quickly enough before Clayton could take aim.

Steven's body hit with such force that the gun flew out of Clayton's hand as he swung it around. The gun went flying across the room and was in the air as Clayton's back cracked into the same doorway Steven had just recovered from.

This time, the door broke open, and both men crashed into the next room. The street lamp just outside the window threw light into the kitchen. Steven saw the gun hit the floor and slide under the refrigerator as the two big men slammed onto the kitchen table.

The table strained against their weight for only a moment. With a crack, it snapped in two, and the two men collapsed to the floor with it.

On the floor, Steven jabbed his knee into Clayton's groin. The big man groaned. Then, Steven lifted his arm and brought his fist down on Clayton's face, breaking the pimp's nose with a crack. Seconds later, it started gushing red.

Clayton kicked up and with one powerful throw from his arms he tossed Steven over his head. Clayton struggled to his feet, facing Steven.

Steven got to his feet and backed away. He knew he was way out-muscled. Sure, he knew a thing or two about leverage, but Clayton Harris was no stranger to street fighting. He didn't like the odds anymore.

Both men were breathing hard, watching each other intently. Adrenalin was pumping hard through their hearts. Both knew that they were fighting for their very lives.

Steven saw a knife lying on the counter and grabbed it. The knife would even the odds against the big man. Too bad he needed Clayton alive. It would be much easier to just kill the bastard.

"What the fuck, old man," Clayton said. "Have you gone fucking nuts?"

"Listen, you son of a bitch, you are going to tell me everything I want to know, or you will be a dead man. And you won't like the way you are going to die."

Clayton maneuvered around the broken table, keeping it between them. Neither was going to take the chance of stumbling over it to attack the other.

"Why did you kill Destinee?"

"That dumb bitch? I didn't kill her. Some crazy senator dude killed her. What the fuck do you care?"

"I happen to know that he didn't."

"You know this? I'm going to kill you. I'm going to break you in fucking two you old fool."

Steven gritted his teeth and threatened back in a guttural voice that sounded younger than he looked. "Tell me the truth, and I might let you live. You thought she was holding out on you, stealing from you. So you had to make an example of her."

"Who the fuck are you, old man? Why do you know so much about her?"

Clayton was tired of the stalemate, he reached down and lifted the remnants of the table and tossed it toward Steven.

Steven threw up his arms to protect his body as Clayton rushed him, using the broken tabletop as a shield from the knife. Steven caught a side of the table with his free hand, tossed it to the side, and took a powerful swing with his other hand. The knife cut deep into Clayton's thigh and immediately the slit in his pants turned crimson red.

Then Steven brought up his leg and gave the big man a kick. Clayton screamed with pain as the knife cut tore open even more.

Clayton fell back against the far wall; Steven raised the knife for another strike, taking the time to plan his attack.

The only thing separating Clayton from Steven was the old refrigerator. Clayton pressed his body against it, and with one thrust from his muscular arms, the refrigerator came crashing down toward Steven, pushing him down to the floor. Steven dropped the knife to protect his body from the full weight of the refrigerator, which landed on his feet, trapping them.

Clayton dove for the now-exposed gun.

Steven lifted the refrigerator just enough to free his legs and then, with a push from both his feet, he kicked it back toward Clayton. It slammed into the pimp's hand just as he picked up the gun.

Steven heard a crack of bone an instant before a shot went off into the floor.

The big, black man cursed as he dropped the gun.

Steven lunged forward.

Landing on top of the pimp, Steven started to pummel Clayton with his gloved fists, his rage fully unleashed at last.

"Why, why did you kill her, you bastard?" Steven screamed like a mad man. "She was just a girl, barely a woman. She just wanted out of the trap you put her in."

Clayton fended off the blows the best he could with his one good hand. Steven felt an uncontrolled wildness come out of him as he tried to break the face of the man who had killed Destinee. Punching him again and again.

In desperation, Clayton made a tremendous thrust with his powerful legs against the wall. This unbalanced Steven enough that Clayton was able to use his good arm to push Steven off of him.

Clayton kicked Steven in the side and then stood, breathing hard through his mouth. He balled up his good hand into a solid fist, preparing to fight to the death. The blood had stopped pouring out his nose because the swelling had closed it but not his leg. He took long heavy breaths through his mouth as he talked.

"I'm telling you—I didn't kill her. You can ask the police. I was out of town, and they checked me out."

The light from the lone streetlamp streamed in through the window. Steven watched as Clayton licked some of the blood off his lips, his face and eyes swollen. "Look, fucker, I don't know who you are, but you have to believe me that I didn't do it. I kind of liked the bitch. I even took care of her mother when she was sick."

"Who was her mother?" Steven demanded.

"Jasmine Sanford."

"Her name was Shatoya Anderson."

"Look, old man, I only know what they tell me. But this I know for a fact. I didn't kill the girl."

Steven contemplated his next move. Clayton was badly hurt, and it was time to take advantage of that. But he was finally getting some answers, so he stood his ground for a moment longer.

"You could have easily had one of your asshole friends kill her when you were gone. Giving you a perfect alibi. Well I'm not the police, and I'm not buying it."

Steven saw a moment of enlightenment in the big man's eyes.

"Fuck!" Clayton cursed as he squinted, examining Steven's face as the light through the window shone on it. "I know who you are. You're that senator. You're the guy that killed her. You're just looking for someone else to blame so you can go free. Just cause you are a rich big shot, you think you can frame an innocent nigger like myself. Just like that cop said you would."

"We both know I didn't kill her," Steven growled.

Clayton's breathing was steadying. Still, he took some deep breaths before saying, "Fuck, man, everybody on the fucking planet knows you did it. Why are you trying to blame me?"

Steven was glad for the dialogue. He hoped to trap the pimp with his own words under the stress of the situation.

"It looks like we are going to have to do this the hard way. If you know who I am, then you know what I am capable of, so you might as well tell me the truth now."

Clayton was thinking about his options when they heard a gunshot outside. The sound distracted Clayton for a second, and that was when Steven lunged once again.

Clayton came up with his good hand swinging, which was just what Steven was planning for. He faked his own swing only to use the big man's momentum against him.

Steven twirled and pounded Clayton on his back with both of his hands clasped like a giant hammer. In the next moment, Steven had the pimp's broken hand in his, and he twisted it hard.

The giant man fell forward in pain.

"Trust me, you will tell me the truth, and you'll have wished that you had done it much sooner."

In the midst of his pain, Clayton started to laugh. "Fuck you. You poor bastard. I didn't do it, or have anybody else do it for me."

With his free hand, Steven grabbed the broken lamp off the floor.

"You had better tell me what you know, this is the pleasant part of what I'm going to do to you."

"Fuck me, but fuck you more. Ha! I do know something you don't. See, I know I didn't kill her. And now I know that you didn't kill her either or you wouldn't be here risking your neck to find out who did. Man, you are so fucked. You can do whatever you want to me, but it won't change the fact that I didn't do it. Whatever you do to me won't help you prove that I did. And it won't change the fact that the police have you cold, man. Ha! You are so fucked!" Clayton laughed some more as he spit out blood from his cut lip and broken nose.

"When you wake up, you might want to change your story," Steven said.

"Don't you see? You're the fool; it's not about Destinee."

"What the fuck are you talking about?"

"Somebody wanted to frame you, and you supplied the victim. Do you really think I got all that DNA shit from you? Hell, I'm just a dumb fucking pimp."

"Destinee scratched me by accident. That's how my DNA got under her fingernail."

"How do you explain your DNA in her pussy, man?"

"What are you talking about?"

"That bitchy detective, Saltarie. She told me they found your DNA inside the girl."

"We didn't; I never touched her."

"Yea right, whatever, but that's what she said when she warned me that you would come here to get me."

"When?"

"A couple of months ago." Clayton groaned as Steven pressed on his hand.

"No, you lying bastard, not that easy." Steven twisted the broken hand harder even though he wasn't quite so sure anymore.

"Fuck you man, fuck you." Steven let up the pressure on Clayton's hand for a moment, Clayton sucked in a big gulp of air.

"What else did she say?"

"There was blood too, your blood on the girl and her blood in your car. Fingerprints too. You are so fucked man." Clayton chuckled.

Steven ripped the electric cord loose from the lamp and then wrapped it around Clayton's wrist as he thought about what he was saying. If it was true, the big man was making some sense; he had lots of enemies, though none he thought capable of such a plot.

"Why should I believe you?" Steven started twisting the hand again. "How do you know all of this? It was never in the papers."

"Listen to me, just listen. Saltarie, that white detective chick, she said that you would come here. She said you were delusional; you told her that if she couldn't find the killer you would. And you told her you knew that I did it."

"Why on earth would she tell you of all people those things?"

"Cause I didn't believe her, and cause I thought it was a trap or something. So she told me why I wasn't a suspect anymore but was in danger from you."

Steven tied off the cord from the broken lamp around Clayton's hands.

"I didn't do it man, I swear! And if you didn't do it, somebody else did. It's that fucking simple."

Shit, Steven thought. What if he was right? The man knew too many details to be lying. If he was being set up to take a big fall by somebody, Clayton was right about something else: that somebody wasn't him.

He had been so blinded by his rage and so convinced that Clayton had killed Destinee, he never considered that he was being framed. Steven cursed at himself for not taking the time to think through the sequence of events.

The pimp could be right. Destinee wasn't the target, never was. She was just a pawn in someone's game to frame him for a murder. Whoever had collected the DNA evidence necessary to frame him didn't care who the victim was as long as he or she could pin the blame for it on him.

Steven reached around to the front of the big man's pants.

"Hey, what the fuck are you doing man?"

Steven unfastened Clayton's belt and ripped it off his pants. With it, he tied the pimp's feet together. The fact was, Steven wasn't a cold-blooded killer.

Steven gaged Clayton, then said, "If I find out you're lying to me, I will be back and I won't be so kind."

It was time for him to leave, but to where? He had to find out if the pimp was telling the truth. If he was, then somebody had followed him, collected his DNA, his blood, and fingerprints. How, he didn't know. But it was no wonder the police were so sure he had killed Destinee. They had much more evidence than Steven could have possibly known.

Clayton was also right that he had supplied the motive and the perfect pawn to be murdered for their plan. *But why? And who?*

Steven searched Clayton's pockets and found his phone. Then he wearily pushed himself off of the prone pimp and stood up. He looked around at the broken home. In the kitchen was a towel. Steven picked it up and tied it around the pimps bleeding thigh as tight as he could.

"That will stop the bleeding."

Then he walked out the door into the cold night air.

Steven looked up and down the poorly lit street. Apparently, nobody had reported the gunshot from outside or inside the home. Or at least the police hadn't responded yet. Anacostia was a rough and tumble place, gunshots were unfortunately fairly common.

Then Steven thought about what he had just learned. Evidently, the Washington he knew was a rough place too. But who would want to frame him that badly to collect his DNA and to kill an innocent woman? *Who could possibly hate me that much?*

Chapter 35

Detective Saltarie went back to the security recording from outside the Billy Goat Tavern, glad that the entire day's footage was sequestered. Unfortunately for Chelle, Destinee had a productive day. Many cars besides Steven Westcott's had stopped. One, she positively identified as Clayton Harris's Cadillac right after the senator and Destinee had their scuffle. Destinee was killed hours later, plenty of time for Clayton to get to the airport. So his presence proved nothing.

Watching hours of grainy time-lapse recordings, trying to match up best guesses of license plate numbers with best guesses of auto make and model was tedious and probably unnecessary, but might become important.

The one lucky thing was that Destinee was at least consistent. She always returned to the area just north of the Billy Goat Tavern. The site was at the outer fringes of the frame, but the camera was able to pick up most of it. It was getting closer to the assumed time of Destinee's death, so the culprit had to appear soon. However, as darkness came, the only light shining on the parkway was from a decorative lamppost. The model and make of cars was becoming difficult to make out. Chelle's eyes were so tired of watching the grainy and dark footage that she even thought one of the cars looked like hers.

It was only when Destinee didn't return to her corner that Chelle had a potential suspect. They played the last pick-up over and over again. The only thing they could determine was that the last vehicle was a dark sedan, and it didn't belong to the senator or Clayton Harris. It certainly didn't prove the senator didn't murder the hooker; it proved nothing more than the fact that Destinee's last hook of the evening on that corner wasn't the senator, or at least not his car.

Chelle had a dark thought. *Could that last car be Detective Harmon's? The size and shape seemed right. It was a sedan like Harmon's department-issued vehicle.*

It was still hours from her supposed time of death, certainly plenty of time for another rendezvous with the senator.

Even if the last vehicle wasn't the killer, finding the last person to see her alive was important. Chelle had been so sure of her case. Now, a lot of clouds were forming in her mind. Maybe that person dropped her off somewhere where she met up with the senator.

Reading the license was hopeless, and even the make and model was questionable in the darkness. All they knew for sure was that the car was a dark-colored sedan. Chelle buried her head into her hands as she stared at the very best still shot they could get. Unfortunately, she couldn't tell if it was Harmon's police cruiser or not. This was the best lead she had in a month, and she was determined to use it. Somehow, she had to find out who the driver of that vehicle was.

Across town that same evening in Anacostia:

Steven closed and locked the door of Clayton's home. With the keys to the pimp's Cadillac in his hand, he had no choice but to add *car thief* to his repertoire. Clayton was gagged and tied securely inside. It would be only a matter of time before he got free and then the largest manhunt the city had ever seen would be afoot.

Steven needed an escape plan, and he needed it fast. Clayton's car was no doubt going to act like a magnet. Steven backed out the drive and then drove away toward the downtown area. Then it struck him that he had nowhere to go. He was headed down the road, but to where, and who? Just an hour ago, he was so sure he would have a full confession from Clayton. Then he would have passed the new information on to Detective Saltarie, and then just wait for his name to be cleared. His freedom had been so near, but now his hopes had all evaporated. He had to get out of the city fast. It was getting late, and many of the stores along the darkened street were starting to roll the heavy steel gates across the storefronts. Steven remembered the resale shop where he had bought his current clothes. It would still be open and would probably be his last chance to make a few purchases; he would have to spare the time.

Across town an hour later:

Detective Saltarie was lost in thought as she decided to call it a night and head home. Her eyes and mind were as tired as she could ever remember. Straining her eyes, looking for faint details on the video monitors all day, and running report after report had taken their toll. Maybe she would have time for a glass of wine at home before dropping onto her bed. Tomorrow was another day, hopefully a slow day for her because a snowstorm was predicted to hit tonight.

The phone on her hip rang. Chelle dropped her hand to answer it, then thought better of it. It was time to call it quits for the night. Whoever it was could leave a message or try again in the morning. She unclipped it from her belt and glanced at the number on the screen. She didn't recognize it. She was just about to turn it off, but her intuition changed her mind. The phone rang once again. Somehow, she knew that if she answered it, it would be the end of the night's sleep she was so looking forward to.

"Hello."

"Hey, sweet thing. This is your old friend Clayton Harris."

Shit, Chelle thought. Why did I answer?

"It's been a long day, Mr. Harris. What do you want?"

"Not that much really, especially seeing as I have some information that you would give anything for."

"You've got my attention for thirty seconds."

"Listen, sweet thing. I will only talk to you. If you get anybody else involved, I'm going to lawyer up. You won't know what I know for weeks. But, if you bring your sweet little ass over here right now, I think you and me will be able to come to an understanding."

"Damn it Clayton! This is no time to screw with me."

"I want a few things from you. A promise or two, that's all. Nothing you can't do, I mean, between friends and all. But only you, in person, and you don't want to wait."

"Harris, this had better be good." Chelle pulled out the concealed red and blue flashing lights next to her seat, slapped it on top of her black Crown Victoria, and turned on the siren.

Chelle didn't trust the pimp but also didn't sense any danger. Still, she called Pat, who was already at home, and gave him a heads up that if he didn't hear from her in half hour, to bring in the cavalpeabodyry.

A few blocks away from Clayton's, she turned off her siren and lights. Attracting extra attention, especially in this neighborhood wouldn't be helpful.

Chelle knocked on the door, one of Clayton's girls opened it. Usually, streetwalkers were cocky when dealing with the police. This girl showed none of that. She looked anxious to have Chelle enter the home. Now that was unusual.

"What the hell happened to you?" Chelle could see the puffed up lips, broken nose and bruised eyes and cheeks of the big man. Not to mention the swollen hand he was tenderly holding with his other.

"I'll tell you, but first, I need you to promise me a few things."

Chelle looked around and saw the busted up furniture and toppled refrigerator. She would eventually get the truth out of Clayton. But she instinctively knew that she didn't have until *eventually* to get it.

"Make it quick. I don't have all night!" Chelle demanded.

"When I tell you what I know, I bet you *will* have all night."

It took awhile to negotiate their deal, but when Clayton told what had happened, Chelle could hardly believe what she was hearing. "You mean he broke into your house, waited in the dark, and then threatened to torture you until you admitted to killing the hooker?"

"I'm telling you exactly that. For an old white dude, he was pretty fast and strong." Clayton showed her his leg wound. "The son of a bitch stabbed me. I was tied up for a fucking hour before the girls came home and found me. That son of a bitch is nuts."

Chelle looked disgusted as Clayton handed her the knife. "Maybe if you don't touch everything, we can get some prints off of these items and prove your story is true."

"Everything is true. Who do you think cut my leg, a surgeon? Besides, he wore gloves the whole time."

"All this blood, is any of this his?" Chelle asked.

"No, I told you, he was quick, and he attacked me in the dark. I didn't have a fucking chance."

"Looks like you had a chance to me. The house is a disaster."

"None of that matters. The fucker took my keys and stole my car."

"You said he was going to torture you. So why didn't he?"

"Cause I convinced him that I didn't do it either."

"What do you mean *either*?"

"The son of a bitch was twisting my broken hand to make me admit I killed the girl. That was when I realized that he didn't kill her."

Chelle slumped against a wall. She thought she was beginning to understand.

"How do you know this?" She asked.

"He really was looking for the murderer. He wasn't just pretending. I know a desperate man when I see one," Clayton said.

"I convinced him that somebody is framing him, and that someone isn't me."

"God help you if you are lying to me," Chelle warned.

"Find my fucking car and my fucking phone and you'll find him, I guarantee it."

"I intend to. What's this?" Chelle pointed at a black balaclava on the floor.

"The son of a bitch was wearing it, but I ripped it off him."

"Don't touch anything until we say you can." If she were right, inside the hat would be her proof. All it would take would be one hair sample left behind and then they could prove if it was the senator's cap. But that would take days.

"One other thing, sweet thing."

"What?"

"He seemed to know the girl's mother. He said her name wasn't Jasmine Sanford, that it was really Shatoya Anderson."

Chelle notified her captain of her suspicions, and he promptly notified the FBI, who notified everybody else. Chelle guarded the house until more police and lab technicians arrived. She also ordered an ambulance for Clayton. It didn't take her long to get the word out to every cop on the street of the description of Clayton's car. She especially wanted them to check the train station, bus depots, and airports.

Senator Steven Westcott couldn't be underestimated. He had disappeared in plain sight once before. She couldn't afford to let it happen again. But, unfortunately, he had quite a head start.

Peabody, Massachusetts:

Lucille Westcott was downstairs folding some laundry when the phone rang. She didn't recognize the number displayed on her cell phone. Still, she answered it.

"Hello, who is this please?"

"Lucille, it's me. It's Steven."

Lucille nearly fainted. "Steven, Steven is that really you?"

Chapter 36

North side of the Anacostia River heading toward Lincoln Park:

On the verge of tears, Steven responded. "I miss you and Tracy so much."

"Oh my god, Steven, you are still alive." Lucille sounded more surprised than relieved.

"Honey, please listen. I don't have much time. Whatever you've heard, it's wrong, they're lies. I didn't kill the girl. Somebody is framing me. I don't know how, but somebody made it look like I killed her, but I didn't. You have to believe me!"

"Oh my god, Steven." Steven heard Lucille pause as if gasping for air.

"Steven, give yourself up. You are just making things worse."

"Honey, I'm so sorry for what I put you and Tracy through. But I can't give myself up. I didn't do it, and I have to find out who did."

"You were having an affair with her," Lucille said.

"No! No I wasn't. You have got to believe me. I was just trying to get some damaging photos back. The pictures were from back in my days in the service, but they could have hurt us all if they made the press."

Steven pulled Clayton's Cadillac into a dark parking lot and drove to the back of a closed restaurant. The sign for Arby's was in place, but the glass was broken and unlit. He put it in park; he knew he was too distracted to be driving.

"So you met with her more than once in a private hotel room, and you didn't tell the CIA or FBI or anybody that you were being blackmailed by a twenty-one-year-old hooker? Come on, Steven, how gullible do you think I am? And what pictures? Of you and her doing what?"

"Not her and I, her mother, it was ages ago. Honey, listen, I can't talk long." He looked at the clock on the dash of the car. The call was risky, but he had to do it.

"Steven, how could you? Just give yourself up before they kill you. You are considered armed and very dangerous."

"Lucille, don't you understand? I didn't do it. I have to find out who did."

"Steven, come to your senses, it's no use denying it. Your DNA, your fingerprints, her blood in your car. My god, Steven, your semen and pubic hair were found inside the poor girl. Christ almighty, your own law would have you convicted twenty times over."

Steven heard the anger in her voice. That was the last thing he wanted to hear, though he should have expected it.

"No, Lucille, that's impossible, we never had sex."

"Give yourself up before you or somebody else is hurt or worse. And don't ever call me again. And don't even think about talking to Tracy, not now, not ever. For her sake, I'm begging you, forget about us."

Steven scanned the area for unusual activity and lowered the window to listen for any sirens.

"Lucille, please ... please. I need you to believe me. You have to. You don't understand. I didn't do it. Please believe me. Somebody is framing me. I need your help. Who would do it? Help me think. Who wants me out of the way that much to kill somebody? Lucille I have to see you. You need to listen to me. I can't live with myself knowing you and Tracy think I'm a murderer."

"Steven, you're delusional. Give yourself up. And in case you haven't heard, I am divorcing you. What you did was way beyond forgiveness. I have to look out for Tracy and me now, and as much as possible, we have to try to forget that you were ever a part of our lives."

The phone clicked, and Steven felt as if he were dangling on the edge of a precipice, and his one reason to cling on to life had just disappeared. He stared at the phone in his hand. He could call her back, but to what end?

Steven powered off the phone, then he looked to the sky and prayed. *Please let this be a dream and please, please let me wake up from it.*

It started to snow and Steven looked at the phone in his hand that he had risked so much to use. What good is a phone, if you have nobody to call? The police, CIA, Secret Service, and FBI had all probably listened to his conversation with his wife—ex-wife, Steve corrected himself. Undoubtedly soon, there would be police cars, and probably helicopters swarming the area, having honed in on the cell phone location. It was time to move on. Cautiously, he pulled back out onto the roadway, fighting back his emotions.

Washington DC was no longer a safe haven for him. Somehow, he had to get out of town. His chances of staying a free man were slim throughout the country, but they were even worse here. Steven pointed the car toward the bus station. It was time to leave.

A fire raged inside of him that was quite different than before. He would be damned if anybody, *anybody*, including his wife, would keep him from his daughter.

Steven felt waves of emotion wash over him. As a soldier trained to control them, he tried to identify the ones that could drive him to make mistakes. Anger seemed to be at the top of the list right now. He knew he had to control it, because anger caused slip-ups. It wasn't just the anger; it was the person he was now angry with. The depth of the emotion was something he wasn't prepared for. How could Lucille turn her back on him like that? A lesser woman he might understand, but he didn't marry a lesser woman.

Lucille was strong, smart and, above all, objective. They had been through so much together; she shouldn't believe the lies against him. She should be the one person he could count on to have his back. She should be working the inside and, in military terms, laying cover for him so he could attack the real target. However, he had learned something invaluably important.

She had confirmed what the pimp had told him. Somehow, his semen was inside of the girl. He was being framed, and whoever was doing it, knew what they were doing. Somebody had somehow duplicated his DNA and incorporated it into somebody else's semen—theoretically impossible. Whoever had done this was sparing no expense.

Steven arrived near the bus station; restraining his anger, he parked behind an industrial building. He stepped out into the cold. Steven couldn't get their conversation out of his mind.

For her to abandon him was one thing, but to threaten him with removing, no, stealing his daughter from his life was quite another. "Fuck her!" He threw the phone to the concrete as hard as he could. Then he ground it into the pavement with his foot.

With an angry kick, what was left of the phone flew across the parking lot. Pieces scattered everywhere.

With renewed vigor, Steven held onto his life or death mission. His daughter would learn the truth about her father, or he would die in the effort. If he weren't successful, living in a cage, unable to unlock the shackles of the lies against him, was not a life he was interested in.

Steven Cowboy Westcott didn't surrender to the enemy that easily. And right now, the whole world was his enemy. "Fuck 'em!" he cursed the world, then, "fuck her," he cursed Lucille one more time. This wasn't over until it was over. Senator Westcott was no more, but look out world, Cowboy was back and he was much more dangerous.

Clayton would no doubt give his exact description to the police, including his attire and facial hair. He grabbed at the bag that contained the extra clothes he had bought at the resale shop in Anacostia. Steven took off his clothes and put on the new/used clothes from the resale shop. He stuffed an old, worn baseball cap into a small backpack, then he flattened the backpack as best he could and put it on. Then he covered himself with a heavy and long overcoat, which he buttoned up tight around his neck to protect against the cold. It wasn't much, but in the short time he had, it was the best he could do.

Calmly and casually, Steven walked two blocks from his car. A bus stop was down just another block, but that wasn't where he was going. He was heading another two blocks away to the Hilton Garden Inn of Arlington.

There was a large construction dumpster sitting alongside a construction site, and he tossed his clothes and the torn winter jacket he had worn for the last months into it and covered them with trash. Then he walked the two blocks and entered the hotel through its restaurant, The Great American Grill. He passed through the restaurant into the main lobby and then headed toward the main entryway like he owned the place.

Steven's plan was to look very much the opposite of his former character. To that end, when he had found a bowler hat at the resale shop, the disguise he now wore came to mind.

When he opened the doors of the main entryway of the hotel and stepped out into the cold, a very dapper-looking, bearded, English gentleman exited. His scraggly mustache and beard were now perfectly trimmed.

His neatly closed umbrella touched the ground lightly with each step and clicked slightly on the concrete walk. The bowler hat was low on his brow as he walked with a confident purpose. Holding his umbrella in one hand, he extended a five out his other to the doorman.

"Taxi, sir?"

"Yes."

"To where, sir?"

"The Air Force Memorial," Steven said, trying to fake a British accent to match his appearance. His hope was that such an outlandish change of identity would fool anybody looking for him. The hat, though unique, would still help shade his eyes from prying cameras.

"Yes, sir." And with a short shrill, the doorman's whistle summoned the next waiting cab. As Steven entered the cab, the doorman repeated the destination to the driver. Steven's hope was that if the police were looking for an old disheveled bum, his disguise as a stately British gent would be as opposite as he could get.

The Arby's parking lot:

As she pulled up to the police tape cordoning off the area, Chelle couldn't believe the amount of activity that was already happening. The FBI certainly had pull she didn't. Two helicopters were hovering over the area with spotlights lighting up any and all potential hiding places. Above them were two more helicopters from the television stations, clearly giving play-by-play reports to their viewers. The senator's face was undoubtedly being shown on all the local stations just to remind everyone of who the police were after. That was assuming somebody already spilled the beans to them about what was going on.

Chelle recognized one of the many FBI agents, who she had met over the course of the investigation; in fact, she would never forget him. At that time, he had quite bluntly, in front of the chief, Harmon, and Pat, expressed great concern for Chelle's detective skills.

"Agent Henderson." Chelle tried to grab his attention with no success. "Agent Henderson," she said louder.

Agent David Henderson turned around and looked disgusted. "Oh, you."

"Yea, me, you know, the police detective who is in charge of capturing Steven Westcott. What do you have?"

"We believe this is the location where he made a call to his wife. He probably pulled around back. We know he was parked for a period of time because the signal didn't move from this area."

"He's long gone; he went south."

The agent looked at Chelle with smirk. "Oh really? I have news for you, the accuracy of a cell phone trace is only relative to the tower that was used to transmit the signal. So you couldn't possibly know that."

Chelle walked away in the direction she had pointed, then stopped. "In fact, I bet I can tell you not only what direction but exactly where he went from here."

"That would be quite a trick, detective, how much?"

"Just to be sporting, let's say one hundred dollars."

"OK, Sherlock. You're on. Prove it."

Chelle continued walking and pointing. "If the call was placed from this parking lot, then he went down the road here."

"You can tell he went down this road right here?" the agent questioned mockingly.

"Yes, exactly, and if you had called me as soon as you intercepted his call, we would have had a chance to catch him."

The agent looked up and pointed to the helicopters. "We will catch him soon, with or without your help. But forgive me if I'm still not convinced."

"About an hour ago, I put out an all-points bulletin for a particular car," Chelle walked away from the road and leaned against one of the cars that had a blue flashing light on its rooftop, "a gold Cadillac that was stolen from a Mr. Clayton Harris about two hours ago, the FBI was notified. That car is now about two miles away from here in the back of an industrial area. And that car was stolen and driven by Senator Westcott."

Chelle held her palm out.

Agent Henderson slapped a one-hundred dollar bill into her hand. "OK, Detective, point taken." His phone rang. "Henderson here. Yes, I know, a gold Cadillac. The local police have already found it. Hold on."

"For a hundred bucks, will you at least tell me where it is?"

Chelle gave him the address as Henderson repeated it into the phone.

When he slipped his phone back into his pocket, he said, "I'll follow you, I assume you know exactly where you're going."

"I do."

Chelle jumped into her black sedan, turned on her own blue flashing lights, raced to the industrial site with Henderson right behind her and the helicopters already on the way.

The helicopters' bright searchlights lit up the building, illuminating any area where the senator could be hiding. Police were there already, searching the buildings for forced entry.

Chelle appraised all the activity and said to Henderson, "He's not here."

"How do you ... ?"

Chelle pointed to the scattered cell phone parts on the pavement around them.

"Want to make another bet, Agent Henderson?"

This time, Henderson chuckled. "No, unless you want to bet this phone didn't belong to the senator. We will check it for prints to confirm."

"I think you'll find it belongs to a man named Clayton Harris. Westcott stole it, and he made the call or calls because he knew we would find the car and track him here anyways," Chelle said over the sound of the circling helicopters. "It was a free pass to make a call or two. In other words, as long as he was stepping back into our lives, he thought he might as well take advantage of the situation.

The air was cold, and Chelle didn't have a hat on. Gusts from the helicopters were moving her curly, shoulder-length hair in intermittent blasts.

"There's a field not far from here, one of the copters is going to check it out with some ground units," Henderson said.

"You won't find him. He knows better than that. There is something else we're missing." Then she had another thought. She pulled out her cell phone and displayed a map of the general area. "There's a bus stop a few blocks from here, south. There is also another one west."

Henderson was looking over her shoulder and immediately was on his phone. The helicopter scouring the small field continued to methodically search it with its spotlight, but the other shot south. Chelle called out to two of her squads standing by and sent them as the ground backup one south and one west.

As soon as the search of the field came up empty that helicopter took off to the west.

"I'll get some agents working the busses and interviewing the drivers," Henderson said.

A black SUV pulled up, and several more agents exited and came up to Henderson. Chelle kept her distance until Henderson motioned for her to join the group.

"This is Detective Chelle Saltarie. She's the lead detective on the case." He turned to her. "We have the call he made. He called his wife. We have it recorded."

"Do you mind if I listen?" Chelle asked.

One of the agents handed Chelle his phone after he pressed a few keys for her. Chelle heard how devastated the senator sounded. And again, he insisted he was being framed for the murder. Of course, what else would he say? Though the conviction in his voice was hard to ignore.

Chelle gave back the phone and asked that a copy of the conversation be forwarded to her.

Chelle looked up at Henderson. "I think this is all a diversion on the senator's part; I don't think he escaped on a bus."

"A penny for your thoughts? I'm all out of hundreds," Henderson asked with a grin.

Chelle smirked.

"Think about it. He called his wife and sped away here, knowing we would trace his call and find the car he stole. He also knew that the bus stops would be our first suspicion, and he knew that we would have to pursue the leads."

"Yea, resources we are preciously short of; this couldn't have come at a worse time for the bureau, what with the peace talks and all going on."

"Exactly. He knew the peace talks would eat up the local enforcement talent. He is very clever. He knows that even if we suspect it is a ruse, we will still have to use those resources in tracking down the buses and following up at all the bus stops and interviewing the drivers and passengers anyways. Divide and conquer. That's why he picked tonight. So now it's over two hours later, and he could be anywhere. But ..." Chelle looked down the street. "But that's not what he did. He wouldn't have taken that chance. There was a reason he drove all the way from the Barry Farm District in Anacostia to here. He was taking us where he wasn't going."

"I don't disagree, but the busses are our obvious play right now. I have to organize my guys; I just don't have time to play all sorts of what-if games right now. We need to make a plan."

Chelle stepped away and lifted her coat collar as the wind pushed at her back. She pictured herself in Steven's place. She imagined the fugitive making a desperate call to his wife. He knew he was giving away his position, yet he took the chance. Chelle scanned the map of the area on her phone. The answer had to be right in front of her.

She imagined the emotional state he must have been in after his wife hung up on him. Some men might find a way to end their own life at this stage. But that wasn't Steven Westcott's method of operation. No, the senator had a plan and would stick to it. Any way she looked at it, several things were fact. The senator was desperate, which meant he was very dangerous, and he believed he had been framed, even if nobody else did. But now, she also knew that he wasn't a cold-blooded killer. He had to have known that by letting Clayton live, he had severely decreased his odds of escaping.

There was no doubt in her mind. The senator wasn't delusional, he was searching for whoever had framed him. Chelle sided with the pimp's logic. She believed that he was innocent. And if he was innocent, there was a killer on the loose.

But he was a fugitive; of that there was no doubt. And it was still her job to catch him. And because she was the one who had made him a fugitive in the first place, she felt especially obligated to bring him into custody safe and sound so she could help him prove his innocence.

Chelle walked the neighborhood, looking for inspiration. The FBI were still having their little powwow. Then, inspiration struck when she saw the Hilton Garden Inn two blocks away from where she was standing.

Chelle tried to think like Steven. In his conversation with his wife, he was pleading with her to help him figure out who could possible hate him so much as to want him arrested for murder. That meant he didn't know who to attack next. But that didn't mean he didn't have a plan. He had to go somewhere to keep from being caught and somewhere he could think about his next step. Chelle looked at the taxi's waiting in line at the Hilton Garden. A taxi would get him there faster than a bus.

She knew the approximate time the senator would have been looking for a cab. If she could locate some cameras, she would only have to search a small window of time.

Then Chelle heard a bellman's whistle. Maybe there was a faster way to find her man.

With photo and badge in hand, she stepped up to the doorman. "Have you seen this gentlemen tonight?" she asked.

"That's Senator Westcott," he said. "No of course not," he answered, looking puzzled.

"He may have been disguised," Chelle explained. "Medium build, may have been bruised around the face. Then Chelle remembered something the pimp had told her. She quickly took out a black pen and drew a beard and mustache onto her photo.

"No, still doesn't look like anybody ... wait, may I?" The doorman asked as he took the photo and pen from the detective.

He quickly traced and then filled in a bowler type hat. Not being much of an artist didn't matter once the brim was covering the senator's hairline. "I don't know, it's possible," he hedged. "There was an English gentleman with an umbrella."

"Do you remember where he went?"

The doorman rather comically acted out opening the hotel door for an invisible customer and calling a make believe taxi and opening its car door for the make believe rider. "Yes, he wanted to go to the Air Force Memorial."

That didn't make sense to Chelle, assuming the passenger was in fact Senator Westcott.

"How long ago?"

The doorman exhaled with a grunt. He looked at his watch and took a guess. "An hour ago maybe, maybe two. I'm not sure."

"What was he wearing?"

"He had on a long dark overcoat, a bit worn maybe, but acceptable. Couldn't tell what else."

Chelle immediately called her partner. "Pat, I need you to get to the Air Force Memorial ASAP and find an Englishman in a bowler hat and long, dark overcoat. Approach with extreme caution. He may be our senator. I'm going to go over the security recordings at the Hilton Garden Inn."

The Air Force Memorial:

Steven knew he was taking a big risk. He maybe had half an hour to an hour head start; it all depended on how fast the tied-up Clayton Harris had been found and how fast the police had traced his call. If he could get to the train station and if he could get a ticket and if he could get to his destination all without being discovered, then he had a chance. In military jargon, his mission had a low probability of success. And if you took such a mission, you made sure you had multiple escape plans. Steven had none.

As the cab pulled up to the curbside of the Air Force Memorial, the three polished, stainless steel equilateral triangles shooting gracefully toward the sky greeted them. Steven thanked the driver, trying hard to sound British or maybe Irish—he didn't know which and hoped the driver didn't know either.

Steven took in the grandeur of the memorial until the taxi was well on its way. To do otherwise would have appeared abnormal. Then he walked a few blocks to the Pentagon Metro Station.

Into the belly of the beast, he thought. Pentagon Metro would be undoubtedly busy with military types and clerks of all sorts. With luck, his circumferential route back to Union Station would throw off the bloodhounds, which would no doubt be shortly on his tail if they weren't already.

Steven could feel his heart race. Despite his English camouflage, he could be recognized at any time. He took several deep breaths to try and quell his heart before he stepped into the crowded station. Walking with his umbrella folded, he kept his head down; despite the crowds, people were polite and tried not to bump into him. The metro had ticket machines that took cash. These machines didn't have built-in cameras, at least Steven's didn't think so. He prayed he was right because there was no way to avoid looking at the machine as he fed it money in exchange for a ticket.

Steven hung in the shadows until just before boarding time. Then he rushed up and into the crowded train. It didn't take long before it shot away from the station, quickly picking up speed until the next stop. At the first stop, Steven's heart pumped harder in his chest until the train was on its way again. Uniformed police seemed to be everywhere. Maybe their presence was always so obvious, but under the circumstances, to him at least, they stood out like politicians at a fundraiser. Steven stuck his head into the only thing he could find, which was a map of the metro stops.

At the second stop, Steven realized he was holding his breath. He forced himself to breathe naturally and tried to will his heartbeats down to a more normal rate.

Eventually, the metro slid to a halt at Union Station. Steven knew what train he needed to be on within the next fifteen minutes. Unfortunately, the only way to buy a ticket with cash was to use an off-site vendor. The automatic ticket machines inside Union Station only took credit cards. Leaving the station and walking to the nearest third party ticket vendor would be a risk, but it was the only way he could buy a ticket.

Steven thought of adding a limp to his gait to suggest age, but that would also draw attention to him. He remembered his special forces training on how to disappear in plain sight. That would be hard to do with the bowler hat, but the hat couldn't be dispensed with right now, not yet. Even if it didn't shield his face 100 percent of the time, it had to certainly minimize any full-face surveillance.

Two policemen were standing near the exit door, scanning the crowd. Steven slowed his step enough so that a crowd behind him would catch up. As the group approached, he slid into the middle of them, cracked his knees a bit, and shrugged his shoulders to shrink his height. Even losing an inch or two would shelter his face by anyone taller. The crowd coalesced at the doorway. He stayed low and soon was nearly pushed out by the swarm of passengers.

The promised snowstorm was on its way; Steven could tell by the sleet falling on him. This was a bad omen. First would come sleet and freezing rain, then heavy, wet, blowing snow. Once out the door, he picked up his pace considerably.

Steven only had minutes to find a third party Amtrak vendor and sneak back into the station. Luckily for him, the first vendor wasn't too far. A street-side magazine and paper vendor advertised Amtrak with the familiar logo. Using the main entryway, Steven rushed back into Union Station.

Chapter 37

Chelle convinced Miss Dobson, who was the manager of the Hilton Garden Inn to show her the videos of the lobby and main entrance. Her first objective was to find the English gentleman in question, but anybody matching the senator's profile within a half hour to an hour of the senator's phone call to his wife would have to be considered a suspect.

Chelle was deep in concentration, watching the videos when she received a call from Pat. "Chelle, I've been up and down the Air force Memorial Mall, and no sign of anybody in a bowler hat. I even enlisted a few uniforms to help. Maybe he changed his mind in the cab and went somewhere else?"

"Or," Chelle said, "he never went there in the first place. It was just a stunt to make us waste time. But if he didn't go there, where did he go? If your wife said she was going to divorce you and never wanted to see you again, what would you do?"

"You mean besides celebrate?"

Chelle didn't laugh. "Smart-ass," she growled. "I'm serious. Where would you go?"

"Home," Pat answered. "But do you think he would really be that desperate? It would be an awful risk."

"You didn't hear his voice. He is desperate. Remember, he has been hiding in some hole for months not talking to anybody. My bet is he is going home because his wife and daughter are even more important to him than the risk of being caught. We better call the local police and tell them to guard his wife."

"You are taking a huge leap of faith here, Chelle. We don't even know if the person we're looking for is the right guy. He could be just some guy with a hat, and nothing more."

Just then, Agent David Henderson stepped inside the small security center. The room was starting to get crowded. It was really nothing more than a side office filled with television monitors and computer equipment.

"Call the local police. I gotta go. I'll call you back," Chelle said to Pat.

Chelle didn't know if Henderson would be upset with her or not for following a hunch without conferring with him first. She collected herself a bit and said to Henderson, "Miss Dobson was kind enough to let me browse through their security footage. I haven't been able to make a positive ID, but I have found an identifiable person of interest. It would be helpful if you could use your sources to trace down the cab driver and find out where the passenger was dropped off," she said. "And if your people have a way of analyzing this footage with face recognition software, that would be helpful as well."

Henderson stepped around a desk to look at the frozen image on the monitor. "You think this man is the fugitive?"

"The time would be about right, and the facial hair and build match."

"Maybe the doorman knows where he went?"

"He did. He said he wanted to go to the Air Force Memorial. We've searched the area already with no success. That's why we need to know where the taxi actually took him."

"Let me see what I can do."

Chelle walked away from the video monitor with another thought. "Miss Dobson, do you have an informational map available? You know, something you might give your guests to help them find their way around."

"As a matter of fact, we do, an excellent one," she said, retrieving a copy from a convenient stack near the front desk.

Henderson watched over Chelle's shoulder with interest as he waited for his call to connect. It didn't take long for Chelle to find what she wanted. "This at least confirms my suspicion. There is a metro very near the Air Force Memorial. If I know our man, I would say he did go to the memorial but then went to Pentagon Metro Station a block away."

Henderson cursed, then asked, "But to where?"

"May I use your computer to access the Internet, Miss Dobson?" Chelle asked.

"Please call me Debbie, and certainly."

Chelle used the computer to pull up a train map and schedule. She put her finger on the map. "He's headed to Boston. The Northeast Regional, number sixty-six, leaves at ten twenty. From there, it's just a relatively short distance to Peabody, Massachusetts, his home town."

Chelle, Agent Henderson, and Debbie Dobson all looked at the clock simultaneously. Chelle immediately dialed her partner. "Pat, I need you to go to Pentagon Metro and look for our man. If you don't see him, take the yellow line to Chinatown, and then the red to Union. I'll meet you there.

Chelle tucked her phone back into her coat pocket

"Hold for a moment," Henderson said into his phone.

Then to Chelle, he said, "Hold on detective, we don't know a thing yet. Nothing. You are just guessing at everything. We don't know that the hat man is our guy. We don't even know if the taxi took him to the Air Force Memorial or Pentagon Station or to the moon for that matter. You think he's taking a train to Boston? That's highly unlikely. This guy evaded us for months; he's not about to ride a train right into our hands."

Chelle stood up and started to button up her heavy winter coat. "Look, David, I would really appreciate it if you could check out the taxi thing. I don't have any other ideas or intuition. If you do, please share. All I do know is that the senator was yards away from here tonight. That is the closest anybody has been to him since he escaped from his office. So if you don't have any other suggestions, I am going to try and get to Union before the ten-twenty leaves for Boston."

"I will see what the bureau can do with the video, and we'll track down the driver ASAP," Henderson said, and then added, "good hunting."

"Miss Dobson, let me introduce you to Agent Henderson of the FBI. I hope you will be equally as helpful to agent Henderson as you have been to me."

Chelle could see the agent was in good hands when Miss Dobson purred sweetly "Agent Henderson, I would be more than happy to help you in any way I can," Agent Henderson wasn't a bad bit of eye candy and Miss Dobson looked totally enthralled to help him in any way she could.

Chelle gave Henderson a sideways glance, and he looked at her with a shrug of his shoulders.

Union Station, Washington DC:

Steven popped open his umbrella; it protected him from the sleet and from any eyes trying to scan his face. He circled around Union Station, losing precious time, but he didn't want to enter it from the same doors as he left. That brought him to Columbus Circle, which was busy with tourists and commuters heading home for the evening. But it was late, and the station wasn't as busy as he would have hoped. Steven paused for a moment, trying to settle himself down. For a few seconds, he stared at Columbus Fountain, trying to appear like a normal visitor.

He heard a siren way in the background and his heart thumped a bit harder and faster. He fought the temptation to find the location of the cameras that were no doubt looking for him with facial recognition software. Steven did his best to hide under the cover of the umbrella.

The sound of the lone siren was getting louder. Ignoring it, and with one last exhale, he crossed a series of busy streets and walked back into the giant stone edifice, closing his umbrella at the last second.

****

Chelle flashed her badge as she ran into the station, leaving her car parked in a no-parking zone, still flashing its lights. She was on the phone with Pat as they both searched the cavernous station.

"The FBI located the taxi driver. He said he dropped the Englishman off at the Air Force Memorial," Chelle updated Pat through quickened breaths.

"He could have easily walked from there to Pentagon Metro. I hope your hunch is right. Why does the driver think he was an Englishman?"

"He said he had an accent. Definitely from England."

"Bloody, you don't say," Pat answered back, huffing it out in his best fake English accent.

"Exactly," Chelle said.

By the sound of his choppy voice, Chelle could tell Marget was running. "I'll be there soon." Then he hung up.

If Chelle was right, then the senator was probably already on the train. Chelle saw an upper balcony; the stairs weren't far, so she ran up them against a descending crowd. The added height would give her a vantage point to scan the crowds.

****

Steven kept his head down and held on to his one-way ticket like it was freedom itself. He stayed just outside the boarding area as if waiting for someone to join him. The train would be a confined space with nowhere to run once he was on it. He didn't want to be cornered sitting in a seat, pinned down with guns pointed at his head. At least in the crowded station he could still have a chance at running. It would be a small chance but a chance nonetheless, and the police wouldn't be able to use their guns.

Steven couldn't help wondering if he was walking into a trap. Nearly two and a half hours had passed since he stole the pimp's car. His time had run out, the police had to be onto him by now. Steven took the final risk by getting into line to board the train.

He tried not to look anxious as he boarded the Amtrak's Northeast Regional out of Union Station. He kept his head down, focusing on the bottom of his umbrella. He had to force himself not to survey his surroundings or assess the people around him. A security team could be closing in on him right at this moment, and he wouldn't even know it.

Steven saw an abandoned newspaper and scooped it up. A few more seats back, he sat and sequestered himself inside the paper, making it quite clear he didn't want to be bothered. With his tipped bowler shielding his face from prying eyes, he could only hope his illusion would be successful.

The paper he buried his head into said, "Historical Camp David discussions between the prime minister of Israel and the president of the Palestinian National Authority begin amid tighter security due to recent bomb threat."

The train started moving, inching its way ahead.

****

"Keep squeezing the area toward the siding of the train. Be ready. If he sees us, we know he will run, and don't underestimate him; he's dangerous," Chelle said to Pat. "Wait, I think I saw him."

"Chelle, what did you say?" The station was suddenly getting crowded and noisy with a new arriving train.

"The hat, I think I saw the hat."

"Where are you?"

"East side of the ramp, upper level."

"Got you. Where? What car?"

"He got into the third car from the back. It was just a glimpse, but it looked like a bowler hat."

Chelle rushed down the stairs and then started running toward the train car. She held up her badge, but it did little good as she began pushing past people in her way. She had already tossed her phone back into her pocket and had her hand prepared to draw her gun out of its holster in a second.

****

The train was picking up speed, and with each incremental movement forward, Steven's breathing got easier. Then he saw some commotion alongside the train, some small woman was pushing her way through the crowd.

His curiosity got the better of him. The woman shoving through the crowd looked directly at him. They locked eyes for a moment, then Steven turned his head back into his paper and prayed she didn't recognize him, but he had certainly recognized the detective.

Chapter 38

The tracks immediately out of Washington were smooth, and the ride was quiet. Most of the passengers seemed tired and glad to be on their way home. Steven knew the riders were mostly commuters and Washington insiders. If he searched the faces, he wouldn't be surprised if he even knew some of them, so he didn't look up from his paper.

The train headed northeast. The Northeast Regional culminated in Boston Massachusetts and was right on schedule as usual. The route to Boston would take about ten hours. Steven could envision the station in Boston and the line of cabs waiting there. From Boston, it was only another half hour by cab to Peabody, Massachusetts and his home and family.

Steven felt he saw a glimpse of recognition on Detective Chelle Saltarie's face during the fraction of a second when their eyes locked. Obviously, he could be just paranoid. Who wouldn't be in his situation? The train was rolling and there was nothing he could do now but wait and pray he was mistaken. Still, he couldn't deny that she was looking for someone on that train, but how could she have possibly known he would be on it? Steven wasn't a believer in coincidences. But the dice were cast; he would have to stick to his plan. The next stop would be New Carrollton, and then on to Baltimore. The detective would have ten minutes to arrange a greeting for him at the next stop. In ten minutes, he would know his fate.

****

Chelle tried to find a quiet corner of the busy station as she pressed the speed dial button on her phone for her captain. Pat Marget was at her side. He had finally caught up with her just as the train pulled out of the station.

"Yes, sir, I know how this sounds, but I'm quite sure ... yes, sir. Positive? No, sir, I'm not. But it was definitely a bowler hat like the man from the hotel. ... No, sir, I don't know that the man in the taxi was the senator."

After placing her phone back into her pocket, Chelle looked at Pat and said, "He told me where I could stick my hunch. I wish he had called it woman's intuition. At least then I could blame it on his sexist attitude."

"Come on, Chelle. What did you think the captain would do? Stop a train and search it. For who? A guy whose hat you didn't like. You know the score. You never had a positive ID. We just can't stop any and every train we think might have a bad guy on it."

Chelle looked at her watch and realized it didn't matter anyways, at least not any more. The train was probably making its first stop at New Carrollton right now and would soon be on its way again.

Her phone rang. It was Henderson. "Detective?"

"Yea?" Chelle sounded winded as if she had just taken a punch to her stomach.

"We got a partial hit on the face. It's an eighty-percent match."

"What's that mean?" Chelle suddenly perked up.

"Just what it sounds like. There is an eighty-percent chance that the guy was our senator."

"Is that good?" Chelle wasn't used to working with facial recognition technology.

"It's better than fifty-fifty and worse than one hundred percent."

"Screw you Henderson!" Chelle let her frustration get the better of her. "I'm sorry, it's just that I think I saw him leave on the train minutes ago. My captain said there was nothing he could do about it because I couldn't positively ID him. Does an eighty-percent match mean we can stop the train and search it?"

Chelle was pacing back and forth, trying to expend some of the adrenaline flowing through her system as she caught her breath.

"I don't know. It's not that simple. An eighty-percent match on a terrorist trying to kill people, I'm sure that would be a go. But this guy is not an immediate threat to anybody. To take the fall for stopping a train with hundreds of people on it? Boy, if we came up empty? Would you risk your career on it?"

Chelle thought for a moment. "This is obviously out of my jurisdiction now. What are the odds that the FBI will monitor the stations it's stopping at?"

"So you want me to risk *my* career. Thanks!"

"Does the FBI want to catch him or not? We know he was out to-night and we followed a trail here. The only trail we have, by the way."

"Yea, a trail, not necessarily his trail. So you want us both to go down in flames?"

Agent Henderson turned his car off onto Columbus Circle and parked it behind Chelle's.

"You know, I don't know if I even care anymore. Like I said, the suspect is now out of my jurisdiction as far as I'm concerned."

"I'll run the eighty-percent probable match up the flag pole and see what happens. I don't even know if we have the people available right now even if they wanted to cover the stations. The peace conference has top priority. Even a runaway senator slash murderer has to get in line behind the Israeli prime minister and a couple of presidents."

"Couldn't you at least tap into the security cameras at each of the stations? The next stop is only minutes away."

Agent David Henderson thought about it as he stepped out of his car with his phone to his ear. "If I can get somebody to listen, maybe we can monitor the stations. But that is one big *if*. Sit tight, Detective, I'm walking in the south entrance right now, by the McDonalds."

Thurgood Regional Airport:

It was dark inside and outside the train as it slowed for its next stop at Thurgood Regional Airport. In the night sky, Steven could see the lights of arriving and departing aircrafts. Many were small, private planes that reminded him of the one he used to fly.

He twisted his umbrella in his hand as the train sped up again. The next stop was twenty minutes away in Penn Station, Maryland, where he'd make his next move. Penn Station was one of the busier stations on the route to Boston, so there was bound to be an abundance of activity for him to blend into.

Union Station, Washington DC:

Chelle was sitting rather dejectedly at a table near the Starbucks inside the station when Agent Henderson found her. She sat alone. Pat had already gone home. She saw Henderson walk past her without saying a word and stood in a short line for coffee. Coming back, he handed her one of the two coffees he had purchased.

"Anything?" she asked.

"We are going to play your hunch a little longer. The techies are going to loop into the live surveillance of any stations along the way that might have video. As I suspected, most of our agents are spread pretty thin right now. The next stop for the Northeast Regional is Penn Station." Henderson checked his watch. "Probably our best shot if they get the proper log-in info in time."

Chelle took a sip of her coffee and stared off at the never-ending activity of Union Station. Professional pride had been a driving force in her desire to be the one to capture the senator. Now she didn't know if that drive was still there.

Chelle looked up and saw Henderson making another call. He hadn't turned out to be such a bad guy after all.

"I'll hang around until the train reports leaving Penn Station if you don't mind. Just in case we, you, get lucky," Chelle said.

Agent Henderson took another taste of his coffee and looked at his watch. "It won't be long." After an awkward pause, he said, "I'm sorry I was so tough on you. You're a good cop. You should check into the bureau after this is over."

"I'll be lucky to land a spot guarding the ticket box at the local theater."

"Sometimes bad things happen to good people," Henderson said.

Chelle laughed. "Yea, sometimes bad things do happen to good people," she repeated, "and it sucks."

Outside Penn Station:

Ten minutes from Penn Station, the train slowed dramatically. Steven's heart raced, knowing it was too early for the train to be stopping. Then he realized that the train was entering the B & P tunnel. It was an ancient tunnel built in the late eighteen hundreds, and the curving tracks required a careful and slow approach into Penn.

Steven walked into the bathroom and locked the door. He quickly took off his overcoat and the small backpack hidden under it. Steven opened the pack and took out an old Baltimore Orioles baseball cap and a pair of glasses. Then he rolled up the coat and stuffed it and the bowler hat into the backpack, filling it.

The long coat had hidden his blue jeans, flannel shirt, and a light jacket blazoned with the big purple winged B. It was an older version of the Baltimore Ravens' team logo. Steven looked into the mirror as he put on the oversized pair of glasses. The transformation was complete. Before leaving the bathroom, he slipped the umbrella into a corner, hoping a passenger would steal it.

As the train slowed to a stop, he walked through the cars with the brim of his baseball cap down. Steven searched for a different seat well away from where the Englishman had sat. As he suspected, the train was busy with people jostling to get off and others trying to find a seat to go farther north.

Steven didn't know he could hold his breath for so long. It seemed like forever before he was breathing again. The train slowly left Penn station and entered another long tunnel heading north. He wouldn't take the chance of staying on the train for much longer. The next stop at Aberdeen Maryland would be his last. Soon, he would put the most dangerous part of his plan into action. Steven glanced at another passenger's watch and guessed that, with an exceptional amount of luck, as the evening approached midnight, he might again be on his way.

Union Station, Washington DC:

Agent Henderson slipped his phone back into his pocket, "Sorry, Detective, no sign of a man in a bowler hat. If he is on the train, he didn't get off at Penn."

Chelle stood and stretched her shoulders. "Well, I didn't think he would get off there anyway. What about the other stops?"

"It looks like we have working cameras along the entire route. I will try to keep my people focused on them."

"It's been another long day; I'm going home. If I don't hear from you, I will assume our Englishman wasn't found."

"It's a ten-hour ride to Boston on the Northeastern. If your hunch is right, that's when we'll spot him. That gives me some time to maybe rustle up a few agents."

"Good hunting and good night." Chelle shook his hand.

Aberdeen Maryland Amtrak Station:

The bearded and mustached Baltimore sports fan didn't look anything like a United States senator might, at least that was what Steven hoped. The train had pulled into the station right on time; it was eleven thirty in the evening and the small group of people departing the train moved sluggishly. Obviously, everybody was feeling the effects of a long hard day, and none had a longer day than Steven. Only for Steven, his day was hardly at an end.

He stepped off the train expecting to be immediately apprehended. Instead, he was greeted by nothing but cold air and a few snow flurries. The snowstorm that had been predicted for this evening seemed to be on its way. Steven hoped they were wrong.

The station was familiar, he had been here before, but usually there was somebody waiting for him with a ride to his destination. Tonight, he would be walking the six and a half miles. Every journey starts with the first step, and so the senator looked up at the falling snow and took his first step toward what he hoped would be freedom.

Washington DC:

The coffee that had tasted so good at Union Station was keeping Henderson awake. He sat in the dark, sipping on a glass of milk that he hoped would calm him. He felt sleepy, yet he knew that his eyes wouldn't close for the night. Too many things kept creeping through his mind. *The detective had good instincts, he thought. Eighty percent.*

The blue light of his DVD player said it was 1:00 a.m. He looked out his apartment window down at the sleeping city below. His thoughts went to the night agents, who were probably bored to death keeping a watchful eye over the sleepy town.

That gave Agent Henderson a thought, and soon he was on his phone. "Jill, hi! It's Dave."

"Henderson?"

"Yea, I couldn't sleep, and I was wondering if you had some spare time."

"That depends on what you want me to do with my spare time," Jill Becker said.

"Nothing you couldn't eventually tell your mother about."

"That doesn't sound like much fun. But ... what do you have in mind?"

"The day guys did an eighty-percent facial match on someone who could be that missing senator."

"You mean the murdering slimeball, Westcott?"

"That's the guy. We traced a phone call he made and thought we had him, but he slipped through somehow. Then we got an eighty-percent match on a person of interest videoed getting into a taxi."

"Don't tell me. You lost him too."

"He got on the Northeast Regional out of Union and we couldn't pursue."

"OK, you have my interest now," answered Jill Becker, who was a friend of Henderson's going back to Quantico, Virginia, when they were both trainees.

"If you could find that file, and then run the same face recognition against all the passengers disembarking from the Regional along the way to Boston tonight, I would be very thankful. The bureau is already tapping into the live video and should have earlier stops recorded somewhere."

"Yea, I think this group could use some structured activities to keep them occupied. Because of the conference, I have more agents hanging around than I need. Of course, if something else comes up, we are dropping your request faster than a hot potato."

"Understood. We think our rabbit might be heading back to Peabody, Massachusetts, through Boston. We are quite certain a bearded man dressed in a dark coat and wearing a bolder hat is the senator in disguise."

"Doesn't matter," Jill said. "Our software will scan every face it comes across."

Aberdeen Throughway:

Steven was beginning to think more and more of himself as the old Cowboy Westcott rather than a senator. On foot, he weaved his way down the four-lane divided roadway. The mature trees and bushes provided him with ample coverage any time he saw the slightest hint of car lights.

The snow had picked up and the roadway was now covered with white. The jacket he had on was too light for the conditions, but it had to do. His destination was only three more miles away, he guessed. At his cautious pace, that meant another hour or more in the cold.

The snow had minimized traffic and had given him additional cover. He was sure nobody had seen him so far and now he was headed into an even move desolate area. It was well after midnight when he saw The Flaming Dragon Tattoo Parlor. He turned left just past it onto Carson's Run road heading north.

As he approached the airport facilities, it seemed deserted. A few security lights lit up some of the parking lot and a series of blue lights dimly lit the taxiway on the single asphalt runway. The hangar for the flying club he had joined had a heated room that would be welcomed. No cars were present, which hopefully meant he would have the place all to himself. The Churchville airport was tucked away nicely in a country setting; it was quiet now, but by tomorrow morning there was sure to be the normal activity.

Cautiously, Steven approached the flying club hangar, leaving tracks in the freshly fallen snow. The wind was picking up and small drifts of white powder were starting to form. No vehicles or foot traffic had been around for a while. That didn't surprise him; in fact, he was counting on it. The small airport wouldn't have any more security than the fence around it and an occasional drive-by from the local sheriff. He typed in the pass code for the small service door, hoping it hadn't been changed. With a click, the door opened, and he felt the welcoming warmth inside.

The small flight room was heated and comfortable and lit dimly by a computer screen still flickering. It had a few small round tables for flight planning purposes. A coffee pot, empty and cleaned was on the counter next to the microwave and refrigerator. Steven didn't turn on the lights, but the room did light up when he checked the refrigerator and saw that it contained an assortment of soft drinks and the leftovers from a party sub. Somebody must have recently earned his or her pilot wings. Hungrily, he opened a Mountain Dew and fisted a leftover ham and cheese sub.

At the far end of the flight room was another small door. Steven opened it, and inside the attached hangar protected from the weather, he saw his prize, or, to be a realist, maybe the vehicle of his death. The Cessna 182 was waiting for him just like he had hoped. Finishing the last bite of his sandwich, Steven stepped back into the cold of the unheated hangar. He took the flashlight that was always tucked in the door pocket of the small plane and checked the fuel levels in the wing tanks. Just as the flying club rules dictated, the last user of the plane was responsible for fueling up the aircraft and leaving it just as they had found it.

Steven went back into the heated flight room and grabbed another fistful of sandwich. While he ate it, he used the flashlight to search for any old aviation charts left lying around. His hope was the garbage can might contain an out-of-date map. He wasn't particular, and anything that he could use to navigate would be welcome.

His hand came out of the garbage with nothing but a sticky wet mess. He needed something to help him navigate around the various airports or airways that could be near restricted areas. Flying into one of those areas by mistake could literally send military aircraft in pursuit, forcing him to land or worse. On the wall was a large aviation map of the United States. It was one of the prized possessions of the club.

Steven found some clean paper in the trash and opened a few drawers until he found a pen. He studied the chart and tried as best he could to memorize the various obstacles between him and his destination and wrote down any appropriate information.

Steven looked at the other prize the club owned. It was an amateur weather station. It wasn't Federal Aviation Administration approved, but it did a fair job of reporting the local cloud ceiling, temperature, barometric pressure, wind direction, and speed. He took a long look at the single parking lot light and saw the snow was still falling. The weather machine reported two thousand foot ceilings. That meant that as long as he stayed below two thousand feet above the ground and the snow wasn't too heavy, he should be able to maintain a visual on the ground and city lights. That would be critical, actually, life-saving. Steven had no reservations about the risk he was going to take.

He had flown at night only once before, but that was with his instructor at his side. If he remembered anything from that lesson, it was that flying at night was a different type of challenge even in the best conditions.

Steven went back into the hangar and pushed open the wide hangar doors.

He had no gloves to warm him as he grabbed the tow bar that was clamped to the front wheel rim. Steven started the small plane rolling by pulling on the tow bar. At first, it was relatively easy, but when the plane's wheels rolled onto the fresh snow, it became much more difficult. The three tires of the single-engine Cessna crunched fresh paths in the snow. The weight of the small plane caused Steven to slip and fall a few times, freezing his hands even more as they became coated with snow. Eventually, he had the plane past the big doors, and he unhooked the tow bar and closed the hangar again. Sitting inside the aircraft, he locked the pilot's door and stared at the array of instruments in front of him. Holding the flashlight with one hand, he went through the checklist, which was a habit drilled into him by his instructor. Tonight would not be the time to cut corners.

The snow was coming down hard and steady. Steven knew that he couldn't let it build up on the airframe or the flying performance of the aircraft would be compromised. The engine started up, and with a flip of a switch, the electrical power went on, and the instruments came to life.

Chapter 39

Steven had to power up the engine quite a bit more than he normally would have just to get the airplane to move down the taxi way and through the building snow. As was his habit, he picked up the radio to make his taxi call and then thought better of it. He placed the microphone back on its perch. Tonight, radio calls would be nonexistent. His hope was that a lone, small aircraft heading away from the Washington area would be of little concern to anybody.

His flight tonight was technically a legal flight. That is, it would have been had he been a licensed pilot. Flying under visual flight rules meant he didn't need to file a flight plan. As long as he stayed out of restricted areas and could see and be seen by other aircrafts, he would be legal.

With a little luck, nobody would know or care that a single-engine aircraft was flying so low across the ground. Because of the weather conditions, he estimated that he would be flying at only a thousand feet AGL, or above ground level. That was quite low for a cross-country flight. It was normally the altitude he would descend to when preparing to land. It would be just another risk he had to take.

Steven taxied to the start of the runway. He was lined up into the wind, and the planes landing light lit up the snowflakes rushing toward him. He contemplated his dangerous decision. There was enough light from the lone pole lamp that he could see snow was collecting on the surface of the wings. He was aware of the fact that even a coating of frost was enough to ruin the aerodynamics of a plane. He was gambling that as the plane gathered speed, the wind would blow off the accumulated snow so the aircraft would fly. What he couldn't see was the critical tail section. And though it was much smaller, he knew it also was accumulating its share of snow weight.

Steven made sure the radio transponder was switched off. When on, the transponder told the controllers on the ground and other aircrafts in flight that a VFR aircraft was in the vicinity and at what altitude. Certainly important safety information, but he didn't want to be seen even on radar if he could help it. In fact, his low altitude and the snow should conceal him. As long as nobody else was as crazy as he was, it shouldn't be a problem.

In position at the departure end of the runway, Steven debated the wisdom of the choice he was making, realizing that every second he hesitated was only making things worse. "Only a fool or somebody as desperate as I am would attempt this," he said out loud. He switched on the landing lights so he could see the runway and pushed in the throttle all the way.

At first, the Cessna didn't seem to want to move, its tires pressing against the building snow. Then, slowly, it inched forward. There was nothing Steven could do but hope the plane would gain enough speed to lift off the runway.

Typically, the two-thousand feet of runway was more than enough for the small plane. But as the plane moved forward, it occurred to him that, under tonight's conditions, it might not be. Halfway down the runway, the plane was going faster, but not fast enough. The airspeed indicator was reading only half of what he needed. Steven started to panic. Usually, he would be in the air by now.

He only had seconds to decide if he should abort or not. If he pulled back on the throttle right now, the plane would probably run off the end of the runway and get stuck in the snow. He would most likely be safe, but his escape plan would be ruined. But if he didn't stop the plane very soon, then he would be committed to a takeoff.

The plane was still gaining speed. Steven glanced at the airspeed indicator; it was finally starting to increase. He looked out at the runway, which was hard to see; the snow made everything look the same.

His glance at the airspeed indicator had cost him. The plane veered left. A wheel caught the edge of the pavement and started to pull the plane into a small ditch running parallel with the runway.

Instinctively, Steven pressed full on the rudder, trying to steer the plane back to the runway. It was too late to abort the takeoff now, but his speed was not enough to lift the plane off the ground either.

The plane popped back onto the runway, or at least what he guessed was the runway. The bright landing light lit up the trees off the end of the airstrip. Until now, the trees had been obscured because of the reduced visibility from the falling snow. Steven knew instantly this wasn't going to work.

The trees were easily fifty feet high; if he took off at all, it was going to be sluggish, and he would never climb high enough to miss them. Too much time had passed; the plane had eaten up too much runway. One way or another, his momentum was going to take him into the trees.

Another glance at the airspeed showed that he should be flying by now. He could only assume that the weight of the snow on the wings combined with the loss of lift because of the nonsmooth airfoil was the problem. That was when he heard a loud swish past his window.

A gust of wind combined with his increasing airspeed had cleared the wings. The airplane dipped left; the right wing wanted to fly. Then, just as suddenly, the left wing cleared and the plane leaped into the sky.

Steven remembered his short field takeoff procedures and hoped it would work in real life like the book said it would. The trees looked too high and too close.

The snowflakes coming toward him looked like a continuous bombardment of tracer fire into the windscreen. He fought disorientation. One good thing about the approaching trees: at least he knew which way the ground was. With his eyes on the trees, he tried to keep the wings level.

Another glance at his airspeed let him know that no matter the temptation, trying to climb any faster would only stall the small plane and make it crash to the ground. It was already climbing as fast as he dared make it.

The trees were coming up fast, but the plane was climbing. Steven felt a vibration; something was wrong. Then there was a shudder. He could only assume more snow had blown off a wing somewhere, but he didn't risk the look. The vibrations stopped, and the plane climbed faster. The gusty winds bounced the small plane around, but Steven hardly noticed. He was concentrating instead on the treetops in front of him. He could see them reaching out to grab his plane out of the sky.

The front light of the plane had the trees clearly and brightly illuminated now. The heavy snow was collecting on their branches. Even if his wings somehow missed them, his wheels wouldn't, and the light plane didn't have the power to push through them.

Steven looked down at the ground where he would probably crash. It was heavily wooded, so he hoped it would break his fall. This was a stupid plan, he thought. That was when a mighty gust came and pushed him up. It was a hell of a ride, but he was above the tree line and still climbing. Frantically, he looked for lights to keep him orientated, but all he saw was darkness and white shrapnel trying to take him out of the sky.

The following morning:

"This is Detective Saltarie, who is this please?"

"Detective, this is Agent Henderson."

This was bound to be interesting. "Agent Henderson, I assume you have some new information."

"It was your guy. You were right."

"I knew it!" Chelle said excitedly into the phone.

Chelle looked up and realized that most of her coworkers had heard her and had stopped what they were doing to listen to her side of the conversation.

"I had some bored night shift people compare photos from all the stops the train made, including Boston. It took some time, but they did an amazing job of piecing together photos to get a full facial picture. Get this, he got off at Aberdeen Maryland."

"Aberdeen? There's nothing in Aberdeen. It's in the middle of nowhere. He probably couldn't even find a taxi at that time of night."

Chelle was aware of the rest of the office staring at her; this was the biggest news in months. They all knew instantly that it was the missing senator being discussed. Chelle twisted her neck to the side to hold the telephone to her ear while she used Google maps to pull up Aberdeen Maryland.

"My thoughts exactly, but it was him, and it is where he got off. Oh, by the way, he switched jackets and hats on the train and was wearing a baseball cap and team jacket and glasses when he got off. He's slick all right, but my people say it's a positive match. We might not know why he got off there, but I'll tell you this, he certainly did. I have everybody the bureau can spare working on this and the national security people as well. They really want this senator back. I'm on my way up there right now."

"If there is anything you would like me to do, just let me know. And, Henderson?"

"Yes, Detective?"

"Please keep me posted."

"Yea, sure. Like you said, nobody knows this guy like you do. I'll stay in touch. And likewise, if you get any brilliant ideas as to why Aberdeen, let me know."

Chelle stared at the computer screen in front of her, already looking for ideas on why Aberdeen. She typed in a name: Shatoya Anderson.

Reidsville North Carolina, 7:00 a.m. the same day:

"Don't turn around, I have a gun pointed right at your back. And do not even attempt to call on your radio," Steven threatened, trying to disguise his voice.

The driver, a detective, didn't panic and did as told. "What do you want?" he asked calmly.

"I want you to find a private place where you can park, and we can talk." Steven spoke monotone and low, almost in a whisper. He had broken into the detective's garage early that morning and then hid in the backseat of the car until they were well away from his home.

"Fuck you, Cowboy, I'll drive wherever the fuck I want. You're lucky I don't kick your white ass out of my car this instant."

"Goddamn it, Jojo, can't you just play along for once. Remember I have a gun pointed at your fat, black ass."

Jojo lit up a cigarette.

"I thought you quit?"

"I did, but took it up again when you started running from the police. I knew this would all eventually end up on my lap. Do you have any idea the trouble we are both in now? I was hoping you wouldn't come here. I'm a cop, Cowboy, I gotta arrest you. I have to, it's my sworn duty."

Jojo took a drag on his cigarette.

"Just stay the fuck down," Steven said. "And could you please roll down your window? The car stinks like smoke."

"Just shut up. How am I supposed to quit smoking when you pull shit like this? Do you have any idea how much fucking trouble I'm going to get in? Why did you come here?"

"Yea, well, it's pretty obvious, *Detective*." Steven emphasized the word like it was a joke. "I must be pretty fucking desperate to come to you for help. And remember, you are in mortal danger if you don't do exactly what I say."

"Yea, yea, whatever."

Jojo tossed out his half-smoked cigarette.

"I didn't do it, Jojo, I didn't. I understand the evidence against me, but I didn't do it." Steven kept his head down behind the backseat.

"But you did know the girl?"

"You know the place in Spring Lake we all went to, you know, where Shatoya worked?"

"The whorehouse? Yea, how is that tied into this?"

"The girl that was murdered had pictures of all the guys who visited that place. Apparently there were one-way mirrors all over it."

"You mean everybody doing everything?"

"You got it, buddy."

"So you were being blackmailed."

"No, not at all. But that is what everybody thinks. She gave them to me, and I destroyed them, all of them."

"Why don't you start from the beginning, fill me in."

"Just keep driving. Remember, I have a gun on you," Steven ordered.

Jojo looked in the rearview mirror, and when he couldn't see Steven, he had to assume he was on the floor of the car. Steven gave him a fairly quick overview of what had all happened.

Jojo turned down an industrial area, someplace he hoped nobody would see them. Then he said, "And the girl turns out to be your daughter by Shatoya. Wow, buddy, I can't imagine the pressure you've been under. You know, I always knew you didn't do it."

"You knew?"

"You couldn't kill a young, helpless woman. That isn't you. You don't have it in you. And you are sure Lucille doesn't know Destinee was your daughter?"

"As far as I know, you and Teddy are the only people who know."

"Do you want me to share that info?"

"It will eventually become public knowledge, but for now, as far as I'm concerned, it's better off not being advertised. I'm thinking that whoever is framing me didn't know Destinee was my daughter. How could they? Until we know more, I think it prudent to not let them or anyone else in on it either. I need somebody inside working on this who has my best interest at heart. Everybody has judged me based on possible motive, circumstantial evidence, and DNA."

"Cowboy, I get it. But don't you think I would have already done anything I could? I looked at the evidence against you. It's pretty bad, and I don't have a clue what to do next. This is a disaster. There aren't many people who would believe this crazy story."

"Tell me about it. You're the only one so far. I wrote everything I just told you down, every name and date I could remember. Pull over and I'll give it to you."

"I don't exactly have the resources of the special forces at my beck and call. I still don't know what I can do to help. But if you have any ideas, I'm all yours. I'll do whatever I can. And talking about resources, how did you get here in the first place?"

"I flew in last night."

"How in the hell could a US senator on every watch list ever created get through airport security?"

"I didn't say commercial airline. I sort of borrowed a plane."

"I didn't think you had your license yet."

"I don't."

"There was a snowstorm in the DC area last night."

"Tell me about it. Let's not talk about my flight down here. It wasn't that pleasant. At least by the time I got here, the snow had let up, and I could see the airport lights."

"So now you add stealing an aircraft and illegally flying to your repertoire."

"Yea, I know, the list keeps getting longer. Find a quiet spot to park, somewhere near Oak Street."

The car jostled a bit as Jojo drove over a rough concrete curb. He didn't see any other cars in the area, so he drove around an abandoned concrete pipe factory and parked in back, well away from prying eyes.

"Any ideas at all?" Steven said. "You must have something."

Jojo turned toward his friend and, looking through the protective grill separating them, said, "It's about the DNA. That's the problem with your new bill. DNA is so easy to get. My DNA is all over this car, and so is yours right now. Anybody can find it, steal it, and plant it somewhere else."

"Not my semen. That's not all over the place."

"That does pose a problem. So the question is, how did your semen get inside her? Want to share with me who does have access to your semen besides you?"

"Nobody, of course, it can't be mine," Steven said.

"I think it was Mr. Spock from Star Trek that wisely said, 'Eliminate the impossible, whatever remains, however improbable, must be the truth.'"

"You and your Star Trek crap. It was Sherlock Holmes."

"No, no, I know it was Spock."

"You're a fucking detective, you should know it was Sherlock Holmes. Never mind, what's your point?"

"If it is your semen, where did it come from, however improbable?"

"It didn't happen unless Lucille murdered the girl and planted the evidence. Not too likely." Steven chuckled.

"Then the only other possibility is that DNA does lie, and it isn't your semen. When I looked at the evidence against you, I noticed something, and guess what?"

"What?"

"It was done by your buddy Paul's company."

"Great, Genepool and Paul are the ones supplying the noose around my neck. And guess who did the paternity test on Destinee? Only he thinks I was verifying Tracy's lineage."

"So do you think Paul would talk to me candidly about the evidence?"

"I don't see why not. My visit here kind of makes it your case doesn't it?"

"I guess I could look at it that way, don't know if my boss will, but what he doesn't know won't hurt him. I want to call this guy Paul from Genepool Medical. Maybe the right questions haven't been asked yet."

"Jojo, I can't thank you enough. I didn't want to get you into trouble, but I didn't know who else to go to. Everything you need is on these papers," Steven said, holding the stray sheets of paper in his hand while still lying down in back.

"Look, Cowboy, if it wasn't for you, I would have been tortured and killed by some sadistic nuts twenty years ago. I have a good life; my family and I will survive. I can't let you go to jail for the rest of your life. So I would rather spend my time keeping you out of jail than spend my time trying to figure out how to bust you out of it. At least I have some new information to work with."

"Thanks, you don't know how much that means to me. I have to go, but before I do, I have to hit you over the head with something."

"What? You're not going to hit me with anything. Are you fucking nuts?"

"It has to look like I forced you into our little conversation and that I knocked you out to steal your money."

"My money!"

"They are going to track my little visit here and put two and two together. They are going to know we talked and you can't lie to them."

"Fuck you, Cowboy, you are not hitting me."

"Just a small bump, I gotta give you a bump or something."

"No bump, no nothing."

"OK, OK, I was just trying to make this easier for you."

"Easier? By cracking my head open. I don't think so. I'll tell them the truth. You were desperate, you begged me to help you with a gun pointed at me. I refused."

"Then give me your handcuffs. Remember I have a gun on you. I'll handcuff you to the steering wheel."

"That's no good. I could still hit the horn or maybe even drive."

"OK, OK, get in the backseat. There must be something here to lock you to?"

"Shit! Cowboy, you will owe me for this. On the floor, there is a ring for locking unruly riders to. You are going to make me look like a fool. I guess I can kiss off being chief."

"Look, we can clean up the mess later, trust me."

"Trust you? Man, I hate it when you say that."

Jojo got into the backseat, making sure nobody was watching. "Just be careful you don't make the cuffs too tight. I might be here awhile."

"That would be the plan. Here is the information, everything except the fact that Destinee is my daughter."

"How can I contact you?"

"I set up an e-mail. Cowboy5810@gmail.com. But as soon as you tell everybody about my visit, you'll be bugged and recorded and your house watched, so you'll have to find some other way of sending it."

"Cowboy, something you should know. Your brother Ernie was released a month ago. He's worried about you."

Steven paused. "Good for him. I wish I could be there for him and help him start over. I hope he can stay out of trouble. Being an ex-con won't make it easy."

"He's a good guy, just slipped a bit," Jojo said.

"You're a good guy too," Steven said as he clicked the handcuffs closed. "Are you sure I can't hit you over the head?"

"I'm sure! What are you going to do now?"

"I don't know. My only lead was the pimp. I don't have another plan. The only thing I do know is the answers lie in Washington."

"I suggest you just lay low and give me some time. Just disappear again."

"Hey, what are you doing?" Jojo protested as Steven searched him.

"I need some cash. I assume you won't mind." Steven took all the cash in his friend's wallet as well as a credit card. "Are you on the take?" He counted the cash. "There's five hundred bucks here."

"Aw, man, not all my cash! It's for Tamara's ring. Our anniversary is coming up, in case you forgot."

"Look, tell Tamara I'll make it up, I promise."

"From the state penitentiary?"

"Find the guy who killed Destinee, and I won't be *in* the penitentiary."

"Armed robbery too! And don't forget assault on an officer of the law, and identity theft," Jojo said.

"Hey, I'm not armed."

"You told me you had a gun pointed at me, that's armed robbery."

"I stand corrected. See you, buddy." Steven ruffle Jojo's hair.

"Cowboy?"

"Yea?"

"How much time do you need?"

"Try to not create a scene for two hours if you can."

"Two hours? Two fucking hours? Are you kidding?"

"You asked. I can't tell you why. Thanks, and whatever happens to me, well ... thanks for being my friend."

Chapter 40

Steven looked around. Nobody was near. Jojo had picked a good spot to hide, and Steven wasn't too far from the car he had taken from the airport. Steven tried to walk normally and not attract attention.

He was buoyed with some hope. At least somebody was on his side now, and that gave him optimism. Nonetheless, he wasn't ready to give up his freedom. So he cautiously walked his way back to the car he had borrowed from the airport.

It was not unusual at all for small airports to offer courtesy cars to transient pilots. Usually, pilots might need to drive to a local restaurant for a sandwich while their plane was being fueled and the airport operator would just toss the pilot a set of keys. In this case, the car was inside a security fence and still had the keys in it for off hours' use. It was time for Steven to take the car back and reclaim his aircraft. Maybe there would be police waiting for him or maybe not. Hopefully, nobody had discovered yet that the small plane was gone.

Steven started up the black Malibu sedan, it was rusted over the wheel wells and the cloth interior was ripped. As an airport loner car it was all he expected. The engine noisily roared to life and he shifted it into drive.

Steven drove to a Walmart. He had given some thought to Jojo's advice. Find someplace to disappear again.

Senator Westcott took the chance and entered the store to do some serious shopping. A half hour later, he filled the borrowed car with necessities he had bought using most of the cash he had left, most of which had been donated by his friend.

Steven then parked a city block away from the airport and scouted the area until he decided it was as safe as it was going to get. Most airports used a series of numbers for their airport security gate that could be easily guessed by transient pilots. Steven took a few guesses and punched in the correct not-so-secret airport code. The security gate opened. In this case, it was the beginning numbers of the address for the airport. He drove the beat-up Malibu to the Cessna and transferred everything into it. Then he parked the car where he had found it.

"So you're the car thief," the friendly airport operator joked as Steven walked boldly into the small office area.

"It was me. I give up," Steven replied with a laugh. "But I do need some fuel. Will you let me off easy?"

"You'd be surprised what we would do to sell some fuel. Want it topped off?"

"That would be great."

"Tommy," the man said into a handheld radio.

"Yea!" came the reply.

"Top off the 182, tail number 182 Mike Delta."

"Copy."

So far so good, Steven thought. But he would have to use Jojo's credit card to purchase the fuel. If the operator paid attention to the name on the card and knew Jojo, he would be in trouble.

"Crazy weather last night, especially north." Steven struck up a conversation, trying to distract the manager while he rung up the fuel.

"Sure was. Where'd you fly in from?"

"North," Steven laughed a bit. "Came in from the DC area just ahead of the storm."

"Looks like things settled down. Headed back or going south for the winter?"

"Headed back."

"Better make sure your airport has been plowed out. It would be a shame to get home and find out you can't land," the manager said as he swiped the credit card through the electronic reader.

"Already checked. It won't be a problem." An unplowed runway would be the least of his worries on this trip.

The manager looked at the slip as Steven signed Jojo's name. "Thank you, Mr. Jones, and have a safe flight."

Steven strolled as casually as he could toward the plane. In another ten minutes, he should be in the air. The next ten minutes might be all there was between life in prison and a shot at freedom.

That same morning in Washington DC:

It was hard for Chelle to concentrate; she was expecting a call from agent Henderson at any moment. Hopefully, they had caught the senator alive and well. This morning, she had found another piece to the puzzle that was Senator Westcott.

She had learned about Shatoya Anderson. She had a record of sorts, nothing serious, mostly for being picked up for hooking. That wasn't the noteworthy part. The thing that was most interesting was that she was arrested in Spring Lake. Spring Lake was near Fort Bragg. Fort Bragg was where Sargent Steven Westcott was stationed at the same time. The file also said the woman had a child, Caucasian.

It was very possible Steven Westcott did know the dead girl's mother. Maybe he *was* trying to help the woman's daughter. Senator Westcott's words haunted her. "I didn't do it, Detective, I have to prove it because I know you won't or can't." Chelle's stomach churned. The last year had been a very productive time for the city's police force. There had been quite a few murders, but most had been easily solved with the use of DNA found at the crime scene and other relatively easy-to-find evidence. Detective Harmon had been especially productive over that time. Chelle was beginning to believe that Senator Westcott had been framed for murder by a serial killer. She wondered if Detective Harmon was that person. And if he was, how could she prove it?

Regardless, the senator was still a fugitive. She had some time, so she was studying Aberdeen. It was nothing, a city of around fourteen thousand, founded by Scots years ago, and named after a Scottish city. It was the home of Phillips Army Airfield and the Harford municipal airport in nearby Churchville. No commercial airports or trains other than the one the senator had taken. Obviously, there was something or someone in Aberdeen the senator needed. Chelle couldn't wait any longer, so she called Henderson.

"Anything?" she said.

"Nothing. He disappeared again."

"What about his wife? Does she know who or what is in Aberdeen that's so important?"

"She claims not, and I believe her. She wants her husband caught so we can put an end to this game. She's beside herself worrying that he is angry with her and will do something violent to her and her daughter. She doesn't believe he's rational."

"What about his office staff?"

"Went there and interviewed everybody. Nothing there either."

"I have an idea. I think I know somebody who might know something: Shannon Johnston."

"I remember her, she used to work for the senator."

"She was his right arm. He didn't do anything without her knowing about it. Her father, who just happens to be the senator's lawyer, made her quit when things started falling apart for the senator. She might know things others don't."

"Let's meet with the young lady and see what we can find out."

Somewhere northwest of the DC area:

Steven looked out at the nearly all-white landscape. He knew exactly where he was, and if no F-16s showed up, he knew where he was going. Finally, he was headed toward home.

Steven left the location-tracking device turned off again. So for the time being, he was just one of thousands of legal VFR flights that flew in the country at any given time, albeit one that had forgot to turn on its transponder.

Steven checked his fuel; it was going to be close. He guessed he was about halfway, and if the winds didn't change against him, he would make it.

Shannon Johnston's apartment that same morning:

Chelle knocked on the door, hoping the young woman was home.

"Who is it?" A woman's voice came through the door.

"Police." Chelle stepped back and held her badge out to the peek hole in the door. "Please let us in."

"I already told everybody, I don't know where the senator is."

"Shannon, open the door now."

Shannon slid off the chain latch and opened the door.

"Shannon, you do remember me?"

"Yes, you're the detective that is trying to arrest the senator for something he didn't do."

Chelle ignored the comment. "This is agent Henderson of the FBI. We have a few new questions to ask you."

They were standing inside Shannon's small apartment. "Please sit, Miss Johnston," Chelle said as she pulled out a wooden chair.

Shannon looked at the two officers and then at the chair she was being offered.

"I'll get right to the point," Chelle said. "Senator Westcott went to Aberdeen. We think you might know why."

Shannon sat down on the chair. It was one of five surrounding her round dining table. Chelle noticed Shannon turn her head away, trying to conceal her eyes.

"Shannon, if you know why the senator went to Aberdeen, you have to tell us," Chelle said.

Agent Henderson was a bit more blunt. "Shannon, you have no protection from withholding information. You are not family, so I would recommend answering truthfully."

Chelle saw Shannon press her lips together tightly and scowl.

"So you do know," Henderson suggested.

Chelle coaxed, "You definitely know something, and we need to know what it is, Shannon," Chelle said. "This is serious. I understand your loyalty to him, but he could be in physical danger, nobody wants to see him hurt."

They both towered over the sitting young woman. Henderson looked down at Shannon and said, "You could be arrested under a multitude of charges, including obstructing national security if you don't cooperate," Henderson pressed. "This is a United States senator we're talking about." Henderson dangled his cuffs in his hand.

Shannon looked at the floor. There was silence for half a minute before she responded.

"He took flying lessons there," Shannon whispered.

"Where?"

"I think they called it Harford County Regional Airport."

Henderson blurted out the same thing Chelle was thinking. "He was looking for an airplane to escape with."

"Last night?" Chelle looked at Henderson with surprise. "In that snowstorm? Maybe he's still there because he couldn't fly out."

Chelle turned back to Shannon and said, "He had a pilot's license? Why didn't we know that?"

"He didn't," Shannon volunteered. "He just started taking lessons. I think he soloed once."

Chelle felt her face turn flush. "Oh my god, if he tried to escape by flying in the storm ..." Chelle didn't finish her thought. "We need to send teams out to that airport at once."

Henderson reached for his phone. "Get the local police up to a place called Harford County Airport. Tell them to proceed with caution but to look for a downed airplane. If there are any agents up that way get them there pronto."

Henderson turned away from Shannon as he continued to talk on his phone. "What? You're kidding? Yea, I can confirm it." Henderson stepped back into the hallway to talk in private. Chelle followed, keeping an eye on Shannon. From the doorway, Chelle overheard Henderson's side of the conversation.

"It looks like he took off out of a small field north of Baltimore. He was taking flying lessons there, a place called Harford County. Tell the FAA to find that plane."

Henderson listened for quite a while before slipping his phone back in his pocket. "The son of a bitch has more lives than a cat. He's got balls. That much I'll give him."

"What? What's going on?" Chelle asked.

Henderson eyed Shannon, then continued in a quiet voice.

"It just came in. Apparently, in last night's storm, he somehow flew a small Cessna to Reidsville North Carolina."

"Why? That doesn't make any sense."

"His friend lives there, don't you guys read the papers?" Shannon said, having obviously overheard. "Nobody else gives a crap about him. Where would you go?"

"She's right, some guy, a detective nonetheless, a Detective Denton Jones," Agent Henderson said. "Flew in last night, hid in his car, pointed a gun at him, and then cuffed him in the backseat of his car and stole his money and credit card, then took off again."

Chelle thought for a bit, then asked, "Did he hurt the detective in any way?"

"No, seems OK."

"And why would he do this?" Chelle asked just as she and Henderson turned back toward Shannon, who was biting her lip.

Chelle folded up her notebook. "And do we know where the senator is now?"

"Used his buddy's card to fill up with fuel, got in his plane, and took off again. We don't know where he is going, but what we do know is that he left Reidsville two and a half hours ago."

"Then we got him," Chelle suggested as Shannon's face turned white.

"Not that simple," Henderson replied. "VFR pilots do not have to file flight plans, and they aren't even necessarily going to show up on radar. What we do know is the range of his plane and that he has to land within the next few hours."

"What about sending out search planes, you know, military jets?"

"We can't send out F-16s to check out every VFR aircraft. Draw a two-hundred or so mile ark around Reidsville. It would be logistically impossible. And if the interception procedures caused a fatal accident with an innocent civilian, we would be tarred and feathered. We know where and when he took off out of Reidsville, that's a plus. Maybe radar recordings can be brought up, and with enhanced analysis, they can pick up a small blip and track it. Chances are, he will be one of the few VFR aircrafts without a transponder on."

"This doesn't smell right," Chelle turned back to Shannon. "I don't suppose you know anything about any of this do you? He didn't just fly all the way to North Carolina to steal some money from an old friend, who just happens to be a cop."

"Maybe he didn't do it," Shannon said, "did you ever think of that? Maybe he is trying to find out who did. Maybe he has to do your job for you because you aren't doing it."

Chelle was thinking the same thing. The senator wasn't just running; he was up to something.

Chapter 41

Back at the station, Chelle looked at her watch. The day was quickly filling up with tasks. She wanted to meet with Mr. Ramon Hayes once again. She had a question to ask him that she had been putting off for too long. Maybe it was because she didn't want to know the answer. Because Chelle wanted honest responses to some pretty blunt questions, she thought some neutral territory would be the best place to meet.

"Ramon, this is Detective Saltarie."

"What a wonderful surprise, Detective. What can I do for you?"

Chelle couldn't believe she was doing this. Ramon was the last person in the world she would have guessed she would be setting a date up with. Chelle took a deep breath and tried to sound casual and friendly.

"Ramon, I was wondering if you would mind meeting me somewhere. I have to be honest with you, I have a few more questions, but I would like to meet someplace more relaxing. I was thinking we could meet at the Billy Goat Tavern. It's not far from the Washington Arms."

Ramon was stunned. He was being asked out on a date. Whatever the pretense was he didn't care. "That sounds very nice. When?"

"Would tomorrow work? Around eight?"

"Yes, I would be honored." *Chelle hated what she was doing, but the manager might be one of the few people who could help her. She tucked a photo of Detective Bruce Harmon in her purse. She steeled herself for what she was about to do, her lips were pursed as if she had just tasted some very bitter medicine. This had better be worth it.*

She was almost out the door for the day when Pat called out to her. She stopped long enough for Pat to catch up. As they walked out the door, he showed her a pile of files in his hand. "I checked on some of the other murders like you asked. I suppose you knew that Harmon was the lead detective on all of them?"

Without waiting for a response, he continued. "Yea, the other thing that is strange is that the victims had a history of using either the Washington Arms or the Saint Claire. I'm afraid you're right. There is something very suspicious going on with Harmon."

Chelle stopped walking, and without turning, said, "Pat, you don't have to be involved with this. This could go badly. You have a family to think of."

Pat grabbed Chelle's arm and turned her to make her look at him. "Chelle, I want to help, but how can I help you if you don't tell me what is going on?"

"If you give me those files, you are helping me. And for now, if I were you, I wouldn't tell anybody about this. If my suspicions are wrong, you don't want to get caught in the middle."

Somewhere over Massachusetts:

The airplane's engine kept up its steady hum; it was running on what must be fuel vapors. Steven looked at his altimeter. He was purposely flying at only about a thousand feet above the ground, hoping radar couldn't see him that low. The fuel gauge on the Cessna was notoriously inaccurate. It was said the only time to believe it was when it said empty, and it had read empty for the last ten minutes. But it didn't matter anymore; it was time for his next flight lesson. He turned the plane into the wind.

Steven pulled the fuel mixture back as far as he could, which cut off whatever fuel was remaining from reaching the engine. Then he went through the engine shutdown procedures. Suddenly, things got very quiet in the airplane.

The sound of the wind rushing past the doors was something the engine and propeller had always drowned out. Now, it sounded peaceful and calming, which was good because what he was about to do would be anything but. This landing, probably the last in his life one way or another, would hopefully be unseen by anybody.

With the engine out, he was a silent glider. It was daylight, but the recent snow hid all references of land contours. Steven concentrated on nosing the plane earthward despite the feeling that he should be doing the opposite. A Cessna 182 didn't make for a good glider, but he kept telling himself that it would fly if he kept the wind going over the wings fast enough. Still, it would only be a matter of time before the plane and the earth intersected.

It didn't take long for the unpowered airplane to descend a thousand feet. Steven cinched up his seatbelt and shoulder harness as tight as he could possibly make them. He kept his airspeed up despite the ground getting closer and closer. The snow made finding a flat and level landing area impossible. Steven wasn't fooled by the smooth appearance of the white blanket; this landing would be anything but smooth.

"Sorry guys!" Steven said, apologizing to the owners of the plane, people who he knew quite well. Reaching for the flap handle, he set it at ten degrees down, and adjusted his speed for sixty-five knots. Then he added a bit more of the landing flaps.

The treetops were getting closer, and he was tempted to restart the engines and find a more suitable landing site. But he quickly rejected the idea; he was committed and as ready as he would ever be.

He turned the fuel selector valve off. Next, he switched off the master power switch to hopefully prevent a fire. The emergency-landing checklist reminded him to crack open the door. Upon a hard landing, the door could become wedged closed. Better to have it wedged open now.

The snow was easier to see now and the white barricades were considerably higher than he had anticipated only minutes earlier. Keeping the plane at a constant sixty-five knots was his only task right now. The plane would land when no more air separated him from the ground, and without power, he couldn't control when that happened.

There was only one thing left to do. He grabbed the rolled-up sleeping bag sitting on the copilot's seat. He set it on his lap, ready to use it to shield his face upon impact. Then, without warning, the windshield became a solid glistening of white. His depth perception was unexpectedly gone. Left or right, up or down suddenly meant nothing. Instinctively, he pulled back on the yoke. The wide-open area where he had chosen to land became a trap. He no longer had any references of height or distance, such as trees or shrubbery. Land and air disappeared into whiteness.

Steven knew the area and had chosen Teal Pond to land on. It was more of a marsh than a pond or lake. He hoped it would be frozen. Habit forced him to glance at his airspeed indicator; he was going too slowly. The plane started to drop. Then the wheels hit the ice of the frozen lake and the plane tipped downward. Steven strained to make out some sort of definition of land as he pulled back even more on the yoke.

The airspeed had dropped below critical speed, and any lift the plane had was completely gone. Steven felt a hard bounce. Luckily, the ice held, and with a thud, the plane bounced again off the hard, frozen surface. It didn't take long for the plane to settle down again, this time even harder.

The nose of the plane fell forward as the wheels plowed into a high drift of snow. Then the propeller caught another drift, and an instant later, the plane flipped over its nose. Steven was flung violently forward, disoriented by the white all around him.

The plane was tossed upside down into the snow. The forward momentum caused the wings to act like skis and the plane skidded for a hundred more feet before they dug into the loose snow, bringing the plane to a stop.

How long it took for him to regain his senses he didn't know. But when he did, he found himself hanging upside down, still strapped into the seat. In a panic to get right side up, he opened his seatbelt latch and dropped onto his head. Steven called himself a couple of choice words for being so stupid. Then, after a few tries at kicking the upside-down pilot's door open, it cracked a few inches. With a few more kicks, it opened enough for him to wiggle free of the plane. His bare hands met the cold snow and frozen lake. Weak and dazed, he stood up, covered in snow.

Late afternoon that same day:

"Hi Paul, thank you so much for talking with me."

"When I heard it was the famous Jojo calling, I had to. If even half the stories Senator Westcott told me are true, you two should write a book."

"The senator has a way of embellishing the facts when it comes to me. And it's usually at my expense."

"Are you kidding? Steven thinks the world of you."

"And I him. That's why I'm calling."

"If there is anything I or Genepool Medical can do to help Steven, I'm in. That is if it's at least close to legal."

Jojo was calling on his personal cell phone inside his car. If he could keep this off the record, he intended on doing just that.

"I don't know if Steven told you, but I am a detective now. I might be obligated to share anything you tell me. Just thought you should know."

"Sure, Detective, I get it. I've been warned."

"Paul, please call me Jojo. Steven and I need your help."

"So you don't think he did it?"

"I've known Steven since training. There isn't much I don't know about him, and I can't believe that he killed a young woman in cold blood."

"It doesn't make any sense, but it was his DNA in the poor girl. I would have to testify to that in a court of law."

While he talked, Jojo watched people coming and going out the gas station he was parked at. His unmarked car drew little attention.

"Paul, if the DNA is his, and he didn't do it. What could be the other possibilities?"

There was a pause on the other line. "There aren't any. It's his DNA, like I said."

"But if Steven said he didn't do it, and we believe he didn't do it, how could his DNA get there?"

"DNA is notoriously easy to collect. Hair on a brush, saliva on a toothbrush, blowing your nose can leave behind nose hairs and mucus with cells in it. Drinking something can leave cells on the rim of the glass. Even touching something like a steering wheel, or book, or telephone will leave enough dead skin cells behind to culture into testable samples."

"OK, so somebody could have collected Steven's DNA and planted it. Unlikely, but plausible," Jojo suggested.

"If we are going on the assumption that the senator didn't kill the young woman, then it wouldn't be just plausible, it would have to be factual. It's the only other way. Except, how do you plant semen? Or rather, how did someone get Steven's semen to plant?"

Jojo watched two male adults enter the convenience store.

"According to Steven, he didn't mess around. And I believe him on that too. That would mean his wife collected it and supplied it to the murderer, which I find impossible to believe."

"I agree, Lucille wouldn't frame Steven, she just wouldn't. Besides, what would be her motive?

"I need to ask a dumb question. How do the police know it was semen?" Jojo asked.

"Semen would be hard to misinterpret. The cells contained in semen would only have one strand of DNA in them; other cells in the body have two. It would be impossible to miss," Paul said. "Unless ..."

"Unless what?"

"Suppose the lab technician assumes it's semen because of where the cells were found or because that was what he was told by the police.

If the technician didn't look, just took the police's word for it, it could be possible to run it through purification, buffer to stabilize, and then set it up in the sequencer all without peering into the cell itself. Especially if someone is in a hurry."

"You're telling me that it wasn't necessarily semen that was found inside the girl?"

"That's right, at least it's not impossible. Theoretically, it could have been any medium that contained some of Steven's DNA."

"If you look real close, could you tell exactly what medium it was?" Jojo asked.

"What you're asking for is an identification of the cell that held the DNA. And yes, absolutely it can be done. In fact, with semen, it would be quite obvious. But what would that help?"

"If it was Steven's semen, then either he is lying or his wife is in on the deception. If it's from some other part of his body, then it substantiates Steven's story that he wasn't having sex with the young woman and that his wife isn't part of the frame up."

"I'll tell you what, Detective, I'll go through the paperwork and talk to the technician involved. I'll go over all aspects of the collection and testing of the samples. I'll assume things are not what they appear to be."

"Thanks Paul. It could be quite literally the difference between life and death for Steven."

Chapter 42

The next day in Washington DC:

Chelle walked into the Billy Goat Tavern. Ramon stood up as she came through the door. She wasn't late. She was right on time. From his half-empty drink, Chelle could see that he had been quite a bit early.

Ramon smiled broadly.

"Please let me help you with your coat." Ramon reached around for her coat with red, cracked, and scaly hands, missing their signature gloves. Chelle noticed a slight hesitation as he lifted her coat off of her. His phobia was possibly worse than she had imagined. He was obviously struggling with the desire to be gallant and the desire not to touch an unhygienic object. Once her coat was off, she couldn't help but notice how the squat, little man tried not to stare at her breasts that were pressing against the buttons of her tight, white blouse.

"Why thank you, Mr. Hayes."

Chelle thought it sweet to be doted on even though she wasn't the doting-on type. She also guessed that Ramon wasn't used to meeting women outside of his job.

Ramon hung Chelle's coat on the coat rack not far from their table. He moved about awkwardly and seemed unsure of what was expected of him. She could see that without his gloves on, everywhere he turned seemed to be another obstacle in his path as he tried not to touch anything around him.

If it was a guess before, now she was quite sure that the hotel manager was out of his element. He seemed nervous and shy. "Thank you, Ramon. I only have a few questions. It shouldn't take long."

"I am in no rush. Would you care for a drink?" Ramon said, trying not to stare at her breasts.

Chelle had purposely worn the tight, white blouse. *Honey for the fly,* she had thought. Now, she felt self-conscious. Chelle wondered if this had been a huge mistake. But she had the suspicion the hotel manager knew more than he let on. Her hope was that in a social setting, his guard would drop a bit and she would learn his secrets.

The waitress appeared and asked for their order.

"A rum and coke," Chelle ordered.

"I will have another coke please, no ice." The waitress left. "Sorry ... I ... I don't drink alcoholic beverages. And you should be careful of ice machines. They don't get cleaned regularly. Not at the Washington Arms of course. I make sure our ice machines are cleaned weekly."

"I appreciate the advice, and no need to apologize, Mr. Hayes."

Their small cocktail table was next to the street-side window; the city lights lit up the street and sidewalk. Chelle looked outside for a moment at the gently falling snow. "They say we are going to get hit again with another snowstorm, and this one is going to be a dandy."

Chelle turned back toward Ramon and nibbled at the bowl of mixed nuts in front of them.

"Try some. They're good." Chelle slid the small bowl toward Ramon.

Ramon stared at the nuts as if trying to solve a puzzle.

"No thank you. Maybe later."

Ramon seemed more than happy to talk about the weather. "We are booked full. People think the airport is going to be closed in the morning, and they're not taking chances."

"I heard the same thing. After midnight tonight, it's supposed to get nasty. Might even turn into a blizzard. Remember last year? The city was basically shut down for a week."

Ramon chuckled a bit, then added, "We had people sleeping in the lobby, waiting for rooms to become available. Of course I wasn't working at the Washington Arms back then."

"Oh, where were you working?"

"The Continental. It's very nice, but the Washington Arms needed my services more."

Chelle assumed that meant an increase in pay. "I remember that week well, the crime rate dropped to near zero. Even the bad guys were forced to stay home."

Chelle and Ramon laughed a bit as the waitress came back with the two drinks.

"Would you mind coming back to wipe the table, it looks a bit sticky," Ramon asked with a very serious expression on his face.

"Sure, no problem."

When Ramon picked up his glass, he saw a smudge, so he set it down again. Chelle looked in the other direction.

"Maybe you will have an easy week then?" Ramon said.

"That would be nice. I have plenty of backlog to keep me busy without any new murders." Then she pointed to an outside video camera. "That helped me to develop my arrest warrant for the senator. That and of course your help, which I want to thank you for. It was more important than you might think."

"I didn't do that much," Ramon said. "You were the one who recognized the fake names he used."

The waitress came back and wiped down the table. Chelle detected a bit of relief in Ramon.

"I'm sure that if I hadn't, you would have. You are extremely aware of who your guests are. You certainly have a talent for it."

"I try my best. I have been working in the hotel industry my entire life and being aware of your guests is very important in making them feel at home."

"Mr. Hayes, may I call you Ray, or Ramon? Mr. Hayes seems so formal."

"Ramon is fine I guess," he said timidly.

"Some people go by their middle name," Chelle added, trying to break the ice, "what's yours?"

"Ruben," he said anxiously.

Chelle took her glass, sipped at it, and took another handful of nuts.

"Ramon Ruben Hayes. Kind of has a ring to it."

Ramon asked, "Have you had any success lately, I mean at catching the senator?"

"I can't tell you anything confidential, but," Chelle moved her chair closer to Ramon and then leaned in toward him, "we are tracking down a few new leads. It will be just a matter of time. We are getting closer every hour."

"I hope you catch him soon. He deserves to go to jail for a very long time."

"He certainly does. That's where murderers belong."

Chelle set her glass down next to Ramon's hand, which was resting on the table.

"What do you think?" Chelle looked her date in the eyes with as much sincerity she could muster. "Why would a man that has so much to live for throw it all away by murdering somebody?"

Ramon fidgeted nervously with his eye glasses, then put his hands back next to Chelle's. He took some time before answering. "I guess some people are evil. I see wrong things happening all the time in my business."

"At the Washington Arms?"

"Not just the Washington Arms, other hotels I've worked at too, all of them in fact."

"What kind of crimes are you talking about?"

Ramon stared at their hands as he contemplated an answer. His lips started to move a couple of times with words that didn't materialize. Chelle thought that maybe the closeness of their hands was distracting him.

"Like the girl that the senator murdered. There are others, many others, that sell their bodies for money. I see them every day. I hate them for what they do. They are sinners."

Chelle reached for her glass, brushing her hand against Ramon's. Ramon looked at his hand as if it had suddenly been turned to gold.

"And what about the men? The men like Senator Westcott, who buy these women?"

Ramon took the napkin from under his coke and used it to hold the drink. Then he took a sip. Chelle felt a bit sorry for him.

"Those men are bad people. They should be arrested. They are sinners too."

Chelle sensed the manager was opening up to her, trusting her. She brushed her leg against Ramon's. "Oh excuse me, I didn't mean to—"

"That's quite all right. No need to apologize."

"We do arrest them, all the time. But to tell you the truth, it doesn't seem to do much good." Chelle didn't think the time was quite right yet to ask her question, so she changed the subject. "Tell me a bit about yourself, Ramon. Do you have any hobbies?"

"I ... I never thought about having one. Most of my time is spent at the hotel. I really don't mind. I guess my work is my hobby."

"How wonderful is that?"

Ramon looked confused, so Chelle rephrased her comment. "How wonderful is it that you enjoy your work so much?"

He responded quietly and slowly, almost reluctantly, agreeing. "Yes ... yes it is, I guess."

Chelle let her leg brush up against Ramon's again, only this time she didn't apologize. She left it in close proximity as they made their way through more small talk.

Chelle could sense that Ramon was becoming more and more comfortable with her. She wondered if this was his first date ever. Ramon talked about some of the other bad things that went on in hotels like spouses cheating.

"I know. I can see where their ring was. I can tell. God says once you are married, you should be faithful."

"You mean the church teaches that?"

Ramon bit at his lower lip and then took a sip of his coke. Something more was bothering him. She decided to let the silence between them do the asking.

Finally, he asked, "Do you go to church, Detective?"

"Please, Ramon, call me Chelle. Not as often as I should. Do you?"

"Yes, often. I talk to God."

"What church do you belong to?"

"I'm Catholic, if that is what you mean, but I can go to any church whenever I want to talk to God."

Chelle decided to probe, albeit carefully. "Does God talk to you?"

"He talks to everyone who wants to listen. He tells me that he doesn't like sinners like the prostitutes and the men who pay them. You should go to church with me sometime."

"That would be nice, Ramon." Chelle realized that she had played her cards a bit too well. The manager was going to be seriously disappointed in the near future. Chelle felt as if she had made a bad mistake. The poor manager was a fish out of water, and she had, was, taking advantage of him. It was time to ask her question and then stop fortifying the charade.

Chelle placed her hand on top of Ramon's. "I'm afraid I have another favor to ask. Detective Marget and I need help catching another killer."

Chelle pulled out the photo from her purse. Ramon used the opportunity to move his chair next to Chelle's, then leaned over to get a closer look at the photo.

"Have you ever seen this man come into your hotel?"

Chelle saw the surprise on his face when he recognized the man in the picture.

"Yes, he has visited often. I believe he is a policeman. I have seen his badge on his belt and the outline of his gun behind his coat."

"Was he there to investigate a murder?"

Ramon hesitated, as if he was breaking some sort of confidentiality that he held sacred.

"You mean like you? No ... never. I shouldn't be talking about this. Hotel privacy needs to be respected, even for bad people."

Ramon had slipped. "Are you telling me this man is a bad person?"

Ramon didn't respond immediately as if he was weighing how to answer. Then he sat up straight but couldn't look her in the eyes.

"He comes in to see some of the hookers. He thinks he sneaks in the back, but I see him."

Chelle reached back into her purse and pulled out another photo. "Was he ever with this girl?"

Chelle sensed eagerness to help her, now that Harmon's visits were exposed, or maybe it was their closeness he wanted to prolong.

"Yes, I do remember her. I even know her name. Well, at least the name she used when checking in. She called herself Tiffany Maddenheart. She would get the room, and then have the guest over. This man was often one of her guests."

Chelle pulled out another picture. "This is the girl that Senator Westcott is accused of murdering. Ramon, do you remember if this same man ever met with her?"

Ramon set the pictures he was looking at gently down into Chelle's hand. Then he took the third from her and turned toward her; their lips close enough to kiss. "He is not a good person. He is not like you. Yes, he would meet with that girl. He would meet others too. He would have sex with them and do drugs with them. You know, cocaine, I think. I would find white powder spilled on the rug sometimes. I usually give them a smoking room on the third floor because they also burn something and inhale it. I can smell it sometimes, even in the hallway. He never checked in, but it was him. I'm sure of it. The girls would get the room, then he would meet them. Are you going to arrest him?"

Chelle remembered the sedan that had picked up Destinee on the day she died. It was a car that looked like hers, which was, in fact, the same make, model, and color all the detectives drove.

"I need proof. I can't just arrest someone."

"I can help you prove it. I can collect things after he uses a room. Things with his fingerprints on them. You use DNA don't you? I could get things with his DNA on them. You could prove he was in the room with girls and drugs."

"I couldn't ask you to do that Ramon."

"I don't mind. He should be caught. He needs to be punished." Ramon took a sip of his coke and stared at the tabletop for a while. "He hits them you know."

"Hits who?"

"The girls. I know they are bad too. But he shouldn't hit them. That's wrong." Ramon was clearly becoming worked up.

Chelle slipped her hand on top of Ramon's. She could tell he was troubled and was serious about wanting to help her.

"How do you know he hits them?"

Ramon stared at the tabletop, looking ashamed. "I can hear them."

"How?"

"From the hallway. I sometimes deliver room service or check on a guest. Then I hear them. Sometimes it's terrible sounds, but I can't stop him. He is a policeman, and I, I am afraid he would get mad at me and arrest me for something." Ramon's face flushed.

"It's not your fault, Ramon. I don't know what I would have done either," Chelle lied; she knew exactly what she would have done, and Detective Harmon wouldn't have liked it one bit. "I might have to ask you to talk to my captain. Would you do that for me?"

Ramon looked up quickly. There was fear in his eyes. "No, no, I can't do that. Only you. I will only talk to you."

"That's OK, Ramon, it's OK. I'll think of another way."

Chelle changed the subject back to the weather and used it for an excuse about why she had to leave. Unfortunately, Ramon could become critical to her in catching a serial killer. That meant she might have to force Ramon into doing things he didn't want to do. Maybe it would soften the blow a bit if he thought he was doing it for her. So for good measure, in case she needed more information from Ramon, she approached the still-sitting Ramon and gave him a short peck on the cheek, guiltily reinforcing the charade. "We really need to do this again," she suggested. "And thank you, Ramon, you have been a big help. I owe you."

Ramon gave a startled nod, barely able to squeak out, "Yes, any time."

"Then let's not be strangers," Chelle added as she turned and walked out the Billy Goat Tavern, a little disgusted at the things she had to do for her job.

Ramon walked the short distance back to the Washington Arms. The winter winds were blowing, but he felt exceedingly warm inside. His date with the detective had gone remarkably well.

Chapter 43

Back at the hotel, Ramon was drawn to room 327. It wasn't occupied, and he used his passkey to enter it. The room looked average. In fact, it looked like most of the other rooms within the confines of the Washington Arms. Only Ramon knew it wasn't.

He opened the nightstand drawer and took out the Bible in it. This Bible was special because it was his. A priest had given it to him years ago. He purposely left it in room 327 so that any guest he ushered to the room had an opportunity to read it just as he had. It was, in Ramon's mind, a chance for sinners to repent, maybe a last chance.

Ramon thought about the Bible in his hand, and then he thought about his wonderful date with Chelle Saltarie and their conversation. Strange that God would bring him together with a detective, but he stopped questioning God's actions long ago. Ramon took off his winter gloves and caressed the book. He used his bare hands to rub over it. He knew there was no reason to worry about his hands because the Bible cleansed everything.

Ramon thought about the priest who had given him the Bible. His name was Father Hales. Ramon's hands instinctively gripped the Bible tightly as he remembered the nightmare of that experience. His mind retreated back in time, forcing him to once again relive that life-changing night.

It was a winter evening in Southern California when a friend of his mother's had stopped by to do what all her other friends did with his mother in the back room. Ramon was ten, but that didn't mean he was unaware of who and what his mother was.

School was his refuge, but at night, he had to put up with the sounds, the terrible sounds. For the most part, the men left him alone and would give him a very unwelcomed pat on the head as his mother took them down the hall. How Ramon hated that hallway. He hated walking past it to his own bedroom; it always made him feel dirty, like the men who came to see his mother. He could still see the dull yellow paint on the walls and his mother taking her new friend in hand.

But it was the sounds he hated the most. The sound of the creaking bed, his mother's cries for more, the men often talking meanly to her and calling her names. Then there was the muffled scream from his mother and a guttural grunt from the man that always signaled the end to the squeaking of the bed frame.

Ramon would turn up the volume of the television whenever his mother's friends came to visit. But it was never enough to mask the sounds. He knew what the sounds were; he had seen movies, movies that a ten-year-old shouldn't see. He and his friend Timmy Lofton had found them and watched them, and he had heard the same sounds.

But that night, Ramon didn't want to hear the sounds. He didn't want to see his mother take her friend down the hall to her room, where countless men had entered, many grungy after a day's work. It was a room he could never bring himself to enter. He was repulsed by its filth, both seen and unseen.

That night, he didn't want to see the money change hands. So he left the apartment angry, and ran down the street as fast as he could. Without a jacket, he ran and ran in the cold and rain. It wasn't until he finally stopped running that he felt the wind whipping at him. He was soaked, the rain was running down his back and arms, and his skin was starting to feel numb.

Looking up, he saw light across the street. It was a church on the corner. Through the beautiful stained glass windows, he saw that some lights were on. He crossed the street as a bolt of lightning flashed and thunder roared.

He slipped up the stairs, not sure of himself. He had never been inside a church. The big, wooden door wasn't latched. He pulled on it, and it took a great deal of strength for a ten-year-old, but it opened and it was warm inside. It didn't take long for him to find a seat at the back of the church on a long, wooden pew. There were strange artifacts around him, and some rather gruesome scenes were depicted on carved sculptures hanging on the walls. The church was lit, but the lighting was dim and threw shadows everywhere. But what struck him most was the big cross at the very front of the church. It was lit up and boldly centered on an ornate wall.

That moment was forever etched into his mind. To this day, he could remember the feeling he had. He wasn't exactly comforted, but he did feel safe, sitting in a protected shadow. He felt safe enough to cry.

Ramon remembered he was starting to warm when a soft hand touched his shoulder, and an old man in a black suit sat next to him. "Are you lost my dear boy?" he asked gently.

Ramon rubbed his eyes dry and looked up. "No, sir. I didn't mean no harm. It started raining, so I came in here."

With a kindhearted look, the man said, "You are causing no harm I can see. You are welcome to stay here as long as you wish. And as long as you don't cause any trouble, you are welcome here any time you want. This is the house of the Lord, and that makes it your house too. But I must ask you—it is my duty to ask—are you in any trouble?"

"No, sir," Ramon's small voice squeaked out.

"I noticed you were crying. Is there anything I can do to dry those tears?"

"No," Ramon answered softly and hesitantly, shocked the old man cared about him.

"Father, Father." A call came from the front of the church.

"Yes, Amanda, I'm back here." The priest rose and patted Ramon on the leg. "You stay as long as you wish. And if you want a friend to talk to, I am always here. But I'm afraid the leader of the church choir has a problem that she thinks only I can solve. But wait, and I will bring you a towel to dry yourself off with."

As it turned out, Ramon visited the church often at night when he didn't want to hear the awful sounds. Eventually, Father Hales and he became good friends, and Ramon even became an altar boy. Ramon learned about the goodness of God and how God cared and took care of everybody, even a small boy and the son of a whore.

Then, one night when Ramon was fourteen years old, a visitor came to see his mother. This time, Ramon knew the visitor. It was one of his teachers.

"Hello, Ramon," Mr. Wells said as Ramon's mother ushered him into their small apartment.

Ramon didn't answer, but he saw the money change hands as well as the wedding ring on Mr. Wells's hand.

"Care for a drink, Frank?" Ramon noticed how his mother's voice turned flirtatious once the money was tucked into her purse.

"That would be nice."

Ramon watched his teacher caress his mother's arms as she took down a bottle of whisky from an upper cabinet and two recently washed glasses out of the sink.

"Your skin is so soft, Maggi," Mr. Wells purred into her ear. "I love your dark skin. Italian?"

"Yea right, if you say so. Didn't know my dad, so you know what, yea sure, I'm a fucking Italian, at least for tonight."

They laughed.

Ramon's mom poured two drinks and handed one to Mr. Wells.

"And Ramon, he doesn't look Italian." Mr. Hayes pointed at Ramon with the same hand that was holding his drink.

"Like mother like daughter, I guess. I don't know who his father was either. Obviously not black or Italian."

They laughed again.

"Ramon, I wouldn't mention to any of your friends at school that you saw me here. That might not be good for your grades." Mr. Wells laughed like he was making a joke. "That would be if you had any friends."

"Frank, don't tease him. Can't you see he's working on his homework? He is such a smart boy."

"I don't think he's very smart; his grades certainly don't reflect it. I do know he is the weirdest kid in class. Aren't you Ramon? I'll bet you don't have one friend at school do you?"

Ramon just looked away in shame.

"He has friends. He goes to church to see his friends."

"Church?" Mr. Wells laughed.

Ramon's mother laughed with him. "Go figure. My weird son is a regular church goer."

"Maybe he's praying for all your sins, Maggi." Mr. Wells laughed again.

Ramon watched his mother drink half of her drink, then she laughed with Mr. Wells and added, "Then he had better pray a lot harder. Come on, let's go to my room and have some fun."

The door to his mother's room closed. Ramon stood up from the table he was working at and clenched his fist. They were laughing at him because he went to church. They were laughing at him because he prayed to God. They were laughing at God.

Ramon retreated into his room, the anger in him growing. Mr. Wells was right, he didn't have friends at school, and nobody understood him. He just kept to himself and most days he was left alone.

Ramon turned on the small television in his room and turned up the volume. He could hear the laughing. Ramon debated about running away; he could run to church. Maybe Father Hales would be there. Ramon took his fist and pounded on his bedding. Why didn't God stop what was going on in the next room? Why did God let his mother do the things the commandments said you shouldn't? What if Father Hales was lying to him? Where was God when he needed him?

Ramon buried his head between his pillows; he didn't want to hear the sounds. Time passed slowly as he cried. Finally, he heard the door slam closed. His teacher was gone and the awful sounds had stopped. Ramon didn't understand, but he knew Father Hales wouldn't lie to him. Father Hales would say to him sometimes, "God works in strange and mysterious ways."

Ramon lifted himself out of the bed. He was going to tell his mother to stop because God didn't like what she was doing and that he didn't like what she was doing.

Ramon marched determined into his mother's room. "Mom, you have to stop. I don't want you bringing men here anymore."

When his mom sat up at the side of the bed to talk to Ramon, she grabbed a pillow to cover herself.

Maggi reached for her half-full glass of whisky. "I do it for you, you know that?" She was obviously drunk, but Ramon didn't care.

"God doesn't want you to take money for sex. It's not right."

"Yea, well fuck God! We gonna just wait around until God pays the rent, buys our food, pays for our clothes?"

Ramon's hands were balled up in fists.

"Father Hales says that God will take care of us if we let him."

His mom laughed and finished her whisky. "I just made more money in an hour on my back then working ten hours at some seedy factory. Grow up, Ramon. There is no God. Now get out of here before I start slapping you around."

"No!" Ramon stood his ground. "Don't talk about God that way."

Ramon's mom took a swing at him. She missed but succeeded at knocking a lamp off the nightstand.

Ramon bent down and picked up the lamp to put it back.

"Get out of here you little pervert. Frank was right, you're a little weirdo. Go pray to God or something. That's right. Why don't you pray to God to make you not such a little pervert."

"I'm not a pervert. I'm not! God wants you to stop."

"Screw you, screw him. I'll do what I damn well please. Now get out of my room you little pervert. I'm not dressed."

"No, no, you will stop!" Ramon swung the lamp still in his hands.

The heavy base hit his mother across the head. She looked at Ramon glassy eyed for a moment and then fell back onto the bed, bleeding from the gash.

Ramon dropped the lamp and grabbed his jacket and ran from the house.

Ramon ran and ran. His feet took him to the only sanctuary he knew. Out of breath, he climbed the stairway into the church. He tugged on the huge wooden door and ran inside.

He saw Father Hales at the front of the church. It was late, and he was alone.

"Father, Father, something awful has happened."

"Ramon, please calm down." Father Hales caught him and held him in a hug until his breathing became a bit less rushed.

"Let's sit." Father Hales sat Ramon on the steps of the alter.

"What is it, Ramon? What's happened?"

"If I tell you, you won't tell anybody will you?"

"A priest must always respect the confidentiality of a confession."

"That means you won't tell anybody right?"

"Yes, of course not."

"My mother was doing bad things in her room with a man."

"Yes, we've talked about this before."

"I told her she had to stop. I told her God didn't want her to do it anymore."

Suddenly, Ramon wasn't so sure telling Father Hales what had happened was a good idea.

"Did you have a fight with your mother?"

"Yes, she said bad things about me and about God."

"I'm sure she will forgive you if you forgive her. I will go home with you if you want. Maybe I can help."

Ramon felt calm. The Father's gentle voice and confident hugs made him feel better.

"I think I hurt her."

"Words can hurt sometimes, but I'm sure she will forgive you. You meant well."

Ramon looked at his old tennis shoes pressed against the marble floor of the church.

"I hit her. A lamp fell and I picked it up and hit her head with it."

"Oh my, Ramon. Is she hurt?"

"She fell and was bleeding."

"We have to go back and help her. We need to call the police and get an ambulance."

Father Hales started to stand. Ramon held his arm back. "You said you wouldn't tell anybody."

"Ramon, we must. Your mother could be hurt very bad."

"The police will arrest me won't they?"

"No of course not, it was an accident."

"It wasn't an accident. I wanted to hurt her. She said bad things about God. Don't you think she deserved to be hurt? She was doing things God didn't like, and she wouldn't stop. So I punished her."

Father Hales stood up. "It is not up to us to decide who to punish. I have to tell the police. I'm sorry, Ramon."

Ramon remembered holding onto Father Hales's arm and not letting go. "No, Father. They'll take me to jail. God doesn't want me to go to jail, does he?"

Father Hales tried to tug his arm out Ramon's grasp. "You won't go to jail Ramon. It was an accident, but we need to see if your mother was hurt badly."

Ramon tugged desperately on the priest. Father Hales struggled to pull away without hurting the young man.

"No, Father, no. God wants her punished. He doesn't want us to help her. It's time for her to be judged by God. You said God will judge all."

"Ramon, let me go!"

The church started to shake and groan, the floor beneath them moved. One of the cables that held the heavy cross above the alter snapped. The cross swung, as Father Hales struggled for footing, it bounced off one side of the alter and struck him on his forehead. Then the other cable supporting it snapped and the huge cross crashed its sharp edge against his chest. Father Hales fell back to the marble, the heavy cross falling on top of him, missing Ramon by only inches. The cross teetered over Father Hales's body. Ramon noticed the blood pooling under Father Hales.

Ramon tried to push himself away, but his hands slid over the blood. He reached up and slowly worked the heavy cross away from him, standing in shock. Father Hales wasn't moving. Ramon reached down with his bloody hands and shook the priest.

"Father, Father. Are you OK?"

There was no answer and no movement. Ramon realized that he was now standing in a pool of blood. He ran out the church with no place to go and nobody to talk to. So he ran back to the only place he could. He ran back home.

Back in his apartment, Ramon ran to his room. Once there, he saw his hands; they were still soiled with Father Hales's blood.

He ran into the bathroom and washed and washed his hands until he could no longer see the red-stained water disappear down the drain. It seemed like he couldn't get all the blood off. It was under his fingernails and stuck in every pore of his hands.

The next morning, there was a knock on the door. Ramon thought it was one of his mother's male friends. He would tell them his mother was sick.

"Go away, Mom's not feeling well."

"It's the police, son. We need to talk to you and your mother."

"Go away, just go away!"

"We can't. You have to open the door for us. We have to talk to you."

Ramon was afraid, but he knew the police wouldn't go away, so he cracked the door open just a bit.

"Mom's not feeling well. She's sleeping."

"Ramon, we know what happened. You were with Father Hales last night weren't you?"

"I didn't hurt him. The church shook and things moved and a cross fell down on him. I didn't do it!"

"Ramon, we know you didn't hurt Father Hales. But we have to ask you a few questions about what did happen."

The two uniformed officers stepped into the room and closed the door.

"Please wake your mother. It's very important."

"I can't, she's sleeping."

"Where's her room?"

Ramon pointed.

The officer knocked on the door. "Mrs. Hayes, this is the police. Please come out. We have something very important to talk to you about. Mrs. Hayes! This is the police, please come out." The officer knocked even harder.

"Are you sure she's in there?"

Ramon nodded bashfully.

After one more try, he opened the door slowly and immediately saw the dead woman.

"Shit!" He called to his partner. "Call the station and get a detective here pronto. She's dead."

Chapter 44

The next morning, Chelle opened the door to the police station, fighting against the cold wind trying to keep it closed. The glass door slammed shut behind her, and she kicked off the snow from her boots and brushed off her coat. Another snowstorm had come into the area, temperatures had dropped, and the wind had picked up. This storm, on the heels of another, was forecasted to turn into a full-blown blizzard.

With her wet coat draped over her arm, she strolled over to Pat's desk, but he wasn't there. A note on his desk said he would be back in an hour. Chelle decided to wait so she could tell Pat in person about her interesting date the night before.

With that date in mind, she thought it might be fun to do an Internet search on Mr. Ramon Ruben Hayes. The search turned up a few names that had the exact match. Then she saw a picture that was undeniably her Ramon Ruben Hayes. With a click, the image and caption expanded.

It was a photo announcing the new manager for the Continental Hotel in Washington DC.

Chelle checked the date. It was dated about a year before she had arrested Deon Michalski for a murder at that very same hotel. Chelle knew everybody even remotely connected with the Continental Hotel and Ramon wasn't one of them, yet she didn't dispute the article. Ramon had somehow slipped through her net.

Chelle could smell a lead from a mile away. This was stinking to high heaven. The statement he had made was sending off alarm bells in her mind. When talking about going to church and talking to God, Ramon had specifically said, "He tells me that he doesn't like sinners like the prostitutes and the men who pay them." When Ramon said he talks to God and God talks to him, he didn't mean it figuratively.

Chelle thought of an old joke: When you talk to God, we call it prayer, but when God talks to you, we call it schizophrenia.

So she continued to dig until Pat snuck up on her and set down a fresh cup of coffee.

"Well, how did your date go?"

"It wasn't a date."

"You met at a bar."

"Yes, a bar just down from the hotel."

"Sounds like a date to me."

"Whatever."

Chelle wrote something on a paper and handed it to Pat. It said, *The manager from the hotel positively identified Harmon as a patron to several prostitutes, at least two of which are now dead.*

Pat read it and handed it back to Chelle and she promptly shredded it.

"He actually ID him?"

Chelle nodded as she wrote *& drugs may be involved* on another slip.

"But there is something else very strange going on. Look at this." Chelle twirled the monitor so that Pat could get a better look at the screen. "He worked at the Continental Hotel and left just before I started working on the Michalski case. Then he went to the Saint Claire and then the Washington Arms. I don't like coincidences. There was something else Ramon said last night that creeped me out. He said when he is in the hallways at the hotel, he hears sounds, terrible sounds. And he said he hates them and that they are sinners and God doesn't like sinners. It sounded to me like he listens at the doorway."

"Chelle, are you implying he is the murderer?"

"All those recent murders involved the same hotels he worked at. I've been going over the Deon Michalski case, and I went over the other cases that you gave me. Not one of the defendants admitted to the murder. In each case, they denied it to the end."

"What do you expect them to say? And Leon Stevens, the executive, did admit to it."

"No he didn't," Chelle corrected. "He was offered a plea deal, and he took it. It shaved ten years off his sentence. He will still be able to see his children and grandchildren before he dies, God willing. Hell, you and I would have taken it too. But he never admitted guilt, which pissed the judge off."

"But, Chelle, it was only because he was guilty in the first place. The evidence was everywhere, blood, and fingerprints, DNA. Motive was proven. The only reason he got the plea deal was that his attorney golfs with the judge. Think about it. This Ramon guy has no motive. All the perpetrators had motive and their own DNA on or in the victim. We recovered the murder weapons, all with fingerprints. In many of the cases, the blood of the victim was on the perpetrator's clothing or car or whatever. And each had plenty of motives. Are you seriously thinking that each and every one of them was set up? And you think that moron did it? Come on ... give me a break. And what about your *other* suspect? You just said this guy positively ID'd him."

"He also said he could get me things with fingerprints on them and Harmon's DNA if I wanted him to. Let's go for a ride and sort this out."

Driving nowhere in particular, but inside the privacy of her police cruiser, Chelle continued.

"I've done some checking on Ramon. There's a police file on him. He lived with his mother, a known prostitute. She died under questionable circumstances. The report says that his mother died from a lamp that fell on her during an earthquake. Suspicious, yes; impossible, no. There was no evidence that there was foul play or a break-in and the boy said he was the only person at home. Her death was ruled an accident. Only he wasn't home during the earthquake itself because he had been in a church with a priest who was killed when a heavy cross from the sacristy fell on him during that same earthquake. The priest's death was also ruled an accident. The young Ramon admitted he was there at the time but was so scared he ran home and hid in his room until the police came. He ended up in a foster home. Soon after, he ran away and wasn't heard from again.

"Don't you see? His mother was a prostitute and he hates prostitutes. He said it quite clearly, and he hates the people in power who use them even more. I'm telling you something strange is going on."

"You think Ramon killed the priest and his mother when he was fourteen?"

"No, not at all, at least not the priest. I saw file photos. Ramon couldn't have possibly had anything to do with the cross falling on the priest. But think about it. Ramon was a regular at the church. He was an alter boy. He was well liked by the priest and others at the church. But his mother was a known prostitute. Ramon was fourteen; he knew what his mother was. Don't you see a conflict here? And not only that. Imagine you are a young boy of fourteen and on the very same night, you witness the death of two people very important to you. Important in very different ways but key influences on your life just the same. That has to change you in a very meaningful way."

"What about Harmon? I thought he was a suspect?"

"He is. I believe he is taking narcotics, and the girls supply it. That would be motive if someone threatened to blackmail him with the knowledge."

"I don't have a hard time with that. I always felt something was strange with him."

"Me neither. We've probably been in a bit of denial ourselves, but the more I watch him, the more suspicious I am. Ramon also told me that Harmon hits the girls during sex. I just don't see any reason he would bring that up if it weren't true."

"Strange, I don't have a hard time believing that either. But does that make him a serial killer? Maybe this Ramon guy is trying to make you look the other way."

"Could be, but if Harmon is getting his drugs through them, and also abusing them, and then somebody decides to play a trump card to stop him? He knows what evidence to collect and how to collect it. So when he has enough evidence to frame somebody else for the murder, goodbye threat, and another collar to add to his arrest record."

"That might explain one girl, but that doesn't make him into a serial killer."

"Assuming he has a sadistic nature, maybe he finds out it's a thrill he can get by with. And if he's the detective in charge of the investigation, he can plant evidence wherever he wants. He's even found a way to do it retroactively."

"Boy, Chelle, that is one big pile of ifs. Do you have any idea how dangerous the waters are you're swimming in?"

"You still want to be a part of this?"

"You certainly have my curiosity. What could possibly go wrong? Yea, I'm still in."

"Funny, suddenly the only guy that isn't a suspect is the one I'm chasing. I want to go back to the Washington Arms, and I would like your objective help. Do you mind?"

"Of course not, I'm sure your boyfriend will be happy to see you again."

Willowdale State Forest:

Steven had hiked about two miles north from the open Teal Pond area inside the Ipswich Wildlife Sanctuary to the three-thousand acre Willowdale State Forest. The Teal Pond area was much too open to hide in. The forest was bigger and the trees provided cover. Steven had come here often as a boy; it wasn't far from where he had grown up.

Some of the finest memories he had were riding the trails with his granddad. Granddad would ride his favorite horse called Lucky, and Steven always rode Amber. As they rode through the forest, Granddad would dole out years' worth of accumulated wisdom.

At the time, he had thought the forest went on forever. They would camp exactly where he was camping right now. Not far was old Hood Pond, a one-hundred acre lake. When he was a kid, fishing for dinner along its banks made him feel like a pioneer.

Yesterday, two feet of snow, some new and soft and some hard and icy, had made the two-mile trudge exhausting. But now, as the wind picked up and the snow blew harder, he was glad he hiked when he did. The trees of the forest shielded him from the worst of the howling wind. The small tent he was nestled into protected him from the rest. Steven had dug down his tent into the snow. That kept the worst of the wind from trying to lift it. According to the radio, the temperature would be dropping to near zero, and with the wind-chill factored in, this storm was very dangerous.

But in the snowstorm was a silver lining. The inverted plane would be covered up by the blowing snow, and his tracks from Teal Pond would also be covered by now.

Every now and then, the top of the tent would snap from a particularly hard gust, but the light fabric seemed to be sufficiently fighting back. A small propane stove provided a little heat for the tent, but more importantly, it had warmed up his soup and water for hot chocolate. Steven was thankful for the creature comforts and, strangely enough, felt somewhat relaxed. He was safe for now, and nobody was coming to look for him here any time soon. Winter survival wasn't hard if you were prepared, and thanks to Jojo's money and Walmart, he was very well prepared. The sleeping bag he was burrowed into said "Rated for twenty below zero." It would be tested tonight.

With nothing else to do, Steven concentrated on his dilemma. He had come to some very disturbing conclusions. There was only one place his semen could have come from and that was from his wife. They didn't want more children and used contraceptives religiously. In fact, besides Lucille's birth control pills, they believed in even safer sex by using prophylactics. As nearly every man in the world did after sex, Steven would toss the used condom in the nearest garbage can. And, like nearly every man in the world, he never thought that he was discarding his most private and personal possession without regard.

He was foolish to accuse the pimp for the murder of Destinee, knowing what he knew now. If it was his semen inside the young hooker, the only way it could have gotten there was through his wife. "Eliminate the impossible, whatever remains, however improbable, must be the truth." The movie quote used by Jojo left a very bitter taste.

The Sanctuary where he had decided to land in wasn't far from their home. He had taken Jojo's advice and found someplace to disappear in. It probably wasn't what Jojo had been picturing, but for Steven, it was perfect.

Chapter 45

Detective Saltarie and Detective Marget waited until evening before visiting the Washington Arms Hotel once again. The snowstorm was in full force and they fought the wind and blinding snow until they were inside the welcoming, warm lobby. Chelle soon saw that their favorite night manager was on duty.

Chelle braced herself for another performance. "Hi, Ramon. How are you tonight?" Chelle looked down, feigning a dash of embarrassment. "I had a nice time with you last night."

"Detective, so nice to see you again. I had a wonderful time with you as well. I didn't expect you to be back so soon, especially during this storm."

"I have to be honest, I have another favor to ask, more for Detective Marget than for me though. I came along, well ... just to make sure my friend here didn't harass you in any way when he asks you some questions. We wouldn't have ventured out tonight if time wasn't such an issue."

Ramon appeared a bit flustered as he tried to conceal his white-gloved hands.

"Mr. Hayes, I understand you are a friend of Chelle's, so I'll keep this short and sweet. I am following up on the murder of a coed, and I understand the suspect stayed here. I need some information on his visits, and I need it now. I'm afraid that if I don't get it soon, Detective Saltarie could be in a bit of trouble for withholding evidence from me."

"I didn't want you to get into trouble, so I didn't mention that you helped me in the past. But now Detective Marget needs the same assistance. What if you and I just sort of browsed the computer like we did last time?"

"I thought Professor Haggerty had already been charged?"

"I see you are familiar with the case, and he has," Pat said. "But his attorney is challenging us on everything. Every fucking thing. I need copies and dates, and I need them now."

Chelle was watching Ramon's face intently, Ramon was so taken by surprise, he didn't know exactly what to say.

"I ... I don't know, I'm not supposed to share that kind of information. Our guest privacy is very important."

Chelle could also see that behind his back, he was trying to remove his gloves as nonchalantly as possible. Undoubtedly for her benefit.

"What if Ramon just looks through the database on our behalf and tells us what he finds? He is very good at picking out discrepancies." Chelle smiled warmly at Ramon to let him know she was on his side.

"I'm sorry, Chelle, that won't do. I guess I will have to get a warrant from Judge Melford, but that will make things all official."

"Ramon, isn't there some way you can help me? I don't want Detective Marget to think we're not being cooperative in his investigation. Couldn't you help him so I don't get into more trouble than I'm already in?"

Ramon looked at Chelle and couldn't resist her pleading eyes. He decided he would have to break the rules for her sake.

"I'm sure the owners would just as well not be officially involved in a murder case. I think there is a way I can get you limited records from the computer that might serve your purposes. I can give you dates and names and time of check-in for the last year. Unfortunately, I have no way of isolating Professor Haggerty's name."

"Oh my god, Ramon, could you? That's all you need isn't it, Detective?" Chelle turned and glanced at Pat.

"I'm not sure, I think I could get more with a warrant," Pat sounded dissatisfied.

"Nonsense, you can make it work. I mean, if you got it right now it would save you a lot of time, wouldn't it? We could have it right now, couldn't we?" Chelle smiled sweetly at Ramon.

"I guess I could copy a file for you. Things seem a little slow right now."

"Then it's settled. Ramon, thank you so much, you have no idea what this means to me."

Ramon decided to leave his hands gloved if he was required to work at the computer. The keyboard clicked and clacked as Ramon typed. He popped in a flash drive and soon, he was finished. He handed Chelle the drive, hoping she understood the necessity for him to wear the white gloves.

Chelle hung back while Pat pretended to be less than satisfied as he walked out of the Washington Arms with the list.

"Thank you, Ramon." Chelle shook Ramon's hand gently as Ramon cursed his gloves. Chelle had a suspicion that one way or another, she would be back, and her next visit wouldn't be so congenial.

The next morning, two days after the crash:

"He just disappeared again!" Agent Henderson sounded disgusted.

"Tell me about it. He seems to be very good at it," Chelle said.

"We tracked all the flights as best we could. We know he landed or crashed somewhere, but we have no idea where. Every airport within his fuel range was checked and double-checked."

"Then he didn't land at an airport," Chelle purposely stated the obvious.

"A plane like that can land almost anywhere it wants to. Any farmer's field would do."

"And if he crashed somewhere?"

"As bad or worse. There are thousands of square miles of uninhabited areas in this part of the country, fields that won't be visited again until spring, and acres and acres of woods and lakes. *If he crashed and if the emergency locator transmitter automatically turned on and if* he didn't turn it off, somebody might hear it and report it. My sources tell me that I shouldn't take that bet. Most the time, if you don't know to look and where to look, then even if it went off, nobody would hear it."

"What we do know is that he loaded supplies onto the airplane before he took off from Reidsville. We have him on video in a Walmart. He knew exactly what he was doing. He bought winter camping gear and food to last him weeks, and a phone. Our best hope is that he uses the phone, we already have its code and can begin tracing it as soon as it's turned on. There might even be a way of making it turn itself on if he didn't pull the battery."

"You can do that?"

"Sometimes, depending on the make."

That same day:

"I'm absolutely sure." Paul sounded sad.

Jojo was stunned into silence. "It was Steven's semen inside the girl, not just his DNA?"

"No doubt about it. I was very, very careful."

"So either Steven is lying, which I'm not buying, or Lucille is somehow complicit in the plot to frame him. And I don't buy that either."

"There are other things that are very strange."

"I don't know how this could get any stranger."

"I found some contamination in the sample that bothers me, but I need your help in researching it."

"I'm all ears Paul; let me have it."

Washington DC:

Agent Henderson had just gotten up and was headed to the shower dressed in only his boxer shorts. He sleepily measured out some coffee and water and started it brewing.

He turned the shower on and was taking off his boxers when his phone rang.

"Henderson here. What? You're kidding." He turned the shower off to better listen to the report.

Luan Mills, an FBI analyst was on the other end of the phone, "A commercial flight reported they heard an emergency locater transmission. The captain was checking his radios and tuned it to the emergency locator transmission frequency out of habit. He was flying an Embraer 190 out of Boston headed to JFK. It could be nothing at all, or it could be your guy. I'll text you the exact location of his aircraft where they heard the beacon."

"Luan, slow down. Run that past me again."

"Every plane has an ELT device on it that automatically sends out a distress signal when it registers a crash. Other pilots from time to time listen to that frequency just in case they hear something."

"So you think this is our guy?"

"It would make sense. It's not far from his home and where you thought he might be headed."

"Thanks, Luan, I'm on my way."

Two hours later, a chartered plane out of Washington had Henderson in Massachusetts. Time was of the essence. After another hour, he was flying low in a helicopter he had locally chartered, heading to the exact coordinates given by the pilot of the Embraer 190. As they listened for the emergency tone, they got nothing but static.

"Why don't we hear anything?" Agent Henderson shouted over the headset.

"Gene Sharp, the helicopter pilot said, the old style ELTs aren't the most powerful even if it is still working. It's twelve hours later; the battery could have gone dead in that time. We'll start at the coordinates and then use a circular search pattern. If the transmission is weak, we might still find it that way. If you are right, and the plane crashed four days ago, the new snow might make a visual sighting much more difficult.

Agent Henderson just nodded and stared out the window. Maybe they would get lucky. Finding this senator was becoming personal.

Chapter 46

Peabody, Massachusetts:

Ernie Westcott didn't presume that he would be able to just waltz up to his brother's house and invite himself in. He had no doubts that whatever happened in the next ten minutes, it was bound to be interesting. Ernie pulled down his worn red and blue New England Patriots hat and drove into the driveway of his brother's home in his beat-up, old pickup. Immediately, two uniformed police approached his car from either side both with their guns aimed at him. "Out of the truck now. Hands behind your head," shouted one of the approaching officers.

He slowly lifted his hands to his head and waited for what he was sure was not going to be a pleasant experience. Within seconds, the rusty, old door was opened and he found himself on the cold concrete drive, facedown on some ice and a knee pressed against his back. Within ten more seconds, he was handcuffed.

"Senator, you are under arrest." The policeman sounded excited.

"I am not my brother," Ernie shouted out, "look at my ID. I'm Ernie Westcott, Steven Westcott's brother. I'm here to see my niece and sister-in-law."

The two officers not-so-gently lifted the cuffed man. "My wallet is in my back pocket, it has my driver's license."

One of the officers carefully holstered his weapon, opened the wallet, and withdrew the state driver's license. Ernie had at least a week's worth of beard that the image on the driver's license didn't have. After a full minute of examining the ID, the officer walked up to the front door and rang the front bell.

Within seconds, Lucille was on her front porch. She stood in the doorway with her bathrobe on. "Ernie? Is that you? What are you doing here?"

"Lucille, please tell these imbeciles that I am not Steven."

"Officers, I can assure you that this man is not my husband. But you might want to arrest him just the same. I'm sure he has done something illegal within the last twenty-four hours," she added harshly, then turned and walked into the house again.

"Uncuff me," Ernie demanded.

"Not so fast. Maybe she's right. Everybody knows that the senator's brother was a no good druggy. Make yourself comfortable in my car while we check you out."

Ernie was walked across the street and placed in the backseat of their squad car. After fifteen minutes, the officers reluctantly pulled him out of the backseat and uncuffed him with a stern warning. "You are on probation; if you don't want to find yourself back in Schuylkill prison, you had better mind your business and manners."

Ernie acted indignant at the officer's comments. His old jacket had somehow torn during the scuffle, and now the pocket hung down sloppily.

"Thanks," Ernie said as he showed the police his torn pocket, then he crossed the street and started up the walkway between the snow banks toward the house.

"She said she doesn't want to see you," the officer said with his hand on his gun.

"Look, I don't want any trouble. I just want to talk to my sister-in-law and maybe see my niece. As you pointed out, I have been gone for a while."

"If we hear anything we don't like, you are going back to prison on violation of your parole."

"What violation?" Ernie protested.

"I'll think of something."

Ernie turned toward the house and saw Lucille watching him. He knocked gently, knowing she was near the door. "What do you want, Ernie?" Lucille asked as she opened the door slightly.

"Hi, Lucille, sorry for the commotion. Can I come in, just for a moment or two? I drove a long way."

"We have nothing to talk about, and I'm not giving you any money."

"I don't want money. I have a job and a truck." Ernie proudly pointed to his rusty, old pickup truck in the driveway. "Please, next to Steven, you're the only family I have."

"I'm divorcing Steven. I'm sure you heard."

"Lucille, just a moment, it's cold out here."

Ernie watched as Lucille's eyes scanned the homes up and down the street. He suspected she was more worried about her reputation then his comfort.

"OK, but just for a moment."

"You're looking good, Lucille."

"What do you want, Ernie?" Lucille demanded.

"Would a cup of coffee be too much to ask? The heater in my truck doesn't work real well."

Lucille made a sound of disgust and walked to the kitchen. She still had her hairbrush in hand as Ernie followed meekly, then asked, "Do you miss him?"

Lucille didn't answer for a while; instead, she silently poured the coffee. She handed him the hot cup. Ernie warmed his hands on it.

"Yes, of course I miss him. Tracy misses him most of all. But we'll get over it. He's a murderer. He is no longer a part of our lives, just like you."

"What if he didn't do it? Have you thought of that? Maybe someone is framing him. I just can't believe he killed someone."

"Of course I thought of it." Lucille sat down at the kitchen table across from Ernie. "I think of it all the time. But I know the evidence against him, all of it. They shared it with me for my cooperation. He did do it; that's the problem."

"He hasn't been convicted yet, so what about innocent until proven guilty?" Ernie said.

"He's on the run; he's a fugitive. Who even knows what he's been doing since? If he didn't do it, why doesn't he give himself up? The longer this goes on, the worse it gets. It's already is a media circus. Our lives are ruined. Tracy will never know what a normal life is like. The press will hound her for years over this. So how do I forgive and forget? Not going to happen, Ernie."

"I don't think he did it," Ernie stated flatly.

"One felon to another, how sweet."

"No, one brother to another. He didn't do it. You know in your heart he didn't. He couldn't."

"You can fool yourself all you want. He knew the girl; I talked to the detective who tried to arrest him. He admitted to meeting with her several times in a hotel. The murder weapon had his fingerprints on it. My god, Ernie, he was fucking the young bitch. There's proof of that too. His blood was on her, her blood was in his car, the list goes on and on, and he had motive. She was trying to blackmail him with pictures.

It's a slam-dunk. And you want to make me feel guilty for admitting the obvious. Sorry, I've been over that for months."

"The girl was Steven's daughter," Ernie said quietly, then set his half-empty coffee cup down and stared into his sister-in-law's eyes to let her know he was serious.

"What? How do you know that? That can't be true. You're lying."

"It will eventually come out. I'm not lying. I can't tell you how I know, I just do. Her DNA matched Steven's. The police don't know yet but will soon, I'm sure."

Lucille sat silently for a while and then got up and absent-mindedly started to brush her hair with the hairbrush she had carried with her into the kitchen.

"How? From who?"

"Way before he knew you, if that's the question. He didn't know he had a daughter; the mother kept it secret from him. She was a girlfriend from his army days."

"Was that why he was with her?"

"Sort of, it's a long story that's getting much longer."

"Even if it's true, that doesn't mean he didn't kill her. That would be all the more reason to. It would be a scandal for a senator to have a daughter who was a prostitute."

"My god, Lucille, this is Steven we are talking about. Do you really think he could murder his own daughter in cold blood? Do you really think he would be screwing his own daughter?"

"If he didn't do it, who did?" Lucille said.

"That is what we need to find out. Will you help me?"

Lucille gingerly placed her hairbrush back on the counter next to the coffee maker, then turned back to Ernie. "If you are telling me the truth, it doesn't change anything. I am still getting divorced. I have to preserve as much of our wealth for Tracy's sake and mine. Steven's going to jail and there is no way I am going to let him drag us into the poorhouse with him.

Ernie got up from the table and poured himself another cup of coffee with his back to Lucille. He was trying to control his anger because right now he wanted to shake some sense into his sister-in-law.

"It's time for you to leave. I'm afraid that our relationship is done, just as Steven's and mine is. Nothing will ever change that."

Ernie set his full cup of coffee down next to the coffee maker and turned toward Lucille. "I'm sorry you feel that way. Steven loved you like no other man ever could. Someday you'll see that, but it will be too late by then."

"Time to leave Ernie, I'll walk you to the door."

Ernie didn't argue as he walked down the hall with his sister-in-law.

"May I hug you goodbye then?" Ernie asked as they stepped into the doorway.

"Sure, why not."

Ernie hugged his sister-in-law. Goodbye, Lucille, and good luck."

"Good luck to you too, Ernie. I want you to know, I don't hate you, or Steven. But I have to get on with my life as best I can. I have to try and make things right with Tracy."

Ernie noticed the two officers watching him closely. He hoped that the hug between Lucille and he would alleviate some of their suspicions about his motives. Ernie hated prison and didn't need any problems from the local police; probation was a very tenuous thing.

As Ernie got back into his truck, he dropped the brim of his hat down over his eyes to avoid eye contact with the police, who were still watching the house closely from their squad car across the street. Slowly, he backed the old pickup onto the snow-covered road and left. Ernie pulled his truck over a couple of blocks away. He slipped the drive lever into park and then carefully slid the hair sample he had taken from Lucille's hairbrush into a plastic ziplock bag. It would soon be in the mail overnighted to someone named Paul at a company called Genepool Medical.

Strangely enough, it had been Detective Denton Jones who had asked him to do the impossible. Ernie had never met Jojo Jones, but he certainly had heard his brother talk about him enough. When Jojo asked if he wanted to help his brother prove his innocence, he couldn't refuse. Jojo had stressed that it was very important that he get a DNA sample from Steven's wife. It looked like Steven was being framed. Now they needed to find out who and why.

Willowdale Forest:

On the third day of the search in the helicopter, Henderson realized that they weren't going to be successful. The senator had escaped once again.

The pilot, Gene Sharp, spoke loudly through the headsets they were both wearing. "The battery on the ELT transmitter is probably dead by now. While I would be happy to have you pay me to fly around this beautiful scenery for another week, it's time to start thinking about ending this search."

Henderson looked at the pilot but didn't tell him his superiors had already come to the same conclusion. They hadn't even wanted him to spend the resources for this day. Instead, he silently looked forward as if he could will the frequency to start chattering.

Then he cupped his ears. He thought he could hear something different over the emergency frequency but wasn't sure. With a question in his eyes, he looked at Gene again. The pilot nodded back; the distinctive wavering tone could be heard. It was faint, but it could be heard.

"We'll mark this latitude and longitude and use it as base unless we pick up a more vibrant tone," he said. "The 121.5 ELT signal bounces off of any hard surface, such as buildings or canyons, so it's hard to know where it's coming from. It's a dumb signal so it doesn't know or tell us where it's transmitting. We have to circle this spot and hope we can get a louder signal."

"How far from here could it be?" Henderson asked.

"It has to be a very weak signal by now. We could be right on top of it. There is no way of telling," the pilot replied.

Henderson did the only thing he could. He scanned the sea of white snow for something that looked like an airplane.

****

The sun had come out, and it felt good on Steven's face as he looked up. But the clear skies meant bitterly cold air again tonight. Steven heard the sound of an aircraft in the distance, which was to be expected because Beverly Municipal Airport was just seven miles to the south. But this sound was different. It sounded like a helicopter.

Steven knew he couldn't stay in the serenity forever. There was a bit of reality to deal with. He had promised to give Jojo some time; it was only four days since he had taken refuge in the forest. A short time, but it seemed forever to Steven.

Steven sat in his tent and looked over his supplies. The food stock he had could last another week, maybe two if he cut his rations. He had plenty of snow to melt for water, which meant that even though he would be hungry, he could go even longer. If he thought his stay would be extended, it would be necessary to trap some of the local wildlife to supplement his food supply.

He looked at the phone off to the side. Another item he had bought at Walmart. He hadn't dared turn it on yet. In fact, as a precaution, he had even taken the batteries out of it. He had to assume it would be traced as soon as it was activated. As much as he wanted to find out if Jojo had learned anything, he knew that he should wait at least another week and a half in solitude before using the phone.

Unfortunately, the only thing Steven could do was think about the little information he did have. And over and over again it pointed to the impossible. Lucille was somehow involved in the frame up. He would wait, but at some point, he would be forced to confront his wife.

Steven heard a sound outside. He peeked out his tent and looked up; the sound of the helicopter was getting closer. It was time for him to disappear inside the small shelter once again. The white tent would blend in with the snow under the canopy of the pines and he would be invisible from the air. And because of the blowing snow, his tracks had been covered. As long as he didn't stray from his campsite, anybody trying to find him would find it next to impossible.

Washington DC:

It was late, and Detectives Saltarie and Marget were still trying to make heads or tails of the computer file Ramon had given them. Going line by line through the list was tedious.

"Need help finding a killer?" Detective Harmon gloated as he walked by Chelle's desk.

"Not yet, but I have some information for you."

Chelle stood up and walked Harmon to a quiet corner. "We have a list of people who stayed at the Washington Arms. The Manager has been extremely helpful. In fact, I ran across something that could help you."

"I don't recall that I needed any help, Detective."

"I see that Tiffany Maddenheart often stayed at the hotel."

Chelle caught Harmon's eye twitch.

"Oh … that is interesting. But not relevant to my case anymore."

"Just thought you would want to know. Maybe you should go and talk to the manager there." Chelle was hoping that if she touched a raw nerve, Harmon wouldn't be able to hide his reaction, at least not quick enough for her to miss it.

"The case is already locked up."

"Just the same, if we find anything interesting, we'll let you know. We know the time Tiffany checked in; maybe the murders are connected."

Harmon's eye twitched again ever so slightly, and his face turned red.

"I'm sure you're chasing a dead end."

Chelle turned, her heart heavy with the truth. She had positively struck a nerve. Bruce Harmon did know the hooker and Ramon was probably telling the truth about him visiting her at the hotel. Though that didn't necessarily make him a killer or even a criminal, it was highly unethical to be in charge of a murder investigation of a close acquaintance.

Was the Detective a drug addict too? Chelle didn't relish the burden she would have to carry by herself until she could know and prove the truth. She walked to the coffee machine and poured two more cups. It gave her time to think and collect herself before rejoining Pat.

"I've started listing the dates Tiffany Maddenheart stayed at the hotel," Pat said as he wrote down another date with a pencil. "I'm not seeing any sort of pattern yet or anything to tie Harmon to her visits."

"If any other names look familiar or suspicious, mark them down too."

Officer Wallace stopped by with some paperwork. "I need you to sign off here, here, and here." He handed the papers to Chelle. "Are you still trying to catch that senator, or have you finally moved on?" Wallace kidded while he waited for Chelle to sign the documents.

"Yes, we are still trying to catch Senator Westcott. But right now, we suspect there is something fishy about the Washington Arms Hotel. Too many murders seem to surround it," Chelle suggested.

Officer Wallace looked over Pat's shoulder and asked. "What are you doing?" Officer Wallace had the ability to stick his nose into everybody else's business and get away with it.

Pat was a little impatient with Wallace but answered anyway. "Trying to locate check-in dates for certain people. Then he turned and suggested, "Isn't there something you need to do, Officer?"

"No, not really. What exactly are you looking for?" He asked as he stared at the list of patrons of the hotel during the last year.

Pat answered this time without looking away from the screen. "Something connecting all the suspects that stayed in the Washington Arms. Chelle doesn't believe in coincidences and over the years, she has made a believer out of me. Something connects all these people besides the hotel itself."

"Do you have a list of names in particular you're looking for?"

"Yes, and we are writing down the date and times they pop up in the check-in list. And I would like to stay with it if you don't mind, Officer."

"I could sort the list for you."

Chelle looked at Wallace not sure she heard right. "What did you say?"

"That looks like a database I run. I could import it into my program and sort it for you. Save you two a ton of time."

"Are you sure?"

"Yea, ninety percent. Why don't you two take a break. I have an idea, but I work better alone."

"Don't screw up this list. You have no idea what Chelle had to do to get it," Pat warned as he smirked at Chelle.

Officer Wallace turned toward Chelle, about to ask exactly what that meant. Chelle scowled at him with a face that said don't even think about it. Wallace turned back toward the computer.

"Don't worry. Just let me play with it for a little while."

Chelle and Pat knew Wallace as a computer geek and, with a bit of trepidation, left for a lunch break. When they came back, they brought back a cold Pepsi for Wallace. As they walked up to him, he was just in the process of printing off a one-page data sheet. "If I give you this," he teased Chelle, "you owe me a day riding along with you."

"I can't promise that, you know that," Chelle replied as she tried to rip the sheet out of his hands unsuccessfully.

"Ah, Ah," Wallace scolded. "You and I both know you can make it happen. This is good," He teased again, dancing the paper close to her face.

"OK, OK, one day. This better be good, very good. Give it here."

Immediately, Chelle and Pat saw the same thing Wallace did.

"I took the list of names you gave me and then had the computer search for only those names or anything substantially close. Then I added in the aliases that the senator used, and wham, this comes out. What are the odds of that happening?"

Pat and Chelle were both mesmerized by the list in front of them. Of course it was so obvious now. Every one of the suspects or victims had stayed in room 327 one or more times.

"We need a search warrant for room 327," Chelle and Pat said to each other simultaneously.

Chapter 47

Willowdale State Forest:

A gent Henderson leaned forward in his seat and massaged his tired eyes with his fingers. The faint ELT transmission remained steady. They couldn't identify exactly where it was coming from, but they had successfully discovered where it wasn't coming from. That had confirmed that somebody had crashed in the wildlife area. Searching it on foot would be extremely difficult because of the recent snowstorms, but Henderson contacted the local police for help anyways.

There was a plane down there, and the sooner it was found the sooner the lone occupant would be found, possibly still trapped in the crashed aircraft. And if that were the case, he would most likely be dead from injuries or frozen from the cold. It was apparent from the winter gear the senator had purchased that he had planned landing in the remote area. What the novice pilot couldn't have planned on was a safe landing.

****

Steven knew that something was up. In the silence of the snow-covered forest, he had heard the helicopter get both closer and farther away over and over again. It was looking for someone or something and there was a good probability that he was that someone.

The sun was starting to set, and the helicopter turned south. Steven guessed that it was going to Beverly Municipal for the evening, but it was sure to be back in the morning. Steven could only guess that the emergency locator transmitter in the airplane had gone off. Unfortunately for him, he hadn't remembered about it until too late. There was no way of walking back to the aircraft to disable it without leaving tell-tale tracks in the snow.

He would be safe enough tonight. The helicopter could circle his small campsite for the next week and still not find him. The problem would be a coordinated search on the ground.

Steven had to assume a search would be initiated possibly as soon as the break of dawn. Once the plane was discovered, the hunt would be on. It seemed that the helicopter was concentrating on an area close to where he crashed the plane. The police would first locate the aircraft. And as soon as they discovered he wasn't in it, they would expand the search area. The snow was too deep to bring in dogs. That was the good news. Snowmobiles would certainly be used and they could easily out-run a man trudging through the snow, and it would be impossible to cover his tracks. Evading the searchers in the morning would take all his skills, learned so many years ago in the special forces.

Day six after the crash:

Agent Henderson's helicopter landed next to Highway 1 on the western side of Ipswich Wildlife Sanctuary. The local sheriff had done a good job of organizing his officers and volunteers for the search. The emergency locator transmitter could no longer be heard. Probably the battery had finally gone dead. Because of the search pattern they flew yesterday, they had a pretty good idea where the center of the signal had originated.

Henderson wanted to make sure they all understood the rules of the game and spoke loudly to the gathered search teams through an electronic megaphone. "Consider the fugitive armed and very danger-ous. He has already severely beaten up a man in his effort to escape, and he has threatened an officer with a gun. He has been trained by the army to be a deadly killer. If he does not comply immediately with an order, shoot to kill or it will be you.

"We have reason to suspect that there is a downed aircraft. He may be trapped inside. If you find such an aircraft, radio for assistance. Do not, I repeat, do not approach it without backup. Work your way to the east. Teal Pond separates the halves of the preserve; we want to flush the fugitive into that area. It is an open area, and I will be watching it from above, and men will be posted on the other side."

****

Steven had heard the sound of the helicopter, it was some distance to the south, but it meant the chase was on. There were only two ways to cover your tracks in the snow. Rule one was to not make them in the first place. Rule two was to make them go where you weren't. He couldn't make his small campsite disappear, so he created several diversionary tracks in the snow. Each path eventually circled around back to the campsite, precisely where he wasn't going to be.

Along the decoy trails, he had buried his tent and supplies. The way he buried them left no visible signs. Any food he had was hidden high in the pine trees along the way. He hoped that any animals, human or otherwise, wouldn't find that either.

Now the hardest part would be where to hide himself. He had two choices there too. It would either be up or down. He could tie himself into the top of one of the tall pines. Or, he could take a lesson from the burrowing animals and find a place to conceal his body under a big enough fallen tree or the rock formation he had found. It had since been covered by snow, creating a small air pocket. The trick would be getting to a hiding spot far enough from his decoy trails without leaving additional tracks in the snow.

Steven knew the odds were against him. Most likely the hunters would use infrared technology to look for his heat signature. The cold snow and his ninety-eight degree body would create an obvious contrast. A rock formation covered with snow would be his best chance to disguise his presence. If he were very careful, and with a bit of help from the wind, his tracks might be covered by the time the police arrived in the area.

He couldn't hide forever. Fatigue and hunger and cold would eventually win out. But the more time he could give Jojo to find the truth, the better. And though it wasn't much to hope for, it was all he had. A 1 percent chance was still better than zero. He figured his chances had grown to at least 10 percent since then. Having Jojo on his side was all the hope he needed for now.

Washington DC:

Armed with a warrant to search room 327, Chelle and Pat headed to the Washington Arms.

"Detective Saltarie, is there something wrong?" Ramon Ruben Hayes was clearly surprised by the serious looking duo.

"Professor Haggerty stayed in room number 327. We need to look it over. Is that a problem?" Pat spoke in a commanding voice.

"There are guests in that room. You can't barge in on them. Think about our reputation. They are entitled to their privacy."

"We really need to see that room," Chelle said, playing the good cop. "Would it be possible to move them to another? It's very important. Detective Marget does have a warrant, but I'm sure you would prefer we don't make a scene."

Ramon was clearly bewildered, eyes flashing between Chelle and Pat.

"Please give me a moment."

Ramon barked a few orders to his assistant and then turned to Chelle. "We have found another room for our guests. Please give us a minute to move them," he said, sounding annoyed.

Chelle and Pat followed the manager to room 327 and stood by as the couple was asked to pack their things and move to a different room. When the man protested, Chelle flashed her badge, and in a very firm voice, said, "Please!"

The young woman in the room left first. It hadn't taken her very long at all to pack up her few things. The much older gentleman left the room with his suitcase in hand, assuring the manager that he would never be staying at the Washington Arms again.

Chelle and Pat entered the room. Neither of them had a clue what they were looking for and stood silently absorbing their surroundings. Ramon walked with the gentleman that had just left the room. He was making quite a commotion, and Chelle felt sorry for Ramon as he tried to placate him.

The bed was unmade and the room obviously used. Dirty glasses and a wine bottle sat on the small desk. A serving tray with the leftovers of a fruit plate along with a knife and leftover cheese and crackers sat on a wheeled cart.

When they were alone, Chelle said, "there has to be something about this room. Look for hidden cameras or microphones."

Chelle walked into the small bathroom. She saw a wet towel on the floor and a wet washrag and hand towel by the sink. But otherwise, it looked quite normal. It was just like thousands and thousands of hotel rooms across the country, even down to the slow-draining sink. Chelle checked the cabinet under the sink, spotting nothing suspicious.

Harmon was inspecting the closet and under the bed.

Chelle had no luck searching behind the curtains as Harmon pulled out drawers and searched cabinets.

"Nothing," Harmon said when Chelle looked at him.

Maybe it wasn't room 327 where the clues were. Maybe it was the rooms adjacent to it. Chelle went out into the hall and listened at the doorway of each of the adjoining rooms. She heard the sound of the morning news coming from both doors.

Chelle looked up and down the hallway, something had to be special about room 327. *But what?* she thought.

Then Chelle noticed a maid finishing up one of the rooms down the hallway. With nothing to lose, she walked down the hallway to talk to her. Chelle showed her badge. The maid, obviously hesitant to become involved, looked unsuccessfully for an excuse to be anywhere but where she was.

"Hi, Janet." Chelle read the maid's nametag. "I'm Detective Saltarie," she said as she slipped her badge over her hip belt. "Could I ask you a few questions?"

"I don't know anything that goes on here, I just clean the rooms," the maid quickly tried to excuse herself from the situation.

"I understand," Chelle replied with a warm smile. "It's just that there is something about room 327 that I can't put my finger on. It's special, but I can't understand why. Does that make any sense to you?"

"No, I clean it every day. It is just like all the rest of the rooms on this floor and all the floors above and below it. This floor or any rooms on it haven't been updated for seven years. I know because I've worked this floor for the last ten."

That wasn't what Chelle was hoping for. She pressed a bit further. "Nothing different about it? Nothing at all you can think of?"

"It has bad drains, they are always plugged. Mr. Hayes checks them often."

"Anything else?"

The maid looked down the hallway behind her and then moved closer to Chelle. "The night manager doesn't think I know, but I do. The managers try to reserve this room for the hookers. It's close to the elevator. They say they don't want them walking all over the hotel."

"I see. Anything else?" That didn't explain why Senator Westcott and the professor ended up in the same room. They booked the room themselves and they certainly weren't hookers. No there was something missing."

Then Janet whispered, "Mr. Hayes uses this room to see if I am doing my job properly. He checks it often, sometimes even before I have had time to clean it. So I always clean it extra careful. Please don't tell him I know."

"I won't tell him a thing, trust me. You have been very helpful, Janet." Chelle turned to walk away and then had another thought. "Janet, do you remember ever seeing this man?" Chelle pulled a picture out of her jacket pocket.

Talking to somebody else at the hotel about Harmon seemed like a good idea. Maybe Ramon was using Harmon to distract her just like Pat had suggested. Chelle had just agreed to do the maid a favor, and she hoped the maid would return it.

Janet looked at the picture and immediately recognized the face. "Yes, he has been here often. I don't think he is a nice man."

"Why do you say that?"

"People don't think I can hear out in the hall, or in the next room, but I can. I don't want to, but the hallway is quiet, and I have to do my job."

"Janet, I'm not accusing you of anything. Of course you can't help but hear. But why do you think this man isn't a nice man?"

"The girls holler at him sometimes and tell him to stop. I can hear him hitting them." Janet's face turned red. "I know it's their job, and they must know he will hit them, but it makes me angry."

"Why would they know he would hit them?"

"It's always with the same three girls."

Chelle produced two more pictures.

"Yes, those are two of the girls. I haven't seen them lately though."

Chelle tried to act as if the information wasn't particularly important. "Thank you, Janet, I appreciate your help."

Walking back into room 327, Chelle immediately got a shrug from Pat as he closed the bureau drawer next to the bed. "If there is something special about this room, I can't find it. In fact, everything seems perfectly normal right down to the Bible next to the bed."

Chelle sat down on the edge of the unmade bed and looked around, still unsure of what she was looking for. There was a reason Ramon had put these people all in the same room. It was just too much of a coincidence.

"Pat?" she asked. "If this was a crime scene, what would we be doing?"

He laughed. "We wouldn't be sitting on the edge of the bed."

"Why not?"

"Preserve evidence 101: don't contaminate the crime scene."

"What evidence?" Chelle had an inkling of an idea, but it hadn't solidified in her mind yet.

"What evidence?" Pat looked around the room "OK, let's play that game. We have drinking glasses and a wine bottle. They most certainly have fingerprints on them and possibly DNA."

"OK. What else?"

"A knife, could be a weapon, and it was used, so it also would have fingerprints and DNA." Pat stood and looked around the room some more. "The garbage, I would carefully collect the garbage into a sterile bag."

"Good." Chelle stood up and went to her purse. She pulled out a pair of rubber gloves, put them on, and then went through the garbage. Disgustingly, she lifted a used condom out, and then dropped it back. "Undoubtedly DNA evidence." She went into the bathroom and searched that garbage as well and pulled out a used tampon.

"Blood sample and more DNA," Pat said.

"And," Chelle lifted a few used tissues out of the bathroom trash basket, "somebody blew their nose—more DNA. The place is littered with evidence."

Back out in the main room, Chelle lifted the knife off the serving tray and examined it. The wooden handle and the overall size of the blade looked very familiar to her. Unusual for cutting cheese or fruit, but in a fine hotel, it added a bit of class.

"Does this knife look familiar to you?"

Pat looked at it for a while. "Oh my god. Yea, it looks identical to the knife that killed the coed."

Chelle searched her memory. Was it also like the one that killed Destinee? Right now she couldn't be sure. Maybe that knife came from this very room, the same room Destinee and the senator stayed in.

Chelle slipped the knife that had just changed from hypothetical evidence to real evidence into a clear plastic bag and sealed it. "Don't let on to the manager what we are thinking. If this knife checks out, we need to talk to the boss and then the judge into another warrant."

"For what?" Pat asked. "I see where you are going, but we don't even have a smoking gun. The knife, even if identical, proves nothing. So the professor stole a knife from the hotel, big deal."

"What if he didn't steal it? What if someone else killed the girl using the same knife the senator used to cut appetizers with? Someone who was very careful to make sure that the only fingerprints and DNA on it were the senator's."

"You mean the professor?"

"What?"

"You said the senator. You meant the professor, right?"

"Yes of course." Chelle realized her mind had been on Senator Westcott the whole time.

She looked around some more. If she found the knife, maybe something else was waiting to be discovered. Chelle thought out loud, "If you wanted to collect DNA to frame somebody, how would you do it?"

They both strolled around the room, looking and hoping something would expose itself as the smoking gun. Chelle rechecked the bathroom and looked at the shower. It had been used. Maybe there was a hair sample left behind? She bent down and found nothing. Then she examined the complimentary comb on the sink and found hair on it— success if you wanted DNA. *What else?* she pondered.

The sink still hadn't drained properly, *Would toothpaste after brushing contain DNA? What if the sink stopper caught some hairs?* Chelle pulled the metal stopper out to examine it. It lifted easily out of the drain and a small screen came with it.

The screen was fitted at the bottom of the stopper. It wouldn't affect the use of the stopper or the drain itself unless it became plugged with debris, such as hair.

"I think I have the smoking gun," she said as Pat rushed into the small room. "This isn't part of a drain, she said, showing him the small screen. "The maid said Ramon comes into the room often to clear the drains. And she said she makes sure to keep this room extra clean because Ramon checks it often."

"Son of a bitch. I'm sorry for ever doubting you."

"I think somebody is using this room to collect DNA and then framing people with it."

"Who? The night manager?"

Chelle wasn't so sure. What if a cop wanted to make a name for himself? What if a cop, a detective named Bruce Harmon, wanted to frame somebody for the murder of a hooker? What if he collected DNA from the hooker's previous guests when he visited them for his own pleasure?

"Maybe. It could be anyone who works here, even a steady patron of the hookers. Could be more than one person. But this room is the key. The maid said the managers like to send the hookers to this particular room. I think we have a serial killer on our hands and innocents have been going to jail for his or her crimes."

"But how can we possibly turn this into an arrest? And who? On what charge? Failure to keep a hotel room free of DNA? Unfortunately, all we have is our suspicions. There is nothing incriminating."

Chelle took a picture of the drain and screen apparatus, then carefully placed it back. If her hunch was right, she didn't want to tip off the guilty party. Then they closed the door to room 327 and walked back down to the lobby where the manager was waiting for them.

"Thank you again for your help, Ramon." Chelle was polite but not near as friendly.

Chapter 48

Y ou have got to be kidding, Detective." Captain Walker laid back in his reclining office chair. "I can't believe your balls! Marget, you tell me, am I missing something here? Could you be the voice of reason? I apparently have completely lost my mind."

Pat, who was standing right next to Chelle started to open his mouth when their captain continued, "You want me to support another warrant to search a citizen's apartment because you found a knife at his place of employment that was like a knife that was used in a murder. A knife that even by your own admission isn't all that special or unique. Not because you have any evidence he committed the murder but just because he works at the same place you found the knife.

The captain started opening his desk drawers and slamming them shut again as he looked for some antacids he knew he had somewhere.

Then he said, "You know, I'll bet between maids and repairmen and check-in clerks, there are over twenty people who work at the hotel on any given day, maybe twice that considering it's open twenty-four hours every day of the week. But wait, you have a suspicious looking drain stopper. Even if that was evidence of wrongdoing, which it ain't, you have the same problem. Anybody in the hotel could have planted it there. Why pick on the night manager? What is the basis? Are you planning on searching everybody's home who works at the hotel?"

Eventually, the captain found his antacids and shook a few into his big hand and slung them into his mouth.

"No, sir, I am basing it on a conversation I had with the manager." As soon as she said it, she knew it was a mistake.

"A conversation? Just what kind of conversation?"

Chelle started to twitch. The captain was a good detective too and sat forward, resting his weight on his thick arms. Chelle could tell he was already suspicious of the explanation.

"One night a few days ago, I met with the manager."

"One night? Oh ... jeesh. You went out on a date with this guy?" Captain Walker pounded both of his palms on his desk at the same time.

"No, sir, of course not. I mean, not really. We ... just had a couple of drinks one night." Chelle knew her goose was already cooked.

"A couple of drinks? Now why on earth did you do that?" The captain was clearly pissed.

"We both thought he knew more and that he would be more open to share in a social setting."

Captain Walker gave Pat a glance.

"Yes, sir, we needed some information. That was how we got the list that showed the room numbers," Pat volunteered, but we didn't think he was a suspect at that time.

Captain Walker stood, his stodgy frame solidly planted behind his desk.

"Can either of you say, *entrapment?* Not only do you not get a warrant, I am ordering both of you to stay away from this guy. And Marget, don't make me regret moving you up to detective."

"Yes, sir!"

"And, Detective Saltarie, and I use that term very loosely, if you want to make it to the end of the new year as a detective, I suggest you ... you ... well, just stay out of my hair for a few months. Take a vacation. Go someplace warm. Forget about this serial killer notion. Christ, Chelle, we already caught the killers in the cases you're talking about, that is, except the senator." The captain glared at Chelle one more time.

"Yes, sir." Chelle knew she had hit a brick wall.

"Now both of you get out of here, jeesh!"

Outside in the hallway, well out of the captain's earshot, Chelle said to Pat, "You know that there are people we charged with murder that probably didn't do it."

"No, I don't know that. In fact, my job and my family and the evidence say otherwise."

"When the professor goes to court, I will tell his defense attorneys about what I know," Chelle said.

"And if you screw it up for the prosecuting attorney, who just happens to be on our side, you will be out of a job."

"I thought our job was justice and arresting the bad guys, not the most convenient person."

Chelle left the station in a huff, she didn't know what she would or could do. Even just thinking about mentioning that Detective Harmon should also be considered a suspect would get her kicked off the force.

The professor was going to be convicted of a murder she didn't believe he did. A United States senator was running for his life, and right now she would give decent odds that he didn't kill anyone either. Too many things didn't make sense. And that was the crux of her problem. Things just weren't making sense. It was something she needed to work out. This was about right and wrong, not her career any longer. But how could she flush out a bad cop?

Willowdale State Forest:

The search of the Ipswich Wildlife Sanctuary two miles south of Willowdale Forest had taken all day. The inverted plane had finally been found. Agent Henderson had rushed to the tail section and dug out the snow around it. The numbers and letters were upside down, but they were quite clear: 182MD. There was no doubt about it now. The senator had survived the crash, removed his gear, and disappeared once again.

Agent Henderson gave the sheriff a pat on the back. "Good job, Sherriff. We have the plane and know where he landed and pretty much when. His home has been watched so he didn't go there. He can't be too far away."

"Because of the winter camping gear you said he had, he's most likely in the state forest two miles north. That would be three thousand acres to get lost in. But even if he heard all the commotion down here and suspected we were on to him, he still couldn't just walk out the forest, there's just no place to go on foot. We would have seen him. Trust me, he's still in there somewhere. Tomorrow, we can develop another search. I know the area well."

"Unfortunately, so does the senator. He's from these parts too."

"You don't have to remind me of that; I voted for him."

Henderson got back into the helicopter for the short ride back to the Beverly Airport. His hopes for tomorrow were not high. *That son-of-a-bitch senator had more fricking lives than a cat.* Now he knew how Detective Saltarie felt.

Agent Henderson called the detective out of professional courtesy and a new respect. "Hi, Chelle. Just thought you would like an update."

"Evening, David. How's it going up north?"

"Found the plane. He landed it and flipped it, but we didn't find him or any blood trail. We think he's hiding in the Willowdale State Forest just north of here. Tomorrow, we are going in shock-and-awe style. Anything new on your end?"

"Nothing, but thanks for keeping me in the loop."

"No problem. I'll keep you posted. We are going to get that SOB this time."

Washington DC:

Chelle decided to make a call that might cost her her job. She walked through the door of her apartment, tossed her keys on the kitchen counter, unbuckled her holster, and put her gun next to the keys. She picked up her phone and called the number she had taken off a police report she had just recently read.

"Detective Jones?" Chelle hesitatingly asked.

"This is, and who is this?"

"This is Detective Chelle Saltarie of the DC police. I have some information for you."

"Information for me? Why do you think I want or need information from you?"

"It's about your friend, Senator Westcott."

"What makes you think he is my friend? He stole my money, held a gun on me, and handcuffed me to the floor of my car."

"And he flew miles and miles out of his way in a very bad snowstorm just to see you. You saved his life in Kuwait and he yours. He came to you for help, and I want to help you help him."

"You sound pretty sure of yourself."

Chelle took a bottle of water out of the fridge and then leaned up against the kitchen counter.

"Listen, I'm not sure of anything lately, but like I said, I have information for you. And I have a request. I need help tracking down the real killer of Destinee Sanford."

"Now you have my attention, Detective. What information?"

"As far as we know, the senator is alive and well. We found the airplane he was using upside down in a wildlife sanctuary near his home in Peabody. He wasn't in it and there was no blood. There was an extensive search for him that came up empty. The FBI agent in charge thinks he's hiding in a forest north of there, and they are mounting a massive search of that area tomorrow morning."

"I'm sorry, but I can't help you. I don't know where he is."

Chelle could tell the detective in Reidsville, North Carolina, wasn't impressed so far.

"There's more. Washington DC has had a series of murders and all of the prosecutions were proven by the extensive use of DNA evidence. Just like the evidence we have on the senator. I have uncovered an unlikely set of coincidences. If we can connect the dots, we could prove your friend innocent."

"Now you really have my attention, Detective."

"The manager of the Washington Arms Hotel, where the senator rendezvoused with Destinee, is the same hotel manager who worked at another hotel where another hooker was murdered. Do you remember the trial of Deon Michalski, the Polish Locomotive?"

"Of course, who doesn't?"

"Michalski was also largely convicted through the use of DNA evidence. Not only that, several people murdered in the DC area and the people prosecuted for their murders stayed in room 327 of the Washington Arms. That is the same room Senator Westcott and Destinee Sanford used several times. I think the manager uses that room to spy on the occupants and collect their DNA so he can frame them."

"That's great, but why are you telling me? Go arrest the guy."

"That's the problem. I have been ordered to *not* pursue this guy. I can't get a search warrant for his home or office. Besides his work history, I have nothing but the fact that many of the murderers stayed in the exact same room at one time or another."

"Why can't you go after the guy?"

"I sort of compromised the investigation by personal contact."

"You mean a good lawyer could get him off?"

"I'm afraid a not so good lawyer could get him off, at least until I have better evidence, which I can't get. I sort of, may have used entrapment to get the information in the first place."

"Detective, I feel your pain, but I'm in North Carolina. What am I supposed to do about it?"

"I don't know, but I have nobody else to talk to about this. If I go near the hotel, I will lose my job."

"OK, I get the picture. You're compromised, and if I want to help my friend, I have to find a way to help you."

"I obviously am not suggesting you do anything at all. I am just telling you what I can't do."

"Detective Saltarie, let me share some information with you. I just found out that the girl Steven is accused of murdering was in fact his daughter. DNA test proved it. Her real name was Destinee Anderson, and her mother was—"

"Shatoya Anderson," Chelle interrupted.

"Yes, so you know that she was Steven's girlfriend back when he was in special forces training. If you talk to the owner of Genepool Medical, Paul Willer, he will confirm it. Tell him I was the one who spilled the beans. The point being, it was Steven's idea to check her DNA against his. So that begs the question. Why would he kill somebody that he suspected might be his daughter? And why would he even want to know if she was his daughter if he was intending on killing her?"

"His Daughter?" Chelle repeated letting the significance settle in her mind. "I knew Shatoya Anderson as Jasmine Sanford, mother of Destinee Sanford. She had a Caucasian daughter. The timing would have been about right."

"I can't tell you exactly why, but he had a hunch about the girl and checked it out. He had it confirmed only days before the girl was murdered. He told me that he had wanted to tell her, and that was why he found her and picked her up the day she died. But something happened, and he never had time to tell her he was her father."

Chelle recalled the letter she had read over and over again. "In his notes, the senator explained that the girl thought she was being watched by her pimp and so she encouraged him to leave her on the curb where he had found her. Their supposed fight was just an act to sidetrack her pimp. But he never said anything about her being his daughter in his notes."

"The notes you are referring to I assume were the ones meant for his attorney's eyes only?"

"They are," Chelle admitted. "But because of the special nature of this case, his attorney was forced by a special magistrate to share them with us."

"Steven told me that he wanted his wife to hear it from him and nobody else. At the time he wrote the letter, he didn't know he would be running for his life before he could tell her."

There was a long silence as Chelle added up the new information. "That would mean the photos were not made up. They came from the girl's mother who was a former lover."

"I was in training with Steven when the photos were taken. I didn't see the pictures, but it makes sense. The people that ran the whorehouse were setting all us soldiers up. Destinee's mother must have ran off with the pictures and changed her name. And as far as Steven could tell, for whatever reason, she never used them to blackmail anybody."

"And that was how her daughter ended up with them," Chelle finished the thought. "What do you know about the scrapbook?"

"It was Destinee's."

"I have already confirmed that. The girl's DNA was all over it. But if she didn't know Steven was her father, why did she make it in the first place?"

"As far as Steven could tell, the girl had a fascination with him. She actually wanted to be lovers, which he claims he refused."

"That's what he said in his letter to his attorney. This still isn't adding up to me and wouldn't to a jury either. What was his semen doing inside the girl and how did her blood end up in his car?"

"I don't have those answers either, at least not yet. But there is one thing different between you and me."

"What's that?" Chelle asked.

"I believe him."

"I'm becoming a believer, but I have a bad feeling about this. I hope we can find the senator before something really worse happens. If by chance you are in DC and want to look into this Ramon guy, I do have his address."

"Detective, I have to go, but trust me on this; Steven didn't do it. I'll be in contact if I find out anything I think you need to know. Oh, and detective, maybe you should text me that address. Just in case I find myself in DC."

"I'll send it right out. And Detective Jones, let's stay in touch."

Chapter 49

Jojo was alone in his police cruiser when his phone rang. "Hi, Paul."

"I did the test."

"Let's cut to the chase. What did you find out?" Jojo asked.

"I'm afraid it's like I suspected. It was Lucille's DNA that contaminated the sample the police gave us on Destinee."

"Does that mean what I think it does?"

"Christ almighty, I can't believe it myself. The sample came from Lucille, it's the only explanation."

"You mean Lucille is somehow involved in setting Steven up?"

"Her DNA is present. It doesn't take much speculation on how it got there."

"But why?"

"Look, I have to report this. This is critical information in a murder case. I'm going to run the test again, officially this time. But I already know it won't change."

Ernie was beyond numb. The unthinkable paralyzed him for a long moment. "Yea, I get it. Fuck, how could Lucille do this to him?"

Without saying goodbye, Paul hung up. Jojo pulled his squad car over and parked. His hands were shaking. He couldn't imagine what Steven would feel when he found out it was his wife that was framing him.

****

Jojo could tell that the instant he walked into the house, his wife knew something was wrong. He took off his heavy winter coat and hung it over a kitchen chair. Tamara was making something in the oven for supper that smelled pretty good, but she stopped working and asked, "My God, hon, what is it?"

Tamara walked up to Jojo and gave her big man a hug. Jojo felt like he needed a hug right then. Jojo and Tamara had been together ever since Jojo's initial training for the special forces. Cowboy was his best man at their wedding so long ago.

"Do you want to tell me about it? Can you tell me about it?"

Tamara understood the demands of an officer not to share certain details of their lives. Other lives could depend on it, or a court case could be lost because of loose lips.

Jojo rubbed the soft, dark skin of Tamar's bare arms. Jojo never understood how his wife's beautiful face had stayed looking so young. In fact, to him, she still looked like the gorgeous piece of brown sugar, as he used to call her, that he had married over twenty years ago. Now, he didn't want to bring tears to her gentle eyes. He didn't know how to tell her what her friend, and his, had done to Cowboy.

"Sugar, I have something to tell you. And it ain't good."

Jojo dropped their embrace and laid his big arms on the back of the chair his coat now hung on and filled in his wife on the latest news.

"I know, it doesn't sound possible."

Tamara was sitting down now. She couldn't stand after she heard that Lucille was implicated in the death of a girl and framing her husband for it.

"Denton, what is happening? I never believed Steven was guilty, but I can't believe Lucille is either."

"Listen, sugar, I got a few calls to make, OK?"

"Yea sure, babes, supper can wait a bit."

Jojo retreated to his office. It was more of a closet with a desk and file drawers crammed in it, but it worked just fine for him.

"Ernie, I just found out something I think you need to know."

Jojo didn't tell Ernie how he knew, just that he did know Steven was in immediate danger of being found. He also confirmed to Ernie what he had learned from Paul at Genepool. Somehow, Steven had to be told.

What he didn't tell Ernie was that the detective who had tried to arrest Steven was suspicious that a serial killer was on the loose in DC. Catching the serial killer would be critical to proving Steven wasn't a murderer. What Jojo couldn't understand was if the detective from DC was right, somehow, Lucille had become involved with a serial killer.

It was a rare evening in the Jones' household in that Tamara and he were quite alone for another hour or so. The kids were all busy at jobs or school functions. Jojo ate dinner in silence thinking of his next move. Tamara also ate in silence; the world she knew wasn't making any sense.

When Jojo was done with his meal, he pushed his chair away from the kitchen table. He didn't know exactly what he was going to do, all he knew right now was he couldn't do it from here. Jojo softly said, "Tamara, I gotta go to DC, Cowboy needs me."

Tamara didn't ask any questions or even try to persuade her husband to not get involved. If Cowboy needed his help, there wasn't a power on earth that would stop him, including her.

Peabody, Massachusetts, later that same night:

"Steeeve, Steeeve ... I know your special forces ass is out there." Ernie Westcott shouted out to the trees. After ten minutes of listening for an answer, he started up the snowmobile and headed to Hood Point. That's where their favorite spot was to camp and fish as kids. It was his best guess as to where his brother might be.

It was well past midnight, and it didn't appear as though anybody followed him. He guessed that he had successfully gotten by the police guarding the perimeter of the forest.

Well inside the forest, he drove slowly and carefully over the virgin snow without turning on the lights of his machine. Lucky for him, the moon was out and its light reflected off the snow, making visibility surprisingly good once his eyes adjusted to the darkness.

"Steeeve. Steeeve!" he called again. "Answer me you son of a bitch. We gotta get you out of here."

"Sorry, Ernie, I had to make sure you weren't followed." Steven came from nowhere.

"Jesus Christ! Don't scare me like that."

Ernie turned off the engine on the snowmobile, rushed over to his brother, and gave him a hug.

"What are you doing here? And how the hell did you know where I would be?"

"Jojo told me. He's wired in somehow to what's going on and knew you were here. I took a few guesses at exactly where you would be camped. Gramps always like this area."

"You've been talking to Jojo?"

"Yea man. He took a big chance calling me. You had us plenty worried. It's good to see you, bro. You look like crap, by the way."

"At least I have an excuse. I've been in the woods for a week."

"Yea, well fuck you too, bro. We just found out about six hours ago that you somehow survived a plane crash. Our information tells us that they have every snowmobiler in the county lined up to flush you out of here tomorrow."

Steven sat down on what was left of a fallen tree, and Ernie sat down on the edge of the seat of the snowmobile.

"Yea ... I figured. I'll be OK. They'll never find me as long as they don't bring dogs, and I think the snow is too deep for the dogs."

Ernie lit up a cigarette and took a welcomed drag. As he exhaled, the smoke combined with the fog of his breath in the cold air.

"You can't stay here. What don't you fucking understand? The forest is surrounded. Get on and let's get out of here."

"And since when have you had a snowmobile?"

"Since about an hour and a half ago. And I have to get it back before it's missed."

"You stole it?"

"Just borrowed it. I'm taking it back, so let's go."

"If it's surrounded, how are we going to get out on this noisy machine?"

"The same way I got in. Remember the old wood culvert? Hardly anybody knows about it and it isn't completely snow-blocked or guarded. The snow and trees suck up the sound pretty well."

Steven looked up at the stars for a while and then back at Ernie. "You are taking one hell of a chance coming here."

"No shit, Sherlock. Hell, if I'm caught out here with you, I'm back in the slammer by noon."

Ernie enjoyed another deep inhale and blew the smoke and his breath into the night air.

"Just go back, I don't want you mixed up in this, Ernie. Start a new life, stay straight, and find a girl." Steven stood up. "Nice seeing you, bro. Thanks for the effort. Now get out of here while you still can."

"Get on the fucking snowmobile. I'm not going without you. We gotta go, it might take us the rest of the night to sneak out of here."

"I told you I'd be all right. I have a plan, and when they don't find me, they'll move on."

Ernie took his last puff then tossed the cigarette into the snow, and it hissed itself out. He looked up at his older brother.

"Steve, you got to listen to me. Jojo told me everything. The girl was your daughter. I get it. You didn't kill anybody. You're innocent. But we have got to get out of here."

Steven sat back down on the old, snow-covered log, sadly looking at his brother.

"Ernie, somebody killed my daughter. I got to know her a little bit, and then I started to sense there was something special about her. I realized it was Rebecca. She looked a lot like my Rebecca. She laughed like her mother but her smile was all Rebecca. And she was hooked on drugs like Rebecca. She ... she wanted a family in the worst way, but she didn't live long enough to find out she had one. I was trying to get her to go to a drug rehabilitation center. She wanted to go; she was going to go. Ernie, believe me, I didn't kill her, but I have to find out who did."

"We know you didn't. And we think we know who did, or at least who was responsible. That's why you have to come with me right now."

Steven stood up.

"Who? Tell me. Who?" Steven looked ready to punch somebody.

"If I tell you who, will you get on the damn machine so we can get out of here?"

"Just tell me."

"Oh fuck ..." Ernie hesitated. "Don't kill me. I'm just the messenger. Remember that."

"Will you tell me already?"

"Lucille."

"What? Impossible ... she couldn't. She wouldn't."

"Paul at Genepool confirmed it was your semen inside of Destinee when she died."

"Ernie, I'm telling you that's impossible."

"Here is where it gets interesting and that's an understatement. Paul also found some contamination of the sample. So Jojo had me get a sample of Lucille's hair; Paul tested it against the third DNA he found in the semen. It matched. It looks like Lucille was involved somehow. That's how the killer got your semen. It was from when you and Lucille made love. Probably from a discarded rubber."

Steven fell back against the nearest tree. "Lucille, no, no ... can't be."

"Please, Steve, we gotta go now. We can sort this out later." Ernie grabbed his brother by the arm and nearly had to drag him to the machine. We'll figure this out, I promise, but we have to get out of here before daylight, or we're both screwed."

Steven sat on the snowmobile. "Hair sample? You saw Lucille?"

Ernie pulled the throttle back and the machine took off through the powdery snow.

****

It was just before dawn when Steven and Ernie returned the snowmobile to where Ernie had borrowed it. The owner probably wouldn't be any the wiser, except he would probably wonder where his full tank of gas had gone.

Ernie had two rooms rented in the local area. One the police knew about, another he hoped they didn't. Ernie dropped Steven off at one and then he went to the other.

Later that morning, Ernie went to a fast food drive through and ordered a coffee, juice, and double breakfast. Once he was certain he wasn't being followed, he drove down the road to the gravel pit where he had been hired. Because of the recent snowstorms, there wasn't any work today, but the police wouldn't know that.

Steven was waiting in a small wooded area when Ernie stopped the truck. The old door creaked a bit as he opened it and got in. It took two tries for Steven to properly close the rusted door.

"Did you get some sleep?" Ernie asked.

"Not much. I couldn't stop thinking about Lucille being involved in this. It just can't be. Thanks for the coffee and grub." Steven warmed his hands on the coffee cup and hungrily ate down the food.

"No problem."

Between mouthfuls, Steven said, "I think my bones are finally starting to unthaw from my little camping trip." Then added, "Listen Ernie, you need to talk to Lucille; you can go back and ask her a few questions. Tell her about her DNA contaminating my semen. Ask her how that could possibly happen. I ... I still can't believe she would be in on murdering someone and framing me for it. It's just not possible. I want to give her a chance to explain."

"I can try," he said, uncomfortable with the idea. "But she didn't want me coming back, and I don't really think she is going to admit to anything."

"Probably not, but if she was in on it, maybe it's time for her to squirm a little bit. We can watch and see who she calls, see who comes to the house, that type of thing."

"I guess it won't hurt to try."

Later that morning:

Lucille Westcott pulled back into her driveway. She waved at the policemen sitting out front in their patrol car. She hated the attention, and was sure her neighbors were quite sick of it also. However, it wasn't the patrolmen's fault either.

She carried in a few grocery bags and walked into the kitchen. As she walked back outside toward the car for the last bag of groceries, an old pickup pulled into the driveway again.

Lucille stood alone on the driveway as the pickup came to a stop in back of her car. The old sports cap was pulled down nearly over Ernie's eyes just like the other day. Lucille watched in disbelief as Ernie got out of his vehicle. Ernie slid out the old truck and walked toward a clearly frustrated Lucille. She saw he had on the same ripped up jacket as the other day.

"I told you not to come back here."

Ernie grabbed the bag of groceries out the car for Lucille.

"Let me help; I have news," he spoke quietly.

Lucille looked at the officers who were clearly interested if she needed or wanted help in getting rid of the intruder.

"This had better be good. And no coffee this time. Tell me what you want to say and then leave." Lucille turned around, not giving her brother-in-law the courtesy of a smile and led the way as Ernie carried the heavy bag into the house.

Once in the entryway, Ernie walked ahead of his sister-in-law down the hallway to the kitchen area. The brim of his hat shadowed his eyes from the morning sun streaming in the two-story foyer window. In a raspy voice, he said, "Let's sit. I have a question for you."

"Ernie! I don't have time, and I want you out the house now."

Ernie set the groceries down on the counter then said, "Steven needs to know how his semen, which came from his bedroom, your bedroom, got inside of the murdered girl. The girl we now know was his daughter."

"Ernie, you're crazy, and I want you out of here right now. And if you know where Steven is, you will have a lot of explaining to do with the police when I tell them what you just told me. I remind you, they're just outside the door, so please leave immediately or I will call them this instant. I don't have to listen to your accusations."

"Maybe you should because your DNA was found in that same sample too," he continued. "There is only one explanation for that. You took the used condom and used its contents to frame Steven."

"You're completely nuts, Ernie. I'm calling the police right now."

Ernie turned and locked eyes with Lucille, then he took off the sports hat.

Lucille fell against the wall. "Steven!" Steven had trimmed his mustache and beard to look an awful lot like his brother, but on closer look, it was easy for Lucille to see through the disguise.

"It is me, and I am not speculating. Not only do I know I didn't do it, I have proof that you were involved. Now, do you still want to get the police? Because I can prove that the semen sample found inside the girl came from here, our bedroom."

"Steven, no, you're wrong. I didn't. I couldn't have."

"Why couldn't you have?"

"I just couldn't; you know that."

"You mean like I couldn't and how you believed me?"

Steven grabbed his wife's arm and held it tight, tight enough to hurt. Then he pointed up the stairs. "Tell me, Lucille, how did my semen get from the bathroom garbage into my daughter. How Lucille?" he shouted. "Because it did. And how did the girl have my DNA, like my hair in her fingernails and other places that were impossible?"

Lucille fell to the floor sobbing. "I didn't, I swear, I didn't do it."

"Somebody did. Who else could possibly be up in our bedroom and go through our trash, collecting my DNA?"

Lucille knew her eyes were giving her away as they began tearing up.

Christ, Lucille, have you been banging someone while I was in Washington?"

"Good lord, I can see it in your eyes."

Lucille sat on the floor, still in shock over Steven's sudden appearance.

"Lucille, you might as well tell me; you can't hide it any longer. Tell me damn it!"

The tears started to drop from her eyes. She felt weak and drained.

"I didn't mean to. It just happened. You were always gone. I was by myself all the time."

"I was alone just as often. Who is he? Who, Lucille, who?"

"Sam."

"Who?"

"Sam Kreiser."

"You and Sam Kreiser? He's a crook! He was fired for taking other people's money. As far as I can tell, the only reason he didn't go to jail was because his company didn't want the bad press and covered for him."

"He was nice to me." Lucille's cheeks were wet. "When he started to help the foundation, we had lunch a few times."

"You shared more than a lunch together."

"He was charming. He made me laugh and feel alive inside again."

"Did he ever come over right after I left?"

"Yes, yes, I'm so sorry. I didn't mean it to happen that way. It just did."

"Does Tracy know?"

"No, no of course not. She was always gone with friends or at school."

"So more than once?"

Lucille looked away. "Yes."

Steven paced the kitchen. He sat down at the table and dropped his head into both his hands. "It doesn't make sense, why would Sam want to frame me?"

"Steven, I swear I didn't know." Lucille lifted herself up slowly and hugged the wall, sheepishly walking toward her husband.

"But why? Why?"

"He wanted me to divorce you. He wanted to marry me."

"But why kill Destinee to frame me?"

"Maybe he thought that if you were in prison, I would divorce you and then we would get married."

"Well his plan is working, you are divorcing me."

"I never stopped loving you, but things were already strained be-tween us. And then when you murdered that girl and ran from the police, I knew it was over for us. I just wanted to move on, for Tracy and I to move on. But I wouldn't, I never wanted to marry him. You have to believe me. I told him I didn't want to see him anymore; it's over between us."

"Lucille, believe me, right now I couldn't care less," Steven looked up and gave his wife a glare that would have melted an iceberg. Then he demanded, "Where is he? Because right now, the only thing I care about is clearing my name."

"He's in Washington this week."

"Where is his office?"

"Corner of Fifth and Indiana, not far from the Capital Grille."

"Lucille, if you care at all about Tracy and I, you will pretend you had another visit from Ernie and let me sort this out."

"Are you going to kill Sam?"

"Of course not. I'm not jumping out of the frying pan and into the fire. But if Sam did this, I need him to confess. For your sake, you had better hope he mans up because the evidence shows it was either you or him. I can promise you this, one of you is going to jail for the murder of my daughter. So you had better give me time to get Sam to confess. Now, I need you to walk me to the door so the police know everything is OK."

****

At the doorway, Lucille opened the door for him and waved at the police with a forced smile. Steven lifted the collar of the torn jacket against his neck and pulled down the visor of the sports cap shielding his eyes. He stepped out into the cold sunshine of the winter day. He had hoped for a different explanation, knowing there couldn't be any. The finality of knowing the truth made him feel nauseous. Whatever happened from here on out wouldn't change the fact that he didn't have a wife to love any longer.

Steven backed up the old pickup and drove to the still-closed gravel pit where Ernie was hiding, wearing Steven's coat and hat.

"How did it go?" Ernie said as he got in.

"It went," Steven huffed. "I don't think Lucille was in on it. But you were right. She has, had, a lover, and he would have had access to our bedroom. He did it because he wanted me out of the way so he could marry her. I don't think she will call the police on me, at least not right away. She seemed pretty confused when I left."

Steven and Ernie swapped winter coats again and Steven gave Ernie back his sports hat.

Ernie looked at Steven with as much sympathy in his eyes as he could muster and said, "Oh shit! Sorry, bro, but it was the only explanation that made sense. It had to be somebody who had access to your bedroom and could get all the DNA samples they wanted."

"Yea, it makes accomplishing the perfect crime easy doesn't it? And to think I sponsored a bill to make DNA evidence even easier to use as evidence." Steven shook his head at the irony.

"Now what, bro?" Ernie said.

"Back to the scene of the crime, I guess. Back to Washington DC. There's a man named Sam Kreiser at Fifth and Indiana who I need to convince to tell me the truth."

"Stupid question time," Ernie said. "Why not just call the police and tell them."

"Tell them what? That I just got my wife to admit to an affair. Big fucking deal; happens all the time. That would be even less reason for her to be a suspect of killing a hooker she thought I was messing with. A woman having an affair isn't likely to be the jealous lover type."

"But you have proof now that the evidence was contaminated and that you didn't do it."

"I'm sorry, but I don't have that kind of confidence in the system. They could come out with reasons for it to be contaminated or leave it out of the trial for one reason or another. Hell, they could make a case that I or Paul or you for that matter did the contamination ourselves. No, I'm not out of the woods yet."

"Why would this Sam guy want to kill Destinee? Hell, all he had to do was show Lucille pictures of you and her together if he wanted her to divorce you."

"Killing Destinee and framing me was the only way to get me out of the way permanently, I guess. I'm in jail, no more senator problem. Besides, killing a hooker is less risky than killing a US senator. Plus, I think Sam Kreiser didn't just want Lucille, he wanted money. He would have told Lucille that he could shelter her assets for her. Once in jail for murder, there would have been very little I could do about what Lucille did with our money. I know it sounds crazy, but it's the only explanation. I still have to prove all of this, and with your and Jojo's help, I am the only person I trust to do it. After what I've been through, trusting the system doesn't seem to be a very good plan."

Steven was still behind the wheel of Ernie's truck, and he ran his hands up and down the steering wheel, massaging it, knowing he had to ask his brother for another favor.

"I need your truck, Ernie. I have to get to Washington ASAP."

"Let's go."

"No, Ernie, you have to stay behind. I'm hanging at the end of my rope. As soon as I expose myself, I'm going to be caught. I just hope I can wrestle a confession out of Sam by then. When they come for you, and they will, tell them you never saw me. I stole your truck, but you didn't know it because you didn't have to go to work and stayed in all day. Either way, by tomorrow morning, call in your truck as stolen."

"What makes you think this Sam guy is going to confess?"

"I'm going to use my persuasive powers. All of them," Steven said through clenched teeth and clenched fists.

"Look, if you beat the truth out of him, it won't be admissible."

"What he doesn't say isn't admissible either. I don't see much choice."

"Let me go with you. I can be a witness."

"Sorry, Ernie, I don't want you any more involved. And I'm afraid you wouldn't be much of a witness. I don't care how many Bibles you swear on."

"Sorry, Steve, it's a risk I will take. I'm going with you."

"But it's not a risk I can take. When I'm arrested, I'm going to need somebody on the outside to help me. So you can't bust your parole. And being caught with me would do that in an instant."

"Damn it, Steve, I want to help."

"You have already done above and beyond, and thanks."

Steven dropped his brother off a few blocks from his apartment and then left for Washington, hoping the old truck would make the eight-hour trip.

Chapter 50

Agent Henderson's Helicopter landed in an open field somewhere near the middle of the Willowdale State Forests. Depending on who you talked to, the manhunt was either going very well or very poorly. From his perspective, it was going poorly.

The good news was that a great deal of the forest had been searched. Also, nobody had been hurt or shot yet. Everybody was doing more or less what they were supposed to be doing. Yesterday's search through the Ipswich Wildlife Sanctuary had been a good learning experience.

The bad news of course, was that they hadn't found the fugitive yet. What they had found were some winter campers, who hadn't heard that a manhunt was underway. They were quickly ushered out of the forest.

The human perimeter net was being carefully monitored and had been since late yesterday. There were a couple of possible holes in the net, but they had been found and fixed an hour or so after daybreak this morning. Every possible entry or exit was monitored. The roads surrounding the forest had police and civilians spaced within sight of each other. If the senator was in the forest, he was trapped inside of it. Of that, Henderson was sure.

But if they didn't find him before dark, guarding the perimeter over the evening would require more resources than he had. Every available citizen and officer was already being used; soon he would have to ask the governor to mobilize the National Guard. That was the only way he could secure the forest after dark.

The following day in Washington DC:

"Don't worry about me." Tamara looked into the visor mirror, checking her abundance of makeup. It had taken Tamara and Jojo a day to make arrangements for both of them to get away. Now, after making the five-hour journey to Washington DC, their plan was set. "You know I can take care of myself."

"Of course I'm going to worry about you. I wish I had never let you talk me into this."

"You needed a trap and some bait for the trap."

"Not my wife."

"Then who? Look, I get it. I'll be careful; I've got Smithy with me."

"That's the point. You shouldn't be in a situation where you might need your gun. And when was the last time you fired Smithy?"

"I cleaned and oiled it. It's good."

"You sure you're up for this? You quit the force five years ago."

"With good reason!"

"Baby, I know why you quit, but this could get dangerous."

"For both of us. I get it. Do you really think I forgot all my training?"

Jojo knew he was losing the argument, again. "No, I just don't want you hurt. Cowboy and I would never be able to forgive ourselves."

"Well I don't see that you or Cowboy have much of a choice. Besides, you said I won't need it."

"Not if you do exactly as I say."

"I promise."

Jojo kissed Tamara goodbye and wished her luck; she did the same and got out the car.

Tamara was wrapped in a full-length coat that covered her less-modest clothing underneath. When the time was right, she would take off the coat and stuff it into her pull bag.

Jojo drove another two blocks and parked. He took a deep breath before walking into the Washington Arms.

"I need a room for a night," Jojo said to a manager at the front desk. One look at the man's nametag and Jojo knew he'd found the right guy. Ramon Ruben Hayes.

"Certainly, sir. Do you wish to charge it or pay cash?"

"Cash, yes cash would be good," Jojo answered nervously.

Jojo pulled out his wallet and frantically searched it. "I guess I can't. I only have about two-hundred dollars, but I need it."

Jojo acted agitated. "I had to buy gas. My wife doesn't know I'm here, and I would like to keep it that way."

"May I suggest the ATM machine?" Ramon nodded toward the machine across the lobby.

"No that's all right, I guess, sure, I mean, yes I'll pay with a credit card," Jojo said, making it seem like he wasn't happy with the lack of a choice.

"I will need to see some identification, sir," Ramon said.

Jojo pulled out his license and handed it to Ramon. His badge was clearly visible in his wallet as he fumbled with his ID nervously.

Ramon's eyes lit up when he saw the badge. "I have room 327 ready for immediate check in. Do you need one key or two?"

Jojo pretended to think about the answer for an instant.

"Might as well take two. You know, just in case one doesn't work right. But otherwise, nope, it's just me, all by myself. Just going to watch a movie all by myself."

"Of course, sir, two keys. If I can be of any further help, please let me know."

Jojo took the keys and replaced his ID and credit card. His ruse had worked.

Once he was inside room 327, he did a thorough search and couldn't find any type of listening or monitoring device. The drain that Detective Saltarie told him about had the small screen in place as she had warned, but that was the only suspicious thing he found. In fact, the room seemed to be exceedingly clean otherwise.

As soon as Tamara knocked on the door, Jojo let her in, and they both stayed in character, not sure if someone was listening.

"Welcome," Jojo said. "Would you care for some pâté and cheese, compliments of the hotel?"

****

It wasn't quite two hours later when Ramon saw the visitor he had been expecting. A very pretty black lady walked through the lobby pulling a small night bag. She took the elevator to the third floor. The ultra-short, skin-tight, shiny, black leather skirt, and the equally skin-tight, bright red, button-down blouse advertised her trade quite well. Especially when the buttons on the blouse, that is the few that were actually buttoned, were straining against the material, certain to pop off at any moment. How the obviously braless woman's breasts managed to stay inside the garment was amazing in itself.

A quick walk by room 327 along with an ear to the door confirmed that the middle-aged hooker was with the detective. Room 327 had recently been fully cleaned, even the drains. He had done them himself. Ramon's heart started beating a bit faster. Possibly, God willing, he would be on another mission for the Lord tonight.

Not too far away:

Steven leisurely sipped at his coffee at a Subway sandwich shop. He could see the Capitol Building in the background, and it reminded him of how much had changed for him. The last months had been nothing short of a nightmare, and he had no clue how he could ever undo the damage to his reputation and the disruption to so many lives that had counted on him.

One thing that was for certain regardless of what happened, he would no longer be a United States senator. From the small radio he had in his apartment, he knew that the governor of Massachusetts was already floating names for his replacement.

The old truck he had borrowed from Ernie had made the trip with no difficulty and was parked at the other end of town at a public library. That was where Steven had used a computer to look up and print out a picture of Attorney at Law, Samuel M. Kreiser.

It was late afternoon, and if he was being tracked or followed, there had been no indication of it so far. He had taken a sightseeing bus to Fifth and Indiana, the location of Sam Kreiser's office.

He had called from a pay phone and confirmed that Sam was in the office today, though unavailable if you didn't have an appointment. It would be quitting time soon, and Steven would be making his own appointment.

It was hard to be patient as the large building across the street started to empty of its daytime residents. Men and women of all ages and sizes filtered through the two sets of glass double doorways. Steven was afraid of losing his quarry in the crowd, so he took his coffee in hand and casually strolled across the busy street.

He watched the corporate parade exit the building. His beard had added another day's growth, and he looked a bit out of place in his white parka as compared to the long dark overcoats that were the uniform of the day. Ernie's ball cap shielded his eyes as he scanned the crowd. Nobody seemed suspicious of him, and after a half hour, his patience paid off.

Steven slouched against a concrete wall as he kept his head hidden behind his hat and his coffee cup. He compared the photo he held with one of the departing residents. There was no doubt he had found his wife's lover. It could be that Lucille had warned Sam or told the police of her husband's intentions. This could all be an elaborate trap. Soon he would know.

Following Sam to his next destination would be the next challenge. Steven waited not far from the taxi stand. Only, Samuel Kreiser didn't get into line for the waiting cabs.

Steven followed from a distance. Maybe the attorney lived nearby, or he had a car in a parking garage. Either would work. All Steven wanted was a few minutes alone with the man. That was all it would take.

Steven stood a mere ten feet from Sam in a crowd of about twenty people waiting to cross the busy intersection. When the light changed, the overcoat he had tagged as Samuel Kreiser crossed Pennsylvania Avenue along with the twenty other people. Steven was shocked when Sam turned the corner and walked alone into the Capital Grille.

Washington Arms Hotel:

The bed squeaked and shook. Anybody who wanted to exercise even a bit of imagination would know what was happening behind the closed door. God had once again sent him a cop, a protector of the people. The squeak of the bed was a sound he hated; it reminded him of his mother and the terrible things she did behind the door.

Ramon listened closer. A man's voice said, "Man, you are good!"

The woman responded, "I am better than good, why do you think I get two hundred dollars an hour."

Soon, he would punish another sinner. This time, it would be somebody paid and trained to uphold the law, somebody just like Detective Bruce Harmon. Unfortunately, Detective Harmon had escaped his own arrest by pinning the blame on a doctor.

Somehow the detective had removed the evidence planted against him for the murder of the red-haired prostitute, and switched it. Ramon didn't understand why God had let that happen. But he knew that God wanted these people punished; he had often told him just that. In time, God would unveil his plan to him, he always did.

Ramon walked away from the doorway, sure that nobody had spotted him listening. If the cop went out for a drink after his tryst, then, God willing, there might be enough evidence left behind that Ramon wouldn't have to wait for another visit. Room service had been requested, and Ramon made sure that clean glasses and a sharp knife were sent up with the wine and pâté.

According to his driver's license, Detective Jones was from a place called Reidsville in North Carolina. The detective had only checked in for one night, so tonight might be Ramon's only chance to do God's will.

As far as Ramon was concerned, he had enough proof to condemn the two perpetrators already. He didn't recognize the prostitute, but it would be easy enough to follow her to her favorite street corner. Picking her up before the night was up shouldn't be too hard.

Then, like the others, he would offer her poisoned drugs, or if they didn't do drugs, he would find another way to make them too sick to resist him. God always provided a way. Ramon became excited as he thought about the college girl. That was what he called the professor's girlfriend.

The college girl didn't want a ride from him at first, but Ramon had convinced her that the rain and wind were going to get much worse very quickly. She changed her mind. After all, she knew him from the Washington Arms, and he wasn't really a stranger. Though she did seem a little taken aback by the rain suit he was wearing from head to toe.

The individual-size bottle of wine that he gave her was laced with a tasteless poison. It made her sick enough that she needed to leave the car to throw up. He had made sure they were at a private area by then. She had struggled a little bit but was too sick to put up a real fight.

After planting the DNA evidence on the body, he took off all of his bloody rain gear and tucked it into a plastic garbage bag. On the way home, he tossed it into a dumpster with his gloved hands.

Just the thought of how the college girl had pleaded with him, how she had begged him to stop slashing her made Ramon's heart pound. Tonight, yes, tonight, would be another good night to do the will of God. God would help him find the new black hooker and he would send her to God for judgment. The policeman from North Carolina would be made an example of. The world would see what happens to policemen when they break the law. He would be punished too. Ramon slinked away from the doorway; he had heard enough to make his own judgment.

****

Jojo whispered into his wife's ear, "Was there somebody listening at the door? I thought I saw a shadow."

Tamara shifted all of her one-hundred-and-thirty-pounds back and forth to make the bed creak and shake some more. "Oh, baby, you are one big hunk of dark chocolate," she cooed loudly and then whispered, "I thought I saw it too. How much longer?"

"Keep making noise," Jojo whispered.

Tamara continued shaking the bed and making lurid comments. Unfortunately, they both still had their clothes on.

Jojo was sure he saw a shadow from under the door. Then it was gone. He waited a bit more, then slowly opened the door. He saw the unmistakable blue sport coat go into the stairwell at the end of the hallway.

"You can give it a rest, luv. It was him, but he's gone now."

Tamara plumped up a pillow to lean against on the bed, smiled at Jojo, and said, "This isn't exactly the romantic evening I had in mind."

"Baby, have I told you lately that you look fabulous."

"Only every ten minutes since I walked in the door."

"That outfit is definitely going home with us," Jojo said.

"Oh yea? Well are you going to pay me two hundred dollars an hour to wear it?"

"No, but I will pay you two-hundred to take it off, at least some of it." Jojo grinned.

"Now what? Do you think he took the bait?" Tamara moved from kneeling on the bed to sitting on its edge.

"I'm sure he was listening. You have to think like a hooker. What would you do next?"

"I wouldn't stay here much longer. I gotta sell my wares. I have a schedule to keep, you know."

"You're right, and I have to check out his apartment. But I don't want you strolling the streets, especially dressed like that."

"How long will you be gone?"

"An hour, hour and a half max."

"The safest place will be right here in the hotel bar. I'll have Smithy and my pepper spray, and I won't go anywhere. I'll be fine."

"I don't know, dressed like that, you won't be alone for long. But I don't want you alone in the room either."

"Don't worry, I won't do anything that could get me arrested, big boy."

"I'm not sure I like it, but I don't see any other choice. Don't let anyone slip you a mickey."

"I'll be careful, just don't be gone too long."

Jojo reached into his suitcase and produced a small camera. "I borrowed this from the department. We use it to catch shoplifters. With both of us gone, if the little weasel does something to the room, we want to know about it."

Chapter 51

Walking into the Capital Grille took special courage. Inside could be any number of people who might recognize him despite the beard and glasses he wore. Steven glanced at his reflection in the window; he hardly recognized himself. He had fooled Lucille, at least for a while. He prayed this would work and his nightmare would come to an end.

Steven tried not to make eye contact with anybody as he scanned for his target. Samuel Kreiser had already found a place at the long bar. Steven slid in between him and another patron. The man on his right apparently didn't appreciate Steven's look or smell and left for the other side of the bar.

Steven saw Sam making a disgusted face at him as well, but he didn't move. Sam hadn't recognized him, at least not yet.

Steven looked in the mirror on the back wall of the bar. He tugged on the brim of his hat and pulled it down over his forehead just a bit more. Steven ordered a beer and dropped a twenty on the bar.

He saw Sam make quick work of his first cocktail and order another. When the bartender left, Steven slipped a ten out of his pocket and put it on top the twenty, assuming that would take care of both their bills.

Steven stood and, breathing heavily into Sam's face, whispered, "Don't make a scene or I will slice your liver in two." He pressed his knife into Sam's side enough to pierce through his clothes and break skin. "My name is Steven Westcott, and I don't have much to lose, what about you?"

Sam's eyes became wide with fear as he froze in place.

"Move, now." Steven urged with the tip of the knife.

Steven and Sam left their drinks on the bar.

Steven was only a half-step behind with the knife pressing through several layers of clothes. Steven noticed just a bit of red showing on Sam's white shirt where the knife was pressing into him.

As soon as they were out the door Steven ordered, "Take a left."

"Senator, I don't know what you want from me. Whatever it is, I'm sure it's a misunderstanding we can work out."

Steven pressed the knife harder with his right hand while he tossed his other arm over Sam's shoulder pressing into him like they were two buddies.

"Keep moving. I just want to have a little chat about my wife. She told me everything."

Very nervously Sam said, "Look, Steven, I'm sorry. It's over between us. I'm sure she told you that. She told me she didn't want to see me anymore."

"Turn into the parking structure. Keep walking, up the ramp."

It wasn't until they found a secluded area, blocked off by two telephone company vans, that Steven stopped and set his phone against the antenna of one of the vans.

"Why, Sam, why?"

"Look, Steven, I'm sorry. She was going through a lot, and I was counseling her. You were gone a lot, and so we would meet somewhere to talk. She's a beautiful woman. Things got carried away. One thing led to another. You understand."

"No I don't!"

Steven took Sam's wrist in hand, and with a twist, Sam was on his knees in front of him facing away.

Calmly Steven said, "I need you to answer a few questions for me, sort of fill-in-the-blanks type things. I'll know if you are lying."

Sam tried to steady himself on the concrete with his free hand. "It's over between Lucille and me, I'm sorry I can't undo the past, but it's over."

"I really don't care, not anymore. Let's talk about something much more interesting. Tell me about how you killed Destinee Sanford."

"What? No way, your DNA was all over her, including your semen. If you think you can pin the blame on me you are way crazier than I thought."

Steven started twisting Sam's wrist.

"No ... no ... Christ, stop!"

"Confession is good for the soul, Sam. And it might also help you live a little longer. You killed her and framed me so that you could take my wife and my money. Isn't that right?" Steven twisted again.

"Shit! Steven, what do you want me to say? Ahhhh!" Sam screamed into a concrete wall.

"Your wrist is getting close to the breaking point, time to come clean," Steven said.

"Jesus Christ, Steven, fuck, fuck, fuck." Sam reached up with his free hand, trying to grab Steven in vain.

"Step by step, how did you do it?"

Steven twisted just a bit more.

"I didn't do it. I'm a fucking lawyer not a murderer."

"Bullshit, that's going to cost you. You killed her. I know you did, and then you framed me for it."

Steven twisted some more and there was a loud crack.

"Ahhhh! No ... stop, no!" It was too late. Sam dropped back on his knees in pain and started to gulp air. "I didn't do it, and I don't know who did."

Steven twisted the broken wrist.

"Please! Please. They made me do it."

"Who made you do it?" Steven demanded.

"This will never hold up in court. You won't get away with this. You are torturing me for information. Hardly admissible."

"How lawyerly of you to explain that to me. No charge I assume. Give me your other hand. Give it to me, right now!"

"I don't know. Ahhhh, shit, shit, stop it." Sam struggled for breath. "OK, OK." Sam gave Steven his other wrist.

"I owed people. I stole some money from a trust, their trust. I didn't think they would miss it. They said if I cooperated, they wouldn't kill me."

"How about I make the same deal with you? Tell me what you know!"

"I can't tell you. They'll kill me. I know they will."

"Who, who will kill you? Tell me or I swear I will crush your other hand."

"Fuck you, Steven, you know that? Fuck you! I can't, lawyer-client privilege, you have to respect that."

"No I don't."

Steven gave a sudden hard twist, there was a loud crack and then Steven placed his hand over the screaming man's mouth. Eventually, Sam regained a bit of composure, and Steven lifted his hand.

"I did warn you," Steven said politely. "You do realize that I have nothing to lose here. So I am quite serious, Sam."

Through short, deep breaths, Sam uttered, "OK, OK. Some guys, big guys, they visited me in my office. I don't know any names. They said if I collected your DNA from your home, I wouldn't be killed. They said they would know if it was yours or not so it better be real. They gave me a file on your wife. Likes, dislikes, hobbies, that sort of thing. And then they told me how I could meet her. So I seduced your wife to get into your bedroom. I collected your hair from a brush in your sink. I found tissue with blood on it and asked Lucille if she had hurt herself. She said you cut yourself shaving so I knew it was your blood. I found a used condom in the trash. I took some knives from your kitchen set, hoping your prints were on them. I took anything I could find that might have your DNA or fingerprints on it and gave it to them."

Steven didn't know if he could or should believe Sam or not. The trouble with forced confessions is they were often lies.

"Somebody wants you out of Washington in a big way. I don't know who, I swear. But if they're from the trust, they have a lot of money. Hell, I thought they would never miss a couple of million."

"Who did you steal from? The trust must have an owner, beneficiaries."

"Don't you think I wanted to know who was threatening me too? A shell corporation owns it and it pays to other shell corporations inside other trusts. Whoever did it, went to great lengths to hide themselves, and they knew what they were doing."

"What was the name of the trust?"

"The Woods Trust of 1955. It means nothing, just another shell."

Steven dropped Sam's hands as a reward. Sam slunk to the concrete floor, withering in pain and staring at his mangled wrists.

"How did they know about Destinee?"

"I had you followed. I overheard a conversation you had with Teddy Johnston in the Capital Grille. I heard something about a sick female friend. My people followed you for a couple of days and saw you shaking up with the hooker. I didn't know they were going to kill her, I just thought they would be interested. Besides, when I told them about the hooker, they already knew about her."

"Who was your spy?"

"Fuck, Steven, my hands hurt, I need a doctor." Sam's voice was laced with pain.

"You can have one after you answer all my questions. Who was your spy?"

"Just an agency I use for domestic disputes. They're called Talbert Investigative. You can check with them, but I just wanted a name and a picture and where she was from. I didn't want her dead, I swear."

"So you didn't care one little bit about Lucille?"

"My life was on the line; you have to believe me. I'll tell you this right now. I will deny everything, you hear me, everything. They'll kill me for talking about them so you might as well kill me now because I will never admit to any of this."

Steven pointed to the cell phone aimed in their direction that he was using to record everything on video.

Sam started a tortured laugh. "A forced confession means nothing. Everybody including me knows you are a trained killer. Of course I will tell you anything you want to hear."

"A person under duress can't make up such a compelling story with certain details. You gave enough new knowledge and inside knowledge to start an investigation. Somebody killed my daughter and somehow it's connected to you and your new friends."

"Your daughter?" Sam said through his whimpering, his hands hanging like broken rag dolls.

"Yes, somebody killed my daughter, and you were an accomplice. I will never forget that!"

"Nothing will stand up in court, nothing. You had better start running, nothing has changed for you."

Steven knew that Sam was right. The confession was next to worthless in a court of law. However, to him personally, it was invaluable. He used the phone to send the video to two people. He typed in his daughter's cell number, hoping she still used it. He might not live through the night, but he wanted her to hear the truth whether through a tortured confession or not. Then he added Teddy's number, signed it with his name, and pressed send.

Sending the message had taken precious time. The FBI, CIA, Capitol police, possibly even Chelle herself were probably triangulating on the phone in his hand.

Steven heard sirens in the distance, but he didn't throw away the phone, not just yet. He ran out the parking garage, leaving Sam crawling on his knees in pain holding his limp hands up uselessly.

Two blocks down, Steven ducked between two buildings and made a call, probably his last.

"Hello," Tracy answered.

"Tracy, it's so good to hear your voice."

"Dad? Is that you?"

"It's me, sweetheart. I've missed you so much."

"Dad, I saw the video you just sent. I knew you couldn't have done it. I miss you so much. Tell the police. Show them the video. Please don't let them kill you, Dad."

Steven walked briskly away from the parking structure. "Listen, baby, always remember I love you more than anything. Your mother and I both have a lot of explaining to do to you. I'm so sorry you had to find out about your mother and Sam this way, but I couldn't take the chance that you might never know the truth. I'm not a murderer, honey, I never was. I had to run away from the police to find out who did it."

"I know, Dad. Are they going to let you go now? Are they going to stop chasing you?"

"Soon, baby, real soon, I hope. I have to go now, this phone won't work anymore, understand?"

"Dad, please be careful."

"Bye, princess."

That was when Steven took his phone and stuffed it into a garbage can. The police would most certainly find it. That was OK because it contained the tortured confession. Steven knew he would still be going to jail, but at least he hoped it wouldn't be for murder. A tour bus came by, and Steven showed his pass and stepped on.

Chapter 52

Ramon looked up when he heard a wheeled overnight case that clicked across the tiled floor. It was the hooker he had seen the night before with the detective from Reidsville. Amazingly, none of the buttons had popped off the tight red blouse yet. He stared at her backside as she sauntered though the lobby.

Ramon followed from a distance and then peeked around the corner as she turned toward the small restaurant and bar area of the hotel. He returned to the front desk, upset and a bit angry that a woman in such a profession should think she was welcomed in his hotel, because she wasn't as far as he was concerned.

About ten minutes later, the detective from Reidsville, North Carolina, approached the front desk and said, "I need a walk to get some air. I was wondering if you could suggest a good restaurant not too far from here," Jojo asked.

"Certainly," Ramon answered, anxious to help persuade the detective to eat off premises. "There are many fine eating establishments not very far from here. There is casual fair right down the block at the Billy Goat Tavern. It is a local favorite and an easy walk from here. I would also suggest Murphy's. If you are looking for something much more formal, they serve fine steaks. Now if you are looking for Italian—"

"No, you can stop there. The Billy Goat sounds just fine."

Ramon gave specific directions and watched Jojo cross the busy intersection on his way to the tavern. Then Ramon checked the bar room one more time. The hooker was still there, probably looking for a new customer. With the current guest of room 327 gone, now was the perfect time for him to inspect the room for the critical evidence he would need to set up the detective for the death of the hooker in the red blouse.

****

Jojo made sure that nobody had followed him to the tavern. Without going inside, he flagged down a taxi. He had agreed with his wife's plan that if she stayed in the hotel in a public place, she would be safe. She also had the car keys and could leave the hotel if she felt it necessary. Tamara also carried Smithy, as she called it, and she knew how to use it.

Jojo needed time to research the night manager, which would also leave the room empty long enough for the manager to do whatever it was he did. Of course it was all speculation on the part of Detective Saltarie, but it was the only lead they had to prove Cowboy's innocence. But if the manager did enter room 327, he would have a record of exactly what he did on video.

****

Tamara was doing her best to be ignored by the bar patron sitting next to her. The big screen television was on a basketball game, and she tried to look involved in the action. Her plan wasn't working.

"That game is over. The Dukes suck this year."

Tamara made the mistake of smiling and agreeing with a silent nod.

****

Ramon finished searching room 327. He had found exactly what he was looking for and more. The detective was secretly taping his liaison with the hooker. Not only was the detective a sinner, he was perverted, and God hated perverts more than hookers. Ramon rushed down to his car to carefully hide the camera he had found and the evidence he had collected.

****

"I sell heavy machinery, gears actually. You know those big diggers that turn on their tracks. I sell the gears that make them turn," the middle-aged black man, George, said. "I've been in this business for so long that the engineers ask me how they should be built."

"Wow, that sounds really interesting," Tamara lied, then turned her head back toward the TV.

George didn't take the hint and offered to buy her a drink. Tamara didn't object, she didn't think she could. She wondered if prostitutes ever punched off the clock.

"You're very kind and a liar," he added with a smile, "but it is interesting to me. The only thing I don't like is the traveling; it gets a bit old after awhile. Going around to different cities every week is a young man's game. I'm getting too old for this."

"So quit. Do something else." She accepted the drink from the bartender.

"Such an easy thing to say, such a hard thing to do. This is what I know, and so this is what I do. I suppose you know exactly what I mean."

It was impossible to miss the inference, but she pretended that she had. Tamara checked her watch. She couldn't assume that her husband would come back in time to rescue her, so she continued to make the best of the situation, hoping things didn't progress further than a simple conversation. Her discussions with George continued on innocently enough for another ten minutes until they were interrupted.

One of the men from across the bar approached her and said. "Hey, sweetheart, I'm feeling a little frisky. What say you and I head off to my room for a little R and R?" The man, who looked to be about thirty to thirty-five and fairly muscular, showed off his room card between his fingers.

Tamara looked up at the younger man and her mouth opened to turn him down.

But before she could speak, George turned on his bar stool and talked softly to the younger man. "Look, son, you've had a bit too much to drink. The lady and I are having a nice discussion, so it's time for you to leave."

"Listen, old man, I think you and the lady have *talked* long enough. It's time for a real man and some real action."

That was when George stood up. "Maybe the lady doesn't want to go with you."

"Did it ever occur to you that she ain't no lady?"

The man's friends from across the bar started to cheer and egg him on. Things were quickly getting out of control. Tamara stood up and smiled at both men. "I do believe it is time for me to leave."

"You don't leave until I tell you to." The young man grabbed her hand. "We leave together."

Tamara twisted her arm away. "I have to leave now. I have another appointment."

"You have an appointment all right, in my room." He grabbed her arm again even tighter.

The rough treatment had gone too far, Tamara knew she had to stop the fantasy right now. She stomped down with her sharp, four-inch heel onto the young man's dress shoes.

He let go of Tamara and reached for the back of a bar stool to steady himself as he lifted his sore foot. The instant the young man released Tamara's arm, she grabbed her empty night bag and purse and raced out the bar before anybody else had time to react.

Tamara was sure that at least one angry young man would soon be after her, so she kicked off her heels so they wouldn't slow her down. Their car was in the parking garage. She looked back and didn't see anybody pursuing her, but she was afraid of being followed into the dark structure.

Tamara put her hand on the grip of her Smith and Wesson inside her purse. She stopped and listened for approaching footsteps before she opened the door to the attached parking structure. Looking down the hallway, she didn't see anyone. As soon as she was on the road, she would call her husband and they could rendezvous.

The fantasy was over; she wanted to go home. With her right hand still holding the grip of her gun, she ran toward her car. At the car, she fumbled through her purse for the keys, listening for the tell-tale echoes of footsteps. She heard none, and her heart started to slow. Then she glanced up and saw a man, and everything went black.

****

Jojo double-checked the address he had been given by detective Saltarie. The apartment building was nothing exceptional. There was no security guard; in fact, the lobby wasn't secured in any way. Jojo looked around and didn't see any cameras watching him either. With a bit more luck, he could get in and out without anybody seeing him. The apartment he was looking for was on the fourth floor. He stood by the elevator, and after wasting about five minutes waiting, he decided to take the stairs.

He worked his way up the stairwell. When he exited on the fourth floor, he could hear a man and a woman arguing in room 434. At least he knew where they were. Otherwise, the apartments were quiet.

Jojo pulled out his set of lock picks and went to work. It was a skill the army had taught him. It was surprising how often it had come in handy. It was a little awkward working with winter gloves, but he wasn't about to contaminate a potential crime scene with his fingerprints.

It didn't take long to open the two sets of locks. The door clicked open. Looking at the door from the inside, he saw two more sets of deadbolt locks. The man obviously liked his privacy.

The apartment was clean, very clean. He would have to be careful. A man who kept an apartment like this would notice anything out of place. He scanned the small apartment and didn't see anything suspicious at first glance.

The bedroom was just as immaculate as the rest of the rooms. Step by step, he went through the bureau drawers. Aside from a drawer filled with white cotton gloves, there was nothing out of the ordinary.

Jojo was sensing a bust, nothing to report to Detective Saltarie. Then he saw some magazines neatly piled on a small, wooden bookshelf.

Jojo scanned the magazine covers. Now that was interesting. All of the magazines were crime and law magazines, like *Forensic Science, New Criminologist,* and various science magazines that explored DNA mapping and collection techniques.

Jojo's heart started pumping. There had to be something else, or at least a clue to where Mr. Hayes kept his real secrets. There must be a key or address or a bill for a storage unit.

Jojo continued to carefully search the apartment. He walked in the bathroom, which was also spotless and void of any incriminating evidence. Mr. Hayes was certainly one clean son of a bitch, he thought as he moved on to the only other door in the apartment. He tried to turn the handle. Strange, it was locked. A locked room in an already locked apartment.

He opened his tool pouch again; his hands were getting sweaty inside the gloves. It didn't take too long. The locked door creaked open just a bit. Jojo proceeded very slowly. It was dark in the room, and Jojo strained his eyes to make out what exactly he was looking at until he found a light switch.

With the flick of a switch, he was nearly blinded by the white walls reflecting the bright lights. The room was immaculately clean, even cleaner than the rest of the apartment, if that were possible.

In a corner was a desk with a white plastic covering on it and two bright work lights. The lights were on adjustable arms. The backside of the table held a microscope, and from the size of it, he figured, a very good one. The room was some sort of a hobby room, and judging from the books he had already seen, Jojo had a good guess at what that hobby was.

He examined the covering on the desk; it was pulled out from a larger role of the material that was mounted on the side of the desk. It was obviously designed to quickly and easily cover the worktable. Just like an oversized role of paper in a doctor's office.

When he opened the middle drawer, it was neatly filled with small precision tools. Miniature pliers, surgery-sharp scalpels, stainless steel picks like you might find in a dentist's office. In a side drawer were empty containers of all sizes. Some extremely small, but everything was exceptionally clean and neatly aligned.

The room wasn't big, but it was organized. Across from the desk was a refrigerator. Jojo opened the refrigerator door with a great deal of trepidation. The shelves were carefully partitioned into sections that contained small, sealed plastic containers. Each was clearly and neatly labeled: blood sample, snot, fingernail clippings, hair, skin cells, semen, and others. Under that descriptions were names. It didn't take long for him to find the two names he was looking for. There was an entire series of samples for Senator Steven Westcott and Destinee Sanford. Strange, Jojo thought, Detective Bruce Harmon's name was on one of the shelves. That was the name Chelle had mentioned as a possible killer.

Beside the refrigerator were shelves with knives—many identical—drinking glasses, wine bottles, and beer cans, all labeled with names. Other potential evidence such as business cards, luggage tags, boarding passes. It was quite a collection.

Jojo reached in his pocket and took out his phone.

"Hello."

"Detective Saltarie?" Jojo asked softly.

Chelle recognized both the voice and the phone number. "Jojo, where are you?"

"You don't want to know."

"Do you have something for me?"

"I'll say. You better get a warrant and get your ass over to Mr. Hayes's apartment ASAP. I found a side room with a worktable and tools and a refrigerator and freezer filled with DNA evidence collected from a good number of people, including Steven and his daughter."

"Get the hell out of there, Detective, and be careful that you do not leave any evidence that you were there or the whole case will go down the toilet."

"Just get a warrant and get this guy. I think you have a serial killer on your hands."

Jojo walked around the room as he talked, touching as little as possible. With his gloved hand he flipped open a cardboard box.

"He has a case of thin rain suits, you know, disposable. The kind that would cover your whole body. He also has plastic footwear and latex gloves. There is enough of the right kind of gear to cover you from head to toe, and easy to dispose of."

Chelle added softly, "Just the things you need if you're going to get splattered with blood and are afraid to get dirty."

Jojo finished, "Or if you don't want to leave your own DNA behind. If this guy isn't a serial killer, I will eat my gun. And, Detective, your other suspect, Detective Harmon, his name is on quite a few labels too. It looks like he was planning on framing your guy."

"If you're wrong about this, my career is over."

"He's a nutcase, trust me."

"I am, gotta go."

Jojo left the apartment as carefully as he had entered. He saw all the pieces of the puzzle fall together, except one. As a manager of a hotel, it would be easy to collect DNA from his guests. The drain screens were added proof of his extraordinary methods. Planting the DNA evidence that had obviously been arduously collected and cataloged on the victims would not have been difficult either. But why?

The farther away Jojo went from the apartment building, the more his thoughts went to his wife, who was still at the hotel. They had set a trap for catching a potential killer. But after seeing and understanding what the hotel manager was capable of, Jojo realized that they had underestimated the man. Tamara was in more danger than they had expected.

Jojo called his wife as he walked down the street, trying to flag down a cab. Tamara needed to know that staying in the public's view at all times was imperative. If the manager took the bait, her life could be in danger already.

Her phone didn't ring back. Soon he got a message that the number was unavailable. There was a restaurant just ahead of him. He saw a taxi pulling over for a couple of riders. Jojo ran to catch up with the taxi and with a quick apology, he flashed his badge and stole it away from an older couple and ordered it to the Washington Arms. He tried not to panic, but he could feel that Tamara was in trouble.

****

Armed with new information, Chelle called Pat.

"Hello, Chelle."

"Pat. We need to talk, now."

"I'm off duty, and unlike you, I have a life. It's getting late, and I'm with my family."

"Pat, listen, I'm offering you the chance of a lifetime. Just trust me on this. We have to meet."

"If I leave right now, my lifetime will be cut short by my wife. What is it?"

"I'm on my way to Judge Melford's house."

"You're not serious. You are offering me a chance of a lifetime to lose my job and my wife all in one night. No thanks."

"I need you on this. First hear me out, then you decide."

"Shit, Chelle. This better be good."

Chapter 53

H ello." Judge Melford answered his home phone.

"Pardon me, Judge, this is Detective Chelle Saltarie. I know it's late, but I need an immediate search warrant."

"I am not on duty twenty-four hours a day, Detective," the judge said.

"Yes, sir. I agree, sir. But this can't wait. I just got a tip, a very good tip that many of the recent hooker murders have actually all been done by one man."

Chelle turned on her flashing blue light and was on her phone racing toward the judge's house in her police cruiser as she talked.

"And just how did you come across this information?"

"It was from a very credible source but confidential, I'm afraid."

"Why didn't your captain call me?"

"Captain Walker doesn't know I'm calling you. I need to search this individual's apartment immediately. We are afraid that he might be on to us. He works at the Washington Arms. The same hotel several of the murdered hookers used. He also worked at the Continental Hotel and the Hotel Astor. All hotels with guests who turned up dead recently. I have very good reason to believe this man was the real killer and framed others, including Deon Michalski, for the crimes by using evidence he collected while working in those very hotels."

"You mean you think Michalski might be innocent?"

"There is a good possibility, sir."

"OK, but if you are wrong, your credibility with me is gone, evaporated."

"Yes, sir. I would stake my career on it."

"Yes you are!"

Armed with a signed search warrant for Mr. Ramon Ruben Hayes's apartment, the two officers raced their cars to the location. Chelle hoped they weren't too late. If the evidence wasn't there, she would be issuing parking tickets for the rest of her career.

When they arrived, backup uniformed officers were already guarding the apartment and a forensic team was on its way. Chelle had called Captain Walker—it couldn't be helped. He was furious of course, but there was nothing he could do at this point. It would have to play out.

Her phone started ringing before she could get out of the car. Just what Chelle didn't need, another phone call, but she answered it anyway.

"Henderson, this is a bad time."

"Well it might get worse. It looks like your boy is back in your jurisdiction. I'm forwarding you a video he made, and it isn't pretty."

"What?" Chelle couldn't imagine having even more on her plate.

"You know that phone he bought in Reidsville? Well, we traced it to a call he made about an hour ago right in DC. The call was triangulated to Fifth and Indiana near a place called the Capital Grille."

"I know the area. But I can't get there right now; I have something more pressing."

"What the hell could be more pressing than catching this guy? I'm telling you he is dangerous. He tried to torture a confession out of a Mr. Samuel Kreiser, who's at a hospital now getting treated for two broken wrists, courtesy of the senator."

"Agent, please listen. I don't think the senator did it. I don't know who this Sam guy is, but we are hunting down a guy we think has been at the heart of five or more murders, including the senator's daughter. I'm on my way to his apartment right now."

"What daughter? I didn't know somebody killed the senator's daughter."

"It turns out the hooker, Destinee Sanford, was the senator's daughter. I don't have time to explain, just believe it. I have to go. We're at the apartment."

"What about the senator?"

"I can't deal with that right now. I'll call you back as soon as possible."

"I'm sorry, Detective. That won't be good enough. We already have people on the way. We have orders to capture him dead or alive. The United States Government is tired of having a rogue senator on the loose. And he has proven once again how dangerous he is."

Chelle hung up and cursed. There just was no way for her to be in two places at once, and right now, she needed to be here at Ramon's apartment.

Washington Arms Hotel:

Jojo ran into the Washington Arms and kept running until he was inside the bar. After a quick glance around the room, his heart stopped in his chest. She wasn't there.

"Did you see a black woman come in here?" He asked the bartender. "Leather dress, red blouse."

The bartender leaned forward and spoke softly. "Yea the hooker was here, but she left in a hurry." Then the bartender pointed to the abandoned high-heeled shoes still on the floor. It's none of my business, guy, but you don't need that trouble. Let me buy you a drink."

"When did she leave? It's important."

The bartender casually looked up at the clock. "I'd say about an hour ago."

"Where did she go?"

"Toward the lobby, she got in a bit of a ruckus and was running from some guy that wanted to buy her services. I guess she doesn't like to screw with drunks."

"What happened?

"She stomped on the guy's foot. He was pretty pissed, but he couldn't run after her. Forget her buddy, she's long gone and probably in bed with some other guy right now."

Jojo took off running again. *She must have gone to the car, but why didn't she call me? Why is her phone off?*

In the parking garage, he quickly found their car, but there was no sign of his wife. He scanned the garage. If she were hiding somewhere, she would have seen him by now.

Jojo slowly circled their car, looking for clues. He found fresh blood on the concrete near the driver's door. It was Tamara's; he was sure of it.

He fought the feeling of nausea crawling over him. He didn't have the luxury of being ill. His wife needed him. On his hands and knees, he searched the floor for a trail. Even one drop of blood could lead him in the right direction. He found more than one. There was a trail of blood that suddenly vanished right where the trunk of a parked car would have been.

He ran back into the hotel and to the front desk, certain of who wouldn't be there waiting. A young woman with a nametag was sorting some mail. Jojo asked through ragged breaths, "Did you see a black woman in a leather dress and red blouse leave the hotel?"

"Sorry, no," the young woman replied.

In a panic, Jojo pulled out his badge and asked again.

"No, I'm sorry," she said.

"Where is the other manager, Ramon? I need to talk to him now!" Jojo yelled.

"He's not here. He was on duty, but he's gone. I don't know where he is."

Jojo raced up the three floors to room 327. Maybe, just maybe Tamara would be there waiting for him. Jojo prayed she was as he opened the door. The room was empty.

Jojo pulled out his phone. "Chelle, this is Jojo. He took her!"

"Took who? Calm down, Detective."

"My wife came with me to DC. We were staying together at the Washington Arms. After I talked to you, I came back and she was gone, and there is blood by our car."

"I don't understand, who took her?"

"I think it was the night manager, Ramon. We were in room 327. He thought she was a hooker and I was a john. I let him see my badge, so he knew I was a cop. It fits his MO of hitting up people in authority."

Frantically, Jojo explained, "We wanted to see what he did in the room when nobody was there. I had a video recorder hidden and it's gone too. He's had about an hour and could be anywhere. We have to find her before it's too late. I think he knows we were trying to catch him."

"Start flashing your badge and search the hotel," Chelle said. "Maybe someone saw him leave. I'll be there in a few minutes. I'm sending some squads to help you. If you find the manager, detain him, and I don't care how you do it. He may have her hidden away somewhere. He's a clever killer and that takes planning, planning takes time. I believe we have some time, but not much."

"Hurry," Jojo shouted into the phone.

****

Chelle understood the danger the detective's wife was in. She had found the evidence. Side by side were the samples from Destinee Sanford and Senator Westcott, Lisa Meyer and Professor Haggerty, Jennifer Stoll and Father Kelly Millen. Chelle recognized other pairs of names, always in pairs. Then she saw a mismatch, Tiffany Maddenheart and Detective Bruce Harmon. Yet the murderer of Tiffany had been a Dr. Joe Lombardo. Detective Harmon had proved that already.

Chelle had looked carefully at the potential evidence collected for Tiffany's death. There was a semen sample from Harmon, hair from both, blood from Tiffany, a knife, drinking glasses, and a small bag of white powder that was marked, *Detective Harmon's coke*. She would have to sort it out later. Chelle ran out the apartment and to her car. She had inadvertently placed another woman in grave danger, and she had to find her before it was too late. That was assuming it wasn't too late already.

National Cathedral, Washington DC:

Steven stared at the giant church. He had been here before. At the time, it had been as an honored guest. In another hour, the church would be closed for the night. But for now, he had a place that appeared safe, at least for a few moments. Steven hadn't planned on visiting the cathedral, but when the tour bus he was on stopped there, he thought it an appropriate place to contemplate his next action. The fact that he was still free to even consider a next move was unexpected. He had imagined he would be captured by now.

Steven walked up the cathedral stairs at the west entrance. Inside, he found a seat. The high-arched ceiling and the hushed voices of late visitors settled his mind. Steven never considered himself an overly religious man, but being surrounded by the majesty of the cathedral and religious artifacts gave him pause just the same.

Steven knew it was just a matter of time now before he was found. He had also settled into the fact that he was done running, inside the church he found peace.

The police probably had seen the video of Sam's confession. It couldn't be used in a court of law as evidence of his innocence, but it would have to raise many questions that would need to be explored. Trying to find Sam's mystery men, the ones who actually killed Destinee, would now be a job for the police.

Steven realized that, though by accident, he was exactly where he needed to be, and he said a prayer to God. Steven prayed that the police would eventually clear his name and that, in time, his life could return to some semblance of normalcy, though he had no idea how that could ever happen.

Yes, his daughter Tracy would see him in jail, but if he were lucky, she might be able to visit him from time to time. She now knew the truth of what happened even if the legal system failed him. Steven pulled out another cell phone from his pocket. It was Ernie's. His hope was that because Ernie had been in prison, the federals hadn't considered him to be a resource for Steven. The phone had been turned off as a precaution. Steven pressed the power button, and the phone came to life.

Back at Ramon's apartment building:

Ramon had collected enough DNA evidence and fingerprints that framing the detective from North Carolina shouldn't be too hard. After all, he and the hooker had been intimately connected just hours ago. It had been God's will that Ramon was in the parking structure securing the collected evidence inside his trunk when he saw the hooker.

The tire iron was conveniently handy. Sneaking up on the distracted woman wasn't hard either. It was all too simple with God's help. So, with the body safely hidden in the tarp he carried for just such purpose inside his trunk, he drove his car to his apartment to get a few tools he needed to properly plant the evidence.

Ramon was about a block away from his apartment when he pulled his car over to the side of the road and parked it. A man was leaving his apartment building who looked suspiciously like the detective from North Carolina. Ramon waited patiently for the man, who was now on his phone, to hurry past him on the opposite side of the street. A streetlight lit up the man's face and Ramon saw that he'd been right. It was the detective.

The man was too distracted to notice him, so Ramon drove away. God was telling him to be careful. So he decided to wait and watch his apartment building from a convenience store parking lot a half-block away.

As he waited, Ramon played the last hour over and over in his mind. He thought back to the moment he swung the tire iron and how quickly the hooker's face bloodied. He wasn't particularly strong, but God had given him the strength to pull her across the concrete and into the trunk of his car. Ramon's heart was still pounding. Doing God's work was exciting and rewarding.

A half an hour passed and he saw nothing out of the ordinary. Ramon locked his car and started to walk across the parking lot toward his apartment. That was when a rush of police cars flooded the area. His patience had paid off. He casually turned and walked back to the small store and purchased a candy bar. He watched from inside the store and saw Chelle and her partner rush into his building.

Seeing the detective was a disappointment. He had thought that Chelle and he had something in common. After all, they both wanted to punish the guilty. But if she was now trying to stop him, that meant she was working for the devil. Ramon listened, and he heard God's voice tell him that she had to be stopped and that he would provide a way, he always did.

Ramon went back to his car and watched from the darkness. It didn't take long before Chelle slid back into her car and rushed off with lights flashing and sirens screaming.

Ramon got into his car and followed. He didn't worry about following her too closely; after all, he knew where she was going. By the time Ramon arrived in the vicinity of the Washington Arms, he could see a much larger police show going on. Once again, Ramon pulled his car over into the shadows blocks away. It was time to wait for God's plan to unfold.

****

The Washington Arms seemed to be a madhouse of activity. Police officers were rushing in from all its entrances and looking for assignments. Chelle Saltarie hoped it was an organized madhouse for Jojo and Tamara Jones's benefit.

Chelle was trying to calm Detective Jones down. "We are doing everything we can. We are searching the hotel from top to bottom."

"I already have!" Jojo said. "What do you think I've been doing? She's not in the hotel and neither is he.

Chelle and Jojo were standing in front of the check-in counter. A terribly frightened young woman was the manager on duty. Customers were looking to her for direction, and she was trying her best to pacify them through the commotion.

"We will have a make and license number shortly," Chelle said. Then she turned to the girl behind the counter. "His cell number, I need it."

"I've already tried it," Jojo said. "He doesn't answer. It goes right to voicemail. He must have it turned off. We can't even trace it."

A blue uniformed officer walked up to Chelle. "Detective, some of the guests want to know what is going on. What do I tell them?"

Chelle's phone rang. "Hello. ... Just make sure forensics doesn't screw this up. ... Yes I know, when I can. And, Pat, get your ass here as soon as possible. Things are getting out of hand."

"Anything, anything at all?" Jojo said.

Another blue uniformed officer came up to her. "Detective, the guests want to know if they are allowed to leave."

Chelle looked at both officers and said, "We are dealing with an apparent kidnapping, and nobody leaves!"

Just then, another call came in for her. She didn't recognize the number displayed and was tempted to ignore it. Two more officers were waiting for her time.

"Hello, who is this?" she asked with more anger in her voice than intended.

"Detective Saltarie, this is Senator Westcott. I'm in DC, and I want to give myself up. But before you signal anybody that I am on the line, listen to my instructions or this won't work for either of us."

Chelle lifted a finger indicating she should be left alone for a moment. Then she stepped away from any listening ears, including Jojo's. "Senator, I know you didn't kill the girl. I know she was your daughter. I'm looking for the real killer right now. But you are still in danger."

Chelle didn't say anything about the jeopardy his friend's wife was in right now. The situation was already fluid enough, and to say anything more might change the senator's mind. For his own good, he needed to be picked up before it was too late.

"It's nice to have you on my side for a change. I'll give myself up only to you and only if you are alone. If you know I didn't do it, then you know that you are in no danger from me."

"Tell that to a Mr. Samuel Kreiser. I watched the video you sent. I can't save you from what you did to him."

"I know. Not your problem. I think we have a lot to talk about, Detective. Here's the plan."

Chapter 54

Tamara woke up in pitch dark with a splitting headache. The air was hot and thin, and she found it extremely difficult to breathe. She felt wetness on her head, but she didn't know if it was sweat or blood. When she realized she couldn't move, her heart began racing. It didn't take long before her lungs demanded more oxygen. The darkness was overwhelming, and she realized that she had been buried alive in a fetal position.

She tried to scream but couldn't. Her lungs couldn't get enough air. Something was covering her mouth. Her hands and feet were tied, her legs pressed into her chest, and her head was folded down toward her feet. She had nowhere to move, her back was up against something solid, and her arms were twisted uncomfortably at her sides.

Then she heard something; it was a siren screaming past. She listened closer and heard muffled sounds. They were the sounds of a city, and she was moving. She wasn't buried; she was in a moving car.

Tamara's worst fear was repressed for now. Her lungs felt like she had been under water for far too long, and they screamed for a solid breath. She knew she had to slow down her heart and will her body to be calm. Tamara concentrated on slow, steady breaths through her nose. When her breathing and heart calmed, she concentrated on her situation.

National Cathedral, Washington DC:

Chelle put Pat in charge at the hotel and left abruptly before too many questions could be asked. She felt bad about leaving Jojo alone, but she had no choice.

She made a quick call from her car. She had the lights and siren off. Though she was in a hurry, attracting attention wouldn't help, so she drove at civilian speeds. "Agent Henderson, do you know where the senator is?"

"We found the phone he was using in a garbage can. He can't be far, but we have no way of tracing him. I'm afraid he's on the run again."

"Keep me posted, I have a few irons in the fire myself right now. Bye." Henderson didn't know where the senator was, that was good. Not telling the FBI where the senator was, well, that was bad, bad for her. But she wanted to have the senator secured safely in her car and to the station before anybody else knew he had been captured.

****

Ramon thought it interesting that Detective Saltarie left the Washington Arms without sirens blaring and lights flashing. In fact, she didn't look like she was in a hurry at all. *If I knew somebody was kidnapped, I probably would be in a hurry wherever I was going.* Something else was going on, something even more important.

Ramon felt God tell him to follow her, so he casually did a U-turn in front of the Billy Goat Tavern and followed from a reasonable distance. Chelle drove northeast on Massachusetts Avenue at a normal traffic pace. That made it easy for him to keep up with. And the detective's car was fairly easy to spot in the crowd of cars. Its size and shape were unique enough among all the colorful subcompacts and SUVs crowding the streets.

When Chelle turned on her signal for a turn onto Pilgrim Road, Ramon laughed out loud. Now he understood God's plan, how perfectly appropriate. The grounds of the church, possibly the woods itself would be a perfect place to end the life of the detective. How ironic to make the officer's demise happen quite literally in the shadow of the National Cathedral, in the shadow of God himself. She deserved no less.

Ramon didn't have to follow the car very close at all. He was certain of its destination. He drove slowly up the roadway adjacent to the giant church he was so familiar with. On one side was the Bishops Garden with its beautiful archways and sculpted gardens. The five-acre Olmsted Woods sat on the other side, it was one of the few old-growth woods left in the DC area. Ramon parked his car well away from the detective's.

He waited a bit until he saw the detective leave her car. As he suspected, it was God's plan. She turned toward the woods. The cathedral and grounds were closing for the night; traffic on the side road became nonexistent. Ramon thought about the woman in his trunk. He assumed she was dead by now. He had hit her pretty hard with the tire iron.

Ramon opened his car door and stepped into the cold of the night. He took his long knife along with him. Slitting the woman's throat would be messy but also quiet. He wondered how God was going to disarm the woman for him because she was certainly carrying her gun. He reminded himself to have patience. There was a reason the detective picked just before sunset to enter a dark woods; he just needed to discover what it was.

****

Chelle parked her car on the roadside opposite the woods where they had agreed to meet. When she stepped out of her car, she reached beneath her winter coat and unsnapped the trigger guard of her holster.

Chelle stuffed her winter gloves into her coat pockets but decided against putting them on, at least for the time being. She was glad she had on her high winter boots. They were more for fashion than practicality, but just the same, they protected her from the deep snow.

Chelle looked up and down the quiet side street down from the cathedral. There was no traffic, and nobody knew she was here. Chelle felt her gun handle, making sure it was at the ready. That gave her some confidence as she crossed the street and entered the woods.

The farther into the woods she went, the quieter it became. Chelle peeked back; the cathedral couldn't be seen anymore. The darkness and the trees combined to erase all traces of its lights from her view.

The snow on the branches and ground acted like thousands of sponges, soaking up the sound around her. She had just walked into the woods a little ways when a call came in on her phone. The ring tone broke into the silence and made her jump because her senses were already on high alert.

"Hey, Chelle," Pat said.

"What have you got for me?"

"His car is a black Impala. Want the license number?"

"Text it to me." Chelle felt a need to whisper in the quiet woods.

"Do you mind if I ask you where you went so fast?"

"Sorry, Pat. I can't talk right now."

"Are you in trouble?"

"I'm OK. I'll fill you in as soon as I can. Let me know the instant you find out anything about Tamara, good or bad."

Chelle hung up and walked deeper into the woods. Each step through the high snow was another chance of tripping over a buried branch or twisting an ankle on uneven ground. Chelle proceeded carefully.

"Detective Saltarie." Steven appeared suddenly in front of her.

"Senator," Chelle said. "For what it's worth, you are doing the right thing."

"I'm not sure about that, but let's get it over with."

"I need to get you to the lock up at the station for your own safety as soon as possible. Besides me, everyone believes you're a threat. You'll be safest there."

"I appreciate your coming here alone."

"I appreciate your caution, but you know I'm going to have to cuff you to take you in?"

"I understand." Steven blew into his bare hands to warm them a bit before they were to be handcuffed. Then he turned around and placed his hands behind his back.

"Put them in your pocket for now, let's get out the woods first. But, if you run or do anything suspicious, I will shoot, and this time, I won't let a vest stop my bullets."

"I'm done running, Detective."

"I know, and I'm sorry about your daughter."

"Thank you, Detective, and I'm sorry for what I put you through. With the evidence against me, I just didn't think I had any other choice."

Chelle and Steven started to walk through the snow toward Chelle's car.

Steven's feet crunched through the thicker snow and broke some of the branches buried under it with small snaps. As he walked, he said, "I sent the video of Sam's confession to my daughter. That's all I needed or wanted. I might not be able to prove that Sam and others did it to the courts, but at least my daughter will know I am not a cold-blooded murderer."

Chelle stayed a few steps behind Steven. Her right hand kept warm under the back of her jacket near her gun, which was in its holster in the small of her back. As they walked, she filled him in on her investigation.

"I wouldn't be so sure about Sam, after all, you did torture him for the confession. His story could be just that, a story to get you to stop hurting him. However, Ramon Hayes, the night manager at the

Washington Arms has an extensive DNA collection in his apartment, including yours and Destinee's."

Steven stopped and turned toward Chelle, clearly confused.

"So you believe it was him and not the people Sam talked about?"

"Sam's story will be checked out, but I am quite certain that it was Ramon who murdered Destinee."

They moved on, crunching their way through the snow. Then Steven stopped again. "You said you saw my DNA in the manager's collection."

"Yes, with my own eyes."

"But he couldn't possibly have my semen. We never had sex."

"Ramon was very clever in placing the evidence. Maybe he has a way to fool the collection process."

"Or he never had it and Destinee was killed by somebody else who did, somebody like Sam's friends."

"We also have video of the last car Destinee got into that night. If we can get enhanced images off it, we should be able to find out if it was Ramon's car or somebody else's. My bet is it will match Ramon's."

The lights from the road weren't far away. Soon they would be in the warmth of Chelle's car, heading for the station.

"There is something else. I'm afraid that I have some bad news for you." Chelle stopped next to a big oak tree, its branches long stripped of its leaves and now covered with snow instead.

Steven turned around.

"Your friend Jojo came to Washington to help you. He tried to trap the killer."

"Oh my god, no. What happened to Jojo?"

"Not Jojo. I'm afraid that he brought his wife along as bait for the trap."

"Tamara, no ... god, no. What happened?"

From behind the oak, Ramon popped out and instantly had a long knife against the detective's throat. Chelle raised her hands to defend herself but felt the knife press against her throat instead. She stopped resisting.

Ramon sneered in disgust. "I'm so disappointed in you, Chelle. You and I could have been a good team. I would frame those animals and supply the evidence, you would capture and arrest them."

The instant Chelle heard the voice, she knew who and why she was being attacked. "Ramon, Ramon it's over. There is a warrant out for your arrest. We went to your apartment. Everybody knows what you did and how you did it. Killing me won't help you."

Chelle saw Steven very slowly move into an attack position. Unfortunately, Ramon must have too because he instructed, "Mr. Senator, start walking, back into the woods. You lead the way."

Steven hesitated.

"Now! Move, now!" Ramon screamed into Chelle's ear.

Chelle winced as the knife cut her a bit. She knew that Steven couldn't take the chance of attacking when the knife was pressed against her neck. Somehow, she needed to give a diversion.

Steven slowly led the way deeper into the darkening woods.

"I saw the detective from North Carolina coming from my apartment. That was when I knew you were setting a trap. But God warned me. He told me to be patient and wait for his plan."

Steven led the three deeper into the woods as Ramon rambled. Chelle saw Steven peek back, but Ramon held the knife too tight against her for him to take any action. She wanted to slide her hand back to her gun but Ramon was tight up against her back.

"OK, this is far enough."

The trio came to a stop, and Chelle saw Steven almost imperceptibly try to position himself for an attack.

"Stay back! One move and the detective dies right now!"

Ramon violently yanked Chelle's left arm behind her back. Chelle gave a small grunt, trying to contain the pain in her left shoulder. Steven froze in place and Chelle prayed he wouldn't force an attack, at least not yet. She still thought there was time to try and negotiate a way out.

Steven held his hands up in surrender and then said, "It's over. They know who you are. Let her go."

Ramon wiggled the knife just a little, and it cut deeper.

Chelle clenched her teeth. She could feel the warmth of blood flow down her neck. She wondered how deep the cut was.

"You know, I sharpened this knife myself. There is an art to sharpening knives. I mean, if you really care to have them razor sharp, it has to be done just right. But I suppose as a former Green Beret, you already know that, don't you, Mr. Senator?"

The knife against Chelle's throat was pressed so tightly she dared not try to speak. Breathing was becoming difficult, and she was afraid of what would happen if she fainted.

"We can work this out," Steven said. "You don't have to kill anybody else."

Ramon laughed. "Do you think this is up to me, or you, or her? It's not; it's up to God. God decides who dies and who goes to jail. I didn't want to kill those people. Do you think I wanted to kill my own mother? Of course not. I'm not an animal. I'm just his instrument in this world." Ramon glanced toward the sky.

"But God doesn't want you to kill innocents. The detective is just doing her job." Steven tried to inch closer, but the crunching of the snow gave him away.

"Back up, Mr. Senator, you don't want to make me do something I'm not ready to do yet. Maybe the detective is doing her job, but now I am doing mine. I am doing the job God gave me to do, a sacred job. Now, Detective, carefully remove your pistol. Very, very slowly."

Ramon slowly let go of her left hand and increased the pressure of the knife using both of his gloved hands, one on each side of her throat. Chelle felt like her juggler was going to be cut at any moment.

Chelle reached back to the gun holstered against her back and slowly drew it forward, tempted to use it despite what would probably happen to her in the process. But she held back that temptation praying for another solution.

"Remove the clip."

With a click, the ammunition clip came loose. Each movement caused the knife to cut just a little deeper. Her captor showed no remorse for her pain.

"Excellent. You follow directions well. OK, Detective, now hold on to the clip and toss your gun to the senator."

Steven caught the gun. The metal was warm in his cold, bare hands.

"Don't hurt the detective; she's on your side," Steven pleaded. "Why kill a detective who catches bad guys? God doesn't like bad guys. He wants them caught."

"That is true. But she wants to prove that I killed those people. You know what that would mean don't you?" Ramon's voice was filling with anger. "It would mean that all of God's work would be undone. All of the people he wanted to go to jail would be free again. People like the football player, who had a family and chose to sleep with a hooker instead, a no good hooker, or a priest who had a girlfriend and broke his vows to God. Or a senator. Ha!" he laughed. "How about a senator that sleeps with prostitutes. God doesn't want you to be free to sin over and over again. Do you really think that is what God wants? Now, Mr. Senator, move the gun to your other hand, that's it. Now toss it back to the detective very carefully and back away."

Steven did exactly as told while looking Chelle in the eye.

Chelle caught the gun with both of her bare hands and realized what Ramon was up to. Her gun now had Steven's prints all over it.

Ramon started pulling Chelle backward with the knife. The movement twisted the knife in just a bit more as she felt her warm blood running down between her breasts.

"Now, detective, put the clip back in and chamber a bullet. If you even think about pointing it toward me, I will slit your throat."

"The girl you killed to frame me," Steven said, clearly trying to stall. "She was my daughter. You made a mistake. I thought God didn't make mistakes."

"Your daughter?" Ramon laughed. "She was a hooker. I know she was. She came to the hotel often. You weren't her only john, you know? She saw many others, including a cop. You know who I mean, Detective; you even showed me his picture. Do you think I can't tell a cracked up hooker when I see one? Chamber a bullet," Ramon said to Chelle.

Chelle loaded the chamber with a bullet she knew would be used to kill her. "Yes, she was a hooker," Steven said. "And she was on crack. But she was my daughter, and I can prove it. She was trying to get away from her pimp. I was trying to help her."

"You're lying. You two were screwing in my hotel. You were making a mockery of your position, Mr. Senator."

"No, we never did. Think, did you ever find any evidence of a sexual encounter? No, you didn't. We just met in the hotel so we could talk and get to know each other. She was trying to repent. She wanted to be a good girl, and she was trying to be better. She didn't want to be a hooker, and she didn't want to be an addict. God wanted her to get better, and you killed her."

"You're lying, and you know how I know? I didn't kill her." Ramon laughed wickedly. "No, I didn't kill her. God did. I didn't frame you. God did. God knows what he is doing, and he doesn't make mistakes. He killed her and framed you." Ramon laughed again, then took the gun from Chelle with his right hand. While holding the knife against Chelle's bleeding throat with his left, he clicked off the safety switch.

"Wait!" Steven shouted. "What about the woman you took from the hotel room today. Where is she? Why would God want her killed? She isn't a hooker. She was with her husband."

"No, you are lying. God sent her to me to be punished. You are all sinners trying to stop me from doing the work of God. Look where we are. Look where God brought us. Was this your decision? Was it mine or the detective's? Did any of us know before tonight we would be here in these woods in the shadow of the great cathedral? Of course not. It was God who decided."

The woods were getting darker; the last of the setting sun was casting long shadows. Mist from the floor of the woods was mixing with the cold air as it sank, creating a temperature inversion and a cold fog over the snow.

"Now, Mr. Senator, you are going to kill the detective that has been chasing you for so long. You are going to kill the person who has been trying to send you to jail. "

"Ramon wait, they saw your apartment. They found your files and the DNA you collected. Nobody will believe I did it."

"Of course they will. My DNA and fingerprints aren't on the gun or bullets. This knife is perfectly clean of my DNA and fingerprints. But shortly it will have yours all over it. Do you really think I could make that mistake? And it isn't a crime to have a hobby of collecting DNA. My hobby is perfectly innocent. And certainly doesn't prove I killed anyone."

"If you kill her, I will attack you and kill you or you will have to kill me. Either way, there goes your frame-up." Chelle knew that Steven was stalling for time, but her time had run out. Soon he would have to rush Ramon. It was his and her only chance.

Ramon laughed again. "I am quite prepared to die for God tonight. Are you? You can kill me, but it still won't change what happened to the woman you claim was your daughter. It won't change the fact that your DNA is on the detective's gun and soon this knife.

"Besides," Ramon shrugged his shoulders. "God will take care of me; he always does. I won't die tonight." Ramon held up the gun to Chelle's head. "Whatever happens will be known in a few seconds."

Steven didn't have any choice, he had to take the chance and attack or Chelle would certainly be dead in another instant.

Steven dared to glance at into Chelle's eyes. She could read his intentions, and she prepared to die.

That was when they all heard a branch snap. Somebody else was very close by.

****

Ramon looked through the mist. A silhouette of a figure was approaching them. The ghost-like aberration was coming closer with arms out. God had sent an angel to help him. Then Ramon's heart started to pound. He knew who the angel was; it was his mother. Ramon could see the blood still flowing from her dark forehead where he had hit her with the lamp. She had come back from so long ago and was wearing her favorite dress.

In the falling shadows of the great church, she was walking closer. God had brought his mother back to talk to him. She was trying to give him a message from God. The ghost tried to speak, and there was nothing but a rasp. Ramon was frozen in time. His eyes were wide, his mouth agape. Why did God send his mother back to him?

****

Steven didn't look back at whatever was distracting Ramon. His muscles, already set to lunge, sprang forward. Ramon's eyes were locked on something behind him, he was so focused that Steven was upon him before he could react.

Steven had rehearsed in his mind exactly how he would disarm Ramon. With his left hand, he grabbed at Ramon's wrist and turned the knife out, away from Chelle's throat.

Ramon tried to turn the pistol towards Steven, who was now behind him, but Chelle reached out with both her hands and twisted the gun out of his hands, and it fell to the ground.

Then, with a crack, Steven had broken his third wrist of the day as he forced Ramon to the ground. Steven held a screaming Ramon face down in the snow by grinding his knee into his back.

Chelle tossed Steven a pair of handcuffs. That was when he realized how badly she was bleeding. The snow around them was splattered with blood, all of it Chelle's.

Chelle held her neck and collapsed to the ground.

Steven tightened the steel around Ramon's wrist as the man withered on the ground in pain. It wasn't until then that Steven looked back at the distraction that had been so valuable. "Oh my god, no," he cried.

Steven ran to Chelle; he rolled her on her back and packed snow around the front of her neck.

"Chelle, listen to me, use the snow to stem the bleeding, freeze your neck if you have to."

Chelle, though looking disorientated, weakly held the snow to her neck.

"Lie very still, I'll be right back."

Chelle nodded.

Steven ran back to what had originally distracted Ramon. A woman, barely able to stand, was leaning against a tree for support.

"Tamara, are you OK?"

"Cowboy, is that you?" a clearly dazed Tamara gasped as she fell into his arms.

"You're safe now." Steven hugged her, rubbing her back and arms vigorously to warm her.

Tamara started crying. "I was kidnapped. A man hit me with something as I was getting into our car. I was locked in a trunk, but I got my hands untied."

Tamara showed her bloody wrist to Steven. "When the car stopped I found the emergency release and opened the trunk and got out. I ran, I ran away from the car as far as I could. I was trying to hide in the woods."

Tamara slumped against Steven, and he picked her up in his arms. Her bare feet were bleeding from the icy snow.

****

Steven carried Tamara to where Chelle was still lying in the snow. He propped her against a tree and hurriedly removed his jacket and covered her with it.

He rushed back to Chelle's side and warmed her cold hands with his as he examined her wound.

"I think it's working," Steven said.

Chelle slipped her hand away from Steven's and found her phone in her coat pocket and pressed a few keys, soon it began ringing.

Pat answered. "Chelle, will you please tell me where you are."

Chelle's mouth felt dry, she tested her voice and choked out, "Pat, tell Jojo his wife is OK, and bring him to Bishop's Garden, we'll be waiting for you. And Pat, don't tell anyone where you're going, just bring Jojo."

"Chelle, what's wrong? You don't sound good."

"Send an ambulance. I'm hurt but safe now. I'll tell you everything when you get here."

****

The paramedics were treating Tamara when Pat and Jojo arrived.

Jojo ran up to his wife and wrapped her in his arms.

Chelle approached Pat with a bloody bandage wrapped around her neck. "I have Ramon cuffed and locked in the back of my car. He tried to kill me."

"Christ, Chelle, you look terrible."

"Thanks, they say I'll be fine, but I'll need some stitches. I want you to meet the man who saved my life."

Chelle made a motion with her hand. Senator Westcott stepped out of the woods and into the ambulance's flashing lights.

"Help me take him in; he's giving himself up. He didn't kill anybody. Just put him in your car before somebody shoots him."

Steven didn't resist as Pat handcuffed him and put him in the back of his car.

It didn't take long before two more police cruisers with lights flashing were on the scene along with another ambulance.

Chelle was immediately placed on a gurney. But before letting the ambulance take her to the hospital, Chelle explained the entire sequence of events to Marget. Then she was taken away from the confusion as police taped off the crime scene and went to work collecting evidence.

Chapter 55

Every day for two weeks, Chelle Saltarie checked in on Steven Westcott. Today, she came to the jail to visit Steven for the last time.

"Senator, you are finally being released on your own recognizance," she explained. "It took a lot of doing, and there is quite a bit of paperwork to do yet. And I hate to say it, you might be back, but for now, you are a free man."

"Thank you, Detective. If you come for me again, I won't run, I promise."

"As a politician, I would think you would have learned not to make promises you can't or won't keep."

Steven laughed. "Not this time. Teddy tells me that things are looking pretty good for me, I mean, considering everything. Besides, going on the run isn't as glamorous as it sounds."

They walked through the steel corridor and through an open door that was usually bolted closed.

"I talked to Mr. Clayton Harris. He was more than willing to sign a statement recanting his previous testimony about you hurting him in any way or breaking into his house."

"How did you do that?"

"It appears that he and a detective within this department were colluding on various things that I can't go into right now. It all came out during an internal affairs investigation.

"But, one of the things that became evident was that Clayton was working as an informant. I agreed that I wouldn't leak that information to the street if he dropped all charges against you."

"No good deed shall go unpunished." Steven smirked.

"Trust me, Clayton has a lot more bad deeds than good."

Chelle ushered Steven into a private conference room with a large plate glass window. Shannon Johnston rushed up to him and gave him a big hug. In his orange jail jumpsuit, Steven hugged her back. Chelle found it hard to hold back her emotions as Steven and Shannon both unsuccessfully tried to hold back their tears.

"I knew you didn't do it. I was so mad at everybody for not believing in you."

"Don't be, the evidence against me was pretty substantial."

"I brought you some new clothes." Shannon wiped away some happy tears. "Detective Saltarie gave me your size, so I hope they fit; she said you changed a bit. And it looks like she was right. You lost weight, Senator."

Steven looked at Chelle, who shrugged her shoulders and gave a sly smile. "I suggested that they buy you some new clothes. I guessed at your size."

"Thanks. Bright orange isn't my color."

"I agree, Senator." Chelle exchanged smiles with Steven.

"There's a mob of reporters outside," Shannon reminded everybody.

"You might consider staying; it's much safer in here," Chelle suggested.

Steven chuckled. "I appreciate your hospitality, but it's time for me to face the music."

"There's a bathroom down the hall you can change in."

When Steven came back, he was wearing a new suit and tie and shiny black shoes.

"You clean up nicely," Chelle said.

Steven tugged a bit on his suit coat. "You seemed to have guessed my size pretty well."

Shannon straightened Steven's tie, even though it didn't need it, and gave him another hug. "Much better," she agreed.

Chelle handed Steven a hot cup of coffee. "Your attorney will be here shortly."

Steven slowly took a sip. "Why does this coffee taste so much better than any I've had in the last three months?"

Chelle and Shannon laughed.

"I have some good news for you," Chelle said. "I just found out this morning that the flying club isn't pressing charges for the theft of the plane. You can thank Agent Henderson for squaring it with them. Once they found out you were innocent and that the insurance company was on the hook for any damages, they were pacified. In fact, they want you back to finish your flight training.

"On the other hand, Mr. Samuel Kreiser is another matter. He wants to press charges against you for kidnapping, attempted murder, and assault and battery. I'm sure he will think of more. I think he is feeling that a strong offense is the best defense."

"I assume you will be filing charges against him for being an accessory to a murder?" Steven said.

"Senator, I tried, I really did." Chelle found it hard to look Steven in the eye.

"But?"

"The Woods Trust of 1955 certainly exists, but that is where the trail starts and ends. Sam was correct when saying it was carefully crafted to protect whoever it benefits. Sam was never charged with stealing from the trust because the money was quickly recovered somehow and then replaced. No harm, no foul. Did it get Sam in hot water? Absolutely! He lost his job. But we can't prove anybody threatened him in any way to frame you. And of course he denies everything he told you because you physically persuaded him."

Steven sat down and put his coffee on the table in front of him. Chelle could see that Steven was trying not to lose his temper. He was brushing his hair back with both his hands and then rubbing the back of his neck.

"What about the car you had on video, the one that was the last vehicle Destinee was seen getting into? It had to be registered to somebody."

"Turns out it was a stolen plate. We don't believe it was Ramon, but we can't prove it wasn't, and his ramblings aren't helpful. After profiling all the killings, I don't think Ramon killed her. Destinee's murder just doesn't follow the random slashing and stabbings that were his MO. Whoever killed her knew what they were doing."

"You mean it was a professional hit?"

"Yes. She died quickly if that is of any consolation."

"Does this mean I am still a suspect?"

"No, not to me at least. But Sam isn't either. He has an airtight alibi."

"So Sam gets off." Steven slammed his fist down on the table, shaking his coffee. "So who the hell did kill her and why?"

"I don't know what to believe. We have a confession of sorts from Ramon Hayes; he claims God is responsible for her death. He has admitted to the murders of numerous people and is quite proud of the fact that he had God's help in framing many prominent figures as lessons to others. The FBI is trying to identify anybody who could have been framed by Ramon, it's a pretty big mess. Your release is because we officially believe Mr. Hayes killed Destinee."

"Well I don't."

"I don't buy it either, but we both need to right now."

"I don't understand."

"The fact is, we have much more evidence that you did it than Sam, or Ramon, or some mysterious group. The only reason you are going free is because the district attorney doesn't think she could get you convicted. Because Ramon collected your DNA along with Destinee's, your attorneys could easily argue that you were framed just like the others."

Chelle sat down next to Steven and put her hand on his arm. "Ramon isn't claiming direct responsibility for her death; he is saying that God did it. She is the only one he isn't taking direct responsibility for. I believe you didn't do it, but I don't think Ramon did either. Sam couldn't have, so Sam's mystery men would be my next best guess. Why? I could only surmise that a US senator, and you in particular, might have enemies capable of doing anything. Maybe it had something to do with the DNA bill you were championing. After all, it would be a game changer. Hell, I could think of a dozen reasons why many people, good and bad, even entire industries, might not want it to happen."

Chelle stood, then leaned on the table. Looking Steven hard in the eyes, she said, "However, that is all beside the point. If we don't pin the murder on Ramon, then you go down. It's that simple. The district attorney wants a win in her column, not a loss. She believes she can get an easy conviction against Mr. Hayes; there are complications in trying you."

"Pretty much comes down to simple math." Steven sighed.

"Senator," she said softly, her eyes apologizing as she spoke. "Either Ramon Hayes is convicted of the death of Destinee Sanford or you. It might not be what you want to hear, but it's the best I can do. I'm sorry."

Steven clutched the coffee mug in his hand. "I suppose true justice doesn't always happen the way it does in the movies. I just have to accept that. I guess Sam and his friends will literally be getting away with murder."

Chelle raised her voice just a bit and said with as much authority as she could muster, "I know what you are capable of and so does everybody else. If anything happens to Sam Kreiser, you will be the main suspect. Please don't put me or you into that situation again."

Steven returned her gaze. "I appreciate your concern, but don't worry. I have been on the run long enough. I don't want to go back to that life. And despite what you might think, I do have respect for the law."

"If it makes you feel any better, I won't let him off the hook so easy. Officially, my investigation on him is over, but he doesn't have to know that. The more questions I ask about the Woods Trust, the more nervous he gets. I'm convinced that somebody does have him plenty scared. He wants this over with too. I think with the proper persuasion, I can have him drop all charges against you if he believes I will drop my investigation on him."

Steven stood and reached out his hand to Chelle. "Again, thank you. I just want to get my name cleared and get on with my life."

Chelle accepted the handshake. "You're welcome, and trust me, Steven, if I find anything to make me reopen the investigation, I will."

"I don't doubt that at all."

"What will you do now?" Chelle asked.

Steven looked at Shannon and grabbed her hand. "Well, if Shannon will help me, I'll go back to work. Officially, I'm still a senator. I don't know if I'm electable again, time will tell, I guess."

"And your family?" Chelle said.

"It's over between Lucille and I. The divorce is still on, and I'm not contesting."

"Give it time, Senator, who knows. For what it's worth, when I talked to her about Sam, she was as helpful as she could be. She hates him for what he did to you and her."

"She should, but it's too late now. And it's not just that. When I needed her most, she abandoned me. Yes she had her reasons, but, well, for better or for worse and all."

There was a knock on the door. Chelle answered. It was Teddy Johnston. Steven and Teddy shook hands. Until now, besides Chelle, Teddy had been Steven's only contact the last few weeks.

"Sounds like Sam is getting away with killing my daughter."

"Sorry, Steven, but I've looked through the case myself. We'll be very lucky if he doesn't bring charges against you. We wouldn't have much of a defense. Temporary insanity maybe; you were under tremendous pressure. I'm sure the detective has told you about our other uphill battle."

"We haven't gotten there quite yet," Chelle said. "I have to share some more bad news with you. When you escaped, you threw your briefcase at me. That is assault and battery against a police officer. Not good. You resisted arrest. You kidnapped Jojo, a police officer, and then you stole his money and credit card. It's all part of his official report. He can't change it any more than I can deny you threw your case at me. You stole his identity. Hell, you were camping without a license. My captain threw out at least a dozen other charges. They add up pretty fast when you're a fugitive. Your escapades probably cost the country millions. I'll bet they repositioned satellites in space to try to find you. The National Guard flew in helicopters and truckloads of men to catch you. Even under the unique circumstances, those charges can't be overlooked, not even for a United States senator. They might even treat you a bit harsher to make an example out of you."

"I suppose we are talking jail time?" Steven asked.

"I'm afraid so, lots of it. Running from the police, whether you're innocent or not, is still a crime."

That was when another officer came through the door and handed a note to Chelle.

"There is someone here to see you." Chelle smiled. "Bring her in," Chelle told the officer. Tracy ran up and gave her father a big hug. With tears in her eyes and emotions cracking her voice she said, "Daddy, I missed you so much. Mr. Johnston said you could come home with us."

"Oh, lord it feels so good to hug you," Steven said as he lifted his fourteen-year-old daughter in a gentle bear hug. "I can't possibly explain how much you mean to me."

"Daddy, do they all know you didn't do it?"

"They sure do. This is Detective Chelle Saltarie. She's the one who figured out who the real killer was." It was a small lie. But for the senator's sake, it would have to become the truth.

Tracy gave Chelle a hug. "Thank you for helping my dad."

Chelle felt bad accepting the compliment, knowing she was as responsible for her father having to go on the run as everybody else.

Teddy Johnston cleared his throat. "There is a mob of reporters outside who are looking for a statement from you. Unfortunately, we have to go through them to get out of here, so here is what I suggest we do ..."

Chapter 56

One week later:

Senator Steven Westcott moved awkwardly as he was ushered into the Oval Office of the president of the United States. Only this morning, Shannon had come into his office with a sealed note from the president of the United States, President Kevin Walker. After signing in, Steven was escorted by an armed guard to the Oval Office.

After a short wait, Steven found himself standing inside the Oval Office itself. He wondered what the protocol was for stepping onto the Great Seal of the president. The unmistakable design was woven into the grand carpeting, covering much of the eight-hundred or so square feet of the room. It seemed unpatriotic to step on such a majestic symbol.

President Kevin Walker looked up and smiled at his secretary and thanked her for showing Steven in. "Senator Westcott, I'll be right with you. I'm just finishing up a few things." The president smiled at his guest, then he concentrated on a set of papers on his desk.

Steven decided to stand a respectful distance away from the president, though he couldn't help but stare at the intricate carvings on the desk. It was a very special piece of furniture, and Steven knew its historic value. It was called the Resolute Desk because it was built from the timbers of the British Arctic Exploration ship, the HMS. Resolute. It was a very special gift from the British.

Steven was afraid he was going to get some sort of presidential reprimand for disgracing Congress and costing the taxpayers an untold amount of money in trying to find him. The senator stood waiting near a small sitting area in front of the president's desk, not sure if he wanted to take his lumps standing or sitting. Either way, he waited for the president to make the first move.

The president finished with his signatures and then stood and walked around his desk. The Secret Service was undoubtedly right outside the closed doors, of that Steven was sure, but this meeting was apparently going to be private between the president and him, which was unusual.

"Relax, Senator, I was fully briefed on your situation. There aren't many in this town that would have a pair big enough to do what you did, including me. I also heard that you believe the man being charged for your daughter's murder isn't the man who did it."

Steven felt his jaw slacken; he was stunned at the president's knowledge.

The president continued, "You may be right, but I don't believe it was Sam or the people from the Woods Trust either."

"You, sir? You know of the Woods Trust?"

"Yes I do. I saw the video of what you did to poor Sam." The president chuckled. "I don't begrudge you, he had it coming; he was messing around with your wife. Care for a drink?"

"Thank you, Mr. President, but I'm afraid I must decline." Steven's heart was pounding. He needed to know more but also knew he couldn't interrogate the president of the United States.

"Nonsense, Steven, you don't want to make the president of the United States drink alone, do you?" The president was already on his way to the small bar to the right of his desk.

"No, sir, not when you put it that way."

"Kevin, please call me Kevin. Would you like a scotch? I believe that's your drink. I just happen to have a wonderful thirty year old Macallan single malt."

"That would be more than fine, sir."

The president smiled, used to people afraid to use his given name.

Steven felt even more awkward as the president poured them each a generous three fingers of the premium scotch. The president walked over to the two opposing couches where Steven was standing, and he handed him a glass.

The president savored his first taste. "I can tell you what he isn't lying about. He did steal money from the Woods Trust."

"Excuse me sir, but who are the Woods Trust and why would they want to frame me for murder?"

"Whoa, I never said they did. I said that you may be right that this Mr. Ramon Hayes wasn't in fact the person that killed your daughter. The important thing is that I believe you didn't kill her either."

"But the Woods Trust, sir? Who are they?"

"Every president knows about the Woods Trust and its founder. Well, at least every president since 1944. It goes way back to the Dumbarton Oaks Conference. You would have to be a real history buff to know about it."

"The start of the United Nations, sir."

It was the president whose face showed surprise this time. "I'm impressed Steven. You are exactly right. It was held at the residence of Robert Woods Bliss, who was instrumental in setting the conference up in the first place."

"Yes, sir, the USSR, China, the United Kingdom, and, of course, the United States were at that first conference."

"Please sit Steven, let's get comfortable."

The president sat on one couch; Steven sat down opposite.

Steven tasted the scotch. Having the drink in his hand did make him feel a bit more comfortable talking privately with the president.

"You know your history well, Senator. However, what most don't know is that Robert Bliss wasn't real fond of the outcome. It became too political for him and well ... by the time things were all said and done, he was disappointed by the final charter that created the United Nations."

"I can understand his disappointment. It's far from perfect."

"As are all things political. Anyhow, he is the one who started the Woods Trust."

"The president took another sip of his drink."

"Why, sir? To what end?"

"It funds a benevolent society. Its mission is what Robert Woods Bliss had wanted from the very first: world peace. Of course, Robert is long gone, died in the early sixties, I believe. But the trust not only lives on, it is a major player on the international stage. To this day, every president is invited to the conferences it still sponsors."

"But why would they want to frame me for murder? And why have I never heard of them?"

"Oh, don't believe a thing that Sam said. In fact, I would suggest you just accept that Sam told you a story. A story that you forced him to make up. As to why you never heard of them before, it's because they prefer to work away from the limelight, and they refuse to be used for publicity purposes. That is one of their strengths. Leaders can meet discreetly—no press and no press releases."

"You mean secretly."

"Inconspicuously," the president corrected. "The organization has the ability to arrange diplomatically private conferences. I assure you, that can be very useful.

The president stood and walked over to a small wood humidor. "Would you care for a cigar to go with your scotch?" the president offered.

"No, sir, I don't smoke."

"Oh yes that's right. I read that in your profile." The president opened the wood top, then he closed it carefully, without taking a cigar. Instead, he walked back to the bar and refreshed his drink.

Walking back, he said, "I have been doing quite a bit of research on you, Senator."

Steven took his time with another sip, contemplating the president's explanation of the Woods Trust and the flavor in his mouth at the same time.

"Take my word for it, the Woods Trust is nothing for you to be concerned about. However, there is a special reason I asked you here. I have a proposition for you, Steven. I need some help, or let me rephrase that. Our country needs your help."

The smoothness of the scotch was still on his tongue, but the experience was soon lost as he grappled with the president's statement.

"I don't know that I am the person you are looking for, sir. I have quite a bit of baggage going along with my name right now. I very well could be going to jail for a period of time, sir."

The president took his seat again. "Oh, you are the person all right. That is exactly what I wanted to talk to you about. I think I have a way we could help each other. But let's not get ahead of ourselves. As you know, our economy is in need of an economic kick in the ass. The Federal Reserve has done about all they can and have already tried every trick in the book. If, or should I say, when interest rates demanded by the creditors of the United States rise to more historic values, nearly twenty-five percent of our tax receipts will go toward interest payment on our national debt. And that will leave us seriously short of funds to pay for nearly everything else. Which will in turn require us to borrow even more money and pay even more interest. In short, a monetary death spiral if we don't change something very quickly.

"I'm told that the main problem is that because we are a mature economy, we won't be able to grow our way out of this predicament. A younger economy can grow at break-neck speeds as it discovers itself and its population progresses from a rural to a manufacturing one. That's the kind of growth China has experienced. We need that kind of growth to get our people from standing in the unemployment line to standing in front of a time clock. But the reality is, it's out of our reach."

"Yes, sir, I couldn't agree more. But, as you say, we can't grow as fast as we need to. That's why I've been proposing job training combined with a bit more fiscal restraint."

"I am aware of your efforts. But, unfortunately, none of it will be enough. Our only way politically out of the mess is to grow our way out. Plain and simple, cutbacks will not be tolerated by the voters. Hell, even a spending freeze would probably get the instigators fired."

Steven took another sip of his drink, as did the president. Steven remained respectfully silent, waiting to be sure the president had finished his thought before replying.

"I'm afraid you're right," Steven said. "Some hard choices need to be made, and the voters won't be kind to the politicians who propose them. Washington has been spending so much more than it has been taking in for so long that the voters think anyone saying spending has to be cut is only crying wolf."

"Well put, Senator. We have built the perfect mousetrap, only we are the mice. But I have an idea. It's a bold idea. If it works, I can't take credit for it. If it fails, I'm certain that this administration will get the blame. However, there is not much of a downside for the country if it doesn't work and everything to gain.

"Politically speaking, we on the other hand should walk away from this idea as fast as possible. We have nothing to gain and everything to lose. But"—the president looked Steven squarely in the eyes—"I hope you and I can put politics on the side for the good of the country and let the chips fall where they may."

Steven tried to read the president. For a lifelong politician to say they were going to put politics on the side sounded insincere. However, Steven felt the president was dead serious. He gulped another taste of his scotch because he didn't know what else to do. Finally, he responded as truthfully as he could.

"Mr. President, with all due respect, without knowing what you are going to tell me, I do not know that I can make that promise."

"Can I trust you?" the president asked as he set down his glass and turned toward Steven. The seriousness in his eyes was unmistakable. "Can you keep a secret? This absolutely has to stay between you and me. This plan will not work if the newspapers get a hold of it. In fact, it has to stay an absolute secret for at least the next five years. I know that national secrets have been entrusted to you before when you were a soldier. Your military record is exemplary. As your Commander-In-Chief, I need that kind of trust in you again. I'm not asking you to agree to my plan, just that you promise not to divulge it to a soul, not a soul. You know there isn't anyone in this damn town that can keep a secret. I am praying that you can. Because as the United States economy goes, so does its national security, and that makes our discussion a national security issue."

"But ... Mr. President ..." Steven stuttered. "Why me? I am in serious trouble with the law. I am being charged with quite a few offenses, possibly some federal crimes as well. I'll probably be going to jail for a period of time, and I certainly won't be a US senator for much longer. You have access to an entire country of experts in any field you want."

The president stood and paced back and forth in front of the Resolute Desk before answering. "You, Mr. Westcott, are very special. I have looked at others, and remember, I am on my own here, nobody but me and one other person knows of this plan. But the set of skills I need are rare, especially when I need to choose an individual who can assert the full authority of the United States Government.

"Keeping you a senator will be critical. You will answer to nobody but me. Make no mistake, I would be sending you into harm's way. There is nobody else I can trust who could possibly handle what I am about to suggest. This request by me, by your country, will be more dangerous than anything you have done in the past."

Steven wanted to stand, to pace the room, but, at the moment, that seemed to be the president's job. Just the same, the seriousness of the president's statement made him feel uneasy just sitting there.

Steven was now very happy for the glass in his hand, and he took a slow, long sip, trying to regain his composure. The ice in his glass had half melted and, to his surprise, the scotch was gone. He set it down on a coaster marked with the presidential seal.

"If I agree to help you, then what? As I told you, I am probably going to jail for evading the police and for what I did to Sam Kreiser. I'm sure he will be suing me for everything I'm worth."

"Oh, haven't you heard?" The president turned to look out the big, curved window at the lit-up White House lawn.

"No, sir. I don't believe I have." Steven uncrossed his legs and leaned forward in his chair.

"Sam's dead. He was in an accident. Died in a car crash along with his driver. Don't worry, nobody thinks you did it. I don't think you will be having any trouble from Sam."

Steven contemplated the suddenly changing circumstances. The odds of his main nemesis suddenly dying in a car crash had to be astronomical. Sam had said they would kill him. But who? The Woods Trust?

The president continued. "Sam's accident was fortunate timing nonetheless. I believe I have a plan for keeping your senate seat, and without Sam's interference, it will be much easier. So if you will trust me, I will trust you."

Steven set his glass down. "Yes, sir. I promise in the interest of national security that I won't tell a soul. This will be our secret, but I am only listening. I promise nothing else, Mr. President."

Chapter 57

Two weeks later in front of the US Capitol Building:

Steven took a deep breath. He was about to tell one of the biggest lies of his life. And for national security reasons, he had to convince an entire country it was the truth. The crowd in front of the Capitol Building was impressive, however millions more would be watching on their televisions.

Outside the Capitol, the reporters and cameramen were all jockeying for the best position they could. With the impressive steps of the Capitol Building behind him, a podium was already in place with lines of microphones attached to it. Atop the camera trucks were large antennas, sending live feeds back to the main stations, and cameramen with mounted video equipment, using powerful telephoto lenses to capture the action.

Steven knew that everyone anticipated his announcement that he was stepping down from his position to defend himself in court. It was commonly known that, though he had been cleared of the murder of his daughter, he was still going to be prosecuted for numerous crimes committed during his flight from the law.

However, because of the people flanking him, it was apparent that something highly unusual was happening. Steven was dressed in a fitted, light-blue, pinstriped suit, a white shirt, and a red tie.

Steven looked over the huge crowd. Despite the number of people, it was so quiet that Steven could hear the warble of a spring robin. On Steven's right was Detective Chelle Saltarie, who was stylishly dressed in a light gray pants suit and purple blouse. Next to her was Captain Walker, dressed in his blue police uniform, and an assemblage of other important people.

To his left was the chief of police for the entire Washington DC area, Chief Margaret Overton. She stepped up to the podium and was the first to speak. The chief of police didn't introduce herself; she didn't feel that was necessary.

"We have called this press conference so that we can explain for the first time, to you, the press, and to the public, an intricate sting operation. Along with myself, Captain Walker, lead Detective Chelle Saltarie, Agent David Henderson from the FBI, and Ms. Lynn Franklin of the CIA are all here to give you any supporting information we can.

"Before we begin, I have to remind you that certain information is restricted because of the ongoing investigation and the prosecution of Ramon Ruben Hayes for multiple murders.

"Months ago, the FBI approached this office with a request for our cooperation in a sting operation to catch an elusive serial killer. When the FBI became suspicious that a dangerous serial killer was behind the tragic death of Senator Steven Westcott's estranged daughter, they enlisted his help to catch the murderer. Their plan was to trap and capture the real murderer using the senator as bait.

"Senator Westcott made huge personal sacrifices and, at times, risked his own life to capture this man who had become so dangerous to our community. Senator Westcott was instrumental to eventually making the final arrest and saving an officer's life."

Then the chief introduced Agent Henderson, Captain Walker, and Detective Chelle Saltarie. All made brief statements collaborating the chief's explanation. Eventually, Steven was introduced. Steven tentatively approached the podium and looked over the crowd and into the cameras with a solemn look.

"I have been very carefully warned not to divulge too much before the trial. After so much effort by so many people, we can't afford to slip up now and say something to interfere with the rights of the accused.

"However, I want to say that, as a father, when I was asked to assist in finding my daughter's killer, I couldn't refuse. My unique position allowed me to work closely with law enforcement personnel to take a serial killer off the streets and to find justice for my daughter. What I did could be best described not as heroic, but as a determined father seeking closure on his daughter's death."

Steven explained some of the details of Ramon's capture and arrest. During the period following his prepared remarks, he had to decline to answer many of the questions that were asked. It was accepted that the lawyers and the courts and the police had their reasons for not letting him divulge certain critical information.

Chelle had told him that Chief Overton was upset that she wasn't brought into the loop much sooner, but being allowed to front the press conference smoothed some of her feathers. She also shared that agent Henderson wished that his supervisors had trusted him with the information as well. He was just told that the sting was being handled at the highest levels and was on a need-to-know basis only.

Eventually, the press conference came to a close. Steven thanked all those around him as he promoted the charade but not without guilt. He was both embarrassed and ashamed in the look that he got from Detective Saltarie. He knew she didn't believe one bit of the farce and wondered what she thought of him for using his position to not only avoid jail, but to come across as the hero.

If only he wouldn't have promised the president that he wouldn't tell a soul about the plan. If only he could share a small part with Chelle—she deserved that. If only he could tell her that this charade wasn't to protect him but rather was critical to the security of the country.

Later that evening:

Chelle had eagerly accepted Senator Westcott's invitation to meet him at the Capital Grille. She had many questions to ask about the sting operation she had participated in. Chelle had certainly heard about the Capital Grille; however, this was the first time she was actually in it.

The bar area was busy and many people had come up to Steven to thank him and congratulate him as she and he walked to their table.

"I'm sorry for the interruptions," Steven said as the maître d' pulled out a chair for Chelle.

"I guess that is the price you have to pay for being a hero."

"You know and I know that what I did, I did for my own reasons. I am not a hero." Chelle took that for as much of an apology for the ongoing circus as she was going to get.

Steven sat down opposite Chelle. The table was big enough for four but was set for two.

"There are people still furious with me for not letting them in on our little plan to catch Ramon. Maybe you could explain it to me again."

"I can't."

"Don't I get an explanation? After all, I am playing along."

"I know you were ordered to, and I'm sorry about that."

"Look, so you pulled some strings, correction, a lot of strings. You did what you had to to save yourself and your senate seat. I get it. Ramon is going to jail for a long time and you're not. I'm actually good with that."

"Chelle, I mean, Detective Saltarie, it's not what you think."

"Please call me Chelle. And what do I think?"

"That I'm just another self-serving politician using my clout to skirt the same laws we write for other people to follow."

"I guess you do know what I think."

"It's more important than that, and I wish I could tell you, but I can't. All I can say is that whatever you're thinking, you're wrong."

"How comforting."

"Look, Chelle, I wanted to meet with you to let you know that I have no ill will toward you at all, and I hope you know it."

"You mean for shooting at you when I came to arrest you?"

"Yea, something like that. You did what you had to, and I did what I had to. Let's leave it at that."

"And I want to thank you for saving my life," Chelle said.

"You have already, many times. And if it wasn't for me, you wouldn't have been in that situation, or Tamara or Jojo."

"Senator, the fact is, you did help us catch a serial murderer."

"Please, Chelle, call me Steven."

The waitress came by and Steven ordered a bottle of wine.

Chelle reflected, "It's strange how things work out sometimes. If you hadn't done what you did, Ramon probably would have gotten away with more murders and more innocent people would have gone to jail."

"I guess, but something is still bothering me. What about Sam Kreiser? He said he would be killed for talking, and all of a sudden he dies in a car crash."

"I don't believe in coincidences either, so I looked into his death. Slippery overpass, his car swerved, hit a guardrail, flipped and landed upside down in the river. He didn't have a chance. I don't know anybody who could pull that off and make it look like an accident. Sam and his driver were in the wrong place at the wrong time, that simple."

The waitress came back with their wine. After she poured them both a glass and left, Steven said, "Still, I can't help thinking that his death was extremely convenient for me, but I wonder who else it was convenient for."

"The only thing suspicious is that we haven't found the body of the driver. Because of his broken wrists, Sam couldn't drive. But it's a big river, the body probably snagged on a sunken log or something. It will turn up eventually."

"Maybe in life we have to accept that sometimes there are coincidences we can't explain," Steven said.

Chelle lifted her wine glass in a salute. Steven followed. They clanked glasses and Chelle proposed, "To letting bygones be bygones."

"And to the future, and the hell with the past," Steven added with another clink of the glasses.

The waitress came by to take their order. Steven ordered the tenderloin, medium, and Chelle ordered the Chilean sea bass.

"I do have something I'd like to share with you that came out of the investigation," Chelle said after the waitress left.

"Oh?"

"I had a third suspect in Destinee's murder?"

"Really? And who was that and why?"

"Remember that internal affairs investigation I told you about?"

"The same internal affairs investigation that got Clayton off my back?"

"The same. It turns out that a detective was planting DNA evidence to frame some of the accused himself. So for a while, I thought he might be the serial killer."

"I'm not following you, why would a detective do that?"

"To make his cases easier for prosecution. He took the lazy way out instead of relying on good police work. He assumed his suspect was guilty and then created evidence to support his arrest. Eventually, with Ramon's help, I got him to confess."

"Ramon?"

"I had my suspicions against Detective Bruce Harmon earlier but couldn't prove anything. That is until I searched Ramon's apartment and found something that didn't make sense. I saw the detective's name on samples next to one of the murdered hookers. That's when I knew Ramon intended to frame him.

"It turned out that Harmon often went to the Washington Arms to meet with his favorite prostitutes. Ramon wanted him to go to jail for murder. What Ramon didn't know of course was that Harmon would become the investigator on the very murder he was supposed to be accused of committing. Harmon removed any evidence that pointed to him and replaced it with evidence that indicated that Doctor Gregory Merrill did it. Unfortunately for the doctor, he was the last person with Tiffany before she was murdered, and his DNA was all over her."

"This sounds even more confusing than my case."

"It kept me confused too. I might have sorted things out about Ramon sooner if I wasn't distracted by my suspicions about Harmon."

Steven asked, "So what happened to him?"

"He tried to wiggle out of it, but when I showed my captain the evidence from Ramon's apartment, he couldn't. There was also evidence that the detective used cocaine, and he tested positive. Once I showed the captain the falsified logs from the evidence lock-up, then the whole thing unraveled."

Their dinners came and Chelle flaked apart some of her bass that was resting over a bed of wild rice while he cut a slice of his thick, juicy steak. Chelle continued, "He was fired of course. And he may be prosecuted for falsifying evidence, but things are so murky already because of all the cases Ramon falsified evidence on that, well, anything could happen, including nothing."

Steven finished savoring a piece of his steak then said, "Do you remember that new law I was working on before I went on the run?"

"I do, S58. Now we just refer to it as the new DNA law."

"Well, obviously it passed. But did you know they took my name off of it. Apparently I was an embarrassment at the time of the vote. For something I worked so hard on, I wish it had never passed. And you know what? I'm glad my name isn't on it.

"DNA evidence is a great tool, but it's too easy to get and plant. I wonder how many innocent people will go to jail because their DNA was found in the wrong place at the wrong time. There still is no substitution for good police work."

Chelle enjoyed a mouthful of her dinner and then said, "Ramon shook up the system pretty good. That might be a good thing, because DNA doesn't lie, but people certainly do."

The End

About The Author

Alan D. Schmitz has recently retired from his business to spend more time writing the novels he loves. He has traveled extensively and has met many colorful characters, all of whom he tries to bring alive through his writing.

Alan's debut novel *Memories Never Die* – a thriller about the evils of terrorism and the struggle for survival – was published in December 2011.

Alan's first novel was 'a put up or shut up' moment from his family members who were tired of hearing about the novel he would write some day. He knew he had success when his wife, Cindy, who had started reading the unfinished novel, wouldn't let him out of his office until it was done. Alan has been writing every since.

To learn more about Alan and to be the first to know when the next book in the Senator Series is published please visit:

www.alandschmitz.com

If you've enjoyed reading *DNA Never Lies*, please consider leaving a review on Amazon, or on GoodReads. Word-of-mouth is crucial for any author to succeed. Even if it is only a line or two, it would make all the difference and would be very much appreciated.